Jack Hig...

Jack Hight has a doctorate in history from the University of Chicago. He lives with his wife, daughter and dog in Washington, DC, where he is currently finishing the Saladin Trilogy. Hight's acclaimed first novel, *Siege*, is also available from John Murray.

Also by Jack Hight

Siege

Eagle

Book One of the Saladin Trilogy

JACK HIGHT

JOHN MURRAY

First published in Great Britain in 2011 by John Murray (Publishers)
An Hachette UK Company

First published in paperback in 2011

2

Map drawn by Rosie Collins

A CIP catalogue record for this title is available from the British Library

ISBN 978-1-84854-299-0
Ebook ISBN 978-1-84854-511-3

Typeset in 11.25/14.75pt Sabon MT by Servis Filmsetting Ltd, Stockport, Cheshire

Printed and bound by Clays Ltd, St Ives plc

John Murray policy is to use papers that are natural, renewable and recyclable
products and made from wood grown in sustainable forests. The logging
and manufacturing processes are expected to conform to the environmental
regulations of the country of origin.

John Murray (Publishers)
338 Euston Road
London NW1 3BH

www.johnmurray.co.uk

For my parents, who let me stay up as late as I wanted,
so long as I was reading.

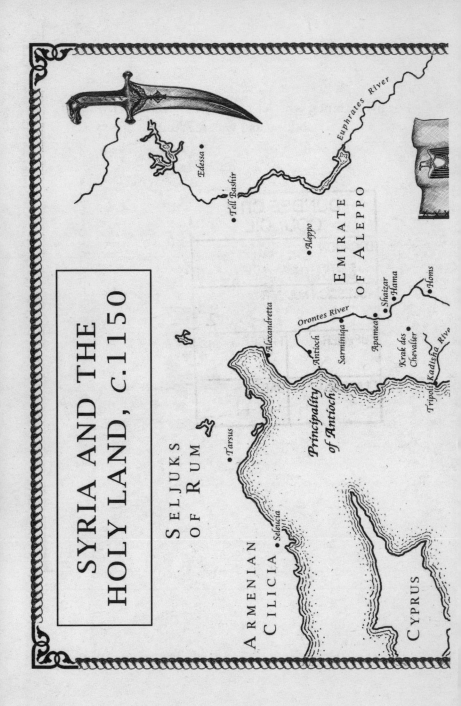

SYRIA AND THE
HOLY LAND, c.1150

SELJUKS
OF RUM

ARMENIAN
CILICIA

• Seleucia

• Tarsus

CYPRUS

• Edessa

• Tell Bashir

Euphrates River

• Aleppo

EMIRATE OF ALEPPO

• Homs

• Hama

• Shaizar

Alexandretta •

Orontes River

Antioch •

Sarminiqa

Apamea •

Krak des
Chevalier •

Tripoli

Kadisha River

Principality
of Antioch

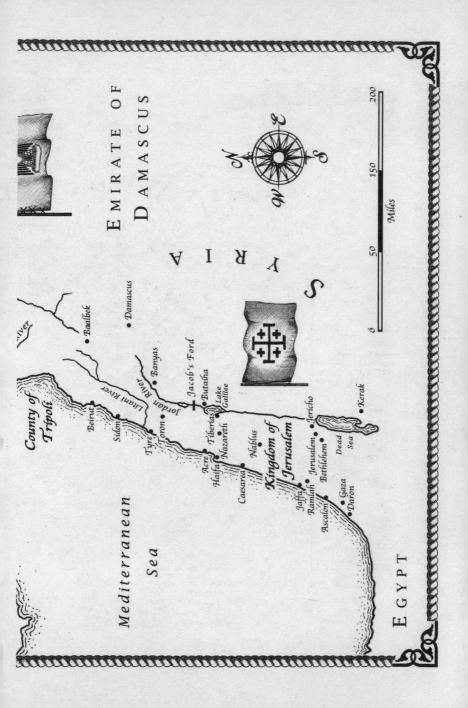

Part I
Eagle

Salah ad-Din, or Saladin as he is known to the Franks, was a Kurd, the son of a despised people, and yet he became Sultan of Egypt and Syria. He united the peoples of Allah, recaptured Jerusalem and drove the Crusaders to the very edge of the sea. He battled, and in the end tamed King Richard of England, who was called the Lionhearted and well deserved his savage name. Saladin was a great man, the greatest man that I ever knew, but when I first met him, he was only a skinny child . . .

The Chronicle of Yahya al-Dimashq

Chapter 1

MARCH 1148: BAALBEK

Yusuf sat in the saddle, his olive-skinned face mottled red and his chest heaving as he struggled to catch his breath. He was having one of his fits, during which the devil himself seemed to grip his lungs and squeeze out all the air. And the faster he breathed, the more elusive the air became. His horse had already recovered from the sprint and was tugging at one of the rare clumps of spring grass that managed to grow on the dusty polo field. On the far side of the pitch, two-dozen boys continued the match without him, the hooves of their horses stirring up a cloud of dust as they swarmed around the kura, a wooden ball made from willow root. Their long mallets waved above the dust, rising and falling as the boys swung at the kura, trying to drive it through the far goal, two half-toppled Roman columns, remnants from some long-vanished structure. A hundred yards past the columns stood the thick city walls of Baalbek, and past them dozens of pale, sandstone buildings clustered around an ancient Roman temple whose tall columns dwarfed the city around it. Over it all loomed the craggy, snow-capped peak of Mount Tallat al Jawzani.

Yusuf closed his eyes and leaned close to the neck of his horse, forcing himself to slow his breathing. He blocked out the whoops and yells of the other boys, concentrating instead on the rapid beat of his heart and the sweet, musky smell of his horse's mane. Gradually, his chest stopped heaving and his heart slowed.

'Yusuf!' Yusuf sat upright and his eyes snapped open. The kura was bouncing towards him across the uneven ground, and one of his team-mates had called out to warn him. Turan, Yusuf's older half-brother and opponent in the match, had broken from the pack and was racing after the ball. Turan was tall and thick whereas Yusuf was short and thin. At twelve, he was Yusuf's senior by two years, and his upper lip already showed the first signs of a man's beard. His horse was larger and faster, but Yusuf was closer. He would reach the ball first.

Yusuf flicked the reins and kicked the sides of his horse, urging it to a gallop. His eyes locked on the kura, and he raised his mallet high. He had begun to swing down in an arc towards the ball when, just before he made contact, he felt a sharp blow against his side as Turan drove the butt of his mallet handle into his ribs. Yusuf slipped sideways, lost his grip on his mallet, and then toppled from the saddle. He rolled as he hit the ground, as he had been taught, in order to absorb the impact. He sat up just in time to see Turan knock the kura through the goal, another pair of tall Roman columns. Turan let out a whoop of joy. Yusuf rose slowly, clutching his side. Dragging his mallet behind him, he trudged towards his horse, which had found another patch of grass some fifty yards off. Yusuf had only taken a few steps when Turan rode past at a gallop, almost knocking him over. Turan gathered the reins of Yusuf's horse and led it back to him.

'You should be more careful, little brother,' Turan said with a grin as he handed Yusuf the reins. 'A true warrior never leaves his horse.'

'A true warrior fights with honour,' Yusuf muttered as he pulled himself into the saddle.

'What was that?' Turan demanded, raising his mallet. He had a dangerous look in his eye. Yusuf wondered if he had been drinking again.

'Nothing.'

'Are you sure, little brother?' Yusuf nodded. 'Good.' Turan turned his horse and spurred away to the centre of the field, where the other boys were waiting. Yusuf followed.

'I have a proposal!' Turan shouted to the other boys. He pointed to the mountains that lay beyond the city to the east. 'We will play until the sun disappears behind Mount Tallat al Jawzani. Those who lose will tend the horses and muck out the stalls for the winners.' The boys on Turan's team, all older, cheered.

'But that's not fair!' Yusuf's younger brother, Selim, protested. Selim was only eight, and at first glance a perfect mixture of his two elder brothers – tall like Turan, but thin and wiry like Yusuf. 'You're already up two to one.' Selim shook his head and turned his horse to leave.

'Fine then!' Turan called after him. 'The next goal wins.' Selim turned back towards the others. 'But the losers will tend the victors' horses for a full week.'

Selim shook his head and opened his mouth to speak, but Yusuf cut him off. 'Agreed.'

The other boys on Yusuf's team looked at him wide-eyed, surprise mingled with anger. They were all older than Yusuf, and they were Turkish, part of the elite warrior class that ruled over the local Arabs. Two years ago, while Yusuf's father was governor of Baalbek, the other boys would have been forced to go along with him. But after the Emir of Damascus conquered Baalbek, Yusuf's father had lost his post, and the boys' respect had turned to scorn. Now when his family visited from Damascus to oversee their remaining lands, Yusuf was just another Kurd, an outsider. The local boys followed Turan because they were afraid of him, but no one feared Yusuf.

Haytham, the oldest boy on Yusuf's team, rode up beside him and gripped his arm painfully. 'What are you doing, Kurd?' he hissed. 'You know we've never beaten them.'

The son of the local emir, Khaldun, put a hand on Haytham's shoulder. 'Peace, Haytham.' He gestured to the sun, which hung huge and molten red just above the mountains. 'We only have to hold on a little longer for the tie.'

Yusuf shook his head. 'No, we only have a little longer to win.'

Khaldun chuckled. 'You're not so bad, for a Kurd.' He turned to Turan. 'We accept your bet.'

6

Turan grinned. 'Then let's play.' He raised his mallet high and swung down in a loop, hitting the wooden kura with a crack and sending it bouncing towards the weathered columns on Yusuf's side of the field. The boys spurred after it, swarming around the ball. Yusuf and Selim kept free of the crowd, circling around to defend their goal. They played better in open space, where their superior horsemanship was to their advantage. The other boys always mocked Yusuf for hanging back, refusing to join the scrum for the ball. They claimed he lacked bravery, but Yusuf did not care what others said, so long as he won.

The mob of riders surged back and forth across the field, now closer to Yusuf and the goal he guarded, now further away. The thick dust surrounding the riders prevented Yusuf from making out what was happening in the melee, but it was clear that Turan was dominating the game, using his superior size to knock other riders aside and get at the ball. Yusuf looked past the players to the mountain behind Baalbek. The sun had just touched its peak, and shadows were already racing across the city, swallowing up the Roman temple and the houses around it. The match was almost over. If he wanted to win, then he had to act soon.

Yusuf looked back to the action around the ball just in time to see Turan rise up amongst the other riders and knock the ball hurtling towards the goal to Yusuf's left. Yusuf responded instinctively, turning his horse with his knees and kicking its flanks to urge it forward. He reached the ball just in time, slamming his mallet into the ground and blocking the rolling kura. Turan's cry of victory died on his lips.

'Selim!' Yusuf yelled as he swung his mallet, sending the ball bouncing to his right, towards his brother. The rest of the boys followed the kura, but Yusuf headed to the left of the crowd. When the ball reached Selim, he sent it bouncing back across the field, past the other riders, to where Yusuf sat alone on his horse. The boys in the crowd turned their horses, but it was too late. There was no one between Yusuf and the far goal.

Yusuf slammed the kura up the field and galloped after it. He was halfway across the field when he reached it, and, without slowing, swung his mallet in an easy loop, striking the ball with a loud crack and driving it on towards the goal. The boys giving chase were still far back, except for Turan. He had broken free of the crowd and was gaining quickly. Yusuf kicked his horse's sides, leaning close to its neck as he raced for the ball. Out of the corner of his eye, he could see Turan closing fast. There was something odd about the way he was riding. He held his mallet at a funny angle, and his eyes were fixed not on the kura, but on Yusuf. Yusuf felt a shiver of fear run through him as he realized that he was Turan's target.

Yusuf was almost to the ball, and now he could hear the pounding hooves of Turan's horse. He took his eye off the kura, focusing instead on Turan's mallet. He would have to time this just right. Yusuf raised his mallet as if he were about to strike the ball. At the same time, he let go of the reins with his left hand, grabbed his horse's mane and slipped his left foot from the stirrup. Turan rode closer and closer, and then his mallet was in motion, arcing down towards Yusuf's head. Yusuf dropped his own mallet and dodged to the right, swinging out of the saddle and gripping the mane of his horse as he clung to its side, one foot in the stirrup. Turan's mallet landed with a thud on the saddle. Yusuf grabbed it, and pulled hard. Turan was off balance after missing Yusuf. He let go of his mallet, but too late. '*Yaha*!' he cried out as he tumbled from the saddle and landed in a cloud of dust.

Yusuf swung himself back upright and reined in his horse beside the kura. He looked back, past where Turan lay, past the approaching riders, to where the last glimmer of the sun was slipping behind the mountain, leaving the field covered in shadows. Yusuf turned back to the ball and swung Turan's mallet hard, sending the kura bouncing through the goal.

'Subhan'alla!' he cried. Hallelujah! They had won. Yusuf dropped the mallet and raised his arms to the sky, a huge grin on his face. He was turning his horse to accept the congratulations of his team-mates, when he felt himself grabbed from behind and pulled from the saddle. He landed hard, knocking his head against the ground. Dizzy, his head pounding, he rose to his feet to find himself facing Turan. Turan was red-faced, his hands balled into fists.

'Cheater! You grabbed my mallet. You broke the rules!'

'You were trying to hit me!' Yusuf protested.

'How dare you accuse me!' Turan growled and shoved Yusuf, who stumbled backwards. 'You're the one who cheated!'

The others had arrived, and still mounted, they formed a circle around Yusuf and Turan. 'Leave him be, Turan,' Khaldun called out.

'But he cheated! He grabbed my mallet. We would have won otherwise.'

'Fine,' Khaldun said. 'We'll call the goal off. Nobody wins the bet. Happy now?'

'I'll be happy when this cheater tends to my horse and mucks its stable.' Turan looked around the circle of boys. 'And all of your horses, too.'

A tense silence fell over the group, and all eyes shifted to Yusuf. 'I didn't do anything wrong,' he said quietly.

Turan jerked his chin up and clicked his tongue to show that he disagreed. 'You lie, little brother.' He stepped close enough that Yusuf could feel his brother's hot breath on his face. 'Admit it. You grabbed my mallet. Otherwise I would never have fallen.'

Yusuf looked to the other boys, then back to Turan. Their eyes met. 'In battle, men will do worse things than grab your mallet, Turan. A true warrior never leaves his horse.'

The words were hardly out of Yusuf's mouth when Turan's fist slammed into his face and white lights exploded behind his eyes. He found himself sitting on the ground, blood pouring from his nose. Turan was standing over him, his fists still clenched and his lips curled back. 'Always so clever, aren't you, little brother?' he snarled. 'You're not so smart now, are you?'

Yusuf could feel the eyes of the other boys on him. He began to struggle for air and fought against the familiar panic. Slowly, he pushed himself to his feet, but he was hardly up before Turan punched him in the stomach, doubling him over. Yusuf was breathing in ragged gasps now, desperate for air.

'That's enough, Turan!' Khaldun shouted.

'Stay out of it!' Turan snapped. 'This is between me and my brother. He needs to be taught a lesson.'

Yusuf wiped the blood away from his nose, leaving a crimson smear on the back of his hand, and slowly straightened. His chest heaved rapidly as he gulped for air, but it was no use. One of his fits had seized him. Still, he forced himself to remain standing and met Turan's gaze. Turan punched him again, catching him in the jaw. Yusuf stumbled but stubbornly kept his feet. He braced himself for another blow, but it never came. Turan had turned away. He and the other boys were watching a rider approach from the city. Yusuf recognized the compact, dark man as Abaan, one of his father's mamluks – Turkish slaves purchased as children and raised as soldiers. The circle of boys parted to allow him to approach.

'What's this?' Abaan demanded as he reined in before Yusuf and Turan.

'He fell,' Turan said, gesturing to Yusuf.

'Is that so?' Abaan looked to Yusuf, who simply nodded. Accusing Turan would only lead to worse later. And besides, Yusuf knew his father. He would care little for Yusuf's complaints. 'Very well,' Abaan said. 'You are to return with me immediately. You too, Selim.'

Turan and Yusuf mounted their horses. As they fell in behind Abaan, Turan rode close to Yusuf and whispered, 'We'll finish this later, little brother.'

Yusuf passed through the gate in the thick stone wall that surrounded his home and rode into the dusty courtyard. Before him was the main building, a low, rectangular structure of tan sandstone. Torches in brackets flickered on either side of the domed entrance way, driving back the advancing darkness. Yusuf dismounted and followed the others to the stables, which were situated against the wall to the left. Four strange horses were there, all of their noses buried in the feeding trough. Judging by how determinedly they were eating, Yusuf guessed that they had been ridden far that day. Visitors, then. But who? Yusuf turned away and followed Turan, Selim and Abaan.

As they walked through the cool, red-tiled entrance way, Yusuf looked up, as he always did. High above, the domed ceiling was tiled in indigo, inlaid with golden stars. A low fountain was set in the floor directly below the centre of the ceiling. Its burbling waters flowed to a channel cut into the floor, and Yusuf and the others followed the channel out to the courtyard at the centre of the residence. Torches had been lit along the walls, illuminating the pool that ran the length of the courtyard. Two men were talking quietly as they paced beside the still waters, their backs to Yusuf. The man on the right stood stiffly upright. He was short and wiry, with darkly tanned skin and short-cropped hair just beginning to grey. Yusuf recognized him immediately as his father, Najm ad-Din Ayub. The other man had unkempt, black hair, and although he was only slightly taller than Yusuf's father, he was much stouter, if not downright fat.

'Your sons are here, my lord,' Abaan called and then withdrew.

The two men stopped and turned. Ayub scowled when he saw Yusuf's bloodied nose and swollen lip. The other man was red-faced, with a gruesome scar across his milky-white right eye. When he saw the boys, he smiled broadly, revealing crooked teeth. It was Yusuf's uncle, Shirkuh.

Yusuf and Selim ran to him, and he gathered them both in his thick arms, lifting them from the ground and kissing first Selim, then Yusuf on both cheeks. 'Salaam 'Alaykum, my little nephews,' Shirkuh rumbled. Peace be upon you.

'Wa 'Alaykum as-Salaam, Uncle,' Yusuf and Selim replied together, as Shirkuh set them down.

Shirkuh's smile faded as he inspected Yusuf more closely. 'What happened to your face, boy? Your nose looks to be broken.'

'A polo match.'

'Polo, eh? Did you win?'

Yusuf smiled, despite the pain it caused his swollen lip. 'I did.'

Shirkuh squeezed his shoulder. 'Well done.'

Turan now stepped forward. 'Ahlan wa-Sahlan, Uncle.' The two exchanged three kisses, the proper greeting between adult relatives. 'I am pleased to see you.'

'And I am pleased to see you—all of you,' Shirkuh replied. 'It has been far too long.'

'Now, go and look after your horses,' Ayub told his sons. 'Your uncle and I have business to discuss.'

'Yes, Father,' Yusuf said, echoed by his brothers.

'I will see you all tonight, at supper,' Shirkuh called after them as they hurried from the courtyard.

The three boys reached the entrance way, but they did not continue on to the stables. Instead, Turan turned right and pulled open the door leading to the living quarters. 'Where are you going?' Selim asked. 'What about the horses?'

'There's time for the horses later, Selim,' Yusuf told him.

'After we find out what they are talking about,' Turan agreed.

Yusuf pulled the door shut behind them, careful to make no noise, and the three of them hurried down the hallway, past sleeping chambers and the weaving-room, with its huge loom holding a half-woven carpet. They turned the corner and raced down another hallway to a heavy wooden door. It was already slightly ajar. Turan pushed it open, and the three of them stepped into a dark room. Hundreds of fleeces were stacked five deep against the far wall, filling the air with their musky smell. The wool was this year's tribute from Yusuf's father's vassals, stored here until it could be worked, sold or sent on to their father's lord, Nur ad-Din, in Aleppo. The stacks reached almost to the ceiling, and at the end of the pile, directly across from the door, the white soles of two bare feet were just visible.

'Who's there?' Turan asked.

The feet disappeared, replaced a second later by a face. It was their sister, Zimat. She was older than all of them, thirteen and already a woman. Zimat was stunningly beautiful, and she knew it. She had flawless skin the colour of golden sand, long black hair and brilliantly white teeth, which she showed now as she grinned at them. 'It's me,' she whispered. 'I've been listening.'

'You shouldn't be here,' Turan told her. 'Get out!'

Zimat did not move. 'Shush, you big ox!' she hissed. 'They'll hear you.'

'This is no business of yours, woman,' Turan grumbled as he climbed up beside her. Yusuf noticed that Turan slid in unnecessarily close to his sister, pressing his side against her. Zimat shot him a warning glance and moved away. Yusuf climbed up next, the raw wool scratching his face and arms as he pulled himself up the side. Once on top of the pile, he crawled forward in the narrow space between the wool and the ceiling, and took his place on the other side of Zimat. She had opened the shutters that covered the window a few inches, but Yusuf could see nothing through the thin crack between them except a sliver of the courtyard pool, flickering torchlight reflecting off its surface. He could just hear the voices of his father and uncle, but they were too far off to make out what was being said.

'What are they talking about?' he asked Zimat.

'Something about a king,' she whispered. 'From a place called France.'

'That is the kingdom of the Franks!' Yusuf said. 'Across the sea.'

'Who are the Franks?' Selim asked as he slid in beside Yusuf.

Zimat rolled her eyes. 'Don't you know anything? They are monsters from over the seas. Bloodthirsty savages who eat children like you!'

'Quiet,' Turan told them. 'They're coming closer.'

Yusuf strained to hear. His father was speaking. 'When will they land, and where?'

'Acre and Antioch,' Shirkuh replied. The two men stopped, and Yusuf could see the backs of their heads through the crack in the shutters. 'As for when, I do not know. Perhaps they have landed already.'

'How many?'

'Thousands. Enough to take Damascus, perhaps even Aleppo.'

'Allah save us,' Yusuf's father said. 'My home and most of what I possess are in Damascus. And if Aleppo and our lord Nur ad-Din fall, then all is lost for us. We have already left two homes behind, Brother. Where would we go next?'

'It will not come to that, inshallah.'

'God willing?' Ayub asked. 'God turned his back on me the day Baalbek fell.'

'Careful, Brother, you speak blasphemy.' The two men stood silent for a moment, then Shirkuh continued. 'The crusade is dangerous, yes, but it is also an opportunity. Nur ad-Din has a task for you. If you are successful, then you will find yourself restored to his favour.'

'You have my ear. Speak on, Brother.'

'Our people are divided. The Fatimids in Egypt quarrel with the Abbasid caliphate in Baghdad. The Seljuks threaten our lord from the north, while Emir Unur in Damascus has allied himself with the Franks. The Christians have exploited these divisions to build their kingdom, but if we join forces, they cannot stand against us. This Crusade can help bind us together. Nur ad-Din asks that you go to Unur and tell him what I have told you. Persuade him to ally with our lord.'

'I will go, but I do not think Unur will listen.'

'He will when the Franks march on his city. Fear will bring him to us.'

'Inshallah.'

'Inshallah,' Shirkuh repeated. 'You should take Turan and Yusuf with you. It is time that they learned their place in the world.'

'Turan, yes, but Yusuf is too young.'

'Perhaps, but there is something special about that one.'

'Yusuf?' Ayub scoffed. 'He has been cursed with fits. He will never be a warrior.'

'Do not be so sure.'

Yusuf did not hear the rest, for Ayub and Shirkuh had moved on, and their voices faded away. 'Did you hear?' Turan asked, his eyes shining. 'Thousands of Franks: this means war! And I am going!'

'I heard them,' Yusuf replied. 'Father said that Damascus might fall.'

'You're not afraid, are you, little brother?' Turan jibed. He exaggerated his breathing, mimicking one of Yusuf's fits. 'Afraid—' gasp '—the terrible Franks—' gasp '—will come and get you.'

'Stop that!' Zimat ordered. 'Don't be childish, Turan.'

'Zimat!' It was their mother calling. 'Where are you? You are supposed to be stirring the mishmishiyya!'

'I must go.' Zimat slid down from the pile of fleeces and hurried out.

17

'We should go too,' Yusuf said. 'If we don't see to the horses before dinner, Father will have our hides.'

Yusuf arrived at the evening meal freshly scrubbed, wearing a white cotton caftan, the ends of the billowing sleeves embroidered red and the middle belted with red wool. His clothes were immaculate, but his eyes were red and his nose swollen. Ibn Jumay, the family doctor, had seen to him, and the Jew's treatment had been almost worse than Yusuf's injuries. First, Ibn Jumay had reset Yusuf's nose, clucking all the while about the dangers of polo. He had then made Yusuf smoke kunnab leaves in order to reduce the pain and bring down the swelling. The pipe was hardly out of his mouth before Ibn Jumay had smeared Yusuf's nose inside and out with a noxious unguent that smelled of rotten eggs. The doctor had said the mixture would prevent infection. It would certainly keep Yusuf from enjoying dinner.

In honour of their guest, the floor of the dining room had been covered with the family's best rug – soft goat hair knotted on to a warp of wool, forming patterns of swirling red flowers and white starbursts against a yellow background. The room was bare of any other decoration, save for a low table that ran down the middle, surrounded by cushions of yellow saffron-stained cotton stuffed with wool. Yusuf took his place at the middle of the table, across from Selim. To his right, Turan sat across from their father, and Shirkuh sat at the head of the table. To Yusuf's left were Zimat and Yusuf's mother, Basimah. She was an older, fuller version of Zimat, still beautiful despite the streaks of silver in her long black hair. Normally, they would not have appeared in the presence of a male guest, but Shirkuh was family.

The meal that Basimah and her two kitchen servants had prepared to welcome Shirkuh exceeded even her usual high standards. Crisp, freshly baked flatbread and a roasted eggplant and walnut dip were followed by a divine apricot stew, the sweet fruit blending perfectly with savoury morsels of lamb. Yusuf sighed. It was his favourite dish, but thanks to Ibn Jumay, everything tasted like rotten eggs. Yusuf ignored the food and listened to Ayub and Shirkuh, desperate to know if he would be joining his father on his mission to Damascus. But as the stew gave way to lentils and roast lamb, Ayub and Shirkuh continued to talk of mundane matters: harvests, the size of their herds and that year's tribute.

Finally, after the last dish had been cleared away, and servants had brought cups of sweet orange juice to refresh them, Yusuf's father cleared his throat and clapped his hands twice to get their attention. 'Shirkuh has brought troubling news. The Franks have launched a second crusade. The French king and queen are expected to land in Antioch any day now. They may be there already.'

'Allah help us!' Basimah exclaimed. 'This means war.'

'That it does,' Shirkuh agreed. 'And it will be all we can do to turn back the Franks. Our spies say they are bringing hundreds of knights, with those accursed warhorses of theirs. We will need every sword that we can muster.'

'I will fight!' Yusuf declared. 'I am old enough.'

Basimah frowned, but Shirkuh smiled at the boy's enthusiasm. Ayub's face remained an expressionless mask as he turned his hard, grey eyes on his son. Yusuf sat up straight and returned his searching stare. Finally, his father nodded. 'We must all do our part. That is why I must go to Damascus. Tomorrow, my men and I will leave for the city. Turan and Yusuf will come with me.' Yusuf could not contain his smile.

'Turan and Yusuf will—not—go!' Basimah stated, her voice rising with each word. 'You will not take my sons to be murdered by those barbarians.'

'Peace, Wife,' Ayub replied, his voice calm and even. 'You forget your place.'

'No, Husband, you forget yours. It is your duty to protect your sons, and yet you propose to lead them like lambs to the slaughter. Do you want them to be taken and sold as slaves? To come of age amidst the infidels?'

'Our sons will not be taken. I am not bringing them to fight, but they are of an age when they must learn the ways of war. They must come to know our enemy.'

'And if Damascus falls, what then? The Franks are savages. They know nothing of God or mercy. They know only blood and the sword. They killed my father, my mother, my brother. They—' Her cheeks flushed, and she looked away. 'They did horrible things. They will not kill my sons!'

'If Damascus falls, then your sons will not be safe anywhere,' Shirkuh said gently. 'You cannot protect them forever, Basimah.'

Basimah opened her mouth to retort, but Ayub raised

his hand, stopping her. 'I give you my word that no harm will befall Turan or Yusuf. They are my sons, too.'

Basimah's head fell. 'Very well,' she sighed. 'Come, Zimat. There is work to be done. Let us leave these men to their talk.' She rose and ushered Zimat out, but then stopped in the doorway. When Basimah turned back to them, her eyes shone with tears. 'I have your word, Ayub. You will bring my children back to me.'

Chapter 2

John leaned over the ship's rail and vomited into the sparkling, clear blue waters of Acre harbour. His company of knights had been at sea for a week, sailing down the coast of Outremer from Attalia, and John had been miserably sick the entire trip. Still, he thanked God that he had not been left behind, prey to hunger, thirst and the devilish Seljuk Turks. They had shadowed the crusading army throughout the long march across the arid lands of Anatolia, swooping down after dark on their sleek horses and riddling the crusaders with arrows before melting back into the night like ghosts. The Seljuks had killed thousands, and when the leaders of the crusade took a handful of men and sailed from Attalia, thousands more had been left to the Turks' mercy. At sixteen, John was only a foot-soldier, but his noble blood had entitled him to a place on the ships. At least it was good for something, he thought, and then puked again.

John wiped his mouth with the back of his hand and looked up at the city of Acre. Ships lined the curving quay, their tall masts bare of sails. On the decks, sailors were busy unloading casks, sacks of grain and bleating sheep. Beyond the ships, the harbour was crowded with market stalls, and past them sat square, dusty-white buildings set one on top of the other. To John's right, the buildings stretched away to a massive tower, part of the wall that protected the city; to his left, they ran uphill to a thick-walled citadel.

'Saxon!' someone barked, and John turned to see the hulking, thickly bearded figure of Ernaut stomping towards him. Ernaut smirked when he saw the trail of yellow-brown vomit on John's white surcoat. 'Stop your puking and get your arse over here. Lord Reynald wants to speak to us.'

John followed Ernaut to the foredeck, where the other men had gathered in their chainmail and surcoats, white with red crusader's crosses on the chest. Ernaut disappeared into the rear cabin and returned a moment later with Reynald. Reynald de Chatillon was a handsome, well-proportioned man of twenty-three. He had sharp features, closely cropped hair and a well-groomed, short black beard. He smiled at them, revealing even, white teeth.

'My men,' he began, 'it has been nearly a year since we left our homes for the Holy Land. Now at last, by the grace of God, we have arrived, and our holy work can begin.' Several of the men sniggered. Reynald had drunk and whored his way through every village between Worms and Attalia. Reynald's eyes narrowed and his smile faded. The sniggering stopped immediately.

'You may be wondering why we have not sailed to

Antioch with King Louis and the others,' Reynald continued. 'Our king has entrusted me with an important mission at the court of Baldwin, King of Jerusalem.' As he was speaking, three of the ship's sailors leapt the short distance to the dockside, grabbed ropes and began to pull the boat tight against the quay. 'As emissaries of King Louis, we must be on our best behaviour.' Reynald's voice was hard-edged. 'I will go ashore to announce our presence to King Baldwin. You are to wait at the docks until we are told where to camp. I want no trouble. That means no women and no wine.' The men groaned. Reynald's hand dropped to his sword hilt, and the men quieted. Reynald was a deadly swordsman. He nodded, satisfied. 'You will wait here,' he repeated and marched off down the gangway the sailors had set up, followed by two sergeants, Thomas and Bertran.

'You heard Lord Reynald!' Ernaut bellowed at the men. 'There's to be no trouble. Now get below and grab your gear.'

John followed the other men below decks. The dank hold was lit only dimly by a shaft of light shining through the hatch above. The huge warhorses whose stalls took up most of the space nickered and stamped, thinking that they were going to be fed. John kept his distance. It was not the size of the chargers that set them apart from other horses, so much as their temperament. It had been John's task during the voyage to muck out their stalls, and he had been bitten, stepped on or kicked more than once.

John headed away from the stalls to the cramped

space where the knights had slept, their thin blankets laid out almost on top of one another. John grabbed the leather rucksack containing his helmet, spare tunic, simple tent, woollen blanket and prayer book. He already wore his most valuable possessions: leather boots and breeches; chainmail armour that hung to his knees; a tattered cloak; a tall, kite-shaped shield slung over his back; a waterskin dangling from his shoulder; and hanging from his belt, his father's sword and a pouch containing a few coppers and his whetting stone.

John climbed from the hold with his rucksack slung over his shoulder and marched down the gangway. Several other men were kneeling on the ground and kissing the soil. John joined them, crossing himself and offering up a prayer to the Virgin for his safe arrival. It seemed like a lifetime since he had fled England with only the armour on his back and a sword at his side. He had joined the crusade in Worms and marched through the great cities of Salonika, Constantinople and Ephesus. Now, at last, he was in Outremer, the Holy Land. He rose and breathed deeply. The usual smells of a port – salty sea air and freshly caught fish – were overlaid with more pungent odours from the nearby market: heavily perfumed women, roasting meats, yeasty bread and burning incense. Joining the other men, John took his helmet from his rucksack and sat on it. The late-morning sun beat down, and he wiped sweat from his brow as he gazed at the market. Only a few feet away, two olive-skinned Saracens in white burnouses – loose-fitting cloaks with broad sleeves – were selling swords and knives. John had never seen anything like the blades, with their polished steel surfaces covered in interlacing patterns in darker grey.

'What are they doing here?' said one of the knights, pointing at the two Saracens. He was a loudmouth named Aalot, nicknamed *One Eye*. He claimed that he had lost his eye fighting the English in Normandy, but John had heard that a vengeful prostitute was to blame. 'I thought we came to fight those sand-devils, and here they are setting up shop in a Christian city.'

'Let it be, One Eye,' Ernaut ordered. 'We're not to make any trouble.'

One Eye spread his hands in protest. 'I'm not making trouble.' He turned to Rabbit, the youngest of the men at only thirteen. His real name was Oudin, but the men had dubbed him *Rabbit*, as much for the way his nose twitched when he was nervous as for his large ears, which were completely out of proportion to his skinny, freckled face. 'I hear the Saracens eat their captives,' One Eye said. 'They cut their hearts out while they're still alive and eat them raw.'

'That's after they bugger them,' another of the men added.

Rabbit's eyes were wide. 'Those are just stories.'

'Don't be so sure,' One Eye insisted. 'You fought in the first crusade, Tybaut. You tell him.'

Tybaut, a grey-haired bull of a man, was sharpening his sword with slow, rasping strokes of his whetting stone. He did not look up as he spoke in a low, gravelly voice. 'You're young enough, Rabbit, that they'd take you as a slave. Then they'd bugger you.' The men laughed. Rabbit's nose twitched.

'It's damnable hot out here,' Ernaut grumbled, interrupting the laughter. 'You, Saxon! Go and fetch me some water.' He tossed John a leather waterskin.

'Christ's blood!' John cursed under his breath as he rose. 'Yes, sir,' he added more loudly.

'Me too, Saxon,' said One Eye, tossing John his skin. Two-dozen more waterskins followed as the other men added theirs.

''Sblood!' John cursed again. As the second youngest member of the troop and an Englishman too, he was subjected to constant ribbing and always assigned the most degrading of tasks. He began to gather up the skins. It would be all he could do to carry them back once they were filled, and that's if he could find a well.

'I'll help.' Rabbit shouldered eight of the waterskins.

'Remember, Saxon: you're only supposed to fill up the skins!' One Eye made a crudely suggestive gesture with his hands, and the men laughed.

'What's he talking about?' Rabbit asked.

'Don't worry about it,' John told him as he began to shoulder his way through the market crowd, a mixture of fair-skinned Franks, bearded Jews, local Christians, Saracens and dark-skinned Africans, all dressed alike in turbans and loose burnouses. Veiled women passed through the crowd here and there, the men giving them wide birth. John passed a stall where a black-haired Italian was showing strips of leather to two clean-shaven Templars in the distinctive surcoats of their order: half-black, half-white and emblazoned with a red cross. Next to the stall, a monk in his black cowl was staring out to sea as he chewed some unidentifiable meat off a stick. John stopped next to him. 'Excuse me. I'm looking for a well.' The monk looked back uncomprehendingly, then spread his hands and said something in Aramaic. John moved on towards a veiled lady in a golden tunic, who was examining glass goblets at the booth of a fat, bearded Jew in a skullcap. 'Pardon me, lady.'

She turned to look at him, wide-eyed. A second later, John was grabbed from behind and shoved roughly aside. He turned to see a tall, thickly muscled Frank in chainmail. 'You're not to speak to the lady,' the Frank growled. He and the lady moved away into the crowd.

John turned to the Jewish merchant. 'Pardon me, sir,' he began in Frankish, but the man shook his head and replied in a language that John did not understand. 'Do you speak English?' John tried. Again the Jew shook his head no, then tried another language that John did not recognize, and then another. 'Latin?' John asked.

The Jew's eyes lit up. 'Of course.'

'I'm looking for a well.'

'There are no wells in the city.'

'No wells?' John asked, dumbfounded.

'There is a fountain, that way.' The Jew pointed down the quay to a shadowy alleyway that led deeper into the city. 'You will find water there.'

'Thank you. Come on,' John told Rabbit, switching back into Frankish. The two headed down the quay towards the alleyway.

'How did you learn all of those languages?' Rabbit asked.

'I was a second son. I was trained to enter the Church.'

'Why didn't you?'

John winced. He gestured to the red crusader's cross sewn to his surcoat. 'I took up the cross instead.'

'Why?'

'None of your business,' John snapped, but his words were drowned out by a shouting crowd just ahead. Men were pressed four-deep around a raised platform, where a skinny young Saracen stood, naked but for a thin loincloth.

An Italian slave merchant stood beside the Saracen, loudly touting his virtues in accented Latin. 'He is strong as an ox,' the Italian declared, squeezing the Saracen's stringy bicep. He slapped the boy, who did not move. 'And docile, too.'

John turned away and headed into the shadowy alleyway that the Jew had indicated. The path twisted left and right, growing narrower and narrower. John had to step over a beggar, who sat with head bowed and hand out. A few feet further on, a scantily clad, buxom Saracen woman stepped out of a dark doorway. 'Only ten fals,' she said in Latin. John squeezed by her, and she turned her attention on Rabbit. 'Ten coppers,' she purred, pressing herself against him. John pulled Rabbit away.

They emerged from the dark passageway into a bright, three-sided plaza. In the centre, water bubbled from the mouth of an ancient stone head and filled a wide pool, where turbaned men and veiled women were busy filling red clay jars.

'Water flowing from stone,' Rabbit whispered. 'How is it possible?'

John strode to the pool and bent over, scooping the

29

cool water into his mouth. 'I don't know, but it tastes blessed good.' He felt a tap on his shoulder and looked up. Rabbit was pointing to the men and women around them. They had stopped filling their jars and were staring at John with undisguised menace. One of them, a tall, olive-skinned man with a long beard and a curved dagger belted to his waist, pointed at John and shouted something in Arabic.

John spread his arms. 'I'm sorry. I don't understand.' The man stepped closer and began to yell what sounded like a string of insults, repeatedly poking John in the chest. 'I told you: I don't understand your dirty Saracen tongue,' John growled. 'Now leave me be.' He shoved the Saracen, who stumbled back several feet. The man's hand went to his dagger hilt, and John and Rabbit both drew their swords.

'I suggest you sheathe your weapons,' someone behind them said in Frankish. John turned to see a young, tonsured man of slight build, wearing black priest's robes. The priest gestured for John to look around him. At least a dozen turbaned men stood around the plaza with daggers drawn.

'Do as he says,' John told Rabbit.

'Thank you,' the priest said. 'We want no violence here.' He went to the angry Saracen, and the two men exchanged words in Arabic. The Saracen and priest kissed one another on each cheek, and the Saracen turned away, apparently satisfied. The priest turned back to John.

'What did the Saracen want?' John asked.

'Oh, he is no Saracen. These men are native Christians.'

'Could have fooled me,' John muttered.

'Syrian and Armenian Christians have lived amongst the Saracens for centuries,' the priest explained. 'They have adopted Arab customs, but they are as Christian as you or me.'

'Well what did he want?'

'He said that the two of you should bathe before coming to the fountain. He fears that you will pollute the waters.' John looked at the men and women around him. They all had clean hands and faces, and were wearing impeccably clean white linen caftans. The priest too had neat hair and clean, trimmed nails. John looked down at his dirty surcoat, still stained with traces of vomit. Rabbit was little better, with matted hair. 'I hope I do not offend,' the priest continued, 'but your odour is rather rank. The bath-house is just over there.' He pointed to a large building just down the street.

'A bath-house?' Rabbit asked. 'What kind of savage place is this?'

The priest smiled. 'You are in a land of savages now, good sir. You shall have to learn to behave as one.' He turned to go.

'Thank you for your help, Father,' John called after him. 'Might I ask your name?'

'William,' the priest replied. 'William of Tyre. I welcome you to the kingdom of Jerusalem, good knights. I hope you find all that you seek.' And with that, the man turned and walked away.

'What now?' Rabbit asked.

John grimaced. 'Now we bathe.'

*

31

John's ears were still burning as he and Rabbit staggered down the narrow alleyway to the harbour, the heavy, bulging waterskins slung over their shoulders. The baths had been worse than he had anticipated. They had entered through the wrong door and found themselves surrounded by indignant, screeching women, who had chased them back into the street, much to the amusement of the men lounging outside in the shade. After finding the men's entrance, they had paid one copper each to a sweaty, bug-eyed man, who told them in thickly accented Frankish to disrobe and then handed them two tiny cotton cloths to wrap around their waists. They were hustled through a small room with a single pool of cold water and on to an enormous pool whose steaming waters occupied an octagonal building with a high, domed ceiling. Windows had been cut high up on the wall, and the light streaming in illuminated men of every race, all naked but for their thin wraps. John had cleaned himself well enough and was just about to climb out when an enormous Saracen servant approached, grabbed his arm in a vice-like grip, and proceeded to scrub him fiercely all over with a long-handled brush. Rabbit was given even worse treatment by a severe old man who grabbed him by the shoulders and repeatedly dunked him under the water.

Their skin raw, John and Rabbit were ushered to the pool of cold water and shoved in. Gasping and shaking from the cold, they were finally allowed to leave. They had retreated to the changing room, where they found that their clothes had been washed in their absence. They practically ran as they left the building. John had to admit, though, that his scalp no longer itched and his hands were whiter than they had been in months. Perhaps the custom was not completely barbaric, after all.

''Sblood,' John cursed as he and Rabbit emerged from the dark alleyway. The market stalls were closing up in advance of the midday heat, and the crowd had mostly gone. Beyond the stalls, the ship they had arrived on was already being loaded with new cargo: large barrels that the sailors were rolling up the gangway. Between the market and ship there was only empty ground. The men of their company were gone.

'You, sailor!' John shouted to one of the men loading the ship. 'Where did our men go?' The sailor shrugged and pointed off down the dock, away from the citadel. John scanned the harbour, but there was no sign of the men. 'Damn!' he cursed, dropping the waterskins.

'We should look for them,' Rabbit suggested.

'Where? In there?' John gestured to the city. 'We have no idea which direction they went. We'd only get lost.'

Rabbit's nose twitched. 'I'm just trying to help.'

John sighed. 'You're right, Rabbit. Maybe the glass seller knows where they went.' John shouldered the waterskins and headed towards the Jewish merchant, who was shutting up his stall. 'Thank you, sir. We found the water.' John pointed to the skins, and the Jew smiled in acknowledgement. 'The men who were there,' John continued, pointing to where the company had been sitting. 'Do you know where they went?'

The Jew shrugged. 'No, I am sorry.' He picked up a string of glass beads and held it out to them. 'Would you like to buy something? A present for a lady?'

'No, thank you.' John turned away to see a knight watching them from horseback. The man wore a black surcoat emblazoned with the distinctive white Hospitaller cross, composed of what looked like four arrowheads, all touching at the tips.

'Looking for something?' the knight asked.

'We are Reynald de Chatillon's men,' John explained. 'We are looking for the rest of our company.'

The Hospitaller's eyebrows arched. 'Reynald's men, eh?' He paused and then pointed along the dockside. 'The rest of your company went that way. They are setting up camp outside the city, just past the harbour gate.'

'Thank you, sir.' The knight nodded and rode on.

John and Rabbit marched along the long harbour, passing tall-masted ships to their right and squat buildings on their left. By the time they finally reached Acre's wall, John's shoulders were burning from the leather straps of the waterskins. The end of the wall was marked by a massive, square gate-tower, which rose up from the coastline. They passed through the gate into a flat, empty space, and then through a second, outer wall. The men were setting up their tents in its shade.

'Where have you been?' Ernaut demanded as John and Rabbit trudged over to the camp and dropped the skins. He unstopped his skin and took a long drink, eyes narrowing as he examined John and Rabbit more closely. 'And what happened to you? You look like two pigs scrubbed up for market.'

John could feel his face reddening. 'Nothing. It took us a while to find water.'

'And they made us bathe,' Rabbit added. John winced.

Ernaut dropped his skin, and water sprayed from his nose as he burst into a fit of laughter. The men nearby also began laughing, and the others approached to find the source of the merriment.

'They made you bathe?' One Eye asked with a wink. 'Tell us all about it, Rabbit. Did the Saxon here scrub you nice and good?'

'No,' Rabbit said. 'There were servants for that.' This produced another, louder fit of laughter from the men.

'Leave him be, One Eye,' John said. 'Come on, Rabbit. Let's pitch our tents.' John stomped away, followed by the men's mocking laughter.

'What did I say?' Rabbit asked.

'Nothing. Just try to keep your mouth shut around them.' John dropped his rucksack and began to pitch his tent on the edge of the camp. He glanced back. The men were roaring with laughter as One Eye bent over, his arse in the air and a quizzical look on his face as he shouted out, 'Is that a bar of soap, Saxon?' John grimaced. The sooner the fighting began the better.

John's shovel dug into the sandy ground, and he leaned forward, scooping up a pile of dirt and flinging it out of the three-foot deep trench where he stood. He paused to push his damp, blond hair out of his face. The June sun blazed down mercilessly from a cloudless sky. When he had first arrived in Acre, two months ago, he wouldn't have lasted an hour under that sun. Now, after weeks of hard labour, he was tanned and fit, firm muscles filling out his bony frame. He had already been working for two hours, shirtless, as he shovelled out a new latrine ditch for the ever-expanding camp. The Germans under the Holy Roman Emperor Conrad had arrived shortly after John's company to swell the ranks of the crusaders. In the past week alone, hundreds more had flooded into the camp outside Acre: Raymond of Antioch and his nobles; King Louis of France with two hundred mounted knights; and hundreds of Templars and Hospitallers from every corner of the kingdom of Jerusalem.

'Get back to work, bath-boy,' One Eye shouted from where he sat on the ground beside the ditch, shaded by a sheet of white linen. John plunged the shovel back into the earth. This time, when he flung the dirt out of the ditch, it hit One Eye in the face.

'You'll pay for that, Saxon!' One Eye spluttered. He brushed the dirt away and jumped to his feet, fists raised, but then froze. John turned to follow his gaze. A group of mounted knights with Reynald at their head was approaching over the barren plain, their horses' hooves kicking up a tall plume of dust. As they rode into the outskirts of the sprawling crusader camp, men began to cheer. John squinted. He could just make out four darker men in white turbans riding in the centre of the knights. They rode stiffly, hands tied in front of them. Prisoners.

'You stay here and dig, Saxon,' One Eye ordered. 'If this trench isn't finished when I get back, then you'll answer to Ernaut.'

'Bastard,' John muttered as One Eye strode away. After a while, the cheering in camp stopped, but One Eye did not return. The sun crawled across the sky, passing its zenith. John was nearly finished with the trench when he heard Rabbit calling his name.

'John!' Rabbit skidded to a stop at the edge of the trench. 'Come on! Get your armour!'

John dropped his shovel. 'My armour? Are we under attack?'

'No, it's not that,' Rabbit replied, his eyes wide with excitement. 'Lord Reynald has captured prisoners. There's going to be a tournament!'

'By Christ's wounds, it's hot,' John muttered, wincing as his hand glanced against the skirt of his scalding-hot chainmail. He followed Rabbit to a spot in the shade of the city wall, where a ring twelve paces wide had been marked off on the dusty ground. A large hour-glass had been placed on a stool, to keep time for betting purposes. Reynald's men stood around the ring, shifting uncomfortably in their hot armour. John and Rabbit elbowed their way to the front, directly across from Reynald and Ernaut. As word spread, other knights came – Hospitallers, Templars, Franks, and Germans – forming a dense crowd, those at the back standing on their helmets for a better view. Others gathered on top of the nearby wall to look down on the sport.

When Reynald judged that a suitable crowd was present, he stepped into the centre of the ring. 'Today, while out hunting, my men and I came across a dozen spies from Damascus, sent here by Emir Unur to gauge the strength of our forces. Their presence in our lands is an outrage, a violation of our treaty with the emir, and they fled at the sight of us. We gave chase, and three fell to our swords. By the Grace of God we captured four more!' The men roared their approval.

'Now, I have heard talk amongst you of our enemy, of their bravery, their skill, their ruthlessness,' Reynald continued. 'I have heard men say they are monsters, savage beasts.' He turned slowly around the circle, meeting the eyes of his men. 'But today you will see that the Saracens are no monsters. They are men of flesh and blood. And they die like any other man!' He turned and called out over the crowd: 'Bring forth the prisoners!'

The crowd turned as the four prisoners approached. They had been stripped of their armour and wore only flimsy linen loincloths. They were unarmed, but Reynald was taking no chances: the prisoners were led by a man-at-arms, sword drawn, and followed by two more soldiers carrying spears. As the Saracens approached, the assembled soldiers jeered and shouted insults at them. The first prisoner was tall and lanky, with olive skin and long black hair that hung well past his shoulders. The second was shorter, spare and compact. He was older, with a greying beard and a pronounced limp, left by some old wound. The third Saracen was a huge man; a good head taller than John, with a round chest like a beer barrel, an ample belly, and upper arms as thick as John's legs. He was bald, and his head glistened in the sun. The last man was dark-skinned and solidly built, with thickly muscled arms and a broad chest crisscrossed with scars. Of all the prisoners, he alone walked straight-backed, his head held high.

The prisoners reached the ring, where they were lined up before Reynald. He examined the four men for a moment, then placed himself in front of the huge Saracen. The other prisoners were led off to the side, where they stood shifting their weight as they eyed the menacing crowd around them. Meanwhile, Reynald had retreated to the edge of the ring and grabbed a sword. He threw it at the feet of the giant Saracen, who picked it up cautiously, as if he feared some trick.

'Ernaut, you hairy oaf!' Reynald yelled. 'This fat-arse is yours.'

Ernaut pulled on his helmet and stepped forth to face his adversary. As Ernaut drew his sword, Reynald turned the hour-glass. An excited clamour went up from the crowd as bets were laid on how long it would take Ernaut to dispatch the Saracen. A few men even took the long odds and bet on the Saracen to win. There was little chance of that. Ernaut was not quite as tall as the Saracen, but he was even broader. And whereas the Saracen had nothing but his sword to protect him, Ernaut carried a shield and wore full-length chainmail.

'Two coppers on Ernaut in under one turn!' Rabbit shouted, waving the coins.

'I'll take that,' a man behind him called.

Rabbit turned to face John. 'Aren't you going to bet?' John shook his head. A fair fight was one thing, but he had little taste for this sort of blood sport. He had come to the Holy Land for redemption, not for this.

Ernaut stepped towards the centre of the ring, and the crowd whistled and jeered as the Saracen backed away. The men surrounding the ring drew their swords, poking at the Saracen and forcing him back into the centre of the ring, where Ernaut waited. As the Saracen inched forward, Ernaut launched an attack, thrusting for the huge man's unprotected middle. But the Saracen was quicker than he looked. He parried Ernaut's thrust, spun away and slashed at Ernaut, who barely raised his shield in time to deflect the blow. The crowd roared as the two men separated. John looked to the glass, which was nearly a quarter empty.

'Finish him!' someone yelled. Others who had bet on a quick end to the fight took up the cry. With a roar, Ernaut raised his sword over his head and charged, bringing his blade down in a deadly arc. At the last second the Saracen sidestepped the blow and with a cry of triumph slashed at Ernaut's unguarded side. The blow should have killed him, but instead it glanced off his armour. Ernaut spun and struck out, catching the huge Saracen in the neck. The man dropped his sword and fell to his knees, blood gurgling in his throat. Then he dropped face first and lay unmoving, his blood pouring out to stain the dusty earth red. There were cheers and curses from the crowd as men settled up their bets. Reynald grabbed Ernaut's hand and raised it high. 'The victor!' he roared. 'A skin of my best wine for Ernaut tonight!'

Whilst the crowd cheered, John stepped forward and picked up the dead Saracen's sword, testing the blade with his thumb. His suspicions were confirmed; the blade had been dulled. It would not cut through hardened leather, much less chainmail. The Saracen had been given no chance.

'Give that here, Saxon,' Reynald said, and John handed the sword over. Reynald turned again to the crowd. 'Bring the next prisoner! The skinny one!'

The lanky Saracen was matched against Tybaut, the old bull of a man who had fought in the first crusade. Tybaut made short work of his opponent, parrying the young Saracen's clumsy first strike and dispatching him with a quick counter-blow to the chest. The older Saracen was next, and Reynald fought the man himself. The Muslim warrior was a confident swordsman, and at first the fight seemed even as he and Reynald traded blows. But the Saracen's limp made him a step slow. When Reynald pressed his attack, the Saracen stumbled, lowering his guard. He was standing just in front of John when Reynald finished him with a vicious blow, nearly decapitating the Saracen and spraying John with gore.

John wiped the blood from his face and looked at his hand, smeared with red. He closed his eyes as memories surged up inside him: his brother's shocked face; the pommel of their father's sword, engraved with the head of a lion; John's own face and hands wet with hot blood. He turned away from the ring and started to push his way through the crowd.

'You! Saxon!' Reynald called. 'Where do you think you're going? It's your turn.'

John stopped. Around him the men stepped back, opening a path back to the ring. John stood clenching and unclenching his fists as he struggled with his dark memories. Perhaps this was how God had decided he would pay his blood debt; here, against this Saracen. He turned and strode back to the ring.

Rabbit's nose twitched nervously as he presented John with his helmet. 'Keep it,' John said as he shed his shield. 'And help me with my armour.' Rabbit helped pull off the heavy coat of chainmail. John removed his tunic too, so that now he wore only his leather breeches and boots. His bare chest was already glistening with sweat under the intense sun. John drew his sword and stepped into the ring where the battle-scarred Saracen stood waiting for him.

Reynald stepped in front of John. 'What do you think you're doing?' he hissed.

'I'll fight him fairly, or I won't fight,' John replied. Reynald looked from John to his opponent. John was lean and fit, but he was still smooth-faced, barely a man. His opponent was an experienced warrior, broad-chested and thickly muscled. Reynald shook his head and opened his mouth to speak, but John cut him off. 'Like you said, he's only a Saracen, flesh and blood. I'll handle him.'

'I like you, Saxon. I hope you live.' Reynald stepped away, leaving John to face his opponent.

The Saracen swung his sword from side to side, testing its weight, and then stood still, his blade held low. John raised his own sword, holding it with both hands. His heart pounded in his chest, and sweat trickled down his face. He could hear men shouting in the crowd. 'Five on the Saracen!' 'The Saracen in one turn of the sands!' 'Get on with it, bath-boy!' Others began to shout his name, and gradually their voices merged into a chant: 'Saxon! Saxon! Saxon!'

John took a step towards his opponent, and the Saracen moved sideways. John pivoted in the middle of the ring, while the Saracen circled around him. A drop of sweat stung John's eye, and he blinked. Instantly, the Saracen attacked, his sword sweeping up from the ground and towards John's groin. John parried, but no sooner had he blocked the blow than the Saracen spun away and launched another slicing attack at John's head. John ducked the blade, but a moment later his face exploded in pain as the Saracen's knee connected with his jaw. John stumbled backwards, stunned, and barely managed to deflect a wicked thrust aimed at his gut. The Saracen resumed circling.

John stood in the centre of the ring, breathing hard. His jaw was on fire, and he worked it side to side to make sure nothing was broken. The Saracen continued to circle, his sword pointed down towards the earth. John had never faced someone who fought like this: always spinning and circling. He had been trained to fight head-on, in a line. He thought back to the countless hours he had spent in practice with his father. John could hear the gravelly voice in his head: 'Keep your distance, find a pattern, break him down.'

The Saracen attacked again, slicing up towards John's face. John raised his sword, but at the last second the Saracen shifted his attack, cutting back down at John's waist. John jumped backwards, and the tip of the blade missed him by inches. He chopped down at the Saracen, but the man was already spinning away. John's sword bit into the dirt, and he barely brought it up in time to block a vicious blow aimed at his chest. The two swords locked, bringing him close to his opponent. The Saracen head-butted John in the face, sending him reeling backwards. John raised his sword to fend off another attack, but the Saracen had moved away, circling again.

John licked his lower lip and tasted blood, metallic and salty. His jaw clenched as anger rose in him, driving away the fear, the pain, and the sound of the chanting crowd until there was only him and his opponent. 'Bastard!' he snarled as he raised his sword and sprang forward, slashing at the Saracen's side. The Saracen parried and spun away, swinging for John's head as he did so. But this time John anticipated the move. He dropped to one knee to avoid the blade, then lunged forward, driving his sword at the Saracen's gut. The Saracen just managed to deflect the blow, but not entirely. John's blade slid past and sliced his adversary's side, leaving a ragged crimson gash.

John stepped back, and this time he was the one to begin circling. His opponent, a grimace of pain on his face, stood holding his sword in one hand and clutching his side with the other, bright blood oozing between his fingers. John charged forward, stabbing at the Saracen's chest. The Saracen parried, knocking John's sword aside, and John reversed his blow immediately, swinging for his opponent's neck. The Saracen ducked the attack and lunged at John, who sidestepped the blow and brought his sword down hard, knocking the Saracen's blade from his hand. John kicked the sword away and stood facing his defeated foe. The Saracen sank to his knees, waiting for the blow that would finish him. John raised his sword, and as his anger faded, the roar of the crowd came rushing back to him. 'Kill him!' someone yelled. 'Finish him!'

John hesitated. Honour and mercy, the virtues of a warrior: that was what his father had taught him. He had not come to the Holy Land to place more blood on his head. He lowered his sword and stepped away. 'I spare you.' The crowd booed.

'Very chivalrous of you,' Reynald said as he stepped past John. In one smooth motion, he drew his sword and brought it down on the captive's neck, killing him instantly. The crowd roared its approval as Reynald hacked down again and again, severing the man's head from his body. Reynald picked up the head and threw it to the cheering crowd. Then he turned back to John and put his arm around his shoulders. 'You're brave, Saxon; a man after my own heart. What's your real name?'

'Iain, my lord. Iain of Tatewic.'

Reynald frowned. 'That's no name for a knight.' Franks could never get their mouths around 'Iain.'

'John, sir. You can call me John.'

'Very well, then, John. You will come to the castle with me tonight, and you will meet our King.'

John spurred his horse as he followed Reynald into the courtyard of the palace of the King of Jerusalem. Reynald was dressed in leather breeches and a handsome green silk tunic. John wore his chainmail and crusader's surcoat: the only clothes he owned that were fit for the occasion. They dismounted, handed their reins to the waiting servants and headed for an arched doorway at the far side of the courtyard.

A sentry at the door blocked their way. 'Your swords, milords.'

'The High Council meets tonight,' Reynald explained

to John as he unbuckled his sword belt. 'Everyone of any importance will be here: the Patriarch of Jerusalem and the archbishops of Caesarea and Nazareth; the Grand Masters of the Temple and the Hospital; the Kings of Jerusalem, Tripoli, France and the Holy Roman Empire, along with their leading nobles. If tempers get out of hand – and they inevitably will – then it is best that no one be armed.'

John handed over his sword and followed Reynald through a wide doorway and into the great hall. He stopped, dumbstruck. Thick, stone pillars – torches mounted in brackets affixed to their sides – ran down either side of the space, supporting a vaulted roof so high that the ceiling disappeared in the darkness. Chairs had been set up in the wide spaces between the pillars. They were filled with bishops in their robes, German and Frankish lords in simple linen tunics, and armoured Templar and Hospitaller commanders, all with their men standing behind them. In the centre of the hall the floor was thickly carpeted with rugs decorated in a dizzying profusion of geometric patterns. But all of this was as nothing compared to the finery of the men and women at the far end of the hall. The flickering torchlight glimmered against gold embroidery, flashed off rings sporting enormous rubies and amethysts, and shimmered on silk caftans in rich red, saffron yellow, bright green and deep sea-blue. At the centre of this luxury were a middle-aged woman and a young man, seated side by side on gilt thrones. The woman, dressed in scarlet silk and wearing a crown of interwoven strands of gold, had wrinkles at the corners of her eyes and mouth, but her long black hair had not a touch of grey. Her jaw was firmly set and her eyes were a piercing blue. The man, who wore blue silk and a heavier gold crown, looked to be half her age. He had a florid complexion, straight hair the colour of straw and a full beard of the same colour. He sat rigidly straight, repeatedly licking his lips.

'They dress like bloody Saracens, don't they?' Reynald whispered. 'That is King Baldwin of Jerusalem and his mother, Queen Melisende. Baldwin's a good man, but don't let his finery fool you. He and Melisende have been hounding our King Louis for money like two Jews. There's our king, there.' Reynald gestured to a youthful man in linen breeches and a green linen tunic fringed with silk. His long chestnut hair and thick beard disguised a rather weak chin. But what caught John's eye was the woman on the king's left. She was a beauty, with flawless alabaster skin, sharp cheekbones and long auburn hair that curled at the end. She glanced in John's direction, and he saw that her eyes were of darkest amber. He looked away, embarrassed.

'Queen Eleanor of Aquitaine,' Reynald said with a smirk. He lowered his voice. 'They say the slut has been sleeping with her uncle, Raymond of Antioch, that man there.' He pointed across the hall to a handsome, square-jawed man with sparkling blue eyes. 'I'm more interested in Eleanor's cousin, Constance,' Reynald continued, pointing past Raymond to a rather plump woman with a pug nose and close-set eyes. 'She is the heir to Antioch. Whoever marries her will have his own kingdom.' He paused. 'Now come, let me introduce you to our king.'

Reynald led the way across the hall and bowed low

47

before King Louis. John did the same. 'I trust that everything is in place for tonight, Reynald?' Louis asked. 'You have Baldwin's answer?'

'I do indeed, sire. He is with us.'

'Good.'

'And who is this handsome knight that you have brought with you, Reynald?' Eleanor asked. John fixed his gaze on the floor.

'May I present John the Saxon?'

'The knight who bested the Saracen captive today?' Eleanor asked.

'The same, my lady.'

'You are far from home, John,' Louis noted. 'Tell me, how does a Saxon come to be in my service?'

John swallowed. 'You—you fight for God, my lord. In serving you, I serve Him.'

Louis smiled. 'I'm sure. And I'm sure you have no great love for your Norman king, either.' Louis dismissed John with a wave of his hand and turned to speak to one of his courtiers. Reynald grabbed John by the elbow and led him to the side.

'He spoke to you, a great honour,' Reynald whispered. 'The council is about to begin. The proceedings are in Latin. They will mean nothing to you.'

'I speak Latin, my lord.'

Reynald arched an eyebrow. 'You are full of surprises, Saxon. Very well. Wait in the back behind those columns. Say nothing and keep out of sight.'

John slipped into the shadows of the side aisle and took up a position at the end of the hall furthest from King Baldwin's throne. He watched as a wrinkled, bald

48

priest in white robes embroidered with gold walked to the centre of the hall and slammed the butt of his staff against the floor three times. 'This council is now in session!' he declared in Latin. He left the floor, rejoining the other religious men, amongst whom John noticed William of Tyre, the young priest he had met at the fountain on his first day in Acre.

King Baldwin spoke next. 'Welcome knights, lords, men of God, kings and queens. You all know why this council has been called. A second crusade has come to our kingdom, led by valiant King Conrad and brave King Louis. Some say the object of this crusade should be the great city of Aleppo. Others wish to attack Damascus. Tonight, we shall decide.' He paused and licked his lips. 'I will now hear arguments.'

Conrad, a stocky, grey-haired German, rose to speak, but before he had said a word, a voice whispered in John's ear. 'I know you.' John spun about to find himself face to face with a blond boy, perhaps three years younger than himself. The boy had pale blue eyes and an aquiline nose. 'You're the brave one, the knight who took off his armour before fighting the Saracen captive. I watched from the wall.'

'Who are you?'

'Amalric.' The boy leaned close and dropped his voice even lower. 'You know that the man you killed was no spy?'

'What do you mean? Lord Reynald said he captured those men spying on our forces. He said they were Unur's men.'

Amalric burst into sudden laughter, and John glanced

about to see if anybody had noticed. Amalric's mirth faded as quickly as it had come. 'Palace rumour says differently. I heard that your Lord Reynald raided a small village this morning, a village within the Kingdom of Jerusalem. He slaughtered everyone – men, women and children – and took those four "spies" as captives.'

'But why?'

Amalric nodded towards the hall, where the handsome Raymond of Antioch had taken the floor. 'You will see.'

'Conrad says that we must march on Damascus,' Raymond began. 'Damascus is rich, as we all know. It sits on the trade route from the East to the Mediterranean, and both its markets and its coffers are always full. It is a great prize, but we must not be blinded by greed.' There were cries of protest from Conrad's and Louis' men. Raymond continued, shouting over them. 'Unur, the emir of Damascus, is our ally by treaty. He fears the growing power of Nur ad-Din in Aleppo, as should we. Do not forget that it was Nur ad-Din who led the army that conquered Edessa, and that Edessa's fall is the very reason for this crusade. Each year, Nur ad-Din brings more cities under his control. His rise threatens us all – Tripoli, Acre, Jerusalem. Our kingdom survives only because the Saracens are divided—'

'Not so!' the Grand Master of the Templars called. He was a lean man, with short dark hair. 'God protects us!'

'Is that why you have spent God's silver expanding your holdings and building fortresses, Everard, instead of spending it on the calling of your order – protecting pilgrims to the Holy Land?'

Everard flushed crimson. 'How dare you? We built those castles to better protect God's children!'

'If you truly wish to protect His children, then you will do as I say!' Raymond shouted back, struggling now to be heard over the clamour of the Templar knights and the German king Conrad's men. 'If we attack Damascus, then we will force Emir Unur to join with Nur ad-Din. We will be sewing the seeds of our own destruction!' Raymond's men stomped their feet in approval.

King Louis stood and waited for the rumbling to subside. 'You speak of Unur as a great ally, a friend. You say he is bound to us by treaty. And yet, this very morning his spies were found outside our walls! This is not the act of a friend. Unur has pissed all over your precious treaty!' Chaos erupted as Raymond's men yelled out in protest, and Louis's men shouted back. Louis raised his hand, calling for silence. 'We would be fools to trust this godless heathen. If we march north on Aleppo, then what is to stop him from betraying us and attacking Jerusalem while we are gone?'

'Hear, hear!' Louis' men were seconded by Conrad's nobles and the Templars.

'See!' Amalric whispered to John.

John nodded. The 'spies' were a ploy to convince the council to move on Damascus. Reynald had held the tournament to eliminate the only witnesses. 'How do you know these things?' he demanded. 'Who are you?'

Amalric placed a finger to his lips. '*Shhhh*.' He nodded

back towards the council floor. 'There's more. Watch King Baldwin.'

Baldwin was shifting nervously on his throne while Raymond concluded: 'If we attack Aleppo, we can crush Nur ad-Din before he grows too powerful. But if we attack Damascus, we will force our enemies to join together.'

'Then we can defeat them all at once!' Conrad declared, and the assembled knights roared their approval.

Raymond turned from the German king in disgust. 'What say you, Queen Melisende?'

The hall quieted. 'This crusade was called to avenge the loss of Edessa,' she said, her sharp voice filling the hall. 'Taking Aleppo will stop Nur ad-Din and allow us to reclaim Edessa. I say we strike there.'

'I say differently,' King Baldwin declared. Melisende sat forward, clearly surprised. 'Aleppo is far. Attacking it will leave our kingdom vulnerable. After today's incident with Unur's spies, I do not believe we can take such a risk. Damascus is close and rich. Once we take it, then we will have wealth enough to hire all the men we need. We will be able to take Aleppo at our leisure.'

'You speak out of turn, Son,' Melisende reprimanded.

Baldwin hesitated, his tongue flicking over his lips. He looked to King Louis, then to Reynald, who nodded encouragement. Baldwin swallowed and spoke: 'No, mother. I am the King. It shall be as I say.'

'To Damascus!' King Louis shouted.

His cry was echoed throughout the hall. '*Damascus! Damascus!*'

'No! No! No!' Raymond shouted, his face red. 'You damned greedy bastards! If you move on Damascus, then you will do so without me!' He looked to Baldwin. 'Think well on that, King.'

All eyes turned to Baldwin. He said only one word. 'Damascus.' The hall exploded into confusion as half the men present roared their approval, the other half their anger. Fights broke out on the floor between Raymond's and Louis's men. In the confusion, Raymond stormed from the hall. John noted that Eleanor began to rise to follow him, but Louis grabbed her arm, holding her down.

Baldwin also left, striding down the middle of the hall. He stopped near the exit and turned to Amalric. 'Come, Brother. We have work to do.'

Giving John a wink, Amalric followed Baldwin from the hall.

Shocked, John stood staring after the boy until Reynald came up and clapped him on the back. 'Let's get back to camp,' he said. 'We've got to pack for Damascus.'

'Damascus,' John whispered. Back in England, men returned from the first crusade had spoken of it as a fabulous city, second only to Jerusalem. 'It will be a great victory for God.'

Reynald grinned. 'Yes. And it will make us rich!'

Chapter 3

Yusuf buckled his new sword belt tight about his waist and drew the curved blade, marvelling at its beauty. It had been made not far from the room where he now stood, in the famed forges of Damascus, and the bright steel was covered with interlacing patterns of darker grey. Yusuf tested the blade with his thumb and winced as the razor-sharp edge drew a thin trickle of blood. He carefully sheathed the sword, then pulled on the conical helmet that his father had given him. It was too large: only his ears kept the hard iron from sinking down over his eyes. Yusuf stepped in front of the polished bronze mirror in his room and frowned. The slate-grey chainmail that he wore was too long, covering his hands and hanging well below his knees, and the tip of the sword hanging from his waist almost touched the ground.

Turan entered behind Yusuf. His new armour was a perfect fit. 'You look like a scarecrow,' Turan smirked, and he slapped Yusuf on the back of the head so that his helmet slid down over his eyes.

Ayub stepped into the doorway. 'You look a true warrior, Turan.' Yusuf pushed up his helmet to see Turan grinning proudly. Ayub looked at Yusuf and frowned.

'When will we fight the Christians, Father?' Turan asked.

'Inshallah, you will not have to fight, not if Emir Unur finally acknowledges Nur ad-Din as his overlord in return for aid against the Christians. I only pray that Nur ad-Din arrives before the Franks.'

'If Nur ad-Din becomes Unur's overlord, will he force the emir to return Baalbek to you?' Yusuf asked.

'Perhaps. In time, I might even be given something more.' Ayub cracked a rare smile. 'But that is for the future. Now, we must look to save ourselves. The Franks are many, and if Nur ad-Din does not arrive in time, the city may fall. You must be prepared to fight, to the death if needs be. I will not have my sons taken as slaves.'

Turan drew his sword and slashed it from side to side. 'I will kill any Frank who dares stand before me.'

Ayub nodded. 'If you must fight, then I am certain you will bring honour to our family. Now come. It is time that you both begin your education as warriors. I will show you how the walls are to be defended.'

Yusuf followed his father and Turan out into the narrow street that ran in front of their home. They turned right, Abaan and four other mamluks marching around them as an escort. Ayub pointed towards a man hammering up boards to cover the windows and doors of his home. 'Little good it will do him if the Franks take the city.'

They reached the city's main street, which was crowded with men and women lugging their possessions in heavy sacks, fleeing east, away from the Christians. A long train of camels passed, each bearing two heavy chests. The caravan was surrounded by heavily armed guards.

'Moneychangers,' Ayub spat. 'Always the first to flee. And taking good men with them.' Once the camels had passed, Ayub turned towards the city's eastern wall. It was squat – as thick as it was tall – and built of brown bricks made from clay dredged from the river that flowed through Damascus. It did not look very imposing. Yusuf followed his father up a ramp to the top of the wall beside the Bab Tuma, the city's eastern gate. From where he stood, Yusuf could see only a dozen troops, staggered along the wall at wide intervals.

'Where are the emir's men?' he asked.

'To the north and west,' Ayub replied. 'The walls are at their weakest here, but the desert offers its own protection.' He gestured past the wall to the dry, cracked earth that stretched away to the horizon. 'No army can last long out there.'

Ayub led them north. As they walked, the wall rose higher beneath them and became more and more crowded with mamluk soldiers. They passed through the upper rooms of the Gate of Peace, where a huge vat of oil sat over a smouldering fire, ready to be poured on any attackers who came too close to the gate. As they neared the Gate of Paradise, the empty waste beyond the wall gave way to fields, then to the lush orchards of Damascus. They continued to the western gate, the Bab al-Jabiya, where they paused to watch the mamluk warriors pouring out of the city and heading into the orchards.

'The orchards are the key to Damascus,' Ayub told them. 'Always remember: strength of numbers, bravery and steel are important, but an army cannot survive without food and water. Whoever controls the orchards controls the lifeblood of the city. The emir will concentrate his forces there. If they are taken, his men will fall back to the walls. They might hold them for several months. But eventually the city will run short of food and it will fall.'

Yusuf gazed over the orchards, which ran for miles towards the rocky foothills of the nearby mountains. It was from these that the Franks would come. Yusuf was looking away when he saw something out of the corner of his eye – the flash of the sun off steel. There it was again. Squinting against the bright morning light, he could just make out tiny figures moving over the hills, headed for Damascus. '*Look*!' he said, pointing.

'The Franks,' Ayub whispered. A moment later one of the sentries in the nearby tower caught sight of the enemy, and a trumpet blast shattered the air, followed by another, then another. 'Allah protect us. They are here.'

John gritted his teeth against the pain in his back and legs as he trudged up the steep hill. His heavy pack dug into his shoulders, his armour chafed against his sides, and his feet were swollen after days on the long march from Acre. He reached a flat spot and sighed in relief as he stepped aside and dropped his pack, letting the other soldiers plod past. He looked back at the long line of men. The mounted knights had mostly passed, leaving the foot-soldiers to slog on, bent under their heavy packs, their spears held aloft and bobbing up and down as they walked. Behind them came a ragged band of pilgrims, with no armour and lightly armed with bows, spears or simple wooden staffs. They had come to pray in Damascus after the Christian victory, but they would fight if necessary. John turned his gaze to the sun, hazy brown through the thick cloud of dust kicked up by the army. Grit was everywhere, in John's nose, his eyes, his mouth. He unstopped his waterskin and held it to his lips, but it was empty. ''Sblood,' he spat. Even his spit was brown.

'Keep moving, Saxon!' Reynald called as he rode past. 'We'll be there soon enough.'

'Easy for you to say,' John muttered under his breath as he shouldered his rucksack. Bone-tired, he walked on with his head down, eyes on the parched, rocky ground before him. He was so intent on putting one foot in front of the other that he did not immediately notice when the slope began to level off. When he finally looked up, he saw that he stood atop the crest of a long rise, with Damascus, the garden of Syria, spread out on the valley floor below. A dark brown wall enclosed a warren of narrow streets that cut between square houses of creamy white and light brown. In the centre of the city, rising above it all, was the dome of a giant mosque. Beyond the walls, a verdant expanse of gardens and orchards – ancient Roman aqueducts rising high above the thick trees – spread west from the city towards the ridge where

John stood. The brilliant green of the gardens was a sharp contrast to the cracked, dry landscape that the crusaders had marched across and which resumed on the far side of the city. A thin stream flowed through those parched lands, entering the city and flowing out again just to the south of the gardens. John licked his parched lips. He could almost taste the cool water.

He marched with renewed vigour as he descended to where the army was drawing up ranks on the plain before the orchard. There he found a dozen men from his company of fifty sitting on their helmets before one of the narrow paths leading into the orchards. They were all covered in dust. Some sat with their heads between their legs. Others stared vacantly ahead. John flung down his pack and sat beside Rabbit. The young man held out his waterskin.

'I saved some,' he said.

John took the skin and shook it, feeling the water slosh inside. He took a sip, just enough to rinse the dust from his mouth. 'By God, that's good,' he said, handing the skin back.

Shortly after the last of the men had joined them, Reynald rode up. The men rose, groaning and cursing at the pain in their feet and backs. 'Well done, men!' Reynald shouted. 'Damascus is almost within our grasp. The kings have decided to push through the orchards to the walls. We are to march through on this path, clearing out any enemy that we find, and reconvene at the river on the far side. Stop for nothing. Any man who breaks ranks to collect spoils will be flogged on orders of King Louis himself. Is that understood?' Reynald glared at the

59

men. 'Ernaut, you will take the lead. I will follow with the rest of the men.' Reynald spurred his horse towards the rear of the troop.

'All right, you heard him!' Ernaut shouted from horseback. 'Let's get going. The sooner we reach that river, the better.'

The company formed into a column, and John and Rabbit found themselves at the front, just behind One Eye and the old crusader Tybaut. They marched down a narrow path that ran between shoulder-high mud walls. The branches of tall walnut trees heavy with nuts hung out over the walls and met overhead, casting dark, ever-shifting shadows on the trail. The air was thick with dust from marching feet, mingled with the smell of ripening fruit. Walnuts crunched underfoot, adding their rich aroma.

Looking beyond the walls and the thick trunks of the walnut trees, John could see plots of green vegetables, rows of vines heavy with ripening grapes, tall palms crowded with coconuts and closely planted trees weighed down with apples and cherries, as well as a variety of exotic fruits: bright yellow and green ones; oblong fruits that ranged from dark red to fiery orange; and dark-brown pods that dangled like earrings.

'It's like Eden,' John said.

'And you can be sure there's a snake somewhere in here,' Tybaut grumbled. 'Just waiting to strike.'

At that moment a long howl of pain came from somewhere off to their left. They all froze, and John dropped his hand to his sword hilt. More cries of agony pierced the silence, joined now by loud shouting.

'What's that?' Rabbit asked, his nose twitching.

'Pick up the pace!' Ernaut ordered from where he rode just behind John.

Tybaut and One Eye moved ahead at a jog, and John hurried to keep up. He could hear shouting all around him now, growing fainter as the walls on either side rose high above them. The path turned sharply to the right, and as they rounded the corner they stopped short before a five-foot-high barricade of logs, laid across the trail.

'Christ, what's next!' Ernaut complained. 'Let's get this moved!'

Tybaut and One Eye put their shoulders against one of the logs, and John stepped forward to join them. They strained, but the heavy log did not budge.

'By God, it's heavy,' One Eye cursed.

'We could go over the top,' John suggested, 'and pull the logs down from the other side while you push from this side.'

'Do it!' Ernaut ordered.

John managed to pull himself up to the top of the barrier and dropped over to the far side, followed by Rabbit, Tybaut and One Eye. They immediately went to the barricade and grabbed hold of one of the logs. 'On three!' John shouted. '*One*, *two*, *three*!' The log shifted, then rolled free. John and the others jumped back as it fell with a loud thud.

'Only a dozen more to go,' Tybaut grumbled.

John grabbed hold of the next log. One Eye, however, was in no hurry. He had wandered over to the side of the trail, where the branches of a fruit tree hung over a mud

61

wall. He plucked one of the oblong, fiery-orange fruits and sniffed at it.

'Get back to work, One Eye,' John growled.

'Cool it, bath-boy,' One Eye replied, leaning back against the wall. 'It's cursed hot, and I'm hungry.' He took a bite of the fruit. It was golden and pulpy inside. One Eye closed his eye as juice dripped from his beard. 'Sweet Jesus!' he sighed. 'It's delicious.' The words were hardly out of his mouth when the iron point of a spear burst from his chest. He dropped the fruit and stared down at the bloody spear tip. A second later the spear was withdrawn, and One Eye collapsed, dead. There was no sign of any attacker.

'Christ! What was that?' Rabbit shouted.

A scream came from the far side of the barricade, then another and another. 'It's an ambush!' John cried out, drawing his sword and crouching behind his shield, his back to the barrier. He pulled Rabbit down beside him.

'Where are they?' Tybaut demanded. Sword in hand, he went and knelt beside One Eye. He touched the wound in One Eye's back, and then looked up to the wall. John followed his gaze and noticed that there were dozens of round holes, each just wide enough for a spear to fit through. 'The wall!' Tybaut whispered. A spear shot through one of the holes, catching him in the shoulder. He cried out in pain and scrambled backwards. Another spear shot out from the opposite wall, catching him in the back and dropping him.

'We're going to die,' Rabbit whimpered. 'We're going to die!'

'Your shield!' John snapped, and Rabbit raised his

shield just in time to deflect yet another spear. 'We're not going to die, follow me.'

John climbed up to the top of the barricade and pulled Rabbit up after him. The ground on the far side was littered with dead and wounded men. Ernaut's horse had been killed beneath him, and he lay pinned beneath it, screaming for help. Four knights were hurrying forward from further down the column. An arrow struck one, dropping him, and the others hugged the walls, only to be cut down by the spears. As John watched, an arrow sank into the barricade just in front of him. He looked past the wall to a tall building set amongst the fruit trees. There, in the windows of the upper floor, stood four archers. One took aim at John, and an arrow whizzed past his ear.

'Come on!' John shouted as he grabbed Rabbit's arm. They scrambled to the wall, which rose four feet above the barricade. John pulled himself up and dropped over the other side. He landed on top of a Saracen, knocking the man unconscious and sending them both sprawling. John sprang to his feet to find himself facing three more men. The closest stabbed at John with a spear. John blocked the blow with his shield and thrust with his sword, impaling the man through the chest. Another man attacked, and John was forced to jump aside, leaving his sword with the dead Saracen. He backed away, his shield raised, as the two remaining Saracens advanced, their spears pointed at him. One of them screamed '*Allah! Allah! Allah!*' and had started to charge when Rabbit landed on him from above, knocking him flat. John rushed the other Saracen, taking advantage of the surprise.

He slammed his shield into the man's face, dropping him. He turned to see that Rabbit had slit the other man's throat. The boy was white-faced and shaking.

John clapped him on the back. 'Well done. You saved my hide.'

'Th-that's the first man I ever killed.'

'You did well,' John replied as he wrenched his sword free from the chest of the dead Saracen. 'We have to deal with those archers.' He pointed towards the tall building before them. 'Are you up for it?' Rabbit nodded. 'Let's go, then.'

John kicked the door of the house open and rushed inside. The bottom floor was empty. He and Rabbit hurried up the stairs on the far wall. The door at the top was locked. John raised his shield, then kicked the door hard. As it swung open, a volley of arrows thumped into his shield. John threw it aside and charged. Four archers stood along the far wall, each frantically trying to nock another arrow to his bow. John slashed across the face of the one furthest to the right, dropping him before his arrow was free of the quiver. The next in line had managed to nock an arrow, but John sliced the man's bow in two before he could shoot, then finished him with a thrust to the chest. He turned to see a third archer kneeling and holding up his bow in a vain attempt to block Rabbit's sword. Rabbit's blade sliced through the bow and cleaved the Saracen's head in two, spilling blood and pink brains on wooden floor. Rabbit turned away and vomited.

The final Saracen, a beardless man no older than John, raised his bow and shot. But the man's hands were shaking, and the arrow flew wide, embedding itself in the wall. The Saracen threw down his bow and drew a knife. As John approached, sword held high, a puddle of urine formed at the feet of the wide-eyed Saracen. 'Drop it!' John ordered, and the archer threw down his weapon.

'No hurt! No hurt!' he babbled in broken Frankish. 'I prisoner!'

'There you are, Saxon,' Ernaut said as he limped into the room, sword in hand. Four arrow shafts protruded from his chest; they had penetrated his mail but not made it past the thick leather vest beneath. 'What are you doing?'

'I've taken a prisoner.'

Ernaut shoved John out of the way and impaled the archer through the chest. He turned back to John. 'We don't have time for prisoners.'

'He could have told us about other ambushes,' John protested.

Ernaut frowned. 'You're a smart bugger, aren't you,' he said as he snapped off the shafts of the arrows protruding from his chest. He pulled off his helmet and wiped the sweat from his forehead. 'God, I could use a drink. We found a path that leads around the barricade. Let's get to that damned river.' He turned to leave, but then stopped in the doorway. 'You two chop off those sons-of-whores heads and bring them with us on spears. Maybe that will make the bastards think twice before they attack us.'

''Sblood,' John cursed as he turned to his gruesome task.

*

65

Yusuf and Turan stood on the wall above the al-Jabiya gate and watched as Muslim troops poured out of the orchard and splashed across the river, heading for the open gate. Behind the troops, a procession of disembodied heads approached through the orchard, bobbing high above the trees. A moment later, the first Frankish knights stepped out of the orchard, carrying spears with the heads of Muslim soldiers impaled atop them.

'They are savages,' Yusuf whispered.

'They will pay for this indignity,' Turan spat.

'Inshallah.'

On the far side of the river more Christians were emerging from the orchards. Most went straight to the waters to drink. A few shouted up at the wall and made crude gestures. Below Yusuf, the gate slammed shut behind the last of the Muslim warriors. Yusuf looked beyond the orchard to the horizon, where the sun was just setting. The battle for the orchards had taken the best part of a day. He looked away from the blood-red sun to see his father approaching along the wall.

'The Franks have taken the orchard, Father!' Turan shouted to him.

Ayub nodded. 'Unur will have no choice now but to ally with Nur ad-Din. He has invited us to dine at the palace. Come, we are expected.'

'Should we change into finer clothes?' Yusuf asked. He and Turan both wore plain white cotton caftans.

'No. Unur prefers simplicity.'

Yusuf followed his father through the city to the emir's palace, a jumble of domed buildings and simpler wooden structures that sat behind a tall wall and deep moat. A dozen mamluks guarded the bridge across the moat. Their commander nodded respectfully as Ayub approached. 'You are expected,' the mamluk said, and the soldiers parted to let them pass.

They entered the palace entrance hall and found themselves before a pair of tall bronze doors guarded by two muscular Nubians. 'Remember,' Ayub said to his sons, 'you are here as guests. Do as I do. Do not speak unless the emir speaks to you first. And if you must speak, keep your answers short. Everything you do and say will reflect upon our family. We can ill afford the emir's disfavour.' Ayub nodded to one of the Nubians, who knocked on the door three times and then pushed it open.

'Najm ad-Din Ayub,' the Nubian declared.

Yusuf followed his father and brother into a large, circular room, brilliantly lit by candelabras mounted on the marble-clad walls that rose to a vaulted dome high above. The dome's interior was covered in ornate script in gold-leaf, with Emir Unur's seal at the centre. Generals and ministers of the emir sat on cushions that had been placed in a circle around the edge of the room. They were already eating, selecting their food from dozens of platters placed on low stands. Emir Unur sat directly across from the door, on a dais that raised him two feet above the others. He wore robes of white silk embroidered with an interlocking pattern of red roses and green thorns. Unur was fit and olive-skinned, with a clean-shaven chin and scalp and crinkles around the corners of his bright, hazel eyes. He smiled broadly when he saw his guests. 'Welcome, Ayub,' he said in a pleasant baritone. 'These, I take it, are your sons?'

'Turan and Yusuf,' Ayub affirmed. The two boys approached and bowed low.

'Fine young men,' Unur approved. 'Sit here, beside me. Eat. Now that you have arrived, we shall have entertainment. Afterwards, we shall talk.' He clapped his hands. 'Bring the girls!'

Yusuf and Turan were directed to cushions just to the left of the emir's dais. Their father took his place on the emir's right. No sooner had they sat down than four young women entered wearing veils and loose, diaphanous silk robes that shifted as they walked, revealing glimpses of firm breasts and long, golden-brown legs. A drummer had entered behind them, and at the first sound of his drum the girls began to dance, circling slowly to the beat. Their arms and feet traced intricate patterns while their waists and hips swayed slowly side to side. One of the girls paused for a moment before Yusuf, fixing him with dark eyes ringed with kohl. Yusuf blushed and looked away towards his father.

Ayub had begun to eat, scooping up stew with a piece of flatbread. Yusuf followed his example, tearing off a piece of the warm bread and using it to scoop up a delicious mouthful of chickpeas, onions and roast lamb. He noticed that Turan had not touched his food. His eyes were fixed on the dancers. Yusuf looked back to the girls, who were each bending forward now, allowing the men to see the curves of their breasts. He shrugged and scooped up more of the lamb. He could not understand his brother's fascination.

The drum began to beat faster, and the dancers moved in time, spinning and leaping. Suddenly they

68

stopped circling and fell to their knees. They shook their chests, then leaned backwards so that the back of their heads touched the floor. Turan was transfixed, his mouth hanging open. Yusuf looked over and saw that his father, too, had stopped eating to watch. The dancers lifted their hips off the floor slowly, then faster and faster, moving to the ever more rapid beat. They rolled over, pushed themselves to their feet and began circling again. They were now a blur of seductive curves and firm limbs. Then, with a final crescendo, the drum fell silent and the dancers fell to the floor, kneeling motionless with their foreheads touching the ground. Only their heaving sides betrayed the recent exertions.

Emir Unur rose from his dais and stepped down amongst the dancers. He walked slowly around the edge of the circle, then touched the shoulder of the dancer opposite the dais. She rose and left the room, head held high.

'Lucky bastard,' Turan murmured, just loudly enough for Yusuf to hear him.

Unur returned to his seat and clapped his hands. The other women left, followed by the drummer. The doors slammed shut behind them. 'Lovely, are they not?' Unur said with a wink towards Yusuf and Turan. 'Even in trying times like these, we should not ignore life's simple pleasures. Who knows when they will be taken from us?' He turned towards Ayub. 'I trust you saw the Franks arrive?'

'I did. My sons and I stood on the walls for much of the day.'

'And how do you rate our chances, wise Ayub?'

'The Franks are many, and now that they have taken the orchards, the city will run short of food. Forgive my impertinence, Emir, but I do not believe you will be able to hold the walls for long. You need Nur ad-Din's help.'

Unur frowned. 'I fear that if I call on your lord to drive off the Franks, then I will only replace one master with another.'

'Perhaps, but a Muslim master, one who will leave you your throne and not pillage your city. All you have to do is acknowledge his lordship and promise to send troops when he calls for them. Is that so much?'

'*Hmph*,' Unur grunted. He looked around the circle at his generals. 'Are you in agreement with Ayub?' One by one, the generals nodded. Unur sighed. 'So be it. Write to your master, Ayub, and tell him to send his army. But warn him that he must hurry if he wishes to win me as his vassal, for I plan to do better than merely hold the city until he arrives.' He turned to face Turan. 'Tell me, young Turan. What would you do in order to drive the Franks away from our city?'

'I would strike now, before they dig in,' Turan replied. 'I would send men out from the eastern gate to circle behind the Franks.' Turan used his right hand to show the movement of the soldiers. 'And then I would attack from both sides.' He clapped his hands together. 'The Franks will be crushed!'

'A bold manoeuvre,' Unur mused. Turan grinned. 'Although one which would leave us with too few men to defend the walls, and which would split our army in order to attack a defensive position. If the Franks learned of our men leaving by the east gate, then they would attack and the city might well be lost.' Turan blushed. Unur turned his penetrating gaze upon Yusuf. 'What of you, young man? What would you do?'

Yusuf took a deep breath. 'So long as the Franks hold the orchards, we are weak. They have food and water enough to last for months, while our supplies will grow smaller every day. We must drive them from the orchards at any cost.'

'Agreed, but how? As I told your brother, we cannot send enough men to drive them out without leaving our walls vulnerable.'

Yusuf's forehead creased as he considered the problem. 'Perhaps there is another way.'

'Indeed?'

Yusuf lowered his eyes. 'But there is no honour in it. It is best forgotten.'

'Speak, young Yusuf,' Unur insisted. 'I wish to hear this idea of yours.'

Yusuf looked past Unur to his father, who nodded. 'If the Franks cannot be driven out, then perhaps they can be lured,' Yusuf suggested. 'Aleppo is a better military target than Damascus. The Franks must have come here because they seek riches. If gold is what they have come for, then give it to them. Pay them to leave the orchards.'

'That is a coward's answer,' Turan muttered. Several of the men in the room nodded their agreement.

'Forgive me.' Yusuf hung his head. 'I should not have spoken.'

'No, it was a wise answer,' Unur said. He turned towards Yusuf's father. 'You have raised clever sons, Ayub. They do you great honour.' Ayub inclined his head to acknowledge the compliment. 'Now I must bid you and your sons goodnight so that I may speak with my generals. We have much to discuss.'

The Frankish camp was set up at the edge of the orchard, near the river. John's troop erected their tents in a clearing and dined on dark brown pods that they shook from the trees. The flesh was chewy but filling, with an earthy taste not unlike the black bread that John had grown up eating. His belly full, he removed his chainmail and crawled into his tent, where he collapsed into an exhausted sleep.

He dreamt of his home in Northumbria, of a crisp autumn day, the sun bright in a cloudless sky. He was walking through a green field of knee-high oats, their stalks rippling in a gentle breeze. He crossed the field towards his family manor, a rectangular building of grey stone, surrounded by a broad moat. His father stood in the doorway, waving to him. But something was wrong. As John approached, his father fell to his knees, blood running from his mouth. Behind him, John's brother appeared. Loud screams echoed from within the manor.

John awoke with a start, but the screaming did not stop. Cries of agony came from outside his tent, joined now by shouts of alarm. John sat up just as a spear ripped through the side of his tent, plunging into the ground where he had lain only a moment before. He grabbed his sword and rushed outside, wearing only his linen tunic. The camp was overrun with ghostly figures, barely visible in the darkness – Saracens in dark armour, stabbing at the tents with their spears. One of the attackers saw John. With a cry, the Saracen charged, his spear pointed at John's chest.

John sidestepped the spear, knocking the point aside with his sword, and then stuck out his foot, tripping the Saracen as he charged past. He hacked down, finishing the man, then looked up just in time to twist out of the way of another spear thrust, which ripped through his tunic. John grabbed the shaft and pulled his attacker to him, impaling the Saracen on his sword. As he pulled his blade free, John looked about for another foe, but he saw only other Christians, some in armour, some still in their tunics. The Saracens were fleeing as quickly as they had come, disappearing back into the dark trees.

'Come on!' John shouted and charged into the trees, weaving between the closely set trunks. He caught glimpses of the Saracens just ahead, and he could hear his own men crashing through the undergrowth behind him. He had not gone far when he heard an arrow whiz past. Another embedded itself in the tree beside him. John took shelter behind a thick tree trunk as the air filled with the buzz of arrows. Around him, the night echoed with cries of pain and curses in French and German.

The arrows stopped and John continued his pursuit. He left the trees and crashed through a row of grapevines. He peered into the dark shadows ahead, but could see neither friend nor foe in the thick darkness, although he could hear the other Christians around him. Then he caught a flash of movement off to his left and headed that way, entering another stand of trees. As he pushed on, the sounds around him faded.

John squeezed between two trees and found himself at the edge of a clearing where two men stood talking. Instinctively, John stepped back into the shadows. The man facing John was a Saracen in a white turban and chainmail. The other had his back to John. 'It shall be as you say,' he was saying. The man turned. It was Reynald.

John caught a flash of steel out of the corner of his eye and ducked just in time to avoid being decapitated. He turned to find himself face to face with Ernaut. 'Ernaut! It's me, John!'

Ernaut stepped back and lowered his sword. 'Sorry, Saxon. I thought you were one of them. It's damn near impossible to see out here.'

'Saxon!' It was Reynald, marching across the clearing towards them. The Saracen was gone. Had John imagined him? Reynald grabbed John's tunic and pulled him close. 'What are you doing here?'

'I was chasing the Saracens.'

Reynald's eyes narrowed as he examined John; then he released him. 'Very well. Since you are here, come with me. I must meet with the other leaders to discuss our response to this attack. Ernaut, you get back to camp and look after the men.'

John fell in behind Reynald. As he walked he looked back to catch a glimpse of Ernaut marching into the darkness, a bulging sack slung over his shoulder.

John and Reynald emerged from a dense grove of apple trees into a clearing that was almost entirely filled by a huge tent. From inside, John could hear the heated voices of many men. At the entrance, Reynald paused and

74

leaned close to John. 'You are brave, Saxon. You will go far with my help. But if you cross me, you will regret it. Do you understand?' John hesitated. What had he seen, anyway? He nodded, and Reynald clapped him on the shoulder. 'Good man.'

They entered the tent, and Reynald shouldered his way through the crowd to where King Louis stood with the German king Conrad and Baldwin, King of Jerusalem. John stayed at the edge of the crowd.

'They came in through your section of the camp!' King Conrad was shouting as he pointed at King Louis.

'You're the one who insisted that we camp here,' Louis retorted. 'There are hundreds of paths through the orchards. It is impossible to guard every one of them. My men's blood is on your hands!'

'How dare you!' Conrad roared.

'Enough! Enough!' King Baldwin shouted. 'This is just what our enemy hopes for. They wish to set us against one another. We must not let them. If you wish to blame someone, then blame me.' He looked to both kings. Neither spoke. 'Very well. We must fortify our position immediately. We will build walls to separate the orchards from the city, and we will post guards.'

'Pardon me, King Baldwin, but is that wise?' It was Reynald who spoke, and all eyes turned to him. 'The orchards will be hard to hold, no matter what fortification we build. We will never be safe from these night-time raids so long as we stay here.'

'What are you proposing?' Conrad asked.

'The walls are weaker on the eastern side of the city. I suggest we move our camp there.'

'After we lost so many lives to take the orchards?' King Louis asked. 'And what will our men eat? The land to the east is desert.'

'We will take supplies from the orchards. We only need enough for a few days. The Saracens do not expect an attack from the east. In less than a week, we will be feasting in the halls of the emir's palace!'

'It is too great a risk, Reynald,' Louis said.

'No,' Conrad countered. 'You should listen to your man. If moving east can bring the siege to an end sooner, then I am for it. I have been too long away from my kingdom already.'

'What do you say, King Baldwin?' Louis asked. 'You know these lands better than any of us.'

'It is true that the eastern walls are weaker,' Baldwin began. 'But moving our camp brings great risk. If we do not conquer the city swiftly, then we will run short of food. And retaking the orchards will be difficult, if not impossible.' He looked around the tent. 'If it were left to me, I would stay and fortify our position here, but I am not the only king present. We shall vote. Those in favour of staying?' Louis shouted his approval and was joined by a handful of men. 'Those in favour of moving camp to the east?' A deafening chorus of approval greeted Baldwin's words. The choice was clear. 'Tomorrow at dawn,' Baldwin declared, 'we break camp.'

On a blazing hot afternoon three days later, John sat in the shade of his tent, his stomach growling as he stared at the unappetizing piece of salted beef he held in his hands. The beef was as tough as leather, and one side was splotched with green. John sniffed at it and wrinkled his nose in disgust. He shook his waterskin and sighed. Only a couple of mouthfuls of water remained to wash down the salty, putrid meat. He was about to toss it aside when his stomach growled loudly. 'By God, I'm hungry,' he muttered to himself.

John glanced over his shoulder, beyond the rows of low tents and past the huge pavilion at the centre of camp that served as a church, to the bulky wall of Damascus, shimmering in the summer heat. After three days of bloody fighting, the wall still stood, and already the army was short of food and water. Moving east had taken them further from the river, and whenever men went to fill their waterskins, the Saracens rode out to drive them off. The fruit and vegetables from the orchards that had not been eaten had already spoiled in the sweltering July heat. This loathsome salted beef was all they had left. John rubbed the tough meat between his fingers, trying to remove as much of the mould as possible. Then, he tore off a piece with his teeth and chewed slowly.

'Get up, Saxon.' It was Ernaut, approaching in full armour. 'On your feet, all of you!' he bellowed to the other men crouched in the tiny squares of shade cast by their tents. 'We're leaving.'

'When?' John asked.

'Now. Pack up and form ranks. We've been assigned to the rearguard.'

John ducked into his tent and stuffed his possessions into his rucksack. Then he untied and removed the tent's woollen covering, revealing its skeleton – two poles at either end that crossed at the top to form triangles, and a longer pole that ran between them. He wrapped the poles in the tent fabric, tied up the bundle and stuffed it in his rucksack. He looked around him as he shouldered the bag. What had been a city of tents only minutes before had vanished, reverting to a dusty plain.

The rest of the company was forming up in a long column, five men wide. As John walked over to join them, he wrapped a long strip of white linen around his helmet, to prevent the blazing sun from transforming the metal into an oven. He joined the column near the end, and Rabbit fell in beside him. A moment later, they set off with Ernaut riding at their head.

'Isn't the rearguard the most dangerous?' Rabbit asked, his nose twitching.

'Don't worry,' John replied. 'Stick close to me and I'll look after you.'

They were marching past the rest of the army now. First came the foot-soldiers of the kingdom of Jerusalem, thousands of men in chainmail packed close together, their ranks bristling with spears. They surrounded King Baldwin and his four hundred knights, whose impatient chargers snorted and stamped at the hard ground. The ranks of Baldwin's men gave way to the tall Germans, who had also formed up around their king. Last of all came the French troops around King Louis and his knights. Reynald rode amongst them, and as John passed, their eyes met.

Ernaut marched his troops to the end of the line and took up his place in the centre of them. John found himself on the outside edge of the column, only a few rows from the end of the long line of warriors. Behind him, the thousands of pilgrims were clustered together in a shapeless mass.

'Listen up, men!' Ernaut roared to his troops as the column began to move forward. 'King Louis has issued strict orders. If the enemy attacks, you're to stay in close formation. I don't care what those bastard Saracens do. If any man leaves the column, I'll have his eyes!'

The column headed around the city to the south, the men of Jerusalem leading the way and the pilgrims straggling along in the rear. After only a few minutes of marching, John was already soaked in sweat and choking at the dust stirred up by the men ahead. He rearranged the strip of linen around his helmet so that it covered his face, leaving only his eyes visible.

The hard ground gave way to sand as it sloped down to the Barada River. John splashed into the water, sighing in relief as it washed over him up to his waist. He filled his waterskin as he waded across, then took a long drink. He lowered the skin at the sound of shouting amongst the pilgrims behind him. Looking back, he saw the southern gates of Damascus swinging open. Hundreds of Saracens on horseback poured out, galloping towards the pilgrims. In a panic the pilgrims rushed forward, eager to cross the river before the horsemen reached them.

'Keep moving, damn it!' Ernaut shouted. 'Tighten the ranks! Shields up!'

John stepped closer to the man in front of him and raised his shield so that it overlapped that of the men before and after him, forming a moving wall. Behind him, he heard screams of pain as the Saracens' first arrows hit home amongst the pilgrims. A few of the faster pilgrims were sprinting past the column now. A scattering of arrows followed them. Most shattered against the hard ground or skittered off the shields of the men in the column, but a few found their mark. John saw one arrow fly straight through a pilgrim's chest. The man kept running for a few steps, then keeled over, dead.

John glanced over his shoulder and saw that most of the pilgrims had been trapped on the far side of the river. The Saracen horsemen had swooped down and encircled them, cutting the pilgrims off from the river and the rest of the column. They were huddled in a mass as the Saracens circled them, firing arrows into the crowd. The pilgrims with bows fired back, but with no armour and few weapons, they had no chance of holding off their well-armed attackers. Already dozens lay dead, their bodies riddled with arrows like pincushions. When the Saracens tired of their bows and closed with swords, the carnage would truly begin.

John raised his voice to address the men around him. 'We've got to go back and help the pilgrims! They'll be slaughtered!'

'Shut your trap, Saxon!' Ernaut shouted back. 'Keep to your places men! If we break ranks, the Saracens will carve us up.'

'But we can't just let them die,' John pressed.

'Better them than us!'

''Sblood,' John growled to himself. 'This isn't right.' He had come to the Holy Land seeking redemption. What better way to achieve salvation than to die fighting to save others? He dropped his rucksack, then stepped from the line and sprinted towards the river and the pilgrims beyond.

'Saxon, I'll have your hide for this!' he could hear Ernaut roaring. But John did not stop. Then he heard another voice, closer behind him.

'John! Wait!' John stopped, and Rabbit came up alongside him.

'What are you doing?' John demanded. 'Get back to the line!'

'You told me to stick with you.'

'So I did.' John drew his sword as he turned back to face the river. A few pilgrims had now reached it, and the Saracens were riding amongst them, chopping men down and staining the waters crimson. 'Come on, then,' John called. 'Let's save as many of them as we can! For Christ!' he roared as he raised his sword and charged.

Yusuf stood on the wall beside Turan and watched wide-eyed as Unur's men butchered the Christian pilgrims. He and Turan were squeezed in amongst a crowd of specta-tors: bearded men in their white caftans and turbans; women in robes and veils. All of Damascus seemed to have turned out to watch the slaughter. They cheered each time a Christian fell. A tall, drunk man beside Yusuf yelled a non-stop stream of invectives at the fleeing Christians. 'Go back to your whore-mothers, you sons of donkeys! Goat-fuckers! Male whores! Bastard scum!'

A piercing wail of agony penetrated the roar of the crowd and the insults of the drunken man. Yusuf spotted the man – a pilgrim on his knees, an arrow protruding from his gut. As Yusuf watched, a horseman rode in close and fired an arrow directly into the wailing pilgrim's mouth. The man's cry ended abruptly as the arrow burst through the back of his head. The crowd roared their approval. Yusuf turned away, sick to his stomach.

He glanced at Turan, who was watching the action intently, his eyes shining and his head nodding at each Christian death. Suddenly, Turan extended his arm, pointing towards the river. 'There's Father!' Yusuf looked and saw Ayub in his distinctive, silvery chain-mail. He sat straight-backed in the saddle, sword in hand as he galloped down the sandy bank towards the river. Several of the pilgrims had managed to reach the water, and a pair of Christian knights had left the column to help them. The knights stood in the river as the pilgrims scrambled for safety up the bank behind them.

Yusuf watched as his father's horse splashed into the river and headed for the larger of the two knights. To Yusuf's surprise, the knight charged straight for Ayub, wading through the waist-deep water with his sword held high. Ayub prepared to deliver his blow, but at the last second the knight seemed to trip and disappeared beneath the water. Ayub reined in his horse, looking for his foe. A moment later, the knight burst from the water beside Ayub's horse. He grabbed hold of Ayub and pulled him from the saddle. As Ayub disappeared beneath the water, the Christian knight pulled himself into the saddle. He slapped the flank of the horse with the flat of his sword and rode downstream to confront another Muslim warrior. The waters behind him stilled. There was no sign of Ayub.

'Where is he?' Yusuf whispered. He grabbed Turan's arm and shouted, 'Where's Father?'

'We've got to help him,' Turan said.

Yusuf shook his head. 'Father told us to stay here.'

'Stay, then. You'd be of no use anyway.' Turan turned away and ran for the ramp that led down from the wall.

'No, wait!' Yusuf shouted as he hurried after his brother. The two sprinted down from the wall and flew through the streets, back to their house. They burst inside to find the building deserted. The warriors had all left to fight with Ayub, and the servants had gone to the walls to watch.

Yusuf banged open the door to his chamber. The suit of chainmail that his father had given him hung from a hook on the far wall, next to Yusuf's sword and helmet. He pulled on the heavy armour and conical helmet, then buckled his sword around his waist. He stumbled towards the stables, clumsy in the ill-fitting chainmail.

Yusuf entered the stables to find Turan saddling a horse. He looked at Yusuf and frowned. 'You should stay here. You'll get yourself killed.'

'I will help to save Father,' Yusuf replied as he grabbed his own saddle and heaved it on to another horse. 'And if I cannot, then I will avenge his death.' Turan smirked, but said nothing as he led his horse to the stable door and pulled it open. Yusuf pulled tight the girth that held his horse's saddle in place, and then followed his brother out into the street, where Turan swung himself easily into the saddle and galloped away, the hooves of his horse kicking up dust.

Yusuf closed the stable door and then struggled to haul himself up into the saddle. Gritting his teeth with a final effort, he pulled himself up and spurred after Turan. The jolting of his horse kept knocking Yusuf's helmet down so that it covered his eyes, and it was all that he could do to catch up with his brother. The two of them raced down the main street and past the towering mosque. They thundered across a wooden bridge that spanned the Barada River where it flowed through the centre of Damascus, and headed for the southern gate. Ahead, Yusuf could see hundreds of people crowded atop the wall. As he and Yusuf neared, several men turned and cheered. Then the gate flashed by, and they were beyond the wall.

Yusuf's horse stopped and reared, shying at the strong scent of blood on the air. His helmet fell over his eyes and he felt himself falling backwards. He reached out blindly and managed to grab hold of his horse's mane, keeping himself in the saddle. He hung on desperately until his horse settled. When he pushed his helmet back from his eyes he saw utter chaos. Unur's warriors had shouldered their bows and closed with swords, and the pilgrims had scattered in all directions. Two Christians in brown robes sprinted by Yusuf's horse, not ten feet away. A horseman galloped after them, slashing left and right as he brought down first one, then the other.

'The river!' Turan yelled, pointing to their right. He spurred forward, and Yusuf followed. They galloped down the sandy bank and splashed into the cold water.

'Father!' Yusuf cried as he peered into the clear waters around him. 'Father!' Dead bodies, weighed down by armour, littered the river bed, but there was no sign of Ayub. Shouting in Frankish drew Yusuf's eyes from the water. Just downstream, eight Christian pilgrims were wading across the river, led by two knights, one on foot and the other on horseback. As Yusuf watched, the one on horseback shouted something, then turned and rode back to gather more pilgrims.

'Bastards!' Turan shouted. 'You will pay for the death of my father!' He drew his curved sword and spurred towards the Christians, who drew together in a compact mass, bristling with spears and pitchforks. Turan charged into them, batting aside spears with his shield and bowling men over with his horse. He lashed out to his right and a Christian stumbled away, his face a mask of blood. The other pilgrims closed around Turan, stabbing at him from all sides. He fought furiously, turning his horse in a circle and knocking spears away with his shield while hacking with his sword. A spear sneaked through his defences and gashed his side. Turan roared in pain but kept fighting.

'Turan, I'm coming!' Yusuf yelled. He cast his bulky helmet aside and drew his sword. He kicked his horse's flanks, charging through the river towards the mass of pilgrims. Two of the Christians – the young knight in chainmail and a wiry, grey-bearded man dressed in tattered linens – turned to face Yusuf. The knight held a sword, its blade flashing in the sunlight, while the old man wielded a pitchfork. As Yusuf neared, the old man smiled madly, revealing rotting, crooked teeth.

At the last second Yusuf veered towards the knight, knocking him aside with his horse. The old man stabbed at Yusuf's chest with his pitchfork, and Yusuf instinctively pulled on the reins, backing his horse so that the thrust missed him. He grabbed the shaft of the pitchfork and pulled, bringing the old man close. Then Yusuf hacked down, cleaving the old pilgrim's head and spilling blood and brains into the river. Yusuf's stomach turned. The man stayed standing for a moment, a lunatic's smile still on his lips despite the sword lodged in his skull. Yusuf was still trying to withdraw his sword when the man fell, his weight yanking the sword from his grasp.

Defenceless, Yusuf looked up to see a lanky pilgrim, spear in hand, wading towards him. The pilgrim stabbed at Yusuf, who jerked back on the reins. His horse reared, and the spear plunged into its chest. One of the horse's hooves clipped the pilgrim in the head, knocking him unconscious. Then, whinnying in pain and fright, the horse fell. Yusuf jumped clear and landed on his back with a splash. He sank beneath the water, his armour pulling him down.

Through the wavering waters, Yusuf could see the bright sun fixed in the cloudless sky high above him. He struggled to rise towards the air, but then collapsed back on the hard rocks of the river bed, weighed down by his chainmail. He began to panic as he grew short of air. Again he tried to sit up, but sank back down. His lungs ached now, and his hands strained towards the light, searching to grab hold of something. Yusuf closed his eyes, forcing himself to be calm. This was no different from one of his fits. If he did not panic, then he would survive. He managed to roll over on his stomach and pushed himself up on his knees. Then, with a last effort, he straightened, gasping for breath as he broke the surface. He knelt in the river, the water touching his chin as he struggled to recover his breath. Then he felt a shadow cross over him and looked up. Standing befor him was a Christian knight, his sword raised high. The knight was beardless and thin – little older than Yusuf himself – and his nose was twitching violently. Yusuf looked past the boy's face to his sword, glinting in the sunlight. He closed his eyes as the sword began its fatal descent.

Nothing happened. Yusuf opened his eyes to see the young knight still standing before him. Only now the boy was staring wide-eyed at his own chest, and Yusuf followed his gaze to see a sword blade protruding from the young knight's armour. The sword disappeared, and the boy toppled to the side. In his place stood Turan.

Yusuf took the hand that Turan offered him, and his older brother pulled him to his feet. 'Thank you, Brother,' Yusuf said. 'I owe you my life.'

'Don't forget it,' Turan said and stepped aside. Past him, Yusuf saw a Muslim warrior in silvery chainmail, facing off against the last of the pilgrims. The warrior sidestepped a spear thrust and hacked down, finishing off the pilgrim. Then the warrior turned, and Yusuf's eyes widened in disbelief.

'Father! You're alive!'

Ayub did not reply. His face was set in a grim mask as he waded over to Yusuf and slapped him hard across the face. Ayub bent down and grabbed Yusuf by the arms, pulling him close so that their faces were only inches apart. 'By Allah, I told you to stay at the walls!' he growled. 'Were it not for your brother, you would be dead. Dead!' Tears welled in Yusuf's eyes. 'Look at you, crying like a woman,' Ayub said with disgust as he released Yusuf. 'At least your brother has the makings of a warrior. You are worthless.' Ayub turned and stormed out of the river and up the bank towards Damascus. Yusuf followed, his head hung in shame.

'Stay together!' John roared at the pilgrims massed behind him. He had managed to rally over three-dozen men and had arranged them in a column four wide, spears bristling on all sides. John rode at their head, leading them at a quick march towards the river. Many of the pilgrims had picked up shields from fallen Saracens, and they held the circular leather bucklers close together, forming a patchwork wall around the outside of the column. But the small shields offered only limited protection from the arrows of the Saracens, who circled the column on horseback, shooting into the mass of men. As John watched, one of the men just behind him went down with an arrow in his leg. Two pilgrims immediately picked him up and carried him to the inside of the column, while another man stepped out to take his place. A second later, that man fell dead, an arrow in his throat. At this rate, John reflected, he would be lucky to reach the main column with a dozen men. 'Pick up the pace!' he shouted back. 'And keep together!'

John turned forward. Ahead, the terrain sloped down to the blood-stained waters of the river. A hundred yards downstream, he saw the group of pilgrims that he had sent off with Rabbit, hoping to get the young warrior safely off the battlefield. John frowned. At least half of the pilgrims were dead, their motionless bodies floating away on the current. Two Saracen warriors were finishing off the last of the pilgrims. Just upstream from them, Rabbit stood with his sword held high, preparing to strike a third Muslim. John watched in horror as one of the Saracen warriors approached him from behind.

'Rabbit, look out!' he shouted, but it was too late. The Saracen impaled Rabbit from behind. He withdrew his sword, and Rabbit slumped into the river. 'No!' John roared. His knuckles whitened where he gripped his sword, and his face flushed crimson. He turned to the man behind him. 'Give me your spear!' The man offered him the weapon, and John sheathed his sword and took it. 'Keep in order and march fast,' John told him. 'If you hurry, you should be able to catch up the column.'

'Where are you going?'

But John was already riding away, his horse kicking up plumes of sand as it galloped down the slope towards the man who had killed Rabbit. The man was walking up the riverbank towards him, flanked by the two other Saracens. He was only fifty yards off now, close enough that John could make out some of his features. He was thickly built, with dark hair, tanned skin and the first beginnings of a beard on his broad face. John raised the spear, preparing to hurl it, when four Saracen warriors rode between him and his target.

John did not slow his mount as the four warriors turned towards him and fired a volley of arrows. One of the arrows embedded in John's shield with a thump. Another penetrated his chainmail skirt and stuck deep in his thigh. John gritted his teeth against the pain, rose in the saddle and hurled his spear. It caught the lead rider in the chest, knocking him from his horse. John drew his sword as he thundered towards the remaining three riders, who had shouldered their bows and now rode with spears in hand. As he flashed past the first man, John swung out and caught him in the throat, killing him instantly. John cried out in pain as the spear of another warrior deflected off his shield and drove into his shoulder. Then, John was past, his shield arm hanging uselessly at his side. He dropped the shield and used his knees to turn his horse to face the remaining two warriors.

'For Christ!' John cried out as he raised his sword and spurred towards the men. They charged him, one on his left and the other to his right, their spears pointed at his chest. At the last second John leapt from his horse, dodging the spear of the warrior on the right and slamming into him. They both went flying, and John heard the Saracen's neck snap as he landed hard on top of him. John rolled off him and rose, standing unsteadily on his injured leg. The final Saracen had wheeled his horse and sat fifty yards off. He spurred his mount towards John.

John raised his sword, then thought better of it. He dropped the sword and stood over the body of the dead Saracen. The final horseman was only thirty yards off now, and John knelt, his head lowered. He could hear the hooves of his enemy's horse pounding closer and closer. The Saracen was only ten yards away when John grabbed the spear of the dead warrior, rose, and with a loud cry, let it fly. The spear struck the Saracen's horse in the chest. The beast collapsed, and the warrior went flying, landing in a heap. John picked up his sword and limped over to finish him. He stood over the Saracen's broken body, then paused at the sound of another set of hooves pounding towards him. He looked up to see a Christian knight with sword in hand, riding straight towards him. It was Ernaut.

'Well met, Ernaut!' John called out as Ernaut reined in beside him.

'You're a tough bugger, Saxon,' Ernaut replied. 'I thought the Saracens would have finished you off by now.'

'Not yet. Help me up.' He held his good arm out towards Ernaut.

Ernaut clasped his hand. Then, as he pulled John close, he stabbed down with his sword, impaling John through the side. 'You have seen too much, Saxon. That will keep your mouth shut,' Ernaut spat as he withdrew the sword. John slumped to his knees, blood seeping from his side and staining his armour red.

As John watched Ernaut gallop away, the world began to spin around him. He felt himself falling, then everything went black.

'Your father wishes to see you.' Yusuf opened his eyes and blinked against the bright morning sunlight. A servant was shaking his arm. 'Dress quickly.'

Yusuf rose and pulled on a linen caftan and sandals. He hurried to the entrance hall, where he found his father and Turan. When Ayub saw him, he frowned and turned away. 'Come,' he told his sons. 'I have something to show both of you: the spoils of victory and the price of defeat.'

Yusuf followed his father out of their home and to the broad square that lay behind the Umayyad mosque. The square was often the site of a produce market. Now it held a market of a different sort. Everywhere Yusuf looked, he saw Christian captives manacled and standing despondently, heads down, or huddled in wicker cages. There were hundreds, maybe thousands of them. The men of Damascus walked amongst them, poking and prodding, inspecting the goods.

'It is as the poet writes,' Ayub told his sons. '*You must choose the point of the spears couched at you; or if you will not, chains.*' He fixed Yusuf with an intense stare. 'Choose always the spears, my son. Better death than this.' He turned to Turan. 'Today, you will purchase your first slave. You fought like a man yesterday. You should have your own servant.'

'Thank you, Father.'

'What of me?' Yusuf asked.

His father whirled on him. 'Were it not for your brother, you would be in a cage like one of them! When you are a man, like Turan, then you may have a slave.' Yusuf felt tears welling up and looked away. Ayub grabbed his chin with one of his calloused hands, forcing Yusuf to look at him. 'No more tears, boy. Only women cry.'

Ayub released Yusuf and turned back to Turan. Yusuf wiped his tears away and followed, trailing behind as Ayub and Turan strolled through the market. 'That one

there is strong enough,' Ayub said, pointing to a towering Frank with long red hair. 'But he is too old. He will
never forget his home, and you will never be able to trust
him.' He walked on and then pointed out another, a
muscular blond boy of perhaps sixteen, who appeared
to be sleeping. 'That one is the right age and he looks
strong enough. But look more closely at the way he
lays there. He is unconscious, not asleep. He has
been injured, probably a wound to the gut. He will not
live.'

Yusuf stopped before the low wooden cage where the
Frankish boy lay on his side, flies buzzing around him.
Yusuf had never seen a Frank this close before. The
slaves in his father's household were mostly black men
from Africa, along with a few Turks. The Frankish boy
had a thin nose and square chin. His face was pale and
covered with sweat, but he shivered as he lay there. The
cost of defeat, Yusuf's father had said. This was it: to
die alone, far from one's home, far from any who might
care.

'You wish to buy the boy?' Yusuf turned to see a short,
thickly bearded man with a heavy coin purse tied to his
belt. 'I'll make you a good deal.'

'I was only looking.'

'You can have him for a song,' the slave merchant
insisted. 'Two dirhams.'

'Two dirhams!' Yusuf exclaimed. 'Look at him. He
won't live out the week.'

'He's hardly injured,' the slave merchant protested.
'With care, he'll live to be older than me.'

Yusuf frowned. 'Not likely.'

'I see you know your business, young master,' the slave merchant said with a wink. 'Very well, I'll let you have him for only six fals.'

Yusuf hesitated. Turan would soon have a slave. If Yusuf could show his father that he too knew how to deal with a servant, then perhaps he would realize that Yusuf too was a man. Yusuf examined the boy. Ayub had said he was the proper age, and he looked like he would be strong enough if he survived.

'I can see you're interested,' the slave merchant said.

'But I have no money.'

The slave merchant gave Yusuf an appraising look. His eyes moved from Yusuf's linen caftan to his belt, and then settled on Yusuf's leather sandals. 'Your sandals. Give them to me and the boy's yours.'

Yusuf looked down at his feet and hesitated. Did he really want to take responsibility for this dying Frank? What would his father say? He was on the verge of saying *no*, when the boy sat up. His hand shot out, gripping the bars, and he stared at Yusuf with clear blue eyes. '*Broðor*!' he cried out. '*Broðor*!' Then he fell back again, unconscious.

'What did he say?' Yusuf asked.

'I don't speak his heathen tongue, whatever it is. It wasn't Frankish. Not German, either. This is an odd one. Allah knows where he's from.'

'I'll take him,' Yusuf said. 'Provided that you deliver him to my home.'

'And where might that be?'

'The house of Najm ad-Din.'

The slave merchant's eyes widened, and he gave a small bow. 'I knew you were no common man. You have a deal, young master.' Yusuf reached down and slipped off his sandals, which he handed to the merchant.

'Yusuf!' It was Ayub, calling from up the street. 'Come here! See the slave your brother has bought.'

Yusuf hurried over barefoot, a smile upon his face.

Chapter 4

Yusuf stood on tiptoes and peered through the open window into the room where the Frankish slave had been brought so the family doctor could inspect him. When the slave had been delivered to Ayub's home in Damascus, Yusuf had been whipped. Ayub had not let him keep the young Frank as a personal servant, but had ordered the new slave be brought back to Baalbek. 'No use in wasting a slave,' he had commented. 'If he lives, then he can work in the fields.'

The Frank lay naked and unconscious on a table. He was well muscled and tall, taller even than Turan. His arms and chest were smooth and tanned brown – where they were not caked in dried, rust-coloured blood – but his legs and the area around his genitals were impossibly pale, the skin as white as freshly shorn wool. His long hair was the colour of ripe wheat and his jaw covered in pale blond fuzz. He was not circumcised.

The Jewish doctor stood beside the table, washing the boy with a sponge. Ibn Jumay, a thin man of almost thirty, with short black hair under a skullcap, long sidelocks and a closely cropped black beard, was the personal physician for Yusuf's family, as well as Yusuf and Turan's tutor. He wiped the dried blood away from his patient's right shoulder, then dipped the sponge in a basin of water and wrung it out. Next, he sponged off the blood caked around the Frank's stomach. There was a small gash in the lower abdomen, and as the Frank breathed, a thin stream of blood bubbled up and ran down his side. Ibn Jumay sniffed at the wound and nodded, apparently pleased. Last of all, he cleaned the blood away from the Frank's right thigh. The flesh around the wound was angry and red. Ibn Jumay poked at the spot with his finger, then bent down and sniffed. 'Infected,' he muttered to himself. 'They let the arrowhead fester inside him for three days, then expect me to perform miracles.'

Ibn Jumay bent down and picked up a brown leather bag, which he placed on the table. He opened it and carefully removed several ceramic bottles, placing them beside the Frank. Next, he took out a leather bundle and unrolled it on the table before him. Dozens of tiny pockets had been cut into the inside of the roll. Some bulged with mysterious contents. Others held wicked-looking knives and strange iron instruments. Ibn Jumay rubbed his hands together, then selected a short blade, a curved needle and a set of pincers that ended in two flat, circular disks. From another pouch, he removed a ball of string.

Yusuf moved to the open doorway, where he had a better view. 'What are those for?' he asked.

'You are blocking the light, Yusuf,' Ibn Jumay said without looking up. He nodded towards the corner. 'Sit there if you must watch. As for these, their purpose is not hard to divine. The knife is for cutting, the needle for sewing, and these—' he held up the pincers, 'are for extracting.'

'Extracting what? And why do you need to sew?'

'Be silent and watch. You shall see.'

The doctor unstopped a square, blue ceramic bottle and poured a small amount of the contents over each of the wounds. The Frank flinched.

'What is that?' Yusuf asked.

'Pure alcohol.' Ibn Jumay held out the vial.

Yusuf inhaled deeply, then coughed. 'It burns,' he said, his eyes watering.

'It will purify his wounds.' Ibn Jumay lifted the Frank's left arm and moved it in a circle while peering into the ragged hole in the Frank's shoulder. 'The tendons appear to be intact. With any luck, he should have use of his arm again.' The doctor took up the curved needle and carefully threaded it from the ball of string. He hooked the needle through the flesh on either side of the wound and pulled the thread through. He continued, expertly sewing up the wound as if he were working with a piece of cloth.

Yusuf frowned. 'Will he not have string stuck in his shoulder?'

'A good question, Yusuf, but this is not string. It is called catgut, although it is made from the dried intestines of a goat.' Yusuf grimaced. 'It will dissolve over time, leaving only a thin scar.' Ibn Jumay finished sewing, cut the catgut and tied it off. Next, he took out a yellowish paste that smelled of rotten eggs. He rubbed it

98

over the wound, which he then bandaged with cotton dressings. 'That will do for the shoulder.' He moved down the Frank's body and again examined the gash in his side. 'Come, Yusuf. Since you are here, you can make yourself useful. Help me flip him over.'

Together, they managed to roll the Frank on to his stomach, revealing another gash in his back. 'He is lucky, this one,' Ibn Jumay noted. 'The sword went straight through, but appears to have missed his vital organs.' The doctor doused the back wound with alcohol, then sewed it up. He and Yusuf flipped the body over again, and Ibn Jumay sewed up the gash in the Frank's stomach, leaving a small gap at the end of the wound.

'Why did you not sew it up all the way?' Yusuf asked as he held the boy upright while Ibn Jumay applied the foul-smelling paste and bandaged the Frank's torso.

'The vile matter inside him must be given a place of exit,' Ibn Jumay said matter-of-factly. 'Otherwise, it will kill him.' He frowned as he moved to the Frank's injured leg. 'Now for the unpleasant part.' He removed the cork from a small red vial, carefully poured a small amount of clear liquid on to a cotton ball and dabbed gently at the wound. 'This is an extract from the poppy plant,' Ibn Jumay explained before Yusuf could ask. 'It helps to ease the pain.'

'But he is unconscious.'

'I am a doctor. It is my duty to not cause unnecessary suffering. And even unconscious, he will feel this.' Ibn Jumay took the tiny knife and held it over the wound in the Frank's leg. He whispered a prayer in Hebrew, then made two short diagonal cuts across the wound, forming an *x*. Blood and pus welled up around the cuts. Yusuf looked away, fighting to keep down his breakfast. When he looked back, Ibn Jumay was just finishing sponging clean the wound. The doctor took up the pincers, then hesitated. He turned to Yusuf.

'Grab his leg here and here—' He pointed with the pincers to a spot just above the knee and another at his groin. 'And hold it still.' Yusuf did as he was instructed. Ibn Jumay moved around the table opposite him. 'It is important that he not move, Yusuf. Hold tight.' With his left hand, Ibn Jumay pulled back the flesh around the wound in the Frank's leg and then plunged the pincers into the hole. The Frank moaned and his entire body convulsed, causing his leg to jerk under Yusuf's hands. 'Keep him still!' Ibn Jumay snapped. Yusuf struggled to hold the thrashing leg in place, while the doctor worked the pincers deeper into the wound. Blood flowed out, dripping on the table and splattering on Yusuf's hands and face. 'Got it!' Ibn Jumay exclaimed at last and pulled out the pincers. Caught between them was a short, barbed arrowhead, dripping blood. 'A cruel piece of work, is it not?' the doctor said. He held the arrowhead out to Yusuf. 'Keep it, as a reminder of the nature of war. You can let go of him now.' The Frank had stopped thrashing and lay still. Ibn Jumay began to stitch the wound closed.

'Will he live?' Yusuf asked, fingering the sharp point of the arrowhead.

'God willing, no. I have never dissected a Frank, and I should like to do so. I am curious to note any differences.' Yusuf frowned. He had purchased the slave, and he felt responsible for him. Ibn Jumay saw his expression and smiled reassuringly. 'But he is young and strong. I fear he shall survive.'

'When will he be better?'

'Only God knows. If all goes well, he should be on his feet before the winter rains. But if the infection in his leg spreads, then I will have to have it off.' Ibn Jumay finished the stitches and looked up. 'In that case, I fear the worst.'

In his dream, John was once more on the battlefield outside Damascus. Rabbit stood in the distance, waist-deep in the crimson waters of the Barada River. A Saracen with his sword held high was approaching him from behind. John screamed and tried to run, but no matter how fast he moved, the river grew no closer. He watched in horror as the Saracen, a mad grin on his face, impaled Rabbit from behind, his bloodied blade bursting from the boy's chest. Then the Saracen's face twisted and transformed into the leering visage of Reynald . . .

John jerked awake to the sound of whistling. He was lying on the floor of a small room, lit only dimly by a shaft of light beaming through a grill in the door. He was shirtless and something warm lay on his stomach. He looked down to see a man bent over his torso. John tried to sit up but the world spun around him and he fell back. The whistling stopped.

'Easy, young man,' a voice said in heavily accented Frankish, the vowels long and foreign, the consonants too guttural. A face appeared over him, darkly tanned with a short beard and kind brown eyes.

'Who are you?' John asked. 'Where am I?'

'Drink this,' the man said, lifting John's head with one hand and holding a cup to his lips. The liquid in the cup was cold and bitter. Despite the unpleasant taste, John drank greedily. His lips were parched, and his throat felt as if he had not had water in days. 'There,' the man said. 'Now for your questions: you are in the home of Najm ad-Din Ayub, in Baalbek. And I am Ibn Jumay, a Jew and for the moment, your doctor.' John began to speak, but Ibn Jumay shook his head. 'Be quiet. Just for a moment.' He took John's wrist in his hand and held it while he looked away to the floor. 'Good, a steady pulse,' he murmured. He looked back to John. 'Now tell me, what is your name?'

'John.'

'Ah, interesting.'

'How did I get here?' John asked.

'You are a slave. You were purchased after the battle in Damascus.' Ibn Jumay offered John another cup of the bitter liquid. 'That was over a week ago. You suffered grave injuries, and you have been incoherent for some time. I had hoped you would die.'

John spluttered.

'I wished to dissect you,' Ibn Jumay explained. 'But no matter. It seems that God has other plans for you, John.' He smiled. 'It occurs to me that perhaps your name is prophetic. John is a Frankish corruption of a Hebrew name. It means *God is gracious*.'

John closed his eyes, suddenly tired. 'I am a slave,' he muttered. 'God has not been gracious to me.'

'Ah, but you are alive.'

John shook his head. He should have died along with Rabbit. He had wanted to give his life for God. Why had He not taken it? John's thoughts slowed. His eyelids grew heavy and his head felt hot. 'I am burning,' he murmured. 'I need to be bled—'

The doctor laughed. 'That is the last thing you need.' He placed a cool, wet cloth on John's forehead, and John felt instant relief. 'You need rest,' Ibn Jumay said softly. 'The drink I gave you will help you sleep. Later, you will be brought food and drink. Eat everything. I will see you tomorrow.'

John tried to respond, but he was already slipping away, surrendering to sleep, returning to his dark dreams.

Weeks passed, time spent mostly in drugged sleep, battling nightmares. The visits of Ibn Jumay punctuated John's tortured sleep. The kind doctor redressed John's wounds and told him of his new owner, Najm ad-Din Ayub. Ayub, he said, was a tough man, but also fair and generous. John could have done much worse.

One day, John awoke to the creak of the door opening and rolled over to see not Ibn Jumay but a slender Saracen with short, greying hair and piercing eyes. He had angular features and his mouth was set in a hard line. John sat up. He sensed immediately that this was not a man to be trifled with. The Saracen stepped into the small room, and Ibn Jumay entered behind him.

'Up,' the strange man said in accented Latin. John stood, wobbling for a moment on his weak right leg. The Saracen stepped close and inspected John, squeezing his arms and legs as if he were a horse. 'Your shirt,' he ordered.

John tilted his head in confusion. 'Excuse me?'

The back of the man's hand flashed out, catching John on the cheek. John ran his tongue along the inside of his mouth and tasted blood. The man leaned close and growled something harsh in Arabic.

'You are not to speak unless spoken to,' Ibn Jumay translated. 'He wishes you to take off your tunic. Do as he says.' John pulled the linen fabric off over his head, and the man leaned close to examine the scars on John's shoulder and torso. Finally, he nodded. He turned to Ibn Jumay, and they exchanged rapid words in Arabic. Then, Ibn Jumay turned to John and spoke in Frankish.

'This is Najm ad-Din Ayub, but you will call him m'allim, master. He has deemed you fit to begin working. Do as he says, and you will be fed, clothed and treated with respect. In time, you may even purchase your freedom. Disobey him, and you will be punished.'

'What good is the word of an infidel?' John spat in Frankish.

Again, the back of Ayub's hand flashed out, stinging John's cheek. 'My word is true,' Ayub said in Latin. 'And if I choose to let Ibn Jumay speak for me, it is only because I do not wish to soil my mouth with your barbarian tongue. Do you understand?'

'Yes,' John said. Ayub raised his hand. 'Yes, m'allim.'

'Good. Follow me.' John limped outside, squinting against the sunshine, which was blinding after weeks spent in the dim confines of his room. As his eyes adjusted, he saw that he was in a walled compound, with a sprawling, white-walled villa at the centre. The room in which he had been kept was one of several in a row built against the wall that ran down one side of the villa. Ayub stopped in front of a doorway that led into a larger room. Straw sleeping mats covered the floor, with hardly any space between them.

'From now on you will sleep here with the other slaves,' Ibn Jumay instructed.

John nodded, and Ayub led on to the back of the villa. He stepped through a low door, and John followed to find himself in a kitchen filled with the mouth-watering smells of roasting meat and exotic spices. The large room had spotless white walls, a red-tiled floor and a low ceiling. John had to duck to avoid the sheep haunches, ribs and even whole goats that hung there. A fireplace eight feet across took up most of the wall to the right. Wood was stacked next to it, and more wood burned in the fireplace, heating a black cauldron that hung from a chain. A thin slave girl with skin of deepest black tended the cauldron, stirring it with a long wooden spoon. Across from John, several narrow tables lined the wall, with a washbasin built into one. Shelves had been built above them, and they held dozens of clay jars. To the left of the shelves, a door led into the villa, and on the left-hand wall, another door led to a pantry filled with sacks of grain. A wide table occupied the middle of the room, and standing behind it was an attractive older woman with long hair just beginning to grey. She scowled when she saw John.

Ayub turned to John and spoke rapidly in Arabic. 'This is Basimah, the mistress of the house,' Ibn Jumay translated. 'You will work for her until you are strong enough to work in the fields. You are to do exactly as she says. Under no circumstances are you to speak to her, or to any other members of the household. Do you understand?'

'Yes.' John looked to Ayub. 'Yes, m'allim.'

Ayub nodded, and he and Ibn Jumay departed, leaving John alone to face Basimah. She stood with her hands on her hips, frowning at him while a fat fly buzzed around the room. 'Mayy,' she said at last. John shook his head to indicate that he did not understand. 'Mayy,' she said more loudly and kicked a wooden bucket so that it slid across the floor to him. ''Ajal,' she added as John picked up the bucket. ''Ajal!'

John hurried outside, bucket in hand. Did mayy mean water, he wondered, or perhaps milk? He looked about, but saw neither a well nor any animals. The space behind the house was a broad expanse of sun-baked earth, closed off on three sides by a high wall. Small trees filled with bright-green fruit grew along the wall opposite John. Buildings lined the wall to the left and right, their red-tile roofs slanting upwards to within four feet of the top of the wall. John started to lug the bucket around the left side of the villa, then froze. If he climbed atop one of those buildings, he would be able to clamber over the wall.

John carried the bucket over to the nearest building and placed it upside down on the ground. He looked around to make sure that no one was watching. Then, standing on the bucket, he jumped and managed to get his chest and arms on to the tile roof. His injured shoulder screamed with pain, but John gritted his teeth and pulled himself the rest of the way up. He lay on the hot tiles, gasping for breath. He had not realized how weak he was. He pushed himself up and crawled to where the roof met the wall. He rose and peered over. A dusty city of narrow streets and closely packed buildings stretched away before him, running down to a square, where there stood a huge Roman temple, its tall columns dwarfing the surrounding buildings. Beyond the temple, the streets sloped down towards a thick wall. Beyond the wall lay a green valley, bordered on both sides by towering mountains. John noted the position of the morning sun, over the mountains to his right. That meant that the kingdom of Jerusalem lay to his left, over the far mountain range.

'You, slave! What are you doing there?' John turned to see a dark-haired boy staring up at him from the ground. 'Come down at once!' the boy demanded in passable Latin. John turned away and placed his hands on top of the wall, preparing to hoist himself over. 'You will never escape that way,' the boy called up to him. 'Even if you get past the city guards and across the valley, you will never survive the mountains. There is no water and the nights are freezing.'

John hesitated. He knew the boy was right. And besides, what did he have to return to? He had fled his home in England with blood on his hands. The Franks had betrayed him. There was nowhere for him to go. There was nowhere he belonged. He turned and scrambled back to the edge of the roof, then dropped down. He landed a few feet from the boy, who was olive-skinned and thin, with deep, intelligent eyes. 'I am Yusuf,' he said. 'What is your name?'

'John.' How, he wondered, could this infidel child speak Latin?

'Ju-wan?' the boy sounded out, a smile tugging at the corner of his mouth. 'A strange name for a man. It means perfume in our language.'

'It's John.'

He looked from John to the roof above. 'I do not advise trying to escape, Juwan. If my father catches you, he will have you stoned to death as an example to the other slaves.'

John felt the blood drain from his face. 'I was not trying to escape,' he lied.

Yusuf clucked his tongue. 'Careful. The punishment for a slave who lies is twenty lashes.' He picked up the bucket and held it out to John. 'My mother will be wondering where you are. There is a well that way, near the stables.' He pointed to the front of the villa.

'You are not going to punish me?'

'Not this time.'

'Thank you.' John took the bucket and headed towards the front of the villa. When he looked back, the boy was gone.

The sun glowed golden red, like iron fresh from the forge, as it set behind the distant mountains. In the dying light John trudged across the courtyard, a stack of wood in his aching, trembling arms. Sweat ran down his face and stung his eyes, for even this late in the day the searing summer heat remained, the air burning his lungs and the ground hot through the leather of his sandals. He moved slowly, every step bringing a stab of pain in his right leg, where he had been injured. His muscles were weak after more than two months of inactivity, and his labours that day had brought him to breaking point. His hands were raw from a morning spent pulling bucket after bucket from the well, and then staggering back to the kitchen, the pail hanging awkwardly between his legs. His lower back ached from mucking out the stalls that afternoon. And he had lost count of the trips he had made to replenish the stack of wood in the kitchen. He gritted his teeth and pushed on through the pain and exhaustion. Escape might not be possible, but the Jewish doctor had said that if John worked hard, he might some day buy his freedom. He clung to that hope.

John trudged into the kitchen to find that Basimah and the kitchen slave were gone. Head down, he headed straight for the wood pile. As he was lowering the wood, his tired arms gave way and the logs fell and rolled across the floor. He began to gather them up when behind him he heard shouting from somewhere inside the villa. He turned to see a girl – no, a young woman – storm into the kitchen. She had high cheekbones, a delicate nose, full lips and flawless, golden-brown skin, the colour of the desert John had passed through on the way to Damascus. Her dark eyes were filled with tears, which she wiped away upon seeing John. He stared, his mouth open. She was more beautiful than Queen Eleanor of Aquitaine, or even than the Madonna in the painting that hung behind the altar of his church in Tatewic.

'Are you well?' John asked finally. The girl straightened

and then looked down her nose at him. She snapped something in Arabic. John spread his hands. 'I don't understand.' He took a step towards her.

The girl frowned and stepped back. She pointed imperiously towards the door. 'Barra. Barra!'

John did not move, and the girl's eyes widened. Her posture softened as she tilted her head to examine him. John tapped his chest. 'John,' he said and smiled. 'I am John.' The girl smiled back, her teeth dazzlingly white against her brown skin.

'Zimat!' It was Basimah, who strode into the kitchen and began to scold the girl in Arabic. John went to restack the wood next to the fireplace. When he had finished, he turned to find that the girl had gone. Basimah stood staring at him, her arms crossed and her mouth stretched in a tight line. Finally, she turned away and went to the cauldron over the stove. She scooped a ladleful of thick, steaming stew on to a plate, added a piece of flatbread and shoved the dish across the table towards John.

'Râh,' she said, nodding to the plate. John took it. Basimah nodded and pointed out the door. 'Râh!' John moved away slowly, expecting to be called back any second, but Basimah let him go. Outside, night was falling rapidly now that the sun had set behind the mountains. A cool breeze brought the scent of ripening fruit. John stumbled through the darkness to the slave quarters, already crowded with a dozen men hunched over their evening meals. Most were dark-skinned Africans, although there were one or two native Christians amongst them. They all eyed John with ill-disguised hostility as he grabbed a mat from near the door and picked his way past them to a space in the far corner. He threw down his mat and sat with a grateful sigh, his back against the wall.

John sniffed at the food he had been given. It had a sweet, pungent smell that was unlike anything he had ever known. He tore off a piece of bread and poked at the stew, revealing tender chunks of lamb amongst the lentils. Using the bread, he scooped some of the stew into his mouth. ''Sblood!' he whispered, his mouth aching as it filled too quickly with saliva. He greedily ate the rest of the stew and had hardly finished when he drifted into an exhausted sleep, the plate still on his lap. For the first time in many nights he did not dream of blood and battle, of Rabbit or of his brother. Instead, he dreamt of the beautiful girl, of Zimat.

That night, Yusuf ate his stew in silence. The family meal was a tense affair, with no one speaking. It should have been a joyous occasion. Mansur ad-Din, the emir of Baalbek and father of Yusuf's friend Khaldun, had visited that afternoon and reached an agreement with Ayub that Zimat would marry Khaldun when she came of age. It was a good match, but Zimat did not look happy. Her eyes were red from crying. Basimah had pushed for the marriage, but she too was upset. She snapped at the kitchen servant when she brought the dishes – this one was too cold, that one not adequately spiced – and ate with her brow furrowed, her eyes burrowing into Ayub. As for Ayub, he avoided her gaze. Finally, he cleared his throat and spoke. 'Turan, tell me of your slave. He serves you well?'

Turan nodded. 'I call him *Taur*' – ox – 'because he is so strong. We practised sword-fighting today. He is good, but not as good as me,' Turan smirked.

Ayub turned towards his wife. 'And you, Basimah? What of the young Frank?' Yusuf looked up.

'Sell him,' Basimah said. 'I do not wish to have him in my household.'

'Why is this?' Ayub demanded.

'He is a savage, a Frank,' Basimah said, her voice trembling with passion. 'He was alone with Zimat today. He saw her unveiled.' Zimat blushed.

'He is a slave,' Ayub said. 'There is no shame in this.'

'But he looked at her brazenly, like a free man,' Basimah insisted. 'Can you imagine what might have happened?'

'I will beat him,' Turan said suddenly, his eyes on Zimat. 'How dare this Frank look at my sister!'

'I do not need you to protect me, Turan!' Zimat snapped.

'Enough!' Ayub looked to Basimah. 'The slave is only a boy,' he said gently. 'Not all Franks are savage.'

'Is that what you will tell Khaldun and his family? Our daughter has been promised and she must be protected.'

Ayub nodded. 'You are right. Zimat, you will stay away from this slave, and you must remember not to show yourself outside the house unveiled.'

'But I was in the house!' Zimat protested. 'And why am I being punished? I did nothing wrong!'

'You will do as I say,' Ayub said with finality. He turned back to Basimah. 'Did the Frank work hard?'

Basimah nodded grudgingly. 'Like a mule. I thought he would work himself to death.'

'There, you see. He will be a good slave. Treat him with kindness, Basimah. Do not seek to take your revenge on this boy. He is not the one who killed your family, who—'

'Do not speak of it,' Basimah snapped. She closed her eyes and sighed. 'I will treat the boy well.' She looked to her daughter. 'But if he so much as touches Zimat, he will die. I will see to that.'

'Allahu akbar! Allahu akbar! Allahu akbar! Allahu akbar!' John awoke to the strident call of the muezzin, beckoning the faithful to morning prayer from his post in a minaret high above the city. Reluctantly, John rolled over and opened his eyes. Most of the other slaves were already gone. Through the open door, John could see that the clear night sky had begun to take on the silvery blue of dawn. Sunrise was only a little while off. John squeezed his eyes shut and pulled his rough wool blanket more tightly about him. Nearly a month had passed since his first day of work, and the nights had turned cold. He huddled there for a moment longer; then, with a sigh, he threw back the blanket and sat up. Basimah expected him before the sun rose above the hills. If he were late, then she would work him harder.

He rose, stretching his arms high above his head to loosen his aching muscles, and then headed outside in only his sandals and tunic, shivering against the early morning chill. Taur, a taciturn Norman slave who had been purchased at the same time as John, was just emerging from his private room, which he warranted due to his position as servant to Ayub's oldest son. Without a word, they fell in beside one another, heading towards the front of the villa. They walked past the stables and turned into a large room built against the wall. The floor was tiled, and on the far wall water flowed from a small opening and splashed into a pool, from where it would flow underground to the fountain in the entrance way of the villa. Other slaves were already busy washing themselves. They were all circumcised, and when John and Taur pulled off their tunics a few still pointed and laughed. Taur growled at them, and they fell quiet.

John took a clay jug from a shelf on the wall, filled it, and dumped the water over his head, gasping at the shock of the cold. Then he picked up a bar of soap and began to scrub himself resolutely. When he was sure he had removed every last trace of dirt and grime, he took up the jug again and rinsed, shivering in the cold. This bracing experience had become a daily ritual; his master, Ayub, gave ten lashes to any of the slaves who failed to maintain a sufficient level of cleanliness. John had already felt the sting of the whip once and was not eager to do so again.

After bathing, John hurried back to his room, pulled on the loose linen pants he had been given, belted his tunic about his waist with a length of rope and headed for the kitchen. Several other slaves were already standing outside, chewing on their breakfast of hot flatbread and talking quietly in a variety of languages. The head slave – a white-haired, black eunuch named Harith – handed John a piece of bread. He stood apart from the others and ate slowly, watching the mountains where the sun would soon rise. His thoughts drifted to Zimat. He had seen her only twice more, both times at a distance. She was unlike any of the women he had known. He thought back to his home in England, and then of his father. His forehead creased; he could not recall the features of his father's face. It seemed a lifetime since he had last seen him. John added up the weeks and months. It had been less than two years. Less than two years since his life had been shattered.

'Those baths will be the death of me,' Taur muttered as he joined John. He tore off a piece of bread with his teeth and continued: 'It's not natural, all this washing.'

'At least we don't have lice any more,' John said. Taur, his mouth full of bread, grunted sceptically. John looked to the nearby mountains, where the sky had lightened to a clear blue. At any moment the bright edge of the sun would rise above the horizon. 'I should go.' Taur grunted a farewell, and John entered the kitchen, where he found the servant girl feeding wood into the fire and Basimah kneading dough. She ignored him, and he stood waiting. He had learned better than to speak first. Finally, she looked up from her work.

'You, stables,' she said, pointing towards the door for emphasis. John sighed. *Yâkhûr* – stables – was one of the first Arabic words he had learned. He had mucked them out more times than he cared to remember in the past two weeks. 'Then water and wood.'

'Aiwa, m'allima,' John replied. Yes, mistress.

Yusuf sat cross-legged in the shade of one of the lime trees that bordered the rear wall of his home, his hand on his chin and his forehead creased as he struggled to remember the Frankish for bird.

'*Merde?*' Turan suggested with a sneer. '*Putain?*' Ibn Jumay scowled at him. It seemed that Turan's skill in languages stopped at foul words like *shit* and *whore*. Behind Turan, his Frankish slave, Taur, guffawed.

'No,' Ibn Jumay corrected in Latin. '*Merde* is what you seem to have between your ears, Turan.' Turan stared at him uncomprehendingly while Yusuf and Selim laughed. Turan punched Yusuf's shoulder.

'What did he say?'

'I said that you need to pay more attention to your studies, Turan,' Ibn Jumay said in Arabic. He pointed again to the sparrow that perched low in the lime tree above them. 'Yusuf? Selim? Can you enlighten your brother?'

Selim shook his head. Yusuf closed his eyes to concentrate. He might not be able to beat Turan when they practised swordplay or wrestling, but at least he could defeat him here. '*Un oiseau*,' he said at last. 'A bird is *un oiseau*.'

Ibn Jumay nodded. 'Good. Now, use it in a sentence.'

'The bird shat on Turan's head,' Yusuf said in Frankish. Ibn Jumay and Selim laughed, and Taur joined in, braying like a donkey.

'What?' Turan demanded. He turned on Yusuf and shoved him, knocking him over. He pounced on top of him and raised his fist. 'What did you say!'

'Calm yourself,' Ibn Jumay said, placing a hand on Turan's shoulder.

Turan shoved him away. 'Quiet, Jew!' Turan's face was red, his eyes blazing. He punched Yusuf hard, then leaned close. 'Tell me, little brother,' he whispered. 'What did you say?'

John strode along the side of the villa towards the kitchen, a stack of logs cradled in his arms. After weeks of hard labour, his arms no longer burned with each load of wood he carried. As the work became easier, he began to reconsider his plight. The Saracens fed him well; indeed, it was the best food he had ever eaten, a far cry from the flavourless meats, black bread and boiled vegetables he had grown up with. And he was treated with respect, if not kindness. The Saracens were not as he had expected.

John was entering the broad space behind the villa when he heard shouting from the trees on the far side of the courtyard. Yusuf, the boy he had met while trying to escape, was pinned to the ground beneath a young man. And not just any man. As John drew closer, his eyes widened in recognition. The thick build, dark hair and broad face with a scraggly adolescent beard: it was the Saracen who had killed Rabbit.

'You bastard!' John growled. He dropped the wood and, fists clenched, headed straight for the man. He was only a few steps away when the young Saracen looked up, and his eyes widened in surprise. John raised his fist to strike, but then someone slammed into his side, knocking him from his feet and landing on top of him. John managed to roll on to his back and found himself staring into the face of Taur. 'What are you doing?' John roared. 'Let go of me!'

117

'Are you mad?' Taur demanded. 'If you touch him, they'll kill you.' He grabbed John's arm and twisted it painfully behind his back as he rolled him over. 'I'm saving your life,' he whispered as he pulled John off the ground, holding him immobile.

Rabbit's killer had risen to his feet. His face was mottled red and he had a murderous look in his eye. 'Kalb!' he spat in Arabic and then punched John hard in the stomach. John doubled over, but Taur pulled him back upright. 'Kalb!' the man snarled again as he swung out and caught John in the jaw, snapping his head back.

'Turan, waqqif!' a voice called out. John looked up to see Ayub striding towards him. Ayub went to Ibn Jumay, and the two exchanged words in Arabic. Then Ayub turned to John and spoke in Latin. 'Take off your shirt.' While John pulled off his tunic, Ayub drew his sword and cut a long branch from one of the lime trees. 'Face the wall.'

John stood with his hands against the wall. He gritted his teeth as Ayub began to thrash him with the branch. The rough bark bruised and cut John's skin. After ten blows, he cried out in pain, unable to hold silent. Ayub stopped, and John slumped to his knees.

Ayub stood over him. 'You are a slave, property. I have control over your life. Never threaten one of my family again. If you will not obey, then you will be broken, like a horse. If you cannot be broken, then you will die. Do you understand?'

John looked to Rabbit's killer, Turan, and then back to Ayub. 'Yes, m'allim,' he lied.

Chapter 5

John raised the scythe and its curved blade flashed against the midday sun before beginning its downward arc, cutting the stalk of wheat off at the base. John straightened as he placed the wheat in the heavy woven basket slung over his shoulder, stuffing it in amongst the hundreds of other sheaves. Then he bent down and grasped the next stalk, the last on the row. He swung down, and the sheaf of wheat came free in his hand to join the others in the basket. With a sigh of relief John eased the basket to the ground and dropped the scythe. He straightened and reached around to touch his back, which was still tender from the whipping he had received. As he stretched, he turned to look out over the twelve rows he had just cut. Where once there had been a sea of golden wheat nodding in the cool breeze, now there was only dark soil dotted with cut-off clumps, stubble on the face of the earth. In the distance other fields of wheat still swayed in the wind, and tiny figures moved through them, their scythes flashing in the sunshine. Past the fields rose the walls of Baalbek, and further still, towering

119

grey clouds loomed over the craggy mountains, promising rain for the first time in months.

John stared at the distant peaks, calculating for the hundredth time his chances of surviving a trip over them. Ever since his encounter with Turan, he had been hiding food under his sleeping mat, in a hole he had dug in the earth floor of the slaves' quarters. He had managed to steal a waterskin and some rope from the stables. He could use the wool blanket he slept with for warmth in the mountains. With another waterskin and a little more food, he would be ready. Getting out of the villa would be easy. As for the city wall, it was built to keep people from getting in, not out. It would be lightly guarded at night, and he could lower himself down with a rope. With any luck, he would reach the mountains before Ayub's men ran him down. Then, he would have to trust in God to make it to a Christian town before he ran out of food and water. But escape was for the future. John had business to finish first. Before he left, he would kill Turan. And before that, he would have to finish with this accursed field.

John gave a final stretch, groaning in relief as he arched backwards, arms stretched over his head. Then he shouldered the basket once more and began the next row. He was half done when he heard the rumble of horses' hooves. He rose to see Ayub riding towards him, flanked by three of his men. As they drew closer, John saw that they had been hunting; a spotted leopard lay draped over the back of Ayub's horse. John lowered his scythe and bowed as Ayub reined in before him.

Ayub looked to the harvested field and then back to

John. 'You work well, slave. You outpace my other workers. Remind me: what is your name?'

'John, m'allim.'

'Juwan,' Ayub said, mispronouncing John's name as all Saracens did. 'I have a task for you, a reward for your hard work. I leave this afternoon for Damascus. Run to the stables and prepare four horses. If you have them saddled and packed when I return from inspecting the fields, then I shall give you one dinar.' A dinar was a gold coin. It could buy John enough food and water for the long trek to the kingdom of Jerusalem. 'If you fail,' Ayub added, 'you shall receive ten lashes. Go!'

John shrugged the heavy basket off his shoulders and began to run towards the city. 'Juwan, stop!' Ayub called. John skidded to a halt and turned. Ayub was pointing to the basket of wheat. 'Do not leave my tools and grain in the field for the thieves. Take them with you.' Ayub spurred his horse off into the fields, followed by his men.

John ran back and grabbed the scythe. Then, with a grunt, he lifted the heavy basket. Gritting his teeth as the weight settled against his sore back, he set off for Baalbek at a jog.

'Of thee did I dream while spears flashed between us, and of our blood full deep did the ashen shafts drink,' Yusuf read, his lips moving soundlessly. He sat against the wall in the shade of the lime trees, a fat book of poetry perched upon his knees. His father was out hunting and Turan had disappeared somewhere, probably practising sword-play with his Frankish slave, Taur. Yusuf had taken advantage of their absence to enjoy a rare moment alone with the *Hamasah*, a book of poetry that Ibn Jumay had lent him. 'I know not – by Heaven I swear,' he continued reading, 'this pang, is it love-sickness, or wrought by a spell from thee? If a spell it be, then free me from my heartache. If some other thing, then none of the guilt is yours.' He closed his eyes and repeated the poem aloud from memory. He was just finishing when he heard a woman's voice raised in a high-pitched, muffled cry. His eyes flashed open and he cocked his head. But he heard only the rustle of leaves in the lime tree.

Yusuf closed his book and stood. The cry had come from the direction of the slaves' quarters, and Yusuf headed that way. The slaves' common room was empty, the slaves having gone to work in the house or fields. All save one. Taur was leaning against the closed door of one of the private rooms, his bulging arms crossed over his chest. Yusuf stopped before the towering Frank.

'What are you doing there?' Yusuf demanded.

'This is my room.'

'Where is your master?'

'Gone to town.'

'Why didn't he take you with him?'

Taur shrugged. 'Ask him when he returns.'

'I will.' Yusuf was turning away when he heard shouting from the room behind Taur. '*Stop! Stop!*' It was Zimat's voice, shrill and panicked. 'Allah forbids this!' Yusuf moved to open the door, but Taur blocked him.

'Out of my way, slave!'

Taur did not move. 'You cannot enter. My master forbids it.'

'I thought your master was in town.' Yusuf stepped close and looked the Frank in the eye. 'If you do not step aside, I will beat you. And do you know what will happen if you strike back? Have you ever seen a man stoned?' Taur's eyes flicked to the side, betraying a trace of fear. 'Move!'

Taur shook his head. 'Do your worst, little one.' Behind him, Zimat screamed, then her cry was cut short.

Yusuf reacted immediately. He kneed Taur hard in the crotch. As the Frank bent forward in pain, Yusuf brought the heavy book of poetry up, catching him in the face. Taur's nose exploded in a fountain of blood. Yusuf dropped the book, shoved him aside and kicked the door open.

Turan stood at the far side of the room, his back to Yusuf and his leather riding breeches down around his ankles. He had Zimat pressed up against the far wall and had torn her tunic down the front, revealing one of her breasts. Blood ran from Zimat's lip. When she saw Yusuf, she gasped and tried to cover herself. Turan turned, and his eyes widened.

'What are you doing?' Yusuf demanded. 'She is your sister!'

'My half-sister. And this is none of your business, little brother,' Turan snarled as he pulled up his pants. 'Leave!'

Yusuf looked past Turan to where Zimat now sat crouched on the floor, sobbing. 'I will not. And if you do not let her go, I will tell Father.'

'You will tell no one!' Turan growled as he crossed the room to Yusuf. His face was flushed and his eyes were bloodshot. His breath reeked of alcohol. 'Remember, little brother, I saved your life. I can take it, too.'

'Do what you will to me, but leave Zimat alone.'

'I will do as I wish,' Turan said and shoved Yusuf hard, sending him tumbling backwards out of the doorway to land hard on his back. Turan was on him immediately, kneeling on his chest. Yusuf squirmed and held up his hands, trying to ward off the blows as Turan began to punch at him. A blow slipped through, and Yusuf's face exploded in pain as Turan's fist slammed into his right eye. A second later, Turan's other fist connected with Yusuf's mouth.

'*Akh laa*!' Turan cursed, shaking his hand. He had cut his knuckles on Yusuf's teeth.

Yusuf took the opportunity to wriggle away. Turan moved to get back on top of him, and Yusuf kicked out, catching his brother in the face. Turan fell back, and Yusuf scrambled to his feet. He could feel his right eye beginning to swell shut, and his lip was split. He stood unsteadily as Turan got to his feet, spitting blood.

'You little bastard,' Turan hissed. 'You'll pay for that.'

'You wouldn't dare. Father will whip you raw.'

Turan sneered, showing teeth red with blood. 'Father doesn't care two straws for you. He wants a son who can fight. What are you good for?'

'Shut up.'

'Father hates you, Brother. He hates your weakness, your snivelling, your—'

'*Shut up*!' Yusuf roared and charged his brother. At the last second Turan stepped out of the way and stuck his leg out, sending Yusuf sprawling face first in the dust. He was beginning to rise when Turan kicked him hard in the side. The air whooshed from Yusuf's lungs, and he lay gasping for breath. But the more desperately he tried to suck in the air, the more elusive it became.

'Having another of your fits, little brother?' Turan taunted. 'Can't cry for help now, can you?' He kicked Yusuf again, catching him in the ribs. Yusuf curled into a ball to protect himself, his arms over his head. His ribs burned and he was suffocating, unable to draw in air. Turan bent over him, and Yusuf could feel his brother's breath hot on his face. 'You're pathetic. I should have let you die in Damascus.' He grabbed Yusuf and rolled him on to his back, then sat on his chest. 'Tell me, little brother,' Turan sneered as Yusuf's face grew red, then purple. 'What is Frankish for pathetic little bastard?'

Yusuf barely heard him. The world was dimming, fading to black. The last thing he knew was Turan's fist slamming into his face.

John strode as fast as his aching legs would carry him through a narrow alleyway in Baalbek, dodging past veiled women and bearded men. He muttered under his breath as he walked, cursing Ayub for making him bring the basket. His lower back ached from the weight and his shoulders were on fire where the leather straps bit into them. He gritted his teeth and kept going. A golden dinar was worth a little pain.

He left the alleyway and entered a dark square that sat in the shade of the ancient Roman temple. He glanced up at the towering marble columns as he hurried past; he had never seen anything so monumental, not even in Constantinople or Acre. Past the temple, John broke into a jog as he turned into the street that wound up hill towards Ayub's home. He circled around to the back gate, where one of Ayub's mamluks stood bored, his spear resting against his shoulder. The man pulled open a small door cut into the larger gate, and John hurried through. He headed across the courtyard towards the granary, a squat building that abutted the right-hand wall. Then he froze.

Ahead of him, Taur sat in a doorway, his head cradled in his hands, blood dripping between his fingers. Past him, Turan knelt over Yusuf. Yusuf was unconscious, his face a swollen, bloody mass, but Turan kept pounding away at him. Beyond them, Zimat stood in another doorway, her lip bloody and her tunic torn. She saw John and moved towards him, but Turan rose and grabbed her arm. 'Where are you going?' he growled. 'I'm not done with you.' He shoved his sister back into the room behind her.

John dropped the basket of wheat and broke into a run. Turan heard him coming. He turned and raised his fists, showing knuckles red with blood. John stopped ten yards away and raised the scythe. At the sight of the curved blade, Turan's eyes widened with fear. He backed away, and John stepped towards him. 'Fight me, you coward,' John snarled, but Turan continued to retreat. 'Fight me!' John shouted as he tossed the scythe aside and raised his fists. Turan stopped retreating.

'Come, dog,' he sneered in barely comprehensible Frankish.

John charged. At the last second Turan stepped to the side, trying to avoid him, but John had anticipated the move. He veered and planted his shoulder in Turan's gut, bowling him over. He landed on top, but Turan used John's momentum to throw him off. John sprang to his feet, and the two boys faced off. John was thickly muscled after months of hard labour, but Turan was larger, with a broad chest and shoulders. His weight would tell if the fight became a wrestling match.

John raised his fists and adopted a fighting stance. He stole a glance over his shoulder to Taur. He did not want to be taken by surprise again. Taur sat watching, his nose a wreck and his face covered in blood. He would not intervene. John turned his attention back to Turan, who held out his right hand, palm down, and made a clawing motion, beckoning John to him. 'Whore. Shit-for-brains,' he sneered in Frankish.

John stepped towards him, and Turan's right fist flashed out for his head. John ducked the punch and swung up, connecting with an uppercut to the chin. Turan stumbled backwards, his sneer replaced by a wide-eyed look of surprise. He shook his head clear and then charged with a roar. John let him come, then delivered a stinging right cross that snapped Turan's head back, stopping him immediately. Turan swung out wildly, and John stepped away.

'Ya Allah,' Turan muttered, wiping blood from his nose with the back of his hand. Then he sneered. He was standing next to the scythe. Turan reached down and picked up the curved steel blade. He growled something in Arabic, then sprang forward, swiping the scythe at John's throat. John jumped backwards, avoiding the blade but tripping over Yusuf's prone form. He fell, and Turan pounced, the blade flashing down towards John's face. John rolled left, and the scythe bit into the earth. The two combatants rose and faced off over Yusuf, who stirred, raising a hand to his face and moaning. John and Turan began to circle his body, each shadowing the movements of the other.

Turan lashed out again, the scythe arcing towards John's face. John ducked the blow, and Turan reversed his attack, swinging backhand. John jumped back, but the scythe grazed his chest, drawing blood. Turan grinned in triumph, but as he completed his swing, John stepped in and grabbed the arm that held the scythe. Then, with this free hand, he punched Turan hard in the jaw. As Turan slumped to his knees, John twisted his arm behind his back, forcing him to drop the scythe. John picked it up and held the sharp blade to Turan's throat. John was facing Zimat, who was still watching. She nodded, encouraging him.

'You killed my friend, you Saracen bastard,' John whispered in Turan's ear. 'May Allah piss on you in the afterlife.' His knuckles whitened around the scythe's handle as he prepared for the finishing blow.

'Stop!' a voice commanded in Latin. John looked up and saw Ayub riding into the courtyard, flanked by two of his men with bows drawn. Zimat hurried away towards the house, her cheeks flushed. John watched her go, then turned his attention back to Ayub.

'Release my son!' Ayub ordered as he reined in before John.

John paused. Why should he let Turan go? John would die either way. He spat at Ayub, then began to draw the scythe across Turan's throat. But John had waited too long. The blade had only just drawn blood when two arrows sank into his shoulder. He dropped the scythe and sank back on his knees in agony. Turan grabbed the blade and whirled on him. But Ayub had dismounted, and he held his son back. Ayub strode up to John and struck him across the face with the back of his hand.

'What have you done?' he demanded in Latin. He pointed to the house, where Zimat had fled. 'What did you do to my daughter?'

Turan, a trickle of blood running down his neck, said something to his father in Arabic, and Ayub's eyes widened. He drew his sword.

'Turan lies!' Yusuf had staggered to his feet. 'It was Turan who tried to rape Zimat,' he said in Latin. 'The Frank saved her.'

Ayub looked from Yusuf to Turan, weighing their arguments. Then, his gaze settled upon John.

'Kill me,' John said. 'I do not care.' Ayub raised his sword, and John closed his eyes. His eyes were still closed when the butt of the sword hilt slammed into his temple, knocking him unconscious.

A shaft of sunshine penetrated the cramped space where John sat slumped unconscious against the wall. He awoke, blinking against the light, and groaned as a wave of pain swept over him. His shoulder throbbed, and his back burned as if it were on fire. He reached back to touch it: the skin was rough and sticky with blood. He had been whipped. He looked about and found himself in a narrow space, too short to do more than crouch and not long enough to lie flat. Across from him, a heavy wooden door had opened just enough to allow someone to slide in a bowl of boiled wheat and a waterskin. Once the food was inside, the door slammed shut, leaving John in total darkness.

'Wait!' John yelled. His stiff joints cried out in agony as he fumbled his way towards the door, his right hand stretched out before him. He cursed as he accidently put his hand in the bowl of boiled wheat. He found the wooden door and began to pound on it with his fist. 'Come back!'

'Quiet!' someone hissed from the other side of the door. 'You'll get us both in trouble.'

John lowered his voice. 'Who are you?'

'Yusuf. I wanted to thank you for what you did. You saved my life.'

'I did not do it for you.'

'Nevertheless, you have my thanks.'

'When will I be released?' John asked.

'My father has declared that you will be kept here for a week with no food and water.'

'Why didn't he just kill me?'

'Were it not for the intervention of my mother, Basimah, he would have. You saved her daughter, Zimat, and that saved your life,' Yusuf explained. 'And do not fear, I will not allow you to starve. But you must conserve the food I have given you. I do not know when I will be able to bring more.' There was a pause. 'Someone is coming. I must go.'

John heard the slap of Yusuf's sandals as he hurried away, then nothing. He began to lean back, then winced as his raw back came in contact with the wall. He sat forward, his head against his knees. It would be a long week.

'You will not make the young ladies of Baalbek swoon any time soon,' Ibn Jumay said as he finished unwrapping the bandages covering Yusuf's face, 'but you are healing nicely. See for yourself.' He handed Yusuf a small brass mirror.

Yusuf frowned at his reflection. His face was still a swollen mess, purplish red around his eyes and almost black around his broken cheekbone. His nose was two sizes too big and now had a kink halfway up. Clear fluid oozed from around stitches that ran under his right eye and above his left. 'I look like a monster.' Yusuf gingerly touched his nose and winced. 'Can you fix my nose?'

'I think it looks rather distinguished, but if you insist, I can reset it. There will be a great deal of pain.'

Yusuf took another look at his nose in the mirror, then nodded. 'Do it.'

'Very well. Hold still.' Ibn Jumay gripped Yusuf's head with both hands, placing his thumbs against either side of Yusuf's nose. 'Ready?'

'Yes.'

Ibn Jumay wrenched the nose back into place. Yusuf's vision went black, and he nearly fainted as pain washed over him. When the wave of agony receded, he looked up to see Ibn Jumay smiling and holding out the mirror. Yusuf's nose was straight once more.

131

'There you are,' Ibn Jumay said. 'Now here's something to ease the pain of your bruises.' Ibn Jumay produced a clay jar, scooped out a greenish, translucent ointment with his fingers and began to smear it on Yusuf's face. The ointment created a pleasant cooling sensation, bringing instant relief.

'What is it?'

'It is an extract from the aloe plant,' Ibn Jumay said as he placed the lid back on the jar.

'Does it bring relief to cuts? Torn skin?'

'Yes, although it is most effective in dealing with sunburn.'

'Can I have some?'

Ibn Jumay tilted his head quizzically. 'What do you need it for?'

Yusuf looked to the ceiling, searching for a plausible answer. 'For later, if the pain returns.'

'You are a poor liar,' Ibn Jumay noted as he handed Yusuf the jar of ointment. He dropped his voice to a whisper. 'You want this for the Frankish boy, I imagine?' Yusuf's eyes widened in alarm. 'Do not worry. I will not tell your father. The young Frank deserves my thanks for saving my best pupil. Tell him to apply a thin layer twice a day. And you will want to give him some of this as well.' Ibn Jumay produced another jar, from which he scooped out a foul-smelling, yellowish paste, which he applied to Yusuf's face.

Yusuf wrinkled his nose. 'What is this? And why does it smell so bad?'

'The smell is sulphur. It will help prevent infection.' Ibn Jumay handed the jar to Yusuf. Then he took a long roll of cotton bandages and began to wrap it carefully around Yusuf's head. 'Remember: leave the bandage on and do not pick at your wounds, or those scars will never heal.' Yusuf nodded his understanding. Ibn Jumay rose and opened the door. 'Now send in your brother.'

Yusuf took the two jars and left the room. Turan was waiting in the hallway, standing stiffly upright. Ayub had whipped him mercilessly for what he had tried to do to Zimat, and Turan's backside was so torn and bloodied that he could not even sit without pain. He sneered when he saw Yusuf. 'How's your face, traitor?'

'It's your turn,' Yusuf said tersely, ignoring the barb. He tried to walk past, but Turan stepped in front of him.

'I saved your life at Damascus, and you betrayed me to save a slave, a Frank. I will not forget what you have done, little brother.' He pushed past Yusuf and entered the room where Ibn Jumay waited.

'I would do it again, big brother,' Yusuf whispered to himself as he turned and headed down the hallway towards his room. He was passing the closed door of his father's bedroom when he heard the loud voices of his parents. Yusuf caught Turan's name, and curious, put his ear to the door.

'What would you have me do?' Ayub was exclaiming. 'He is my son!'

'You have other sons,' Basimah retorted.

'A poet and a whimpering child,' Ayub said, his voice thick with disgust. 'Turan is a man, a warrior.'

'He is an abomination!'

'You have never liked him. You always preferred your own children.'

133

Basimah said something in a low voice, which Yusuf could not hear. Then: 'I raised him as my own after his mother died, but this is too much. Look at what he did to Yusuf, what he tried to do to Zimat. I will not share my house with that animal!'

'You will do as I say, wife!'

'Or what? You will beat me as Turan beat Yusuf? Or perhaps you will rape me as he tried to do our daughter?'

'Turan is a man, filled with young blood. And you know how Zimat teases him.'

'How dare you!' Basimah screamed, and Yusuf heard a loud slap. 'Do not pretend that this is her fault. It is your son who has defied Allah.'

'And he has been punished: thirty lashes from my own hand.'

'That is not enough.'

'What then? What would you have me do?'

'Send him away. Let Shirkuh deal with him in Aleppo.'

There was a long moment of silence. Yusuf was just beginning to move away from the door when he heard his father's voice again. 'Turan is my first-born son. I will not send him to be raised by another. But you are right; something must be done. It has been too long since I attended Nur ad-Din's court. I will go next week to Aleppo, and I will take Turan with me. We will be gone for several months. I will speak with Turan. I will teach him to rule his passions. And I swear to you by Allah that when we return, he will never touch our daughter again.'

'Very well,' Basimah said. 'But if you are wrong, Ayub, then I promise you, I will kill Turan myself.'

Yusuf moved away from the door and headed down the hall to his room. He had heard enough. Zimat would be safe from Turan. Now, Yusuf only had to find a way to prove his father wrong. He, too, would become a warrior.

John sat slumped against the wall shivering despite the heat. 'One hundred sixty-five' he rasped, his throat so dry he could barely speak. 'One hundred sixty-six.' In the blackness of the tiny cell, which stank of his piss and shit, time seemed to expand and stretch with no beginning and no end. Some time ago – maybe hours, maybe days – John had begun to count his breaths as a way of keeping track of time. When he reached a thousand, he would make a scratch on the dirt floor with his fingernail. Eventually, he had lost track of the number of scratches in the darkness. But that did not matter. The counting had taken on a meaning of its own. 'One hundred and seventy-six—one hundred and seventy-seven.'

Yusuf had not visited for days, and John, with no sense of time to guide him in his rationing, had run out of medicine, then food, then water. First, the fiery burning in his back had returned, along with shooting pains that spread out from his left shoulder, where the arrows had struck. Then came a ravenous hunger that gradually transformed into a gnawing pain in his gut, accompanied by uncontrollable shivering. But worst of all was the thirst. John's mouth became so dry that even swallowing hurt. His lips swelled and cracked. His skin crawled, and his head ached with a searing pain, as if someone had driven a hot iron deep into his brain. Then the visions had begun.

Shapes appeared to John in the darkness. He had seen Zimat, flashing her brilliant smile and beckoning him to come to her. The image had been so real that he had fumbled towards her, smashing his forehead against the door. Zimat's image had dissolved, to be replaced by others. John had seen Turan, his knuckles covered in blood, sneering at him. He had seen his father, his face pale and stretched in agony as he hung from the gallows, but living still, his eyes burning into John. And he had seen his brother, Harold, his face bathed in blood, his finger pointed accusingly at John. John had squeezed his eyes shut, but the images remained. He sought refuge in fitful slumber, but the ghosts of his past continued to haunt him.

Counting helped to keep them at bay. 'One hundred and ninety-nine—two hundred,' he croaked, focusing on the numbers. But another image intruded upon him regardless. He saw the door flung open, then daylight flooding the cell. John closed his eyes and shrank back. 'Two hundred and one,' he rasped, desperately trying to hold on to his sanity. But this was no vision. Rough hands grabbed him, pulling him out into the light and holding him upright. His stiff legs, bent for so long, refused to straighten. He kept his head down, away from the sun, and his eyes squeezed shut. Someone slapped him, jerking his head to the side. John cracked open his right eye and saw Ayub standing before him.

'So you have survived,' Ayub said in Latin. 'Allah favours you, slave. Perhaps he guards you for some purpose. I do not know. But I do know that if you ever touch my son again, not even Allah's favour will protect you. Do you understand?'

'Yes, m'allim,' John croaked.

'You will have three days to recover. Then you will resume your duties.' Ayub turned and walked away. The men on either side of John released him, and he dropped to the hard, sun-baked ground. He lay there for a moment, then rolled on to his back, letting the bright sun wash over him. After a time he cracked open his eyes and drank in the endless expanse of blue sky.

'You look like hell.' John looked over to see Taur walking towards him. The Norman's nose, swollen and purple, was flattened and shifted to the right of his face.

'You don't look so good yourself.'

Taur grinned. 'The Jew doctor says my nose makes me look distinguished.' He put his arms under John and gently lifted him off the ground. 'Jesus, you're light, nothing but skin and bones.' He wrinkled his nose. 'And you stink. Come on, let's get you cleaned up.'

Yusuf stood in the doorway of the kitchen and looked out on the rain beating down on the muddy courtyard. Chill weather had blown in from the north, bringing with it the first rain of the year. There would be rejoicing in the town. Yusuf wondered if it was also raining on the road to Aleppo, where his father was taking Turan. Yusuf's jaw tightened at the thought of his brother. Turan was why he was here, peering through the rain at the barely visible form of Juwan.

Juwan was standing in the centre of the courtyard, his

arms spread wide and his head back. Yusuf had never seen such bizarre behaviour. Rain was good, a blessing from Allah, but only a fool stood outside in the cold and wet. Perhaps the Frank's time in the cell had made him mad. Yusuf would find out soon enough. He had been waiting two days for a chance to speak with the slave alone, and now his chance had come.

Yusuf lowered his head and ran out into the rain. By the time he splashed his way to the Frank's side, he was soaked, his tunic heavy with water. Juwan did not move. Yusuf saw that his eyes were closed. 'Juwan!' he shouted. The Frank lowered his arms and snapped upright. His posture relaxed somewhat when he saw that it was Yusuf who had addressed him.

'John,' the Frank said. 'My name is John.'

'Yes—Juwan,' Yusuf said, speaking Latin. 'I wish to speak with you. Come.'

Yusuf led the way across the courtyard to the shelter of the lime trees, where the dense foliage kept out most of the rain. Yusuf brushed his wet hair back from his eyes, then began to wring out his caftan. 'What were you doing out there?' he asked.

'The rain reminds me of my home.'

'And where is that?'

'England. It is an island far from here.'

'I have heard of it.' Yusuf shivered as a chill wind blew a gust of rain under the trees. 'I hope it is not always so cold.'

John smiled. 'No, not always.' His smile faded as his eyes took on a distant look. 'My home is lush and green. There is no sand, no dusty earth. Grass grows everywhere.

Cold rivers flow through fields full with crops. Dense woodland abounds, with towering oaks. In winter, deep snow covers the land. It is beautiful.'

'Why did you leave?'

John's eyes narrowed and his mouth hardened to a straight line. 'For the crusade, to fight for God.'

'I see.' Yusuf paused. The key moment had come, and he carefully weighed his next words. 'You are a great warrior, Juwan. I saw you at Damascus the day you were captured. You took on four men and killed them all.'

'Yet I ended up here.'

Yusuf did not catch the bitterness in John's voice. 'Teach me to fight as you do,' he said. 'Help me to beat Turan.'

John watched the rain for a long time, his forehead creased in thought. Finally he shook his head. 'No.'

'But you owe me your life! My father would have killed you had I not spoken out against Turan. You would have died again in that cell had I not brought you food and water.'

'And Turan would have killed you had I not stopped him. We are even.' John began to turn away, but Yusuf placed a hand on his shoulder.

'No, we are not. I saved your life before, in the slave markets of Damascus. It is I who purchased you. You would have died had I left you there.'

'Then it is you who made me a slave,' John said, his voice hard and unforgiving. 'For that, I owe you nothing.' He stormed off.

'Wait!' Yusuf called after him. 'Juwan, I command

you to stop!' But John kept walking and disappeared into the driving rain.

John sneezed violently, holding the pitchfork with one hand while he wiped his nose with the back of the other. His eyes watered as he took the pitchfork and scooped up another pile of hay, dropping it down from the loft to the stable floor. '*Ha-choo*!' John sneezed again. He had been back at work for a week, and before he left, Ayub had removed him from the fields, assigning him full time to the stables. John loved being around the horses but dreaded feeding them; he was violently allergic to hay. He wiped his nose again, then turned and thrust the tines of the pitchfork into the high pile of straw.

'Salaam,' a woman's soft voice called out. Greetings. John turned to see Zimat standing just inside the stable entrance. She wore a belted caftan of saffron yellow, with red silk embroidery around the neck and sleeves. Her long black hair cascaded down her shoulders, a stray strand hanging over her veiled face. Her eyes were downcast.

'Sa—sa—*ha-choo*!' John replied, an explosive sneeze cutting off his greeting. Zimat giggled. John could feel his cheeks starting to burn. 'Salaam, Zimat,' he managed. Her laughter faded, and they stared at one another in silence, John gripping the shaft of the pitchfork as if he were drowning and it were a lifeline.

'Ija la-taht,' Zimat said at last, motioning for John to come down. He tossed the pitchfork on the pile of hay and climbed down the ladder from the loft. When he reached the stable floor, he found Zimat waiting for him, close enough that John could smell her heady scent of spice and citrus, close enough that he could have reached out and smoothed back the lone strand of hair that fell across her face. He met her eyes, and she looked away, then back to him. She took a deep breath and began to speak, a flood of Arabic rushing out. John's rudimentary understanding of the language was not up to the task. He found himself staring at her dark eyes, her slender waist, the curves of her hips beneath the tightly belted caftan. He wondered why she had come to him. What would her mother think? She stopped speaking, and John's eyes snapped back to her face. Zimat was looking at him expectantly, her eyes wide.

'I'm sorry. I don't understand,' John said in Latin. He shrugged his shoulders to signal his incomprehension. 'Lâ 'arabi.' No Arabic.

Zimat lowered her eyes and shifted from foot to foot. Then she looked up at him through her thick eyelashes. 'Shukran,' she whispered as she pulled down her veil. She stepped forward and kissed him quickly on the cheek, her lips soft and warm. John stood dazed as she turned and hurried away. At the door of the stable, she turned back to him and smiled. Then she was gone.

Yusuf stood in the courtyard behind the kitchen, a bow in his hands. The bow was a compact but formidable weapon, formed in the shape of a rounded *m*. It had a wooden core reinforced with layers of horn on the inside of the curves and of sinew on the outside. Yusuf took an arrow from the quiver on his back, nocked it, and strained to pull back the bowstring as he focused on his target, a small circular shield that hung on the wall thirty paces off. He inhaled and let his breath escape slowly as he sighted along the arrow. He let fly and the arrow hit the centre of the target with a satisfying *thwack*, the steel tip driving straight through the shield. Yusuf smiled and reached back to grab another arrow.

He sighted along the shaft and was about to release it when out of the corner of his eye he saw Juwan approaching. Yusuf lowered his bow. 'Salaam, Juwan.'

'John,' the slave replied. 'My name is John.'

'Ja-ahn,' Yusuf said, struggling with the strange vowels.

'John,' the Frank repeated.

'John,' Yusuf managed.

'Good. You should know my name if I am going to teach you how to fight.'

Yusuf grinned. 'You have changed your mind?'

'There is one condition.'

Yusuf's smile faded. 'What is it?'

'If I teach you to fight, then you must teach me Arabic.'

Yusuf nodded. 'Done.'

John presented his right hand, and after a moment's hesitation, Yusuf did likewise. The Frank grabbed Yusuf's hand and squeezed it tight. 'It's a deal.'

'Then let us waste no time,' Yusuf replied, rubbing the hand that the Frank had gripped as if it were dirty. 'Let us begin.'

'First, a question: what does *shukran* mean?'

'Thank you. It means thank you.'

Chapter 6

Yusuf's sword arced downwards and met John's blade with a metallic ring that echoed off the walls of the ancient Roman temple. The two swords locked, and Yusuf stood face to face with John. After months of practice, Yusuf had added muscle to his wiry frame. The sword, which just a year ago he had struggled to lift with one hand during the battle for Damascus, he now wielded with ease. Still, he was no match for John's size. Yusuf strained, but the two swords inched closer to his face. He gave a final push, then disengaged and spun away, but not before John's sword snaked out and caught him a stinging blow on the side. The weapons were blunted, and Yusuf wore a leather vest for protection. But the blades could still bruise well enough, and Yusuf was sure that this blow would leave its mark. He refused to acknowledge the stinging pain as he circled with his sword held high. One of the first things John had taught him was to show no weakness.

'You must act more decisively,' John said, wiping sweat from his eyes with the back of his hand. The stones of the temple were hot under the summer sun. John had stripped down to his leather breeches, but he was still glistening with sweat. 'Always keep your distance when fighting a larger opponent. Keep moving.'

Yusuf nodded. They were inside the Roman temple that sat at the heart of Baalbek. Walls composed of huge blocks of stone rose high all around them, reaching up to the clear blue sky. The peaked roof of the temple had long since collapsed, the rubble carted off and incorporated into the walls of the surrounding buildings. What remained was a perfect practice arena: a space some twenty yards by thirty, close to the villa of Yusuf's father, and best of all, hidden from prying eyes. In the afternoon, while the other boys played polo on the fields outside Baalbek, Yusuf came here to practise. As soon as he had finished his work in the stables, John sneaked over the villa wall to join him.

John wiped more sweat from his eyes, and Yusuf took advantage of the distraction to attack. He feinted a low thrust, which John moved to block. Then Yusuf spun right and slashed down at John's side. But John had already moved. He sidestepped the blow and punched Yusuf hard in the shoulder, knocking him stumbling backwards.

'Don't let your opponent trick you into an off-balance attack,' John cautioned. 'And never over-extend yourself.' Yusuf gritted his teeth and nodded. He knew John was right, but his constant advice grated. 'And never forget this,' John added, 'the most important lesson my father taught me: an angry warrior is one step away from a dead warrior.'

Yusuf grunted in response and attacked with a vicious overhead chop that John parried. Yusuf brought his sword down, cutting at John's shins, but he jumped the blow, then slapped the flat of his sword against Yusuf's knuckles. Yusuf dropped his blade, shaking his hand and cursing.

'You must never allow your emotions to get the better of you.' John tossed his sword aside and raised his fists. 'Let's continue.' They began to circle, mirroring one another's movements. Yusuf was breathing hard after half an hour of swordplay, but John was hardly winded. 'Don't be in a hurry,' John advised. He stepped forward and jabbed, but Yusuf skipped back out of the way. They continued circling. 'Remember: find your opponent's pattern, break it down, then attack.'

John charged as he finished speaking, his arms out to grab hold of Yusuf. Yusuf stood his ground. He hit John with a quick jab to the jaw, ducked his arms, then spun away, a smile on his face. 'You move like an ox,' Yusuf taunted in Latin.

'Good,' John grunted, feeling his lower lip. His hand came away red with blood. 'Taunting is a good way to unbalance your opponent.'

'And you are as dumb as an ox, too,' Yusuf added in Arabic.

'Don't overdo it,' John growled. He approached Yusuf more slowly this time, keeping his hands up. Yusuf let him come, ducking and bobbing his head as John had taught him, so that he would not present an easy target. John swung high, and Yusuf ducked the punch, stepping in and delivering a right to John's stomach. Yusuf stayed in close, hitting John twice more in the gut. But Yusuf's fourth punch never hit home. John's hand clamped down on his wrist. John spun Yusuf around and twisted his arm behind his back, wrapping the other forearm around Yusuf's throat. Yusuf struggled to escape but could not break John's iron grip.

'When fighting a larger opponent, you must rely on quickness and deception,' John spoke into Yusuf's ear. 'Strike and then move away. If you let him get close, you are lost.'

'You haven't defeated me yet,' Yusuf growled. He bit down on John's forearm.

''Sblood!' John cursed. He pulled his bleeding forearm tight against Yusuf's throat, choking him. 'A wise warrior also knows when to admit defeat.'

Yusuf's face turned bright red, but he continued to struggle. Finally, when his vision dimmed and he began to see spots of light swimming before his eyes, he went limp. 'You win,' he croaked. John let him go, and Yusuf fell to his knees, gasping for air. From the mosque nearby, the muezzin began his rhythmic chant, calling the Muslim faithful to their evening prayers.

'I must go,' Yusuf said between heavy breaths. He rose and collected the swords, hiding them under one of the loose flagstones that formed the floor of the temple. 'I never miss evening prayers.'

John nodded as he picked up his tunic and pulled it on. 'I should return as well, or I will be missed at the evening meal. You fought well today, Yusuf.'

Yusuf smiled. Compliments from John were hard-earned. 'Tomorrow we will meet in the stables,' Yusuf said. 'And I shall teach you.'

'Until tomorrow, then. Ma'a as-salaama.' Go with safety.

'Allah yasalmak.' God keep you safe.

John poured a bucket of water into the horse's trough, and the chestnut stallion came to the edge of its stall and bent its head to drink. John scratched the horse between its ears, and it nuzzled at him, searching for a treat. Disappointed, the horse returned to the water. John leaned against the stall and watched it drink. He loved the compact, graceful Arabian horses. They were smaller than the bulky European chargers he had grown up with, but were surprisingly strong for their size. Yusuf said that they could carry more weight because their bones were denser. For the same reason, they rarely went lame.

John gave the horse a final pat, then hung the bucket from a hook next to the stall. His work in the stable was done. He still had to restock the kitchen's wood supply, but he would have plenty of time to do so after his lesson. John climbed into the hayloft and sat to wait for Yusuf. Almost immediately, he began to sneeze. The loft was not the ideal place for their studies, but at least it was private.

A moment later, Yusuf entered the stables carrying two leather-bound tomes. 'Greetings, John,' he said in Frankish, then clambered up into the loft, the heavy books clutched under one arm.

'Salaam, Yusuf.' John had always had a gift for languages; he had learned Latin and Frankish with a rapidity that astonished the monks who had taught him as a child. His gift had not deserted him, and he had picked up Arabic quickly. Yusuf's Frankish had improved just as fast. Now, they spoke to one another in a mixture of the two. 'More reading?' John sighed, eyeing the books.

'If you can speak but cannot read, then you are little better than a savage.'

'I can read Greek, Latin, Frankish and English.'

'But not Arabic, the holy language.' Yusuf handed the larger of the two books to John. Graceful, curving Arabic letters had been carved into the leather of the spine.

'*The Chronicle of Damascus*,' John spelled out. While he spoke Arabic well enough, he found it devilishly tricky to read. The flowing, snaky script seemed to blend together, making it difficult to determine where one letter ended and another began.

'It is a history written by one of our greatest scholars,' Yusuf told him. 'Today's topic will be of some interest to you; we shall read of the first crusade and the siege of Jerusalem.'

John opened the book at the marked page and squinted at the ornate, flowing script. 'The army of the Franks—' he read slowly, 'more than ten thousand men strong, arrived before the walls of the Holy City on the ninth day of Rajab in the four hundred and ninety-second year since the flight of the Prophet Mohammed from Mecca to Medina.' Yusuf nodded and smiled encouragement. 'The Frankish . . .' John's eyebrows knit in frustration.

'Warriors,' Yusuf supplied.

'We would say *chevaliers* – knights,' John murmured.

He turned back to the text. 'The Frankish warriors are said to have—'

'Wept.'

'—to have wept to see the city that they had travelled so long to reach. They were led by Raymond of Toulouse, a giant of a man and a fierce warrior, and Godfrey of Bouillon, who would become King of Jerusalem. The Franks surrounded the city and lay—What is this word, here?'

'Siege,' Yusuf translated into Latin.

'They lay siege. The Franks dashed themselves against the walls of the Holy City, but the mighty walls did not fall. Hunger and thirst plagued the Franks. In desperation, they marched—'

'Barefoot.'

'—barefoot around the walls of the city, calling on God for aid. On the walls, the defenders of Jerusalem also prayed to Allah, asking for victory. But it was not to be. The Franks built tall towers, constructed of wood from the very ships they had used to reach the Holy Land, and used these towers to break through the walls. The Holy City fell.' John looked up with a grin. 'I wish I had been there to see it. That was a glorious day.'

Yusuf frowned. 'Read what comes next.'

'The Fatimid emir fled with his army, and the Franks entered the city. The horror of their deeds will never be forgotten. Men, women, children: all were put to the sword. The slaughter was worst on the Temple Mount, where blood flowed in—in—'

'The blood flowed in torrents,' Yusuf supplied. He took up the narrative from memory. 'Women were dragged from their homes and raped. Children were torn from their mothers' arms and cast into the air to be impaled on the swords of the Franks. The Franks entered the Al-Aqsa mosque and killed all they found there, staining this holiest of places with blood.' Yusuf's voice shook with passion. 'In the Jewish quarter, they forced the Jews into their houses of worship, which they then burned. Those who escaped the flames were cut down by waiting warriors. Smoke hung dark over the city. The cries of sorrow could be heard for miles. The emir, hearing them as he fled, fell down and wept, cursing himself for his failure.'

John shook his head. 'The writer is a Saracen. He lies.'

Yusuf opened the second book that he had brought and read a nearly identical tale of carnage. John interrupted him. 'What does this prove?' Yusuf closed the text and handed it to John. '*Gesta Orientalium Principum*,' John read from the title page. His eyes widened. The author was William of Tyre. 'I have met this man. He is a priest.'

'A Christian,' Yusuf agreed.

John said nothing. He had been told that the taking of Jerusalem was a glorious victory. The priest in Cherbourg who preached the second crusade had referred to the victory again and again, calling on the people of the town to take up the sword and surpass the feats of their forefathers. The priest had not spoken of slaughtered women and children, or of streets flowing with blood.

'That is the nature of your great victory,' Yusuf said. 'The Christians are savages, animals.'

'Not all of them. Our faith is one of love and forgiveness. It is Jesus who told us that if our enemy strikes us, we should not strike back, but offer him our other cheek.'

Yusuf nodded. 'Your Jesus said much of great wisdom. He is counted amongst our prophets. But tell me: do the crusaders follow his teachings? They burn crops, kill women and children. They know nothing of medicine or literature. They do not even know enough to bathe. They are fanatics who blindly follow the Cross. Even you, John, you followed this pagan symbol from your home all the way to these lands. And why? To murder and pillage in the name of God. But your crusades are no business of God. Allah turns his back on such savage deeds.'

John frowned. Much of what Yusuf said was true. In his months in Ayub's household, he had learned that the Saracens were nothing like he had been told. They were cultivated, learned and frequently kind, even to their slaves. Compared to Yusuf and his family, the men and women that John had known in Tatewic did seem like dirty savages. And it was true that many of the men who had accompanied John on the crusade to Damascus had fought for spoils or adventure, not for God. Even he had not truly come east to fight for Christ. He had joined the crusade to escape his past. But that did not make him a savage. 'The Christian knights are men of honour,' he said. 'Savages have no honour.'

'Honour?' Yusuf scoffed. 'Your knights have the honour of men who sell their fellow soldiers for a sack of gold. I was at the emir's court in Damascus during the siege. The emir paid your men to move from the orchards, and they did. Such men know nothing of honour.'

John thought of the night long ago when he had seen Reynald in the clearing meeting with the Saracen. He thought of the heavy sack that Ernaut had carried. The facts fell into place. Reynald was the man the emir had bribed. That was why he had sent Ernaut to kill John: to eliminate the only witness to his treachery. John's jaw clenched in anger.

'Your knights are brave,' Yusuf continued. 'But it is the bravery of animals, not of men. They fight to satisfy their appetites, not for honour, and certainly not for God.'

John shook his head. 'There are men of honour among us.' He put the book aside and rose, brushing straw from his pants. He stepped past Yusuf and climbed down the ladder.

'Where are you going?' Yusuf demanded as John headed for the stable door.

'I have had enough for today.'

John poured water over the back of the last of the five horses that Ayub's mamluks had taken hunting that day. He had avoided Yusuf for the past week, ever since their lesson in the hayloft. Once Yusuf had come to seek him out early in the day while he was rubbing down one of the horses, but John had ignored him. He was not yet ready to confront Yusuf. His time in Baalbek had opened his eyes to another way of life. It was raising uncomfortable questions about much that he had taken for granted. Yusuf had given voice to

152

those questions, and now all that had been so certain – John's faith, the righteousness of his cause, the superiority of the Christians – seemed suspect.

John finished washing the sweat from the horse's back and proceeded to scrape its coat clean. When he was done, he patted the horse a final time, grabbed his tunic from where it was slung over the stall door, and left the stables. He was passing through the narrow space between the east side of the villa and the outer wall when he heard a high-pitched giggle and froze, his pulse quickening. He looked about and saw Zimat, peeking out through the shutters of one of the rooms in the villa.

'Salaam,' John said as he hurriedly pulled on his tunic.

'Salaam. I liked you better with your shirt off,' Zimat added in Arabic. 'I have never seen a Frank shirtless.'

John's eyebrows shot up. He approached the window. 'Haven't you?'

Zimat's golden cheeks flushed crimson, but she did not move away. 'You—you speak our tongue,' she managed. 'How?'

'I am not a total savage.'

'I never said you were.'

'But it is what you think of us, is it not?' John insisted. 'We are fierce warriors, monsters, savages.'

'That is what I thought,' Zimat admitted. 'But you are different.' She met his eyes. 'You saved me.'

John looked away. 'I only did what any knight would do.'

'But you risked your life. You were lucky not to have been executed.'

'I would do it again.'

'I know.' Zimat turned away. 'Someone is coming,' she whispered as she looked back to John. 'I must go.' But she did not move. John stared into her dark eyes, and she met his gaze without blinking. He leaned forward to kiss her. Zimat slapped him. 'How dare you!' she snapped and slammed the shutters closed.

John touched his cheek where she had slapped him, and a grin spread across his face. For just before the shutters had slammed shut, he had noticed that Zimat was smiling.

Yusuf sidestepped a punch from his younger brother Selim and grabbed his arm, spinning Selim around and placing him in a headlock. Selim struggled for a moment, then gave up and went limp. 'Never over-commit against a larger opponent,' Yusuf told his brother, then released him. The two boys stood with their hands on their hips, breathing hard. Yusuf wiped the sweat from his forehead as he looked up to the hazy-blue autumn sky, framed by the tall walls of the temple. The sun had sunk behind the west wall. They had been training for well over an hour.

'You did well today,' Yusuf told Selim. 'You can go.'

'You always send me away early,' Selim pouted. 'I want to stay.'

Yusuf shook his head. 'What I do now, I must do alone, Brother.'

Reluctantly, Selim trudged out of the temple. Yusuf had brought him there every day for the past week. If John would not help him, then Yusuf would find other ways to train. Selim was still only a boy, but sparring with him was better than nothing. And teaching, Yusuf had found, forced him to think more carefully about what he was doing. Together, they practised swordplay and afterwards trained for hand-to-hand combat. Each day after Yusuf sent Selim home, he ended with the hardest exercise of all.

Yusuf took a drink from the waterskin, then walked to the centre of the temple and sat cross-legged on the worn stone floor. 'Amânt-Allah,' he whispered as he closed his eyes. God protect me. The first time he had tried this exercise, he triggered an attack that left him gasping on the floor of the temple until he lost consciousness. His other efforts had been only slightly more successful. Still, he would keep trying until he conquered his weakness. Yusuf closed his eyes, took a deep breath, and held it. He counted silently: 'Wahad, tnain, tlâti, arb'a, khamsi.' As he used up the air in his lungs, he felt the familiar panic. He could hear the thumping of his pulse in his temples and his heart began to race. He kept counting, forcing himself to remain calm. 'Tlâtîn!' he whispered as he reached thirty and allowed himself to breathe. But he did not gasp for air, even though his lungs burned as if he were suffocating. He forced himself to breathe slowly and evenly. Gradually the feeling of suffocation faded. Yusuf grinned in triumph. For the first time, he had fought off one of his attacks.

Yusuf rose, slung the waterskin over his shoulder, and left the temple, skipping down the stone steps. He dodged through the crumbled remains of the temple complex and entered the street leading to his home. There, he slowed his pace, enjoying the perfect weather.

The heat of summer was gone, but the winter rains had not yet come. It was the best of seasons, and the street was filled with men working outdoors and women in veils chatting as they kneaded dough or sewed. Yusuf weaved between them as he walked up the hill to his home. The guard at the front gate nodded as he entered.

Yusuf passed through to the inner courtyard of the villa, where he washed his head, face and arms in the shallow pool. Then he went to his room to collect the book of poetry that sat beside his bed. There was still time for some reading beneath the lime trees before evening prayers. He headed down a shadowy hallway and into the kitchen, where he sneaked a piece of khubz – hot flatbread – from the kitchen slave, who complained half-heartedly. Yusuf popped the warm bread in his mouth and stepped out into the courtyard. John was waiting just outside the kitchen door.

'What do you want?' Yusuf asked as he brushed past without stopping.

John fell in behind Yusuf. 'I wish to apologize. It was the truth in your words about my people that angered me, not you.'

Yusuf stopped and turned to face John. 'Then why did you avoid me?'

'I did not wish to hear what you had to say, but ignoring you will not change the truth: many of my people are indeed savage, as you say. But I will show you that some of us have honour.'

Yusuf nodded. 'Very well, come with me. I was just going to read from the *Hamasah*.' Yusuf held up the thick book and smiled. 'It will be an ideal lesson. There is nothing less savage than poetry.'

Yusuf led the way to the stable and up into the hayloft. He opened the *Hamasah* and leafed through the pages. 'I will read,' he said. 'Listen carefully and tell me what the poems mean to you. This one is called the "Song of Maisuna". She was a queen who married young. Listen.' He turned to the book:

> *The russet suit of camel's hair,*
> *With spirits light, and eye serene,*
> *Is dearer to my bosom far*
> *Than all the trapping of a queen.*
> *The humble tent and murmuring breeze*
> *That whistles thro' its fluttering wall,*
> *My unaspiring fancy please*
> *Better than towers and splendid halls.*
> *The rustic youth unspoilt by art,*
> *Son of my kindred, poor but free,*
> *Will ever to Maisuna's heart*
> *Be dearer, pamper'd fool, than thee.*

Yusuf looked up. 'What does this mean to you?'

'The queen is unhappy. She misses the simplicity of her home, of her people. She despises the luxurious life of her husband, the king. She feels trapped.'

Yusuf nodded. 'This poem is famous amongst my people because it speaks of a truth: luxury makes one weak. The simplicity of the nomad, with only his tent and his camels, is honoured above the wealth of princes.'

'Yet your princes live in great palaces.'

'Yes, because such things are necessary to rule, but the wise ruler lives as a nomad within his grand halls.'

'I am sure,' John laughed. 'And do nomads recite poetry?'

'Of course, what better way to pass the cold nights in the desert?' Yusuf flipped through the pages of the book. 'Ah, this is one of my favourites. A love poem to ward off the chill desert night':

> *Leila, whene'er I gaze on thee*
> *My altered cheek turns pale,*
> *While upon thine, sweet maid, I see*
> *A deep'ning blush prevail.*
> *Leila, shall I the cause impart*
> *Why such a change takes place?*
> *The crimson stream deserts my heart,*
> *To mantle on thy face.*

Yusuf looked up to see that John's tanned face had flushed crimson. Yusuf laughed. 'John! You're blushing.'

'I am not,' John said, looking away.

'You are, my friend. Has some maid captured your heart?'

John refused to meet Yusuf's eye. 'I am a slave,' he muttered. 'What does it matter?'

'Slaves may marry if their master approves. And perhaps one day you will be free.' He leaned closer to John and whispered conspiratorially. 'Tell me. Who is it? A slave girl?' John shook his head. 'A girl from town, then,' Yusuf said, grinning. 'You must be careful, John.

Her father will not take kindly to the attentions of a Frankish slave.'

But John shook his head once more. 'It is not a girl from the village.'

The smile fell from Yusuf's face. 'I see.' There was only one free woman in the villa who might have captured John's heart. 'Zimat,' Yusuf said, his brow furrowed. 'She is promised to a friend of mine, Khaldun. They will be married in three years, when he is a man.'

'I did not know.'

'Even if she were not promised, you could never be with her.' Yusuf's voice was hard. 'It is forbidden. Put her from your mind. If you so much as touch my sister, you will die.' He met John's eyes. 'I will kill you myself.'

'I understand.'

'Good. Let us continue. You read the next one.' Yusuf handed the heavy book to John, who bent close to the page, biting his lip as he puzzled out the words of a poem about the incompatibility of pride and achieving true glory. Yusuf feared that John would not heed his warning. He was headstrong, and Zimat, well, she had always been unmanageable, unwilling to stay in her place as a woman. Yusuf had heard Ayub say more than once that he could not wait to marry her off so that protecting her honour would no longer be his concern. Yusuf feared she would do something foolish, and it would cost John his life.

John scooped up a shovelful of manure and trampled straw from the stall floor and dumped it in a wheelbarrow. Yusuf had taken his friend Khaldun and several mamluks on a hunt, leaving John to muck out the stables.

He added another shovelful to the wheelbarrow and paused for a break, leaning forward on the shovel.

'Salaam.'

John turned to see Zimat, dressed in a loose white caftan and wearing a veil. 'What are you doing here?' he whispered, looking past her to make sure that they were alone. 'You should go.'

Zimat did not move. 'You are a fickle man,' she said as she ran one of her slender fingers along the edge of the stall next to her. 'You did not seem so eager to be rid of me the last time we met.'

'I mean it,' John insisted, setting aside the shovel and wiping his grimy hands on his tunic. 'If we are seen together, then I will be beaten, or worse.'

'Then we had best not be seen.' Zimat stepped past John and inside the empty stall that he had been cleaning. John hesitated for a moment, then followed her.

'Are you mad?' he hissed. 'Yusuf has forbidden me to see you.'

'I will not be ruled by my brother.'

'And what of your father?'

Zimat frowned. 'My mother says that men are all the same. They use us for their pleasure and expect us to serve them. They never think of our desires. My father is that way. He cannot wait for me to be married so that he can strengthen an alliance and obtain my bride wealth. He cares nothing for my feelings.'

'Then you do not wish to marry the man to whom you have been promised?'

'I have never met Khaldun, but he is a man like any other. He will treat me as property. But you are different.'

She met John's eyes. 'I never thanked you properly for saving me from Turan.'

'I told you, I need no thanks.'

'But I wish to thank you nonetheless.' Zimat raised her veil and smiled shyly, her eyes downcast. She took a step towards him, close enough so that John could smell her sweet, spicy scent. The hair rose on the back of his neck. He knew he should walk away. Yusuf could return at any moment. But John did not move.

'Have you ever kissed a woman?' Zimat whispered.

John felt himself flush red. 'There—there was a girl in England . . .'

'Did you love her?' Zimat pouted.

'No. She—she was not half so beautiful as you.'

A smile played at the corner of Zimat's mouth. 'You are not so terrible yourself,' she said and kissed John. Her lips were soft and dry. Without thinking, John put his arms around her waist and pulled her towards him. He held her for a long moment, and then she pulled away.

'I should not have done that,' Zimat said, her eyes now wide with fear. She looked down at her white caftan, stained brown where John had held her. 'My caftan—what will I tell Mother?'

John reached out to comfort her and left a brown smudge on her cheek. 'I—I'm sorry,' he mumbled as he wiped his hand again on his tunic.

'I should leave,' Zimat said as she pulled her veil over her face.

'You don't have to go.' John stepped closer, but she slipped past him and out of the stall. Perhaps it was for the best, John thought as he watched her hurry from the stable. Then, he closed his eyes and touched his lips. Despite the risk, he longed to see her again.

'Lighter armour is better,' Yusuf insisted. He was sitting across from John in the hayloft. The book they had been reading – another history of the first crusade – had been laid aside. 'Our warriors can fire arrows from horseback as well as fight with sword or lance. They can attack and retreat swiftly. Your knights are slow and clumsy.'

'But they are also strong,' John replied. 'Your arrows cannot penetrate their armour. And when the knights charge as a group, nothing can stand up to them.'

'Then why stand?'

'But if you retreat, you are lost.'

'Not necessarily.' An idea struck Yusuf, and he leaned forward, gesturing excitedly. 'Our warriors are more mobile. What if they retreat before your charge, then circle back around on each side, outflanking you?'

John said nothing, his forehead creased in thought. 'It might work,' he grumbled.

'It will work!'

'Yusuf!' They both looked to the stable entrance. Ayub was standing there, holding his horse by the bridle. Turan stood behind him, along with half a dozen mamluks. They had returned from Aleppo. 'What are you doing with that slave?' Ayub demanded. 'Come down here, both of you!' The two boys scrambled down the ladder and stood straight-backed before Ayub. He glared at Yusuf for a moment, then turned his hard grey eyes on John. 'You have neglected your duties, slave. You will be whipped, but first, care for our horses.' He handed the bridle to John, who led the horse into its stall and began to unsaddle it. The mamluks also led their horses into their stalls, leaving Yusuf to face Ayub and Turan.

'Please, Father' Yusuf started. 'It was I who took the slave from his duties.'

Ayub turned towards his son. 'And why was that? What were you doing in the loft with that slave?' Behind Ayub, Turan snickered.

'He is teaching me to fight. In return, I am teaching him to read and speak Arabic.'

'Teaching him to read?' Ayub asked, his eyes wide. 'He is a slave, and a dangerous one at that. You should not even speak to him! Go to your room and stay there until I decide what is to be done with you.' Yusuf began to leave, but had hardly stepped out of the stables when Ayub's voice called him back. 'Wait! Come back here!' Yusuf returned to stand in front of his father. 'You say the slave is teaching you to fight?' Yusuf nodded. 'You will show me.'

Ayub turned to his men. 'Leave us,' he ordered. 'You too, Turan.' He looked to John. 'Come here, slave! You will fight my son. Fight to the best of your ability. If I suspect you are holding back, then I shall whip you.'

'Yes, m'allim,' John said. He turned to face Yusuf and dropped into a fighting crouch. Ayub backed away, and Yusuf and John began to circle a few feet apart, their fists raised. The space was tight, a square of hard-packed earth ten feet by ten, with stalls close on either side. Yusuf knew the close confines would give his larger opponent an edge. If John got a hold of him, then the fight would be over before it began.

John sprang forward and threw a vicious left hook at Yusuf's head. Yusuf ducked the blow and circled away to his right, but John anticipated the move. He stepped sideways, mirroring Yusuf's movement, and delivered another punch. Yusuf just had time to flex his stomach before John's fist slammed into his gut. Yusuf took the blow with a grunt. He snapped off a jab that caught John on the chin and spun away.

Again, however, John was on him instantly, charging forward with his shoulder lowered. Yusuf did not have time to avoid him. He levelled a straight jab that caught John square in the nose. John stumbled back, blood running down his face, and Yusuf charged, planting his shoulder in John's chest. John went down, and Yusuf landed on top of him. He rolled free immediately, springing to his feet before John could grab him. John rose more slowly, wiping the blood from his nose and leaving a red smear on the back of his hand. He raised his fists and again moved towards Yusuf.

'That is enough!' Ayub called. The two boys lowered their hands and turned to face him. He studied Yusuf for a long time, then nodded and turned to face John. 'Remind me: what is your name, slave?'

'John.'

'No more stable work for you, Juwan. You will be my son's servant. Attend to him at all times.'

'Yes, m'allim.'

Ayub nodded again, then turned and walked away. Yusuf smiled. It was as much praise as he had ever received from his father.

Chapter 7

'Allahu akbar! Allahu akbar!' The penetrating voice of the muezzin woke John. He rolled over on his straw mattress and reached up to pull open the wooden shutter. Only a faint predawn light filtered into his tiny room. As Yusuf's private slave, John was entitled to a thicker blanket, the straw mattress and his own room – spare and small, but all his. However, he still had to wash with the other slaves. As the muezzin continued his call – 'Al-salatu khayru min an-nawm', prayer is better than sleep – John rose and headed for the baths. Taur was already there, and he greeted John with a grin. 'Look who decided to get up. Did you get your beauty sleep, Saxon?'

'Obviously, you didn't get yours,' John replied as he pulled off his tunic and took a clay jug from the wall. The other slaves stepped respectfully out of John's way, allowing him access to the water. He filled his jug and dumped it over his head. ''Sblood, that's cold!' he exclaimed. At least the bathing chamber was heated; a small fire in another chamber ran heat through clay pipes beneath the tile floor.

'What's your master got you up to today?' Taur asked.

'The usual: more studies, more sword practice. You?'

'I can't say.' John raised his eyebrows, but Taur offered no elaboration. John shrugged. It was none of his business anyway. He tried to avoid Turan as much as possible.

John finished washing and towelled dry. Still, he shivered as he stepped outside. Autumn had come, and a chill mountain air had moved down to blanket the town. He entered the villa and headed along the hallway to Yusuf's room. The door was open. Inside, Yusuf knelt on a prayer rug, facing a mark on the wall that showed the direction of Mecca. John leaned against the doorframe and watched. Yusuf placed his palms on the ground before him and bent forward until his forehead touched the prayer rug. After a moment, he sat back on his heels. All the time, he quietly murmured the words of the rak'ah, the Muslim prayer ritual. 'Surely you are the most praiseworthy, the most glorious,' Yusuf concluded in a louder voice. He turned his head to the right and although he was looking directly at John, he seemed not to notice him. 'As-salaamu alaykum,' Yusuf whispered. Peace be with you. He turned to the left and repeated, 'As-salaamu alaykum.' Then he began to roll up his prayer rug. 'Greetings, John,' he said as he rose and placed the rug in the corner.

'Morning.' John pointed to the rug. 'Do you ever grow tired of that?'

'Of what?'

'Of all that bowing and scraping?'

'Do the Christians not kneel and bow their heads to pray?'

'We kneel, yes, but we do not grovel before our God.'

'He is not *your* God, John,' Yusuf corrected. 'There is only one God. And when I prostrate myself before Him, it is not to grovel or beg for favours. It shows my submission to His will. That is my faith.' Yusuf tilted his head in thought. 'From what you tell me, your religion requires you to submit to the will of priests of whom you must beg forgiveness. If one must grovel, as you say, is it not better to grovel before God than before other men?'

'Perhaps,' John grumbled.

Yusuf grinned triumphantly. 'I will make a true believer of you yet. Now come. We have much to do today.'

'And what sort of God do you think was worshipped here?' Imad ad-Din asked. Yusuf and John had met him on the steps of the temple late that afternoon after practising swordplay. Only twenty-four, Imad ad-Din was already a learned imam – a poet, scholar, legal expert and private secretary to Yusuf's father, Ayub. Recently, he had also taken over from Ibn Jumay as tutor of Ayub's children. He was a handsome man with a thick beard, sharp cheekbones and an aquiline nose that gave him a hawk-like appearance. The resemblance was heightened when, as now, he fixed his intense brown eyes on his two pupils.

'The god of war?' Yusuf hazarded. Imad ad-Din shook his head.

'The god of love?' John suggested.

Imad ad-Din smiled. 'No again. Come, I will show you.' Their teacher led them to the back wall and pointed to the faint remains of a mosaic, barely visible in the dim light that managed to penetrate the clouds gathering overhead. Yusuf had noticed it before, but had thought little of it. The mosaic of red and gold tiles pictured a man in a short tunic – or perhaps a leopard skin, it was difficult to say – lounging in the shade of a tree. He was crowned with leaves and held a shepherd's crook in one hand and a goblet in the other.

'Bacchus,' Imad ad-Din declared. 'The god of wine. The lewd rites associated with his cult took place right where we stand. Here his followers would re-enact the life, death and resurrection of Bacchus, before sharing wine in his name.' He turned to John. 'Not unlike how you Christians worship Jesus.'

John frowned. 'Bacchus is a pagan god. It's not the same.'

'At first, the Romans considered your Jesus to be a pagan god,' Imad ad-Din mused. 'But you are right: the ceremonies are not precisely the same. For it is written that after they had become drunk on wine, the worshippers of Bacchus engaged in wild orgies, where every possible perversion was committed.'

'The *bacchanalia*,' John said. 'It is a Latin word that remains with us.'

'Indeed.' Imad ad-Din shook his head. 'Is it any wonder that the Roman Empire fell?' He turned away from the mosaic and led them back towards the front of the temple. 'What do you take from this, Yusuf?'

'To beware of the dangers of wine and women. The

Prophet was wise in this. He forbids drink to the faithful and sought to tame the lustful hearts of women.'

'Excess is a dangerous thing,' Imad ad-Din agreed. 'But life would be only half as sweet without women and wine. What do you think, John?'

They had reached the front steps, and John gestured back to the temple. 'We can build nothing so magnificent today. The Romans may have been depraved, but their empire was the greatest the world has ever known.'

'But they fell,' Yusuf insisted. 'Their glory did not last.'

'No, it did not,' Imad ad-Din agreed. 'But what was the cause of their fall? Was it their depravity, or was the Romans' lack of honour perhaps the reason for their greatness? After all, their empire did last for over four hundred years.'

'Virtue counts for little amongst men,' John said. 'I have seen honest men hanged from the gallows, while liars and scoundrels rule over kingdoms.' His hand went to his side, where Ernaut had stabbed him long ago at Damascus. 'I have seen traitors paid in gold, and brave men made slaves.'

'But no kingdom can last like this,' Yusuf countered. 'A king who bases his rule on treachery will find himself betrayed. The righteous ruler will create a kingdom that endures.'

'Tell me, Yusuf,' Imad ad-Din said. 'Do you believe an empire can be created that lasts forever?'

Yusuf nodded. 'I do.'

'And how would you keep this empire together?'

'When I am king—'

'When?' Imad ad-Din chuckled. Yusuf only nodded. 'You are a Kurd, Yusuf,' Imad ad-Din cautioned. 'You must know your place.'

'Very well,' Yusuf murmured. 'If I were king, I would rule with justice and moderation, and I would enforce the laws of Islam. This will prevent the perversions that undermined the Romans.'

'And what if the leader himself becomes perverted? Or if his heirs are unjust?'

'Only the greatest of men should rule, and he must pick his heirs carefully.'

'The Greek Plato believed something similar,' Imad ad-Din noted. 'You truly believe such a man can exist?'

'I know it.'

Imad ad-Din stroked his beard. 'Perhaps. But history shows that one great man rarely follows another. What happens to your empire after the king dies?'

'Maybe empires are not meant to last,' John offered. 'Perhaps greatness in one's own time is all that can be hoped for.'

'Indeed,' Imad ad-Din approved. His words were punctuated by the roar of thunder. As Yusuf looked up to the dark sky, a drop hit him, splashing off his nose. Another hit and then another. Lightning flashed across the sky, and an instant later rain began to pour down. Yusuf and Imad ad-Din hurried to take shelter in a corner of the temple, where a portion of the roof remained. John remained standing in the rain, his face turned towards the heavens.

'That is enough for today,' Imad ad-Din shouted over the rain. 'The emir in Damascus has sent for me, and it will be a long ride in this storm. I will return in two days, and we will resume your studies. Until then, think well on what we have said today.'

'Aiwa, ustadh,' Yusuf replied. Yes, teacher.

Yusuf went to John, who grinned at him. 'Just like home!'

Yusuf shook his head in wonder at his strange friend. 'Come!' he shouted. 'We must return home. There will be feasting tonight to celebrate the first rains of the year.'

The two boys sprinted out of the temple. Yusuf pulled himself into the saddle of his horse and gestured for John to mount behind him. They rode off at a canter, the horse's hooves splashing in the ankle-deep water flowing down the streets. By the time they arrived at the villa, dusk had fallen. They stabled the horse and headed straight for the kitchen and its warm fires. Inside, preparations for the feast were already underway. Pots hung over the fire releasing mouth-watering smells. Bread was baking in the oven. And people were everywhere: kneading dough at the long table in the middle of the room, chopping vegetables, carrying pails of goat's milk in from the pantry and adding wood to the fire. Basimah stood in the middle of it all, her hands on her hips as she issued orders. When she noticed Yusuf and John, she frowned.

'What are you two doing there dripping on my kitchen floor?' she demanded. 'The governor of Baalbek is coming tonight. Go and make yourselves presentable.'

John stood against the wall in the dining room, directly behind Yusuf. The low table was crowded with food:

crisp, freshly baked flatbread; a steaming vegetable stew; and whole, roasted partridges that had been marinated in a mixture of yoghurt, mint and garlic. John's mouth watered, but he would have to eat later with the other servants. For now, his role was to stand silent behind his master, ready to do anything he was asked.

Half a dozen of Ayub's mamluks, led by Abaan, sat at the foot of the table. Yusuf and Selim sat near the table's head across from Khaldun, the eldest son of Mansur ad-Din, the governor of Baalbek. John studied Khaldun with special interest, for he was to be Zimat's husband. She had met him for the first time that evening, before the men went to the dining room and the women retired to the harem – the section of the house forbidden to visiting men. Khaldun was thin, with long black hair and pinched features. His father was a plump man with an exceptionally long, curly beard. He sat to the left of his son, and to his left, at the head of the table, was Ayub. The space between Ayub and Yusuf was empty. Turan had not yet arrived.

Ayub frowned as he looked towards the door for at least the tenth time. 'I apologize again for my son's tardiness,' he said to the governor. There were footsteps in the hall, and Ayub's face brightened. 'Ah, this must be him.'

But it was not Turan. The doctor Ibn Jumay entered, followed by a Frank in dark priest's robes. The priest was thin and tan, with a narrow face and brown, tonsured hair. John's eyes widened in recognition. It was the same priest that he had met his first day in the Holy Land, all those months ago.

Ibn Jumay bowed towards Ayub. 'Greetings Najm ad-Din. And to you, Mansur ad-Din. I apologize for my late arrival. The rains slowed my return from Jubail, and I did not learn of your invitation until I reached home. I came straightaway.'

'You are welcome at my table, Ibn Jumay,' Ayub said. He looked to the priest and scowled. 'And who is this that you have brought with you?'

'I am William of Tyre,' the Frank declared in passable Arabic.

'I met him in Jubail,' Ibn Jumay explained. 'He is a priest and my guest at my home in Baalbek.'

'If he is your guest, then he is welcome here,' Ayub said, although his gravelly voice sounded far from welcoming. 'Sit, both of you.' The *mamluks* made room at the centre of the table, and William and Ibn Jumay sat down across from one another.

Ayub held up a piece of round flatbread. 'We shall begin without Turan. We feast tonight to thank Allah for the rains He has sent us.' He broke the bread in half. 'To Allah! And may our crops grow tall and our livestock fat under this rain.' He dipped his bread in the stew and ate. The others at the table followed suit.

Mansur ad-Din was toying with his beard as he examined the Frankish priest. 'Tell, me. What brings you to my lands, William of Tyre?'

'Curiosity. I have long wished to see the temple of Baalbek. It was a Christian church once. I was at the home of William of Jubail when Ibn Jumay visited to treat the lord's son. Ibn Jumay offered to escort me to Baalbek, so I came.'

'It is dangerous for a Christian to travel in Muslim lands,' Ayub noted. 'You might be taken for a spy.'

'I am a man of God. I carry no arms, and I mean no harm.'

'If you carry no arms,' Mansur ad-Din noted, 'then you will be easy pickings for bandits and thieves upon your return.'

William smiled. 'God will watch over me.'

'*Hmph*.' Ayub's forehead creased. 'When you return, I will send two men to escort you back to Christian lands.' He looked to Ibn Jumay. 'How did your patient fare?'

Ibn Jumay sighed. 'Not well, I fear. He is dead.'

'You could not cure him? I have never known you to fail before.'

'Oh, I could have saved him from his illness, but I could not save him from his own people.' Ayub's eyebrows arched questioningly, and Ibn Jumay continued. 'My patient was a knight, the nephew of the lord of Jubail. His thigh was cut in one of their tournaments, and an abscess formed. By the time I arrived, it had grown so large that the man could no longer walk. I applied a poultice to his leg, and the abscess opened and began to heal.'

'So how did he die?' Ayub asked.

Ibn Jumay frowned. 'A Frankish doctor arrived. He called me a charlatan and had me chased from the sick man's room, but I listened at the door. This madman asked the knight if he would rather live with one leg or die with two. When the knight replied that he would rather live with one leg, the doctor sent for a man with a sharp axe. It took two blows to sever the leg. Blood was everywhere. The Frankish doctor could not stop the bleeding. I watched the knight die while a man-at-arms held me back.'

'Bloody savages,' Mansur ad-Din muttered.

'Not all our doctors are such butchers,' William noted. 'But alas, there are some such among us. We have much to learn from your people.'

'The Franks do not seem interested in learning,' Ayub replied. 'Only in taking. Look at what happened at Damascus. The ruler befriended you, and yet you sent your crusaders against his city.'

'There are many among us who did not wish to attack Damascus,' William said. 'Queen Melisende believes that there can be peace between our peoples. Her son, Amalric, believes the same.'

'But Amalric is not king, nor is Melisende. Baldwin rules in Jerusalem.'

'He rules alongside his mother. She is still the true power, even more so after the failure to take Damascus.'

'A woman ruling over men!' Mansur ad-Din scoffed.

'But a wise woman,' William countered.

'*Hmph*,' Mansur ad-Din snorted. 'Still a woman.'

At that moment, Turan entered with Taur trailing behind him. Both walked stiffly; John guessed they had ridden far that day.

'Where have you been?' Ayub snapped at Turan.

'I was in town. I was delayed by the rain. I apologize.'

'Apologize to our guests, who you have insulted.'

Turan bowed. 'My apologies honoured governor, Khaldun.'

175

Mansur ad-Din, his mouth filled with partridge meat, waved his hand dismissively. 'It is of no matter.'

Turan sat down, and Taur took up his place next to John. Ayub studied his son. 'Tell us, Turan. What were you doing in town?'

Turan hesitated, his eyes roving the room as if searching for the answer. 'I—I was with friends, practising swordplay.'

Mansur ad-Din brightened at this. In his younger days, the governor had had a reputation as a swordsman. 'My son tells me that you are quite fearsome with a sword, Turan.'

Turan sat up straighter. 'None my age can best me.'

'And what of you, young Yusuf?' Mansur ad-Din asked. 'Are you also a terror with the sword?'

'Yusuf prefers books to swords,' Turan sneered.

Yusuf ignored him. 'I try to cultivate my mind as well as my body. I believe the two can be equally dangerous weapons.'

'Well said,' Khaldun murmured.

'Indeed,' Mansur ad-Din agreed. He turned to Ayub and began to speak in a low voice, a signal that the others at the table could talk as they pleased. Soon the room was buzzing with conversation.

John took advantage of the opportunity to whisper to Taur. 'Where were you really?' Taur smiled slyly, but did not reply. 'Surely you were not in town all day,' John insisted. 'You were stiff as a priest's cock when you walked in here.'

'I cannot say,' Taur whispered back. 'My master would kill me.'

176

'He doesn't have to know,' John offered, but Taur shook his head and refused to speak.

The next morning Yusuf was shaken awake by the mamluk, Abaan. Yusuf looked to the shuttered window in his room. No light filtered through. 'Your father requests your presence in the interior courtyard,' Abaan said. He began to leave, then stopped in the doorway when he saw that Yusuf had not yet moved. 'Now!'

Yusuf rolled out of bed and pulled on his cotton pants, tunic and a brown caftan. He slipped on his sandals and belted his caftan around his waist as he walked down the cool, shadowy corridor to the courtyard. He entered to find his father waiting in the dim predawn light, his arms crossed and his face a blank mask. Turan stood next to him. He sneered at Yusuf, who scowled back. Next to Ayub and Turan was a third man – a Bedouin, one of the nomadic people who wandered the wastes beyond the villages, driving their flocks from pasture to pasture. The man wore a caftan of rough cotton and a white turban, tied in place with a black ribbon. He was very short, with a thick black beard, beak-like nose and penetrating grey eyes. The man's mouth was set in a thin line. As Yusuf approached, his father turned to the shepherd. 'Is this the one?'

The Bedouin's forehead wrinkled as he examined Yusuf. 'I cannot be sure. But it was one of your sons, of that much I am certain.'

Ayub frowned and turned to face his sons. 'Waqar here is the sheikh of his tribe.'

'Ahlan wa-Sahlan, Waqar,' Yusuf and Turan said, welcoming him. The sheikh did not reply.

'Waqar has come to lay a serious charge against one of you,' Ayub said.

The shepherd nodded. 'Yesterday, I rose before sunrise and rode into Baalbek with my sons to trade. When I returned that night, I found that my camp had been raided. There were at least two men. They killed one of my goats and raped my young daughter. She was to be married this spring, and now she is worth-less. My brother chased the intruders off, and in their hurry they left behind a horse. It bore the brand of Najm ad-Din.' The shepherd pointed an accusing finger at Turan, then at Yusuf. 'One of you did this. I demand justice!'

'Forgive my impertinence, yâ sîdi,' Yusuf said to the shepherd, addressing him respectfully as *sir*. 'But perhaps it was one of my father's men who did this terrible crime. The horse alone proves nothing.'

'It was no man,' Waqar spat. 'My daughter swears that the one who shamed her was no older than she.'

'It was Yusuf!' Turan burst out. 'Yusuf and that Frankish slave of his. They must have done it.'

'He lies!' Yusuf protested.

'Silence!' Ayub roared. 'You shame me with your childish behaviour.' He turned to Turan. 'Explain yourself. Why do you say that Yusuf did this thing?'

'Because I could not have done it, Father. I was in town all of yesterday. My friends, Idiq and Rakin, will vouch for me.'

'What do you say to this, Yusuf?'

'I was with Imad ad-Din yesterday afternoon. I could not have raided this man's camp.'

Ayub's mouth set in a hard line as he looked from one of his sons to the other. 'One of you is lying. Admit your fault now, and I will be lenient.' Neither Turan nor Yusuf spoke. 'Very well,' Ayub said. 'You will be judged, and judged harshly. I will sell the slave of whichever of you did this deed; he let you commit this crime, which makes him as guilty as you. And whoever did this will marry the sheikh's daughter and will pay the bride gift out of his inheritance.' He turned to Waqar, who was smiling at his good fortune; to be connected by marriage to the household of Nur ad-Din was more than he could have hoped for. 'The local imam, Imad ad-Din is a wise man. He returns from Damascus tomorrow, and I will ask him to judge the case. Tonight, you will be my guest. Tomorrow, you shall have justice.'

Yusuf sat cross-legged on the floor of the dining room and listened as a rooster's crowing broke the morning silence. Despite the early hour, the room was already full with men who had come to hear his case. The long, low table had been removed to create space for an impromptu court. At one end of the room, Imad ad-Din sat on a pile of cushions, his expression stern. To his left sat Ayub and to his right the Bedouin Waqar, who maintained a permanent scowl.

Yusuf sat before them, with Turan on his left. Immediately behind Turan were the men he had brought as witnesses: his friends Idiq and Rakin, his slave Taur and a bearded man that Yusuf did not recognize. Only

John sat with Yusuf. The back of the room was crowded with his father's men, Abaan at their head.

Imad ad-Din cleared his throat, and Yusuf turned his eyes back to him. 'The case before us is not clear,' the imam began. 'Both of the accused claim to have been in Baalbek when the crime was committed. Today, we shall find the truth of the matter. Turan.' Imad ad-Din beckoned Turan forward. 'State your case.'

'I was in town all of yesterday in the company of Idiq and Rakin,' Turan said, gesturing to his two friends. 'My slave and I left shortly after morning prayers. We took two horses from the stables. We returned with two horses in time for the feast. My father saw me there. I could not have done this shameful deed.'

'I see.' Imad ad-Din paused, his brown eyes burrowing into Turan, who lowered his gaze to the floor. 'I have examined your father's stables. I found a horse there that does not bear the brand of your father. Do you know where this horse might have come from, Turan?'

'I do not know. Ask Yusuf.'

Imad ad-Din ignored the suggestion. 'You were in town all of yesterday, you say? Tell me, what were you doing?'

Turan hesitated. His eyes flitted from his father to the floor and back. 'I was at a tavern.' Ayub frowned.

'A tavern?' Imad ad-Din asked. 'Which one?'

'Akhtar's.'

'A place of ill-repute, gambling and prostitution,' Ayub growled. 'Such conduct does you little credit, Son.'

'Nevertheless,' Imad ad-Din said, 'if Turan was at Akhtar's then he could not have also raided Waqar's camp. Turan, you may sit.' Turan smirked triumphantly as he took his seat. 'Idiq, Rakin,' Imad ad-Din called. 'Come forward.' The two young men approached. They were Turan's frequent companions when he smoked hashish, local boys with wispy facial hair and pimply faces. Rakin stood with his head down and his hands clasped before him. Idiq held his head high and met Imad ad-Din's gaze. 'Idiq, do you swear that you were with Turan all of yesterday?' Imad ad-Din asked.

'Yes,' Idiq said confidently.

'And you, Rakin?'

'I was with him all day,' Rakin affirmed in an adolescent warble.

'And you passed the day at Akhtar's?' Both boys nodded. 'Did you win at the tables?'

Rakin's forehead creased, and he looked to Turan. Idiq looked equally unsure. 'We—we did,' Idiq said at last.

'How much?'

The two boys looked at each other. 'Three dirhams,' Rakin said. 'Idiq was lucky at dice.'

'I see,' Imad ad-Din mused. 'I notice that you have your purse with you, Idiq. May I see it.'

'I—I—' Idiq stuttered.

'Come, give it here, boy,' Imad ad-Din insisted. Idiq handed the purse over. Imad ad-Din opened it and shook the contents into his hand. 'Four fals,' he said, holding up the cheap copper coins. 'Where did your winnings go?'

'Women,' Turan interjected. 'We spent them on women.'

'Silence!' Imad ad-Din snapped. 'You were not questioned, Turan.' He turned back to Idiq. 'You spent this money on women?' The boy nodded. Imad turned his penetrating gaze upon Rakin. 'Tell me about the woman you purchased, Rakin.'

'She—she was beautiful,' Rakin stammered.

Imad ad-Din nodded. 'I am sure. Of what did her beauty consist?'

Rakin stared up to the ceiling, as if he might see a picture of the woman painted there. 'She had brown eyes—and brown hair—and brown skin. She had very large breasts.'

'And were they brown as well?' Rakin's blush deepened. He nodded. 'Very well,' Imad ad-Din said with a frown. 'You may both sit.' Imad ad-Din dipped a quill in ink and wrote something, then turned to Turan. 'Do you have anything to add?'

'Akhtar, the owner of the tavern, is here,' Turan said, gesturing towards a thin-faced man seated cross-legged behind him. The man had thinning black hair, light skin and dark rings under his eyes. His rather gentle features were marred by a cleft lip. 'He will vouch for my story.'

'Come forward, Akhtar,' Imad ad-Din said. The tavern owner unfolded his long limbs and rose.

'Your Exthellenthe,' he lisped and bowed to Ayub, who nodded back. Akhtar turned to face Imad ad-Din.

'Were Turan and his friends at your tavern yesterday?' Imad ad-Din asked.

'Yeth.'

'And what did they do there?'

'They gambled, thmoked hashish and had women. As usual.'

'Turan is a regular client?' Akhtar nodded. 'And what of this brown girl? The prostitute?'

'Buthayna,' Akhtar said. 'She is from Africa, and she doeth have very large breast-th. You can come to my tavern and examine her, if you like.'

Imad ad-Din grimaced. 'That will not be necessary. You may sit.' He turned to Yusuf and waved him forward. Yusuf kept his head up and met his teacher's gaze. 'Turan presents a strong case,' Imad ad-Din said. 'What do you have to say in your defence, Yusuf?'

'I was with you, ustadh, all afternoon. Before that, I was in Baalbek with my servant, John, practising swordplay. I could not have done this crime.'

'John, is this true?' Imad ad-Din asked, looking to the slave.

John stood. 'Yes, ustadh. It is as my master says.'

'He lies!' Turan spat. 'The word of a slave means nothing.'

'That is enough, Turan,' Imad ad-Din admonished. He turned back to Yusuf. 'But he is correct. A slave's word stands for nothing in court. Did anyone else see you practising?'

'No,' Yusuf admitted. 'We practised in the Roman temple. No one saw us.'

'How convenient,' Turan snorted.

Imad ad-Din ignored the outburst. 'And after our lesson, how did you return from the temple?'

'I rode.'

'And your servant?'

Yusuf opened his mouth, then froze. The truth was that John had ridden with him because of the rain, but if he spoke true, then it would only condemn him. After all, Waqar had captured one of Ayub's horses. It would look as if Yusuf and John had raided the camp, then been forced to ride back together. 'I—I—' Yusuf stuttered.

'I saw you and John ride away on the same horse, Yusuf,' Imad ad-Din said.

'The case is settled then!' Waqar burst out. He pointed a stubby finger in Yusuf's direction. 'It must have been the young one!'

'No!' Yusuf protested. 'I did not do it.' He breathed deeply, trying to remain calm. Everything pointed to his guilt: the testimony of Akhtar; Yusuf's own lack of witnesses; his return with John on a single horse – that was it! 'I can prove my innocence!'

'That's ridiculous!' Turan spluttered.

Imad ad-Din held up a hand to silence Turan. 'Explain yourself, Yusuf.'

'Ustadh, you met me at the temple after afternoon prayers,' Yusuf said.

'So?' Turan interjected. 'This proves nothing. You could have raided the Bedouin camp in the morning.'

'On the contrary,' Yusuf countered. 'Waqar has told us that he was camped in the mountains, several leagues up the Orontes River. Even had I pressed my horse, it would have taken me from sunrise to nearly midday just to reach Waqar's tents. Then, if I turned and rode straight back, I would have arrived just in time for my lesson.'

'I do not understand,' Ayub said. 'By your own admission, then, you could have done this crime.'

'No. Imad ad-Din has said that my slave and I returned on one horse. He speaks true. There is no way that we could have ridden from this man's camp on one horse and arrived so quickly, much less would we have had time to rape his daughter or to roast and eat a goat.' Yusuf gestured towards Turan, whose face had begun to turn red. 'By his own admission, Turan left early and was gone all day. He had more than enough time to commit this crime.'

Imad ad-Din stroked his beard. 'Very clever, Yusuf.' Yusuf exhaled in relief, but then Imad ad-Din continued. 'But this proves nothing. I saw you leave the temple on one horse, but that does not mean that you could not have ridden back from the Bedouin camp on two. And besides, I cannot place your reasoning – no matter how clever – above the word of three men. Do you have anything else to add before I pass judgement?' Yusuf's mind raced, but he could think of no way to prove his innocence. 'Very well,' Imad ad-Din sighed. 'Turan, come forward. I am prepared to deliver my verdict.'

Turan rose to join Yusuf. 'Who is the clever one now, little brother?' he whispered under his breath.

Imad ad-Din cleared his throat. 'Yusuf, I find that—'

'Wait!' Yusuf interrupted. 'I have something to add.' He glanced at Turan. 'My brother spoke true about one thing: he could not have committed this crime.'

'What do you mean?' Imad ad-Din asked, his eyes wide.

Yusuf looked to the floor. 'I—I cannot say.'

'Speak!' Ayub told him. 'I command it.'

'Very well.' Yusuf looked to Waqar. 'The beauty of your daughter is well known. Turan never would have ridden so far to be with her.'

'And why not?' Imad ad-Din asked.

Yusuf took a deep breath. 'I know my brother. He has no feeling for women.'

'What!' Turan cried.

'He might be interested in the goat, yâ sîdi, but not your daughter.'

Turan raised a fist and took a step towards Yusuf. 'You lie!'

'I speak the truth,' Yusuf shouted over his brother. 'Turan would never have touched her.'

'You lying bastard!' Turan shoved Yusuf, knocking him to the ground and stood over him, his hands clenched into fists. 'I had the girl! More than once! You are the goat-fucker!'

The room fell silent. All eyes fixed on Turan. His face reddened as he realized what he had said. 'You bastard,' he growled at Yusuf. 'You tricked me!' He lunged for Yusuf, but Ayub's man Abaan grabbed him from behind and held him back.

As Yusuf rose from the floor, he looked past Turan to his father, who was shaking his head in disgust. 'Imad ad-Din, what do you say?' Ayub asked.

'Turan has admitted his guilt. Let justice be done.'

'But Father—' Turan began.

'Silence!' Ayub snapped. He rose and everyone in the hall did likewise. Ayub turned to Waqar. 'We are brothers now. My oldest son will marry your daughter.' He placed his hands on the shepherd's shoulders, and kissed him three times on the lips. Waqar nodded, speechless. There were tears of joy in his eyes.

Ayub turned from Waqar and approached Turan. 'You disappoint me, my son. Maybe marriage will cool your blood.' He marched out of the hall, leaving Turan red-faced.

Yusuf leaned close to his brother. 'Congratulations on your marriage, Brother,' he whispered, then followed his father from the hall.

Yusuf stood shivering in the courtyard of the villa, his ceremonial white-silk caftan pulled close about him. The winter had been long and hard, and even now, in April, the weather was unseasonably cold. The dozens of guests – men on one side of the courtyard and women on the other – looked miserable as they stamped their feet and blew on their hands while waiting for the wedding ceremony to begin. But none looked more miserable than the groom. Turan stood next to Yusuf, wearing a pure-white caftan, belted with a length of saffron-yellow silk. His turban was also held in place with yellow silk. Last night, at the henna ceremony, the little finger on his right hand had been painted with intricate, swirling patterns in dark brown. His sparse, adolescent beard had been filled out with kohl. He looked every bit the perfect groom, except for the grimace stretched across his face.

A cheer went up from the crowd, and the frown on Turan's face deepened as his bride-to-be, Sa'ida, rode through the gates of the villa on the back of a camel led by her smiling father, Waqar. Sa'ida was also dressed in white, with only her hands, feet and eyes showing. Her eyes had been outlined with kohl and her hands and feet decorated with henna. Yusuf guessed that she had also used powders to lighten her face, because the skin around her eyes was ghostly pale. Either that or she was simply frightened of what was to come. Indeed, her wide eyes, which were locked on Turan, spoke of something close to terror.

The camel stopped, and Waqar helped his daughter to dismount. He took her arm and led her towards Turan. She stopped before him, and Turan presented her with a necklace of beaten gold, his bride gift. The rest of her bride price – fifty fleeces, ten sheep, two fine horses and ten dinars – had already been delivered. Turan placed the necklace around Sa'ida's neck, and Yusuf noticed that she flinched when his hands touched her. The two then turned to face Ayub.

'I call on all of you to witness this marriage,' Ayub called out to the crowd. He turned to his son. 'Turan, will you take this woman, Sa'ida bint Waqar?'

Turan nodded. 'Yes.'

Ayub turned to Waqar. 'Waqar, will your daughter accept my son, Turan, in marriage?' Sa'ida looked positively terrified. Her hands shook, and her wide eyes scanned the crowd as if looking for help.

'Yes!' Waqar bellowed. 'She gladly accepts.' The crowd cheered, and Waqar grinned.

'Let us have feasting and celebration!' Ayub shouted. The crowd cheered again and servants rushed forward to serve the men. The women retreated to behind the villa, where they would have their own celebration.

Yusuf stepped forward and took Sa'ida's trembling hands. She was crying. 'You are welcome in our family,' he said, then lowered his voice. 'If you need a friend, you may come to me.' She nodded her thanks, and Yusuf turned to Turan. He grasped him by the shoulders and kissed him three times on the lips. 'Congratulations.'

Turan did not thank him. Leaning close, he whispered in Yusuf's ear: 'You will pay for this, Brother.'

Chapter 8

'By God it's hot,' John grumbled, wiping sweat from his brow. He and Yusuf rode along the dusty path that ran east from the city of Baalbek and into the foot-hills of the mountains. John turned in the saddle and looked back to where Yusuf's brother Selim rode, fol-lowed by the women – Zimat, Turan's new wife Sa'ida and four female slaves, all veiled. Abaan and two other mamluks brought up the rear, leading a pack-horse. Behind them, the retreating walls of Baalbek shifted and wavered as heat rose from the parched earth. John turned forward again and rewrapped his turban, covering his face to protect it from the sun.

'You look a proper Muslim, now,' Yusuf told him.

'Anything to keep that cursed sun off. It feels as if it could burn straight through my skin.'

'We will be at the spring soon enough. It is a paradise. You will forget all about the sun.'

The road sloped gently upwards towards the moun-tains, and they began to pass ruins on their right-hand side – huge arches of stone, built one on top of another, supporting what looked like a road high above the ground. There were frequent gaps where the columns had collapsed into jagged piles of rubble.

'What is that?' John asked.

'An aqueduct. The Romans built it to carry water from the spring into town.'

'A road for water,' John murmured in wonder. They left the aqueduct behind as the path swung sharply uphill and entered the shadows cast by towering cedars. After a few minutes the road levelled out, and they entered a shadowy clearing carpeted with lush green grass. At the far end of the meadow a half-fallen wall and a few marble columns – the crumbled remains of an ancient temple – stood beside the dark waters of a spring-fed pool.

'Come on!' Yusuf shouted. He slid from the saddle and ran towards the water. When he reached it, he leapt through the air with a whoop of joy and landed with a splash. Selim followed close behind, hurling himself head over heels into the pool. John dismounted, gathered up the reigns of the horses, and led them across the clearing. The women followed, giggling over Yusuf and Selim's antics.

John tethered the horses to a column and left them to crop at the lush grass that grew up between the stones of the ruined temple. He turned to see Yusuf emerging from the spring, his dripping tunic clinging to his thin but muscular frame. Behind him, Zimat, Sa'ida and the other women were standing at the edge of the pool, gasping as they dipped their feet in the water. Yusuf shook himself, sending water flying at the girls, who shrieked and retreated.

Yusuf turned back to John. 'What are you waiting for?'

John looked at Yusuf's clinging tunic, then glanced over to where Zimat stood watching. He shook his head. 'Later, maybe.'

'At least take a drink,' Yusuf insisted.

John approached the pool and knelt down. As he bent forward to drink, Yusuf shoved him from behind, and John tumbled into the pool. The shock of the freezing water took his breath away, and he broke the surface gasping. As he pulled himself out of the pool, he noticed Zimat staring.

Yusuf approached, grinning. 'Not hot any more, are you? Come on. Let's eat.'

Abaan and his men had unpacked food and laid blankets on the ground in the centre of the clearing. They all enjoyed a meal of fresh peaches, bread and goat's cheese, washed down with cold water from the spring. When they had finished, the men left the clearing to allow the women to bathe. Yusuf posted Abaan and the other mamluks on the road to protect their privacy. He left Selim with them and took John aside. 'Come with me. I have something to show you.'

John followed him along a narrow animal track that ran uphill to the west of the clearing. The shouts and laughter of Zimat, Sa'ida and their slave girls faded as John and Yusuf headed deeper into the forest, pushing through the branches that crowded the trail. Finally, Yusuf stopped at the edge of a sunlight-dappled glade. The golden light played upon a throne of white marble, streaked black here and there by time and weather. On either side of the throne lay two bulls sculpted from stone, and upon the throne was seated a statue of a bearded man, naked but for a crown of leaves. His nose was missing, but the face was still stern and strong, with a square jaw and thick eyebrows. John's eyes widened. The man on the throne looked just like the depiction of God painted on the stained-glass windows of his church back in Tatewic.

'Who is it?' John whispered.

'Zeus,' Yusuf replied. 'Or Baal, as the local Phoenicians called him. Imad ad-Din says that this spring was sacred to the Phoenicians long before the Romans arrived. They built the temple and left this statue as well.'

John stepped forward and touched the weathered stone of the statue's face. He looked up as a peal of high-pitched laughter penetrated the clearing. Peering through the trees beyond the statue, John caught a glimpse of long, athletic legs and then a firm bottom, framed between two tree trunks. Yusuf must have led them in a circle around the clearing, which they had then reapproached through the woods to the west of the pool. John flushed red and glanced at Yusuf. His eyes were fixed upon the distant trees. John looked back, and the figure was gone. More scantily clad forms flitted past. Then there was a splash and high, loud laughter. A second later, a face appeared, staring back at them from between the distant trees. It was Sa'ida, a dark bruise on her cheek. A moment later, Zimat's face joined hers. Her eyes met John's.

'We should go,' Yusuf said as he grabbed John's arm and pulled him away.

John followed Yusuf back down the path, cursing as he stumbled over a root. His mind was still back in the clearing, filled with images of long limbs, that perfectly shaped bottom and Zimat's face. He was still thinking of her when they reached the road where Selim and the mamluks were waiting. John stopped short when he saw that Zimat and the other women were also there. Zimat had not dried thoroughly, and her caftan clung to her left side, revealing the outline of her breast. John stared dumbly at her, and she returned his gaze. He felt himself turning red.

'It grows late,' Yusuf said, giving John a hard look. 'We must return to Baalbek.'

The party returned to the clearing, where Abaan and his men packed up their supplies. Yusuf helped Sa'ida into the saddle, and John hurried to help Zimat. As he took her foot and lifted her up, she leaned over and whispered, 'Meet me tonight, in the stable loft.'

John lay in his small room and stared out of the open window at the night sky, strewn with innumerable stars. He had stayed awake, his mind busy with thoughts of Zimat, while one by one the sounds of the villa had faded. Now, only the song of the cicadas could be heard. John took a deep breath and threw off his blanket. He was fully dressed. He went to the door and opened it, wincing as the hinges creaked. He froze, his heart pounding in his chest, and peeked out. No one had stirred. Relieved, he slipped outside, carefully shutting the door behind him. He paused to cross himself, and then crept towards the stables, keeping to the dark shadows thrown by the wall.

One of the tall double-doors to the stable was slightly ajar. John slipped through the crack into the inky darkness. 'Hello?' he whispered. He listened, but heard only the hum of the cicadas and the nickering of a horse, lost in a dream. 'Zimat?' There was no reply.

John tiptoed forward, his hand held out before him as he groped his way towards the ladder that led to the loft. He found it and climbed up, pausing at the top. He saw only the dim outline of the piles of hay. Then he caught a movement out of the corner of his eye. 'Zimat?'

'John?' It was her voice.

'It's me,' John said as he clambered into the loft. Zimat moved towards him and in the darkness they collided, their foreheads knocking together with an audible crack.

'Akh laa!' Zimat cried out as she fell back.

'Are you hurt?' John whispered as he moved forward to comfort her, only to trip over her legs and fall on top of her. He quickly rolled off and began to apologize, then stopped as Zimat burst out laughing. Her mirth proved contagious, and John found himself laughing with her, laughing so hard that his eyes watered. Finally, they fell silent, sitting side by side and gasping for breath.

'I am glad you asked me to come,' John said when he had recovered his breath. 'After our kiss, I did not think you wanted to see me again.'

Zimat glanced at him, then looked away. 'I was afraid. I had never kissed a man before.'

'And I had never kissed a woman.'

'But what about the English girl?'

'I lied.'

'I guessed as much. I felt your knees shaking.' Zimat turned to face him. 'Tell me, John: what do you see when you look at me?'

John stared at Zimat, the outlines of her face only dimly visible, her eyes twin pools of darkness. 'I see a beautiful woman, the most beautiful I have ever seen.'

Zimat turned away. 'Is that all?'

'No.' John reached out and gently touched her chin, turning her face back towards him. 'I see a generous heart; you are kind even to your slaves. And I see a proud woman, but also one who is afraid. You want more than your place in life offers, but you are afraid to take it.'

'Yes.' Zimat nodded emphatically. 'How did you know?'

'Because I feel the same.'

Zimat moved closer, her side almost touching his. 'I am not afraid now.'

'Nor am I.' John took her hand in his.

'Your hands are rough.'

'Yours are soft, like the petal of a rose.' John raised her hand to his lips and kissed it. Zimat giggled.

'You missed the mark.' She leaned close and kissed John. Her lips were moist and soft, her breath sweet.

John closed his eyes, his head spinning, then pulled away suddenly. 'But I am a Frank. Are you sure?'

'That is why I am sure. You see me as I am. No man of my people will ever do the same.' Zimat reached out and pulled him back towards her. John kissed her hard, and she opened her mouth to his. His arms encircled her, pulling her close against him so that he could feel the soft curves of her breasts against his chest. His hands moved down her back, then grabbed one of her firm buttocks. She gasped.

'I'm sorry,' he mumbled. 'I did not mean to—'

'No, do not stop.' Zimat took his hand and placed it on her breast. John kissed her hungrily, while with his other hand he reached behind her back and gently laid her down in the straw. He began to kiss her cheeks, then her neck. He pulled open the front of her caftan to reveal her breasts, the dark nipples hard and erect. He took one in his mouth, and Zimat moaned softly. John grasped her thigh, and his hand moved up under her caftan, between her legs. She reached out to stop him.

'I must remain a virgin.'

'I—I understand,' John replied, his voice choked with passion. He pulled away.

Zimat reached out and drew him back down to her. 'But that does not mean you must stop. There are other things we can do.'

John lay asleep in the straw of the loft, Zimat in his arms and her head upon his chest. She shifted, pressing herself closer against him, and he smiled. Then, his eyes snapped open at the sound of a loud wail from outside the barn. Daylight filtered in through the thin cracks between the boards that made up the ceiling. 'What was that?' John wondered.

Zimat awoke and sat up, pulling her caftan around her bare shoulders. 'Ya Allah! It is daylight. I must go.' She pulled on her caftan and headed for the ladder, then froze as another horrible cry penetrated the barn.

'Something is wrong,' John said, rising and pulling on

his own caftan. 'I will check to make sure that you will not be seen.'

Zimat nodded, and John stepped past her and hurried down the ladder. He cracked open the barn door and peered out. Most of the household was crowded around the well, only twenty feet from the barn doors. Basimah was on her knees, her head in her hands. Ayub and Yusuf talked quietly beside her. Slaves and servants kept a respectful distance.

'What has happened?' Zimat asked as she joined him at the door and peeked out.

John shook his head. 'I do not know.' In the courtyard, Basimah began to wail again.

Zimat turned to face John. 'If we leave together, we will be seen. You go first. I will come out when it is safe.'

'Will I see you again?'

Zimat flashed him a brilliant smile. 'Yes. Now go.'

John stepped out and almost ran into Turan, who was heading along the wall towards the well. 'Watch where you are going, Frank!' he roared, shoving John aside. Turan started to move on but then stopped and examined John more closely. He picked a piece of straw off John's tunic and twisted it between his fingers. 'What were you doing in the stables, slave?'

'I—I sleep there sometimes,' John lied. 'It is cooler than my room.'

'*Hmph*, with the other animals.' Turan headed on towards the well, and John followed.

'It was dark last night,' Ayub was saying to Yusuf as John and Turan approached. 'Perhaps she did not see the well and fell in.'

'Perhaps,' Yusuf said. His eyes narrowed as he noticed Turan.

'What has happened?' Turan asked.

Ayub put his hand on Turan's shoulder. 'I am sorry, my son. It is your wife, Sa'ida. She is dead.' At this, Basimah began to wail again, her loud keening drowning out the cries of the rooster, which had just begun to crow the dawn.

'How?' Turan asked.

Yusuf's gaze burrowed into Turan. 'We are not sure—yet.'

'Do you wish to say something to me, Brother?' Turan flared.

'That is enough!' Ayub snapped as he stepped between them. 'This is a day of mourning. I will not have your petty squabbling.' He turned to Turan. 'I must speak with you.' Ayub led Turan a few paces away, and they spoke in low voices. After a moment, Ayub called the head slave, Harith, over to join them.

John stepped past Yusuf and peered into the well. Sa'ida floated at the bottom, her pale, broken body barely visible in the gloom. John turned away. 'Perhaps she killed herself,' he whispered to Yusuf. 'I would not blame her.'

'No, he did it,' Yusuf snarled, gesturing towards Turan. 'I am sure of it.'

John nodded. He made a show of looking about, then turned back to Yusuf. 'Have you seen your sister, Zimat?'

Yusuf's face paled. Basimah looked up from where she knelt. 'Zimat?' she whispered, then her voice rose to a scream. 'Zimat! Where are you my child!'

'I am here!' Zimat called, hurrying over from the direction of the barn.

'Thank Allah!' Basimah cried as she rose and embraced her daughter.

Turan and Ayub walked back over to the well. Turan went straight to John, grabbed his right arm, and twisted it behind his back. John began to struggle, but Yusuf shook his head. He turned to his father. 'What is this?'

'Turan says the Frank killed his wife, then hid in the stables. Harith has confirmed that John was not in his room last night.'

John shook his head. 'But—'

'Silence, slave!' Ayub snapped. 'Turan will stay here and prepare his wife for burial. Yusuf, you will leave now to inform Sa'ida's father of this tragedy and to present him a gift in recompense for the loss of his daughter. You will bring him back with you, and when the two of you return, the Frank will be executed. That should appease Waqar.'

'But John is innocent!' It was Zimat, and all eyes turned to her. She blushed and lowered her gaze.

Ayub frowned. 'This is no business of yours, Daughter. I have spoken. It will be done.' He nodded towards John. 'Take him to the cell.'

Yusuf reined his horse to a stop as the city of Baalbek came into sight. Waqar and the five mamluks who accompanied him also halted. It had taken them nearly a week to find Waqar, who had taken his herds to summer pastures in the mountains north of Hama. Yusuf had welcomed the delay. Every day he spent searching for

Waqar meant another day that John would live. But now, after four days of hard riding, they had reached Baalbek.

'At last,' Waqar muttered. 'I will gut the Frankish bastard myself.'

Yusuf grimaced and spurred his horse forward, riding at a fast trot. He and his men passed through the city gate and wound through the town to the villa. As he rode into the courtyard, Yusuf saw Turan speaking with their uncle, Shirkuh, who had just arrived and was still covered with the dust of the road. Turan saw Yusuf and his eyes narrowed. Shirkuh grinned. 'Nephew!' he roared.

'Ahlan wa-Sahlan, Uncle,' Yusuf said as he slid from the saddle. He put his hands on his uncle's shoulders and exchanged the ritual three kisses on the lips.

'You greet me as a man now,' Shirkuh noted. He squeezed Yusuf's arm, feeling his hard bicep. 'And by Allah, you are a man. Soon enough, it will be your turn to join me in the court of Nur ad-Din.'

'My turn?'

'Your father has decided that Turan is old enough to begin his service to his lord. I have come for him. We leave tomorrow for Aleppo.' Shirkuh looked past Yusuf to Waqar. 'And who is this?'

'This is the Bedouin sheikh Waqar, father of Sa'ida,' Yusuf informed him. 'Waqar, this is my uncle, Shirkuh.'

'As-salaamu 'alaykum,' Waqar called out as he dismounted.

'Wa 'Alaykum as-salaam, sheikh. I mourn with you for your loss,' Shirkuh replied, and the two men exchanged kisses. 'Now come, all of you. Let us go in for refreshments. I am eager to see my brother.'

Turan shook his head. 'Later, Uncle. I must speak with Yusuf.'

Shirkuh frowned. 'But you insult our guest.'

'My most sincere apologies, Sheikh,' Turan said, bowing to Waqar. 'After tomorrow, I will not see my brother again for many months.' Waqar nodded.

'Very well,' Shirkuh said. 'But do not be too long.'

Yusuf followed Turan around the side of the villa to the rear courtyard, where Turan turned to face him. 'I have a score to settle with you before I go, little brother.'

'And I with you.' Yusuf raised his fists. 'You killed Sa'ida. Admit it.'

'Who will make me? You?' Turan turned in place as Yusuf began to circle around him. 'Careful, Brother, your Frank is not here to save you this time,' Turan said as he casually cracked his knuckles. Yusuf sprang forward and snapped off a jab, catching Turan in the jaw. Turan stumbled back, surprised. 'You little bastard!' He brought his fists up and began to circle, mirroring Yusuf.

'Why did you kill Sa'ida?' Yusuf asked. 'Did she laugh at the size of your zib?'

Turan's face flushed red. He stepped forward and swung for Yusuf's head. Yusuf ducked the clumsy blow and punched Turan twice in the gut before moving away, leaving his brother doubled over, hands on his knees.

'I must have gotten close to the mark,' Yusuf taunted. 'Or was it that you could not get it up?'

'I will kill you!' Turan roared. He charged towards Yusuf, who stood his ground. At the last second, Yusuf jumped to the side and smashed his fist into Turan's face before tripping his brother and sending him sprawling in the dust. Turan rolled over, furious, but Yusuf was on him immediately. He slammed his knee into Turan's gut as he knelt over his brother and punched him in the nose, feeling a satisfying crunch. He hit Turan again and again, as his older brother vainly tried to defend himself. Turan's nose was gushing blood and his lip was split, but Yusuf kept punching. He bared his teeth as the anger and frustration built up over so many years boiled over within him.

'You bastard,' Yusuf growled as he swung down. '*Bastard*! *Bastard*! *Bastard*!' Yusuf swung again, but this time Turan caught his punch. He yanked Yusuf's arm, pulling Yusuf off his chest. Yusuf tried to shake free, but Turan's grip was like a vice. Turan rose to his feet and spun Yusuf around, putting him in a headlock. He pulled his forearm tight across his brother's throat, choking him.

'I did kill Sa'ida,' Turan whispered in Yusuf's ear. 'It was that bitch's fault my zib would not rise. And it's your fault I married her in the first place. Shall I kill you, too, little brother?' He squeezed tighter. Yusuf's face was shading from bright red to purple, and he was start-ing to see spots of light dancing across his vision. 'No smart replies now, eh? Can't talk your way out of this.'

Yusuf snapped his head backwards and Turan fell back, hands over his face. Gasping for air, Yusuf spun around to face him. But the air would not come. It was one of his fits. *Not now, not now*, Yusuf thought to himself. He dropped to his knees, his chest heaving as he struggled for air.

Turan smirked, despite his swollen right eye and the blood running from his nose. 'What's the matter, little brother? Trouble breathing? And you wonder why I am Father's favourite. You're pathetic.' Yusuf closed his eyes, shutting out Turan. He forced himself to breath evenly and slowly. He could defeat this. He must not try to catch his breath; it would come to him if he was patient. He opened his eyes and got to his feet.

'Still fighting?' Turan sneered, his teeth stained red with blood. 'You should have stayed down.' He surged towards Yusuf, who threw a jab, catching Turan in his bloodied nose. Yusuf slipped away and started circling. He grinned. His breathing had returned to normal.

'I'll wipe that grin off your face,' Turan hissed. He stepped forward and threw a windmill punch. Yusuf ducked the blow and then unleashed a combination: two quick blows to the gut and an uppercut that snapped Turan's head back. Turan stumbled backwards, his arms down. Yusuf stepped forward and threw two hard punches to his brother's stomach, driving the wind out of him. Then Yusuf reared back and put all his force behind a straight cross that caught Turan square on the jaw. Turan's legs gave out, and he sank to his knees, his eyes glazed. Yusuf looked past him and saw Shirkuh, watching impassively as he leaned against a corner of the villa.

Yusuf put his hands on Turan's shoulders and leaned close. 'You will admit what you did to Sa'ida.'

'It was an accident,' Turan mumbled, his head down. 'I didn't mean to hurt her.'

'Louder, Brother. I did not hear you.'

'It was an accident!' Turan cried. 'I shoved her, and she fell. She hit her head on the table.'

Yusuf's face wrinkled in disgust. 'You are my brother, or else I would beat you to death like the animal you are.' He let go of Turan, who slumped to the ground and lay unmoving in the dust. Yusuf headed towards Shirkuh. 'You heard what he said, Uncle. He killed Sa'ida.'

Shirkuh nodded. 'Your father suspected as much. That is why he asked me to come for Turan. The boy needs to be taught a lesson.' He gripped Yusuf's shoulder. 'I wouldn't have believed it if I hadn't seen it myself. Turan is nearly twice your size, and you made him eat dirt.'

Yusuf nodded towards the cell where John was being kept. 'The Frank, John, taught me.'

'He taught you well. I will speak to your father and see that he is released.' Shirkuh drew a dagger from his belt and handed it to his nephew. The pommel was carved in the shape of a fierce eagle's head. 'Nur ad-Din gave this to me. He said I was like the eagle descending upon the hare, the terror of the Franks. Now it is yours.'

Yusuf drew the dagger from its sheath and the dark-grey blade glinted in the sunlight. 'Thank you, Uncle.'

'You have the makings of a great warrior, Yusuf. Our lord Nur ad-Din has need of men like you. Soon enough, it will be your turn to join him in Aleppo, little eagle.'

Part II
Saladin

'Leaders are not born; they are made.' Saladin told me this. I do not know if what he says is true for all, but it was true for him. And the making of Saladin the Great was no easy thing. It almost killed him . . .

The Chronicle of Yahya al-Dimashq

Chapter 9

John gripped his spear in both hands as he crept along a game trail, weaving through the tall cedars on the slopes above Baalbek. To either side, a dense undergrowth of ferns, shrubs and saplings disappeared into the early morning mist. Ahead, Yusuf crept forward, scanning the ground for signs of their quarry: a black panther that had killed three villagers in the past month. They had first caught sight of the huge beast two days before. Now they had found its trail again.

John paused as Yusuf bent down to examine the ground. In the two years since Turan left, Yusuf had added muscle to his thin frame, and in the last few months he had developed the beginnings of a black beard, which he filled out with kohl. John thought back to the reedy boy he had first met years ago. That boy was gone. Yusuf was becoming a man.

Yusuf looked up from the trail and waved John forward. He approached and crouched beside Yusuf, who poked at the earth and raised two fingers wet with blood. 'This kill was recent,' he whispered. 'We're close.'

Yusuf took his bow from his shoulder and nocked an arrow. They walked in silence as the sun rose above them, burning off the mist and dappling the undergrowth with light. John caught a sudden movement out of the corner of his eye and froze, his spear extended towards the woods on his right. Yusuf drew his bow taut. There was another flash of motion, and John spotted a deer bounding away from them, followed by its faun. The deer stopped, looked back for a second, then disappeared into the distant trees. Yusuf grinned sheepishly as he relaxed his bowstring. They moved forward again, but John stopped almost immediately.

'Fresh droppings,' he whispered, pointing to a pile of dung glistening in a patch of sunlight to the side of the trail.

Yusuf nodded, then gestured to the branches above. 'Keep your eyes open.' After its kill, the panther would have dragged its prey up into a tree in order to eat in peace. The cat's black coat would make it difficult to spot in the shadows. John and Yusuf crept forward and John noticed more signs that the panther had passed this way: the broken branch of a fern on the side of the trail; a trace of blood on a leaf; a single paw print in the dust. Then the traces ceased. A dozen feet ahead, Yusuf stopped and looked back. 'I see no more sign.'

'Perhaps the panther left the trail,' John suggested. He took a step into the dense foliage to his right.

'Don't move!' Yusuf hissed and pointed to a branch over John's head. John looked up and saw two unblinking, golden eyes peering back at him. The panther was stretched out on a limb directly overhead. The beast was huge, easily five feet long and thickly muscled beneath its glossy black fur. It yawned, revealing long canines, startlingly white against its black coat.

John looked back to Yusuf, who had drawn his bow and was sighting along the arrow. John whispered a prayer to the Virgin, then added another to Allah for good measure. Yusuf let fly, and the arrow buried itself in the panther's right hindquarter. The animal screeched in pain. It's golden eyes moved from the arrow in its side to John. The beast roared and leapt.

John raised his spear, but the panther slammed into him, knocking it from his grip and flattening him. The huge cat swiped at John, raking its claws across the forearm that he raised to defend himself. Yusuf came running, and the panther looked to him. It snarled, then limped away into the woods. John sat up, gripping his left forearm, where three parallel gashes oozed blood.

'Are you all right?' Yusuf asked.

'I'll live.' John extended his right hand, and Yusuf pulled him to his feet.

'Forgive me, Brother. I missed.'

John waved away the apology. 'Come on,' he said as he bent down to pick up his spear. 'It's getting away.' Yusuf grinned and drew his dagger with the eagle hilt. He charged into the underbrush after the panther, and John followed at a jog. Leafy branches slapped against him as he ran through the forest. John leapt over a fallen tree, then ducked a low-hanging branch. Yusuf was just ahead, and John accelerated to catch up, but then skidded to a stop when he noticed a fresh smear of blood on the front of his tunic. He turned and examined the bush he had just passed. Sure enough, the leaves were splattered with blood. The trail led off to the right.

'Yusuf!' he shouted. 'This way!' John set off, scanning the ground ahead for signs of his quarry. He veered left as he noticed blood on a fern. There were no further signs, and John slowed, then stopped, scanning the brush around him. He felt the hair on the back of his neck rise. The beast was close; he could feel it.

There was a roar behind him, and John turned just as the panther slammed into him, bowling him over and landing on top of him. The panther dug its claws into John's shoulder and roared, its long canines only inches from his face. He could feel the animal's hot breath. And then Yusuf slammed into the panther from the side, knocking it off of John. Yusuf sprang to his feet, but he had lost his dagger in his attack. Defenceless, he faced the big cat. It swiped at him, and Yusuf backed away so that John lay between him and the panther. The beast roared and sprang for Yusuf.

With a cry of his own, John rolled and extended his spear, impaling the panther through the chest just before it hit Yusuf. The cat fell heavily, taking the spear with it. John scrambled away as it thrashed on the ground, screeching in agony. The panther's cries quieted as its lifeblood flowed from it, and then it lay still, dead. John pushed himself to his feet and looked across to Yusuf. They stood silent for a moment, the only sound the song of a nearby sparrow, and then Yusuf began to laugh. John joined him, and soon they were both bent over, roaring with laughter.

'Yusuf,' John gasped between laughs, 'you should have seen your face when it leapt for you.'

'My face? When it hit you, you looked as if you were going to piss yourself!'

Their laughter faded as quickly as it had come, and they stood silent, staring at the mighty beast they had slain. John winced as he felt his right shoulder; his tunic was torn and bloody. Yusuf approached and gripped his other shoulder. 'Thank you, John. I owe you my life.'

John shrugged. 'I only did my duty, m'allim.'

Yusuf met his eyes. 'Do not call me m'allim. I am your friend.' John nodded. 'Now come.' Yusuf stepped forward, grabbed the spear with both hands and wrenched it free. 'Let us take our prize home.'

Yusuf rode through the streets of Baalbek, leading the horse over which the dead panther had been slung. As he and John wound up the hill towards the villa, people came out of their homes and lined the streets to see the beast, some staring open-mouthed, others cheering. The women stayed in the background, silent and veiled, but more than a few fluttered their eyelashes at Yusuf as he road past. He had a smile on his face as he left the road and trotted through the gate into the villa.

As Yusuf dismounted in the courtyard, his father came out to greet him, followed by Shirkuh. 'Uncle!' Yusuf shouted. He went first to greet his father, then turned to Shirkuh, who gripped him by the shoulders. 'Ahlan wa-Sahlan,' Yusuf said, and the two exchanged kisses.

'Well met, young eagle.' Shirkuh looked past Yusuf

and nodded towards the horse that carried the black panther. 'What have you caught?'

'See for yourself.'

They gathered around the panther. Shirkuh whistled appreciatively and reached out to stroke the glossy black fur. 'I've never seen one so big. It will make a fine cloak. Where did you kill it?'

'The slopes of Mount Tallat al Jawzani, but I was not the one who slew the beast.' Yusuf gestured to John. 'It was John.'

'Ah, yes. I remember him,' Shirkuh murmured. 'A useful man.'

'My lord is the one who tracked it,' John said quietly.

Shirkuh slapped Yusuf on the back. 'Well done, nephew.'

Yusuf nodded. 'And what brings you to Baalbek, Uncle?'

'You, Yusuf. You are coming with me to Aleppo. It is time that you begin your service to our lord, Nur ad-Din.'

Ayub stepped forward. 'Nur ad-Din is a man who values first impressions, Son. If you please him, then you will go far. You can become an emir, perhaps even the commander of his armies, like your Uncle Shirkuh.'

'Or more,' Shirkuh added. 'It is no secret that Nur ad-Din has no son.' Shirkuh turned to Yusuf. 'I have told him great things of you, young eagle. Do not disappoint me.'

That night, John lay in the straw of the stable hayloft, Zimat pressed against his side, her head upon his chest.

He looked down at her, trying to create a memory that he could carry with him. Zimat had, if possible, grown even more beautiful in the past two years as new curves appeared at her hips and breasts. She propped herself up on her elbow and turned to face John. A tear ran down her face, glistening silver in the moonlight. John gently brushed it away.

'Do you remember our first kiss,' he whispered, 'when you came to me in the stable?'

'Of course.'

'Why did you come?'

'To thank you. You saved me from Turan.' A trace of a smile curled her lips. 'And I was curious. You were so different from any of the men I had known.'

'More handsome?' John suggested playfully.

'No.' She laid her head back on his chest. 'It is the way you looked at me. In the kitchen when we first met, you met my eyes and did not look away. My father would have had you whipped had he seen you.'

John stroked her hair. 'I did not know any better.'

'It is not just that you did not lower your eyes.' Zimat looked up and met his gaze. 'I felt like you saw me, truly saw me, as someone to love, not as something to possess.'

John frowned. 'I could not possess you if I wished to. You will be married to Khaldun next spring.'

'No!' Zimat took his hand. 'I cannot bear it. We will run away. You will take me far from here.'

John looked away. 'We cannot.'

'We can! I know where my father keeps his gold. I can take enough for us to reach Jerusalem.'

'It is not the money. Your father is a powerful man. No one would take us in. There would be nowhere for us to hide between here and the Frankish lands. We would be caught, and I would be killed.' John met her eyes. 'And perhaps you too.'

'I am not afraid to die. Better that than to lose you, to live as Khaldun's slave.'

'I will not be responsible for your death,' John told her. 'And there is another reason: your brother.'

'He is your master. You owe him nothing.'

'No, he is my friend, and I owe him my life.'

Zimat turned away. 'You do not love me.' She began to sob, her shoulders shaking.

John reached out and gently touched her cheek, turning her face towards him. 'You know I do,' he said as he welcomed her into his arms. He held her tight, her head against his chest, and they lay in silence for a long time. When Zimat finally pulled away, John's caftan was wet with her tears.

She met his eyes. 'I want to lay with you John, as a wife lays with her husband.'

'But—'

Zimat put a finger to his lips. 'I do not want my first time to be with Khaldun. I want it to be with you.'

'Are you sure?'

Zimat nodded and slipped her caftan off her shoulders.

Yusuf stood in the courtyard behind his home and listened to the rhythmic chant of the muezzin calling the faithful to pray. For the first time since his tenth birthday, he would not complete his morning prayers. Shirkuh had declared that they would leave at sunrise, and already the sky behind Mount Tallat al Jawzani was brightening, shading from pink to smouldering orange and incandescent white. Yusuf looked away from the mountain and turned slowly, taking in his home one final time. His gaze lingered on the leafy lime trees, under which he had spent so many summer hours reading; on the cell where John had been confined all those years ago; on the door to the kitchen, emanating comforting smells of yeast and spice.

'Yusuf!' John called, and Yusuf wiped away tears before turning to watch him approach. John had filled out since Yusuf had first met him. Now twenty, he had a broad chest and thickly muscled arms. 'Our horses are ready,' he said. 'They are waiting for you.'

Yusuf nodded and headed for the front courtyard, followed by John. Their horses – two saddled and two more packed with Yusuf's possessions – stood near the gate, next to Shirkuh and his men. Yusuf's family was gathered in front of them.

Yusuf went to Selim, who had screwed up his face in an effort to master his emotions, and placed his hands on his brother's shoulders. 'I will see you soon, Brother. In two more years, it will be your turn.' Selim nodded but did not speak. Yusuf embraced him. 'Allah yasalmak.'

He turned next to Zimat. She would be married soon, and then she would be gone from his life, part of another man's household. Indeed, this might be the last time they saw one another for many years. Zimat's eyes were distant, looking past Yusuf, and tears ran down her cheeks.

'Do not cry for me, Sister,' Yusuf said.

Zimat flushed red, and her eyes snapped back to Yusuf. She leaned forward and kissed him on the cheek. 'I shall miss you, little brother. May Allah bring you fortune.'

Yusuf moved on to his mother. 'You will do great things, Yusuf; I know it,' she said. She bit her lip, holding back tears, then embraced him. 'Always come back to me, my son.'

'I will,' Yusuf murmured, his voice choked with emotion. He faced his father last of all.

Ayub stood with his back straight, his face betraying nothing. He placed his hand on Yusuf's shoulder. 'Remember, my son: you serve Allah first, our lord Nur ad-Din second, and your family third.' He withdrew his hand and held out a bundle of folded cloth. 'You are a man now. This is yours.'

'What is it?'

'Look.' Yusuf unfolded the cloth to reveal a banner, white with a golden eagle in the middle. 'Always carry it when you ride into battle,' Ayub said. 'Do not dishonour it, and do not dishonour your family.'

'I will make you proud, Father.'

Ayub nodded. He grasped Yusuf's shoulders and kissed him three times on the lips. 'Go,' he said gruffly.

Yusuf turned before his father could see the wetness in his eyes and went to his horse, pulling himself into the saddle. Shirkuh waved farewell and then spurred his horse out of the gate, followed by his men and John,

leading the packhorses. Yusuf took one last look at his
family, then turned his horse and followed. He did not
look back.

NOVEMBER 1152: ALEPPO

John dug his heels into the sides of his horse, urging it up
the last few steps of the steep hill. Ahead, the other riders
had stopped at the top of the rise. They had ridden far
over the past five days, following the winding course of
the Orontes River to the city of Hama and then riding
north across the dry, barren plains to Aleppo. John's
horse was tired, and it whinnied in protest. 'Almost
there, girl,' he coaxed, patting the mare's neck. He
tugged on the lead rope that ran from his saddle to the
two pack-horses behind him, urging them to keep pace.

As John crested the hill and reined in his horse beside
Yusuf, he saw why the other riders had stopped. Aleppo
was laid out before them in all its splendour. To the east,
the brown desert stretched away to the horizon, the
empty waste dotted with the minuscule forms of travellers making their way towards the city. To the west,
verdant orchards lay to either side of the sparkling river
that flowed past Aleppo. Directly before them, the hill
sloped down to a thick wall that towered over an
approaching caravan, the heavily packed camels ant-like
in its shadow. Beyond the wall rose a city many times the
size of Baalbek. White-walled, flat-roofed buildings sat
one on top of the other, covering the rolling hills. Here
and there, slender minarets rose above them. And

looming over it all was the great citadel that crowned the rocky hill at the city's heart.

'It is called *the white city*,' Shirkuh declared. 'Not because of its virtue, I assure you. The court is filled with intriguers, and the streets are thick with thieves. But it is a great city, nonetheless.'

'What has happened to the walls?' Yusuf asked, pointing to the right, where several long sections of the wall had been reduced to rubble. Looking closer, John saw that the city was littered with half-ruined buildings, their roofs collapsed and walls crumbling. 'Was there a siege?'

'The crusaders have besieged the city many times,' Shirkuh replied. 'But it was not they who did this. In the year of your birth, Yusuf, a mighty earthquake struck the city. Thousands died. The walls are still being rebuilt. Nur ad-Din says the earthquake was a sign of Allah's anger over the presence of the crusaders. He has vowed to drive them from our lands.'

Shirkuh spurred his horse forward. John followed the others along the well-beaten trail that wound down towards the city. They rode into the long shadow of the walls and towards a gate framed by two bulky towers of unequal height. Scaffolding covered the left-hand tower, and workers scurried over it, placing heavy stones to add to the tower's height. At the base of the right-hand tower was an arched gateway, wide enough for six men abreast to ride through. Merchants crowded around the entrance, hawking their wares.

'Sharp blades!' a lanky man in baggy robes cried. He held up a dagger, the shining blade marked with whirls of darker grey. 'Of the finest Damascus steel.'

'Slaves!' shouted another merchant, whose curly black beard hung down to his plump belly. He pointed to a half-dozen Franks who stood chained together beside the wall, their heads down. The men were shirtless, and their ribs showed clearly on their gaunt frames. The slack-faced, dirty women looked little better off. John's jaw tightened. The slave merchant mistook his attention for interest and stepped closer. 'Fancy a Frankish lady to keep your bed warm at night? Only fifty dirhams.' John spat at the slave merchant's feet and rode on through the gate.

The gate did not lead through the wall, as John had anticipated, but rather to a square chamber dimly lit by smoky torches set in brackets on the walls. John noticed a grate in the low ceiling, through which boiling oil could be poured on would-be attackers. An arched doorway to the left brought him into a long room with a high ceiling of cross-vaulted stone. The room, which ran parallel to the wall, was lit by high windows on the city side. They cast light on a throng of merchants and travellers whose loud voices echoed off the stone walls and created a deafening roar. John followed the others through the room, then through two smaller chambers before they finally emerged into the city. A crowded dirt road curved away before them, running between close-set, tall houses.

'The gate has been rebuilt to make attack more difficult,' Shirkuh was explaining to Yusuf as they rode down the street. 'If they break through the outer gate, attackers will find themselves in a confined space, attacked from above. They will have to break through three more gateways to enter the city.'

Shirkuh continued talking, but John lost track of his words amidst the din of the crowd. He turned his attention to the people he was passing. To his right, a Bedouin shepherd with staff in hand was driving four bleating sheep towards market. Past him was the first in a long line of heavily laden camels, all slowly chewing their cuds as they plodded forward under the prodding whips of their drivers. Beyond the camels, John noticed two men standing in a doorway, passing a smoking pipe between them. In the window of the floor above them, a veiled woman was beating out a rug. John caught her eye, and she retreated inside, banging the shutters closed behind her.

The road they were following curved to the left and entered a broad square. Everywhere men crowded around carts, haggling over a dizzying variety of wares: fresh fruits; vibrant blue, red and yellow rugs covered in geometric designs; even vials containing a home-made elixir that the seller promised would cure all ills. To the right, the covered alleyways of a souk opened on to the square. Each alleyway specialized in a particular good, from gold to cotton cloth to spices. Yusuf had told John that the souks of Aleppo were famed throughout the East. It was said that anything one desired could be purchased there.

A sudden commotion ahead drew John's attention away from the market. A swarm of young, half-naked children appeared from out of the crowd and pressed around the horses, forcing them to stop.

'Fresh fruit, yâ sîdi?' one of them yelled at John, holding up a mango.

Another pushed a waterskin towards him. 'Cool water?'

Others simply begged, holding out their hands and repeating: 'Money, yâ sîdi? Money?'

One of the boys tried to slip his hand into John's saddlebags, and John caught his wrist. The child cringed, his eyes wide with fright. John released him, and the would-be thief scurried off into the crowd. He was instantly replaced by another child.

Ahead, Shirkuh threw a shower of glinting coppers off to the side, and the children raced towards them, shouting with excitement as they scrambled on the ground, wrestling one another for the coins. John urged his horse past them, following the others out of the square and into the shade of the citadel. High above, he could see guards walking the limestone walls, which were set with towers at regular intervals. The walls rose directly from steeply sloped, bare white rock. At the base of the hill, the dark waters of a moat some twenty feet across added another layer of defence. Four guards in chainmail and pointed helmets, spears in hand, stood blocking the drawbridge across the moat. They stepped aside as Shirkuh approached. 'Morning, men,' Shirkuh called as he rode past, the hooves of his horse sounding loud on the wooden bridge. Yusuf came next, nodding towards the guards. He was followed by Shirkuh's three men and then John, to whom the guards gave a hard look. John ignored them, urging his horse up the brick causeway that led to a large gatehouse, only half built and still covered in scaffolding. At the top, four more guards stepped aside to let the group pass, and John followed the others into the citadel.

What he found there surprised him. He was facing an oval-shaped expanse of flat land, easily three hundred yards long and one hundred yards wide. A maze of verdant orchards and gardens covered the expanse to his left. Off to his right, an enormous palace was built against the far wall. Other buildings – barracks, stables, kitchens, storerooms – were built into the walls that surrounded the space. And in the middle of it all was an expanse of closely cropped, green grass where two-dozen riders were thundering back and fourth in pursuit of a wooden ball. John recognized the game they were playing as polo. He had seen Yusuf play it in Baalbek.

John reined in his horse just behind Yusuf and watched as one of the players brought his mallet down and with a loud crack, sent the wooden kura hurtling towards the left-hand goalposts. Several riders spurred after the ball, but two outraced the rest, galloping close to John and the others. One was tall and thickly built, light-skinned and with a thick chestnut-brown beard. The other was darker, tall and thin, with only a few wispy black hairs on his chin and cheeks. The riders were neck and neck as they galloped towards the kura, their mallets raised high. At the last second, the dark-skinned rider pushed ahead and veered his horse towards the other man, cutting him off. He then brought his mallet down with a triumphant yell and sent the ball hurtling through the goalposts.

'Who is that?' Yusuf asked.

Shirkuh smiled. 'That is our lord, Nur ad-Din.' He kicked his heels and trotted on to the field. The others followed, John bringing up the rear.

'*Ho!* Shirkuh!' Nur ad-Din roared as they approached. 'Well met!' Close up, John saw that Nur ad-Din had brilliant, golden eyes and a full-toothed, bright smile. John looked past him and was surprised to see that the rider who had contested him for the kura was none other than Turan. While Nur ad-Din rode up to Shirkuh and grasped his arm, Turan guided his horse towards Yusuf.

'As-salaamu 'alaykum, Yusuf,' Turan said, greeting his brother formally.

'Wa 'alaykum as-salaam, Brother,' Yusuf replied stiffly, and the two leaned across their saddles and exchanged the ritual kisses.

'*Ah!*' Nur ad-Din turned his gaze upon Yusuf. 'So this is the young eagle that you told me of, Shirkuh? He doesn't look like much.'

'Nor did you at his age.'

'True enough. Tell me: do you play polo, Yusuf?' Yusuf nodded. 'Then we shall see if you merit the praise your uncle has given you. You will play on my team.' Nur ad-Din raised his voice so that all those on the field could hear him. 'Two gold dinars to whoever scores the next goal!' The men cheered, and Nur ad-Din turned back towards Yusuf. 'Let us see what you are made of, young eagle.'

Yusuf sat astride his horse, mallet in hand, and watched as the crowd of riders surged up the pitch towards the far goal. He held back, keeping free of the melee and saving his horse's strength. It had already carried him thirty miles that day, and Yusuf knew his mount would only be good for one or two short bursts. So he stayed near his own goal and watched as the other riders jostled against one another in the fight for the kura. Nur ad-Din forced his way alongside the ball and swung, but missed. There was a loud crack as an opposing player hit the kura, sending it out of the crowd. Turan was waiting for it. He slammed the ball downfield towards Yusuf and galloped after it.

Yusuf ignored his brother; his eyes were fixed on the kura. He spurred towards it and hit the ball smoothly, sending it bouncing back up the field. A split second later, the handle of Turan's mallet slammed into his gut. Yusuf grabbed his horse's mane and managed to stay in the saddle. He reined in and sat doubled over, gasping for breath.

'Welcome to Aleppo, Brother,' Turan sneered as he rode past.

Yusuf looked past his brother and noticed Nur ad-Din watching him. He gritted his teeth and straightened, then spurred after Turan. A crowd had again formed around the kura, and this time Yusuf headed straight for it. His mount was tiring fast, and Yusuf kicked at its sides, squeezing the last bit of effort from it as he weaved through the other riders towards the centre of the melee, following Turan. Turan reached the kura first, but as he swung at it, Yusuf slammed his horse into Turan's mount. Turan missed, and Yusuf hit the kura up the field. He saw Nur ad-Din charging for the ball, and Yusuf steered to the right, keeping clear of the other riders. Nur ad-Din reached the kura first, but the crowd was on him instantly. Nur ad-Din managed to hit the ball, but it glanced off a horse and rolled straight to Yusuf. There was no one between him and the goal.

Yusuf raised his mallet, but then hesitated. He spotted Nur ad-Din alone and sent the kura hurtling towards him. As the ball reached him, Nur ad-Din swung his mallet down and sent it flying through the goalposts. He let out a loud whoop and raised his arms in victory.

'Well done, Yusuf!' Nur ad-Din called as he rode over. 'You have saved me two dinars, and for that, you shall have the honour of dining with me tonight. You will meet my wife, Asimat, and we shall see if you are as clever with words as you are with a polo mallet. But I warn you: Asimat is harder to impress than I.'

Yusuf stood at the window of his room – part of Shirkuh's suite in the palace – and looked out over the city that was now his home. His room faced east, away from the setting sun, whose dying light cast the white-walled buildings of the city below in soft pink. The ululating chant of the muezzins reached Yusuf as they began the call for evening prayer. It was a Friday, and the streets filled with men and women headed towards the mosques. Yusuf moved from the window and went to the small washbasin in his room to perform the ritual ablution required before prayer. He filled the washbasin from his waterskin and then carefully washed his arms, face and hair, repeating the ritual three times. He dried himself off with a cotton cloth, then unrolled his prayer mat.

'In the name of Allah, the Most Gracious, the Most Merciful,' Yusuf began, when he was interrupted by loud knocking. The door swung open to reveal Shirkuh.

'Come,' he said. 'It is time to dine.'

'But what about evening prayers?'

'Allah will wait. Nur ad-Din will not.'

Yusuf followed his uncle out of the room and down a long, dim hallway. 'I thought Nur ad-Din was a religious man.'

'Our lord practises religion in his own way. Instead of prayers, he offers victories over the Franks. Which do you think Allah values more?'

They reached the end of the hallway and ascended a steep staircase. At the top, Yusuf found himself in an open, marble-floored room. To his left, a row of arched windows looked out over the city. Opposite the windows was a large double door guarded by three mamluks. Shirkuh approached and allowed the guards to search him for weapons. Yusuf did the same.

'How are your wives, Marwan?' Shirkuh asked the man searching him.

Marwan grimaced. 'Three wives is three too many.'

'I couldn't agree more,' Shirkuh chuckled. 'That is why I have none.'

The search concluded, and the guards pulled the doors open. Yusuf followed Shirkuh into a large room that was a double of the one they had just left, with arched windows on the far wall looking out over the citadel grounds. But this room was not empty. Braziers burned in the corners and a thick rug – saffron-yellow with geometrical designs in blue and crimson – lay spread across the floor. Cushions were stacked in a circle on the rug and low tables had been set up at intervals between the cushions. Nur ad-Din sat across from the door in a caftan of red silk. To his left was the woman who had to be his wife, Asimat. Upon seeing her, Yusuf felt his pulse quicken. She was surprisingly young – perhaps a few years older than Yusuf – and her milky-white skin was flawless. She had wavy, chestnut-brown hair that framed a long, thin face with a delicate nose and full lips. Her dark eyes met Yusuf's, and she did not look away. Yusuf forced himself to look back to Nur ad-Din.

'Shirkuh! Yusuf!' Nur ad-Din smiled and raised a goblet towards his guests. He gestured to the young woman. 'This is Asimat.' Yusuf bowed to her, and she nodded back. 'Do not be deceived by her beauty, Yusuf. Her tongue is sharp.'

'A wise wife is a great asset, Husband,' Asimat said quietly.

'True, but a quiet wife is a greater one still,' Nur ad-Din replied with a laugh. He gestured to the cushions. 'Please, sit.' Shirkuh took a seat to Nur ad-Din's right, and Yusuf sat directly across from Nur ad-Din. As soon as they were seated, servant girls carrying platters of food entered through a side door. One of the servants, a thin girl with skin as black as ebony, placed a tray beside Yusuf. It held steaming flatbread, a bowl of yoghurt dip and a fragrant lamb stew that smelled of mint. Another girl placed a goblet on Yusuf's table and filled it with red wine. 'A toast to you, Yusuf,' Nur ad-Din said. 'Welcome to Aleppo and to my table.' He quaffed his wine, and Shirkuh followed suit. Yusuf lifted his goblet and hesitated, gazing at the crimson contents. He glanced at Asimat, who had not drunk. Then he placed the cup aside.

'You do not drink,' Nur ad-Din noted. 'Is it that you are unhappy to be in Aleppo?' He smiled. 'Or is it the company you find objectionable?'

'N—no my lord,' Yusuf stammered. 'I do not drink wine. Allah forbids it.'

'You are a man of conviction, and you are to be commended for it.' Nur ad-Din clapped his hands. 'Servants! Bring water for young Yusuf!' As a servant hurried in, Nur ad-Din took a piece of bread. 'In the name of Allah,' he murmured and scooped up some of the stew. He took a bite and chewed on it thoughtfully, then pointed at Yusuf with what remained of the bread. 'Yusuf has spent some time in Damascus, Asimat.'

Yusuf turned towards Nur ad-Din's wife. 'You know the city?' he asked.

'I grew up there. My father was Emir Unur.'

'I met your father during the Christians' siege. He seemed a good man.'

'That he was,' Nur ad-Din declared. 'He was a worthy adversary, may Allah have mercy upon him. Not like the current ruler, Mujir ad-Din.' Nur ad-Din frowned, then threw back another cup of wine. 'The snivelling brat.'

'I hear that you know the *Hamasah* by heart,' Asimat said to Yusuf, changing the subject. 'Is this true?'

'It is, my lady.'

'Excellent,' Nur ad-Din said. 'You shall entertain us with a poem. There is one I particularly enjoy. It is a story of vengeance, where a man lays waste to the tribe who killed his uncle.'

'The *Ritha of Ta'abbata Sharran*,' Yusuf said. 'I know it well. The tale begins with the death of the uncle:

On the mountain path that lies below Sal'
  lies a slain man whose blood
  will not go unavenged.
He left the burden to me and departed;
  I have assumed that burden
  for him.

Asimat smiled, and Yusuf paused as he felt his throat go suddenly dry. 'Impressive,' she said, nodding for him to go on.

Yusuf swallowed and continued: 'Bent on vengeance am I, his sister's son.' While the others ate, moving through course after course, Yusuf recited the long tale; how the uncle had led raids on the Hudhayl tribe; how the Hudhayl had fallen on him and killed him when he was alone in the mountains; how his nephew had ridden forth and avenged the murder in bloody fashion. As the last dishes were being cleared away, he concluded:

The hyena laughs over the slain of Hudhayl;
  you see the wolf grinning
  above them.
At morn the ancient vultures flap about, fat-bellied,
  unable to take flight, they tread
  upon the dead.

Yusuf fell silent. Asimat applauded, and he flushed red.

'So let it be for all our enemies,' Nur ad-Din declared and drained his goblet of wine. He turned to Asimat. 'You may go now, Wife. We have business to discuss.'

Asimat rose gracefully, and Yusuf watched her leave. When she was gone, he looked back to Nur ad-Din. He was watching Yusuf carefully. 'You have impressed my wife, a rare feat. Your uncle spoke true when he praised your learning.'

'Thank you, my lord.'

'I have need of wise men around me. I am a warrior, not a thinker. Perhaps you can turn your wits to a problem I am having with one of my emirs, a eunuch named Gumushtagin. It, too, is perhaps a question of vengeance.'

Yusuf paled. He had only just arrived in Aleppo, and already Nur ad-Din, ruler of Aleppo and Mosul, was asking him for advice. His future might well depend on the quality of his answer. 'I am your servant,' Yusuf managed. 'I shall help as I am able.'

'Good. A little over a year ago, I named Gumushtagin emir of Tell Bashir as a reward for his service. He governed well enough for a time, but recently I have received disturbing news.'

Shirkuh nodded. 'My spies tell me that Gumushtagin is in talks with the Seljuk sultan Mas'ud. If Gumushtagin allies himself with the Seljuks, then they will threaten both Mosul and Aleppo.'

'Why not simply remove him?' Yusuf asked.

'It is not so easy,' Nur ad-Din replied. 'Gumushtagin is well loved by his men. If he is removed, they might revolt, and an uprising would give the Seljuks an opportunity to invade. I will never be able to fight the Christians if I am constantly having to defend my northern borders.'

'Perhaps Gumushtagin's loyalty can be bought,' Yusuf offered.

'He has been paid,' Shirkuh said. 'But the Seljuks offered more.'

'Yet something must be done,' Nur ad-Din said. He leaned forward, his unblinking golden eyes fixed on Yusuf. 'Tell me: what do you advise?'

Yusuf looked to Shirkuh. His face remained an impassive mask; there would be no help from that corner. Yusuf took a deep breath. 'You must make Gumushtagin want to leave Tell Bashir.'

'How?' Nur ad-Din queried. 'Explain.'

'Offer him something better, the governorship of Bizaa perhaps.'

'But he is a traitor!' Shirkuh interjected. 'And Bizaa is wealthy, with twice the men of Tell Bashir.'

Yusuf nodded. 'That is why he will accept. More importantly, Bizaa is close to Aleppo, and the people there have no loyalty to Gumushtagin. Once he is there, you can remove him at will if he proves disloyal.'

'And Tell Bashir?' Nur ad-Din asked. 'The men that Gumushtagin leaves behind will not welcome a new emir. There could be trouble.'

'Then you must send someone you trust to take command, somebody who can take matters in hand. If he fails, then you have lost nothing. You are back where you started. If he succeeds, then Tell Bashir will be secure.'

Nur ad-Din smiled. 'Again, I am impressed.' He turned to Shirkuh. 'You did right to bring your nephew to me. He has a bright future before him. I will need men

233

like Yusuf soon enough. The time is coming to drive the Franks from our shores.' He paused to take a gulp of wine. 'Keep me informed regarding your nephew, Shirkuh. I am curious to see how he gets along with your men.'

John sat alone amidst the dark shadows of his room and looked out of the small square window to the bright crescent moon. The chamber – one of several dozen identical rooms located in an outbuilding beside the palace – was only three feet by six, barely large enough for the straw mattress that covered the floor. There was no door for privacy. Shirkuh's men had shown John to the room in the slaves' quarters shortly after they arrived and told him that Yusuf would send for him if he was needed. John had waited, alone with his thoughts, while the light faded from the sky. His stomach had begun to growl, and John wondered if he should leave the room to look for food. But where? He had no idea where to go.

A loud bell began to ring somewhere close by, and John heard the tramp of feet in the hallway. Several men filed past his room. John rose and went to the door just as two black men were walking by – one bald and dark as the night sky, the other a rich brown like freshly turned earth. John noticed that they each carried a clay bowl. 'What is happening?' John asked them. 'Why is the bell ringing?'

The darker of the two men examined John. 'Our master has finished dining,' he said at last. 'It is the servants' turn to eat.'

John followed the two men through low-ceilinged,

shadowy hallways to a long room crowded with a bewildering mixture of men – native Christians, Turks, Egyptians, Africans, but no other Franks. They stood with bowls in their hands, waiting to be served from a huge black cauldron that hung from the ceiling on the far side of the room. The room buzzed with conversation, but as John entered, it fell silent. All eyes turned to him.

A tall, heavy man with a double chin approached John and stood looking down at him. 'What do you want?' the man asked in a high, reedy voice. John guessed he was a eunuch.

'To eat.'

The eunuch chuckled briefly, then his expression hardened, and he spit at John's feet. 'You will not eat with us. You are unclean, ifranji. Go.'

The dark slave that John had followed to the room stepped forward and put a hand on the eunuch's arm. 'Leave him be, Zakir.' He handed John a bowl.

Zakir shrugged off the other slave's hand, then slapped the bowl from John's hand so that it shattered on the floor. He met John's eyes. 'I said go.'

John could feel the eyes of every man in the room on him. He knew that he could not back down. If he showed weakness, then he would have no peace so long as he was in Aleppo. He sighed and spread his hands. 'I want no trouble.'

The eunuch sneered and reached out to shove John from the room. John moved quickly, grabbing the man's arm and twisting it behind his back. As Zakir spun around to relieve the pressure on his shoulder, John wrapped his free arm around the eunuch's throat and pulled tight, choking him. The other slaves watched silently as Zakir thrashed and clawed at John's forearm to no avail. Finally, the eunuch fell still, and John released him, letting him slump to the floor unconscious. No one moved.

John stepped forward, and the other slaves parted as he made his way to the cauldron. The slave with the ladle looked at John for a moment, then filled a bowl with steaming stew and handed it to him.

'Thank you, Brother,' John told him, then turned and left. He would eat in his room. Alone.

The next morning Yusuf, dressed in chainmail and with his sword at his side, followed Shirkuh out on to the expansive lawn that had served as a polo field the day before. Turan had already drawn up fifty mamluks in ranks to form a large square. The men wore identical armour of hardened black leather and conical steel helmets. They had bows and quivers slung over their shoulders and held long spears in their right hands. Although bought as slaves, each mamluk was freed at age eighteen, when they entered the service of their lord as warriors. They occupied a place of honour within the citadel. Those who fought well could hope to become emirs in their own right. All hoped someday to earn enough money to settle and raise a family of their own.

Yusuf trailed behind his uncle as he walked between the ranks, starting at the back row. The men straightened as Shirkuh passed, and he nodded to each of them. He spoke to a few, commiserating over injuries, praising their exploits in recent raids, or joking about their luck with women. Near the end of the final row, he stopped before a slump-shouldered, thin man with a sallow complexion.

'I hear you won at the tables last night, Husam,' Shirkuh said.

'That I did, sir.' Husam grinned, showing a smile missing several teeth.

'You have not yet spent all of it on women and drink, I hope.'

'Not yet, sir.'

'Good. Then tonight you shall come to the palace and give me a chance to win some of your fortune from you.'

'Gladly, sir, but only if we use my dice.' The men around Husam chuckled.

'You use your dice, and I will use mine,' Shirkuh said with a wink, and the men all laughed. Shirkuh moved away and stood with Yusuf and Turan flanking him. 'Men, this is my nephew, Yusuf ibn Ayub!' Shirkuh's deep voice carried to the furthest ranks. 'You will treat him with respect. He has come from Baalbek to serve as one of my commanders. He is already a fearsome warrior; cross him at your own risk.' Several of the men smiled at this. Shirkuh turned to Yusuf and spoke more softly. 'I am needed at the palace today, Yusuf. I am leaving you in charge.' He winked. 'Take it easy on them.' Shirkuh turned to Turan. 'Show your brother how we do things.'

Shirkuh strode away, leaving Yusuf and Turan to face the troops. The mamluks were grown men, many old enough to be Yusuf's father. He swallowed, then opened his mouth to speak, but Turan spoke first. 'You heard what Shirkuh said,' he shouted. 'Take it easy on my little brother. No laughing behind his back. No calling him names.' He winked and grinned. 'Pipsqueak, son of a donkey, man-whore, bastard, bugger: I don't want to hear any of that.' There was scattered laughter amongst the men. 'When he drills you, you will do exactly as he says. But before we train, I say we go to Sakhi's for a round of wine. I'm paying!' The men roared their approval, and Turan grinned. The carefully ordered ranks dissolved as men headed for the gates.

'Wait!' Yusuf shouted. 'Halt!' The men reluctantly shuffled to a stop. Yusuf glared at Turan. 'Shirkuh said we were to train, not drink. And besides, alcohol is forbidden.' There were threatening grumbles amongst the men at this. 'There will be plenty of time for drink later, after training,' Yusuf amended.

Turan smiled. 'Very well, Brother, if that is what you wish, then go ahead. Train them.'

Yusuf nodded. 'All right, men! Back in your ranks!' The mamluks filed sullenly past Yusuf and lined up in sloppy, uneven lines.

'Who does he think he is?' someone whispered.

'Little bastard,' another grumbled.

Yusuf flushed with anger. 'That's enough talk!' he snapped. He marched up to Husam, the gap-toothed, lucky gambler in the first row. 'Straighten up!'

'Yes, sir,' Husam replied and straightened. Yusuf moved on down the line, and as soon as his back was turned, Husam muttered: 'You little bugger.'

Yusuf whirled around. 'What was that?'

Husam shrugged, his eyes wide and innocent. 'What was what, sir?'

Yusuf frowned and turned away. He continued down the line, meeting each man's eyes, and the men straightened as he passed. He was near the end of the first row when he tripped over someone's leg, stumbled, and fell to his hands and knees. He rose immediately, glowering at the closest soldiers. 'You call yourselves warriors?' Yusuf roared at them. 'You are a disgrace! The Franks will tear you to pieces!'

'The little bugger has a temper,' a voice called from the centre of the ranks.

'Who said that?' Yusuf demanded. The men all stared ahead, giving away nothing. The blood started to roar in Yusuf's temples and his jaw clenched. He pushed his way through the rows of warriors in the direction of the voice.

'Careful, he is a fearsome warrior,' another voice sniggered from behind Yusuf.

Yusuf pushed his way back to the front of the ranks and turned to face the men. 'Who said that? I demand to know who said that! Face me!' he yelled, his voice breaking at the end.

A huge, muscle-bound man pushed his way forward. He was a head taller than Yusuf, and his neck was easily as thick as Yusuf's thigh. 'I said it,' the man rumbled. 'What are you going to do about it, little man?' The other men laughed. Yusuf glanced over his shoulder to Turan. He was laughing, too. Yusuf was red-faced with anger and on the verge of losing control. He closed his eyes and concentrated on controlling his breathing.

Gradually, the pounding in his temples faded. He opened his eyes and met the gaze of the man before him.

'What is your name?'

'Qadir.'

'You will return to the barracks, Qadir. I will deal with you later.'

'Make me.'

Yusuf's jaw tightened. 'Pardon me?'

'You heard me. Make me.'

Yusuf nodded to the two men on the front row nearest to Qadir. 'You two, escort Qadir to the barracks.' The men did not move. 'My uncle will not stand for this,' Yusuf growled.

'What do you know of Shirkuh?' Qadir sneered. 'I have fought beside him for ten years. I saved his life twice. What have you done, little bugger?'

Yusuf reacted without thinking. He lashed out, punching Qadir hard in the gut. It was like hitting a wall. The huge mamluk did not even move. His huge hand clamped over Yusuf's wrist and twisted, forcing Yusuf to his knees.

'Let him go, Qadir,' Turan said. Qadir released Yusuf immediately.

Yusuf rose to his feet. He met Qadir's eyes, then looked past him to the men. 'I will not forget this,' he promised, then turned and strode away towards the palace.

Turan's voice followed him: 'Now men, let's have that drink!'

Yusuf paced the marble-floored antechamber outside Nur ad-Din's apartments as he waited for his uncle to emerge. The guards before the door watched him, their faces impassive. As he paced, Yusuf thought of what he would tell his uncle, and a smile curled his lips as he imagined the various punishments Shirkuh would devise for his troops. But Yusuf's legs grew tired from pacing, and still Shirkuh did not appear. Through the arched windows, Yusuf saw the shadow of the citadel lengthen and then deepen as dusk gathered. Finally, the doors to Nur ad-Din's apartments opened, and Shirkuh emerged. 'Uncle!' Yusuf greeted him. 'I must speak with you.'

Shirkuh examined Yusuf for a moment and then nodded curtly. 'Come with me.' Yusuf followed him out of the antechamber and down a staircase. 'Well, Yusuf?' Shirkuh asked as he descended. 'What do you have to tell me?'

'Your men are insolent, and Turan is worse. They must be punished.'

'Do not tell me how to deal with my men,' Shirkuh snapped as they entered a long corridor.

'But they insulted me! They refused to obey.'

'I know what my men did. Husam told me. You were lucky to avoid a beating.'

'But Turan—'

'Turan is the least of your worries.' Shirkuh stopped and turned to face his nephew. 'There will always be men in the ranks like Turan. You must learn to deal with them.'

'But how? The troops would not listen to me. They laughed at me.'

'Then let them laugh. You cannot expect to command

their respect instantly. They are hardened warriors. Some of them were fighting for me before you were born. You must earn their respect, and you cannot do so by insulting and threatening them.'

'What then?' Yusuf grumbled. 'Should I buy them drink, like Turan?'

'Forget Turan! He is a drunkard who wants the men to love him. He will never be great. But I expect more from you, Yusuf. Today you lost control. You must never lose control before your men. They will never respect you if you do.' Shirkuh paused and took a deep breath. 'Nur ad-Din has asked me to send you back to Baalbek.'

Yusuf lowered his head. He had only just arrived and already he had failed. He thought of the men's laughter as he had walked away. They seemed to be mocking Yusuf's dreams of greatness. He clenched his jaw as he fought back tears. 'I am sorry, Uncle.'

Shirkuh gripped his shoulder. 'Do not be too hard on yourself, young eagle. Leaders are created, they are not born. I reminded our lord that he was no better when he was your age, and I have persuaded him to give you a second chance. He has agreed that you are to command the citadel at Tell Bashir.'

'Tell Bashir? But that is the property of the eunuch Gumushtagin.'

'Not any more. He has been given Bizaa as you suggested. But the men he left behind in Tell Bashir remain loyal to him. Nur ad-Din fears that they will open the city to the Seljuks. It is your task to ensure that this does not happen.'

Yusuf straightened and met Shirkuh's eye. 'I will not fail you, Uncle.'

'You had best not. I gave Nur ad-Din my word that you would succeed in Tell Bashir. If you fail, you will disgrace both of us.'

'I understand.'

'Good. You leave tomorrow.' Shirkuh grasped Yusuf's shoulders with both hands. 'Remember, Yusuf. Always remain in control. Never show weakness. Most importantly, treat your troops as men. And never forget: you must be one of them before you can lead them.'

Chapter 10

NOVEMBER 1152: ON THE ROAD TO
TELL BASHIR

Slate-grey clouds hung low in the sky as John rode out of Aleppo through the Bab al-Yahud – the Jew's gate. John was happy to leave the city behind; he had never felt more foreign and alone than he had in the slaves' quarters of the citadel. Perhaps Tell Bashir would be better. At least Yusuf would be in charge there. John glanced to where his friend rode beside him, his head held high. They followed a Bedouin guide named Sa'ud, and behind them came three men leading pack-horses, then six mamluks surrounding a mule that carried an iron-bound chest. John knew that the key to the chest's heavy lock hung around Yusuf's neck. Back at the citadel, he had allowed John to look inside. The chest contained two thousand golden dinars, enough to buy John's freedom many times over – surely enough to ensure the loyalty of the men at Tell Bashir.

Ahead, the road was little more than a beaten track, the wind whipping up swirling plumes of sand. John pulled down one of the folds of his turban to cover his face and keep out the dust. The trail sloped down to run parallel with the tiny Quweq River, which wound its way north through broad plains. They passed orchards, the trees heavy with oranges and limes. Beyond them were fields of harvested wheat – black earth dotted with the yellow stubs of cut stalks – and also fragrant fields of bright-yellow saffron. Past the fields, the rocky desert stretched away to the horizon, where a sheet of rain fell from the dark sky. As the storm came closer, John could see the rain sweeping down the river, disturbing its placid surface. He unwound his turban as the first cool drops hit him. A moment later, the skies opened up, soaking his tunic and turning the road to mud. John turned to Yusuf and grinned.

Yusuf shook his head. 'The rain will slow us. You won't be smiling if we don't make it to the inn and have to sleep in the open.'

'That's why we have tents. Besides, we can't get any wetter.'

'It's not getting wet that worries me; it's the bandits. There are only twelve of us. That is enough to fight off most raiders, but the rain will dampen sound and make it hard to see. It will make us an easier target.'

John's smile faded. He looked at the road stretching across the empty plain ahead and saw only a distant camel train. 'Are bandits really such a danger?'

Yusuf nodded. 'There is an old saying: *the companions chosen are more important than the route taken.* Only fools travel alone, and even large groups are sometimes attacked. When my mother was young, she was part of a caravan of over forty that was raided.'

'Why doesn't Nur ad-Din do something about it?'

'There is little he can do. The raiders often attack far from where they live. Some are Franks from the Christian lands. Most are Bedouin. After their raids, they vanish into the great desert. None dares follow them there.'

They rode on in silence, following the course of the river. John was more alert now, scanning the road ahead for potential ambushes. When they came to a small settlement – a few single-room homes mixed with tents – he gripped the hilt of his sword as they passed, ready in case bandits burst forth. The rain slackened, then stopped, and a few rays of sun broke through the clouds. Around noon, they came to a larger settlement, built where two tributaries flowed into the Quweq from the north. The village had a mosque, and John led the horses to the river to drink while the others went inside to perform their afternoon prayers. Afterwards, they ate a simple meal of flatbread and goat's cheese, then crossed the Quweq over a rickety wooden bridge. They left the river behind, following one of its tributaries north-west. The tributary, dry most of the year, was now full of muddy, turbulent water, which had cut a deep channel in the sandy soil. Desert grasses and wild flowers grew near the channel, but there were no crops. After a time, they left the tributary behind and rode across barren desert.

'How does our guide know the way?' John asked Yusuf.

'The desert is the Bedouin's home. They can read its signs, see things we cannot.'

They saw no trace of human life until just before sunset, when they heard the familiar, wavering cry of a muezzin calling the evening prayer. A moment later, they crested a small rise and saw a u-shaped building built around a well. It was a funduq – an inn that served caravans. Yusuf's shoulders relaxed visibly when he saw it. 'We made it,' he said and spurred his horse through the gate. John followed and found himself in a courtyard lined with wooden stalls on the right. Most of them were occupied by a horse or camel. A murmur of conversation – punctuated by a woman's loud laughter – came from a door to the left. It opened, and out stepped a dark-skinned man with a bright smile and large, gold loops in his ears.

'As-salaamu 'alaykum, travellers,' he said, giving a small bow.

'Wa 'alaykum as-salaam,' Yusuf replied as he dismounted. John also dismounted and took the reins of Yusuf's horse.

'I am Habil, and you are welcome at my funduq,' the man said. 'You can stable your horses here. Beds are through that door behind you. There is food and drink in the tavern.' He waved to the door through which he had just come. 'Three fals each for a bed and horse stall. Food and drink are extra.'

Yusuf took a dinar from the pouch at his belt and tossed it to Habil, whose eyes went wide at the sight of the gold piece. 'That should be sufficient for me and my men.'

'Yes, yes!' Habil bowed again. 'You can have all the food and wine you want.'

'I do not desire wine. Where is the mosque?'

'Yes, of course, the mosque. It is that way.' Habil pointed to a door at the far end of the courtyard.

Yusuf nodded curtly. 'You may go now.' Habil bowed and re-entered the tavern, and Yusuf turned to John. 'Care for my horse,' he said, then spoke to the mamluks. 'You will take turns guarding the gold. I want two men with that chest at all times. We will leave after morning prayers.' Yusuf crossed the courtyard and disappeared into the mosque. Shirkuh's men led their horses into the stalls and unsaddled them. Most of the men headed into the tavern, but two stayed behind in the fading light. They carried the chest into one of the stalls and sat on the straw-covered floor while John groomed Yusuf's horse in the next stall along.

John took a comb, hoof pick and cloth from one of the saddlebags and then removed the saddle. He slid his hand down the horse's right foreleg, squeezing just above the hoof, and murmured 'fauq' – up. The horse lifted its leg, and John carefully picked out the pebbles and grit that had gathered in the sole of its hoof. When he had finished with the hooves, he used the cloth to wipe the dirt from the horse's face and ears. Then he took up the brush and began to scrape the dirt from the horse's coat. He was nearly done when he heard a voice from the next stall.

'What do you say, Nathir? Do you think he'd notice if we took a few dinars for ourselves?' one of the mamluks said.

'The chest is locked, Jareh.'

'I could pick it. My father was a locksmith. He showed me how.'

'It's not worth it. Yusuf will have your hands if he catches you.'

'Then we won't let him catch us, will we?'

John stopped brushing. In the silence, he could just hear the sound of metal scraping on metal. He tossed the brush aside and walked over to stand in the entrance of the next stall. Jareh was on his knees, his back to John as he probed at the lock with his dagger and a needle. Nathir stood over him, watching. He looked up, and his face paled. He tapped Jareh's shoulder.

'What?' Jareh asked. Nathir pointed, and the other mamluk looked over his shoulder. He sat on the chest and met John's eyes. 'What do you want, ifranji?' John returned the man's stare, but said nothing. 'Yusuf's watchdog,' Jareh grumbled.

'Careful, Brother,' John told him.

'I am not your brother, ifranji,' the mamluk spat. He tapped the blade of his dagger against his open palm. 'If you speak of this to Yusuf, you are a dead man.'

John shrugged. 'I only wished to warn you: Yusuf knows the precise number of coins in the chest. If even one goes missing, he will know.'

'I told you!' Nathir slapped the back of Jareh's head, then looked to John. 'Shukran.'

John nodded and walked out into the courtyard, which was all dark shadows now that the sun had set. Yusuf was still at his prayers, and the sounds of revelry from the tavern had grown louder. Looking through one of the tavern windows, John saw a mamluk grab a buxom young woman – a prostitute, no doubt – and pull her on to his lap. He kissed the girl, and John turned away, battling bittersweet memories of his last night with Zimat. He went to a small door that he guessed led to the sleeping hall. But when he pushed it open, he found himself in a small candlelit chapel, a wooden cross hanging from the far wall. Two benches sat before an altar, and on one of them was seated a priest in brown robes. The priest turned, and John saw that he was very old, the skin of his face mottled and wrinkled. His eyes were covered with a milky film, and he looked towards John without seeing him.

'Greetings, Son,' the priest said in Latin.

'Hello, Father.' John closed the door and crossed the room to sit beside the old man, who stared ahead, saying nothing. 'What are you doing here?' John asked.

The priest smiled, revealing a mouth in which only a few teeth had survived. 'This is my church.'

John feared the old man might be crazy. 'But these are Muslim lands.'

'Yes, but they were not always so. I came here more than fifty years ago, with the first King Baldwin. We conquered these lands and made a new kingdom for God. I have been here ever since. When the Saracens retook these lands, I stayed. I was old and blind; too much trouble for my fellow Christians to bother taking with them, and not worth the effort for the Saracens to kill.'

'The Saracens treat you well, then?'

'They let me be. There are native Christians and Franks who pass through with the caravans. Just yesterday, two-score Franks stopped at the inn. I prayed with them, offered them confession and absolution. Do you wish me to pray with you?' The priest held out a wooden cup. A few copper coins rattled in the bottom. John added another. 'Bless you, Son. Do you wish to confess your sins?'

John shook his head. 'It has been a long time, Father.'

'It is never too late to find forgiveness.' The priest placed a hand on John's back. 'Tell me.'

John lowered his head and looked at his hands. For a moment, it seemed as if he could still see them covered with blood. 'I do not wish to be forgiven for what I have done.'

'And why is that?'

'I killed my brother.'

'Why?'

John's jaw clenched as long-buried memories came to the surface. 'He sold my father to the Normans. They strung him up as a traitor. I watched him die . . .' John felt tears in his eyes and wiped them away.

'It was vengeance, then.'

'Yes. But it was not justice.'

The priest nodded. 'I understand. I too killed someone I loved.' John looked up, surprised. The priest smiled. 'I was not always the old man you see now. Once I was young, with a beautiful wife.' He sighed. 'I found her in bed with my closest friend. I killed them both, with these hands.' He held up his hands, gnarled and wrinkled. 'I stabbed them to death, and then I ran away. I entered the priesthood and ended up here.' The priest turned his blind eyes upon John. 'I hated myself. I wanted to die. But hating myself did not bring them back. And it will not help you, either. God does not want our hate, but our love. It took me a long time to learn that. Too long.'

The priest fell silent, and they sat side by side while

the candles on the altar burned down. Finally, John knelt before the altar and bowed his head. He prayed silently, then rose and added a silver coin to the old priest's cup.

'Thank you, Father.'

'I will pray for you,' the old man replied. He held out his hand towards John and made the sign of the cross. 'Go with God, my son.'

The sun had not yet risen when Yusuf and the others rode away from the funduq, quickly leaving it out of sight in the pre-dawn gloom. The innkeeper had warned them that bandits had struck several caravans nearby, and Yusuf had decided to leave early, skipping prayers in the hope of slipping past unseen in the darkness. No one spoke, and the only sound was the faint clip-clop of their horses' hooves over the dusty ground. Yusuf kept his hand on his sword and scanned the dimly visible terrain around them for signs of danger.

The darkness gave way to soft, morning light as the sun rose dull red before them, revealing a barren land-scape, unmarked by a single tree or boulder. Low, rolling hills rose up ahead, and the dusty track they followed headed straight for them. Yusuf spurred his horse forward next to their Bedouin guide. 'If there are bandits about, those hills would be the perfect place for them to set an ambush,' he said. 'Is there another way?'

Sa'ud shook his head. 'The hills stretch for miles in either direction. Going around will cost us at least a day. Better to push straight through.'

Yusuf nodded. 'Very well. But we will ride fast and

avoid the hilltops so as not to be seen.' He raised his voice. 'Have your weapons ready, men.' Yusuf took his short, curved bow from where it was tucked into the saddle behind him and strung it as he rode. He then slung it over his shoulder, along with his quiver. The other men did the same.

Sa'ud spurred his horse to a canter. Yusuf kept pace, John beside him and the other men bringing up the rear. The track they were following snaked into the hills, and the sound of their horses' hooves echoed loudly off the steep slopes on either side. Yusuf scanned the hilltops as they rode, expecting at any moment to see a bandit staring back at him, but there was nothing. He breathed a sigh of relief as they rode free of the hills and into a broad valley, which sloped downwards to a sparkling river. More hills rose on the far side of the water.

Ahead, Sa'ud kept up the pace, but then reined to a stop as he reached the edge of the wide, shallow river. His horse immediately plunged its muzzle into the stream and began to drink. 'We should pause to water the horses,' he suggested. 'There will be no more water until we reach Tell Bashir.'

John rode up beside Yusuf and leaned close. 'I don't like this. We are too exposed here. We should move on.'

Yusuf scanned the hilltops on either side of the river and saw nothing. Beneath him, his horse was wet with sweat and breathing heavily after the long canter. 'Our horses will not last much longer without water,' he said. 'And I'd rather face bandits than walk through the desert to Tell Bashir.' He raised his voice. 'We will let the horses drink, but be ready to ride, men.' Yusuf dismounted and led his horse to the edge of the river, where he stood holding the reins while it drank thirstily. He unstopped his waterskin and also drank, keeping his eyes fixed on the hills on the far side of the river. He saw nothing and turned to examine the hills they had just traversed. He was just looking away when out of the corner of his eye he caught a flash of sunlight on steel. He looked back, but saw nothing.

John walked over, leading his horse. 'I think we're being watched.'

Yusuf nodded. 'I saw it, too.' He turned to shout to the men. 'Saddle up!' Yusuf was pulling himself into the saddle when two dozen riders in chainmail broke from the hills behind them and came thundering across the valley. 'Follow me!' Yusuf shouted. He grabbed the lead rope for the mule carrying the gold and then kicked his horse's sides, sending it splashing across the shallow river. As he emerged on the far bank and urged his horse towards the hills, Yusuf glanced back over his shoulder. The bandits were approaching the river, but it looked as if Yusuf and his men would reach the hills before they crossed. Just behind Yusuf, John was yelling and pointing forward. Yusuf turned to see another twenty bandits pouring from the hills ahead of them, only a hundred yards away. They had bows in hand, and they reined in and released a volley. Yusuf heard the arrows whiz past, and there was a cry of pain behind him. He turned to see one of Shirkuh's men fall from the saddle, the feathered end of an arrow protruding from his chest. Yusuf veered to the left, riding away from the archers and up the valley floor. John and the mamluks followed, spreading out to create a barrier between Yusuf and the bandits.

'We can't outrun them!' John shouted. 'Not with the mule. We have to leave it.'

Yusuf shook his head. 'Without the gold, we won't even get into Tell Bashir.' He looked back and saw that the archers were almost within range. The other bandits had splashed across the river and were angling across the valley, gaining fast. 'We'll lose them in the hills!'

Yusuf turned his horse and headed for a gap between two sheer rock faces. John and Sa'ud followed, while the mamluks pulled up behind them to block the passage and protect their escape. Yusuf kicked at the sides of his horse and pulled at the lead, urging the mule to keep pace as he cantered along a narrow trail that snaked between the steep-sided hills. Behind him, he could hear shouts and cries of agony as the bandits reached the mamluks. Then the shouting stopped, replaced by the thunder of hooves as the bandits charged after them. The rumbling grew steadily louder, and then an arrow hissed past Yusuf. The bandits were almost upon them.

Up ahead, the trail turned sharply to the right. Yusuf rounded the corner and shouted '*Stop*!' He reined in, and John and Sa'ud pulled up beside him. 'Quick, your bows!' Yusuf turned his horse and swung his bow from his back. He nocked an arrow and drew the bow taut. The first bandit rounded the corner, and his eyes went wide. Yusuf let fly, and the man dropped from the saddle, an arrow in his throat. Four more bandits rounded the corner in quick succession. John fired first, taking the lead rider out. Sa'ud's arrow also found its target. Yusuf hurriedly nocked another arrow and let fly. The arrow lodged in the chest of the leading bandit's horse, causing it to rear and throw its rider. The other bandit pulled up short as the injured horse – whinnying and eyes rolling – reared again and again, blocking the narrow path.

'Come on!' Yusuf yelled as he grabbed the mule's lead rope and cantered away. Soon, he could again hear the rumbling of horses' hooves, and then the shouts of the bandits as they closed in. An arrow whizzed past Yusuf's ear and shattered on the rock face ahead of him. He looked back and saw that the nearest bandits were only a dozen yards behind him. As he watched, Sa'ud's horse was shot beneath him, collapsing and sending Sa'ud tumbling. The pack mule brayed loudly as it took an arrow in the flank. It stumbled and fell.

'The gold!' Yusuf exclaimed as he pulled back on the reins.

'Forget it!' John shouted as he rode past.

Yusuf hesitated for a split second, then spurred after his friend. Arrows were whizzing all around him. One sank into the rump of John's horse, which slowed immediately. Yusuf rode up alongside him. 'Quick, get behind me!' John grabbed Yusuf's arm and swung himself on to Yusuf's horse. '*Yalla*! *Yalla*!' Yusuf shouted as he urged the last bit of speed from his tired mount.

''Sblood!' John grunted as an arrow slammed into his shoulder. Another grazed the flank of Yusuf's horse, and it whinnied in pain. 'They're right on top of us!' John yelled. 'No, wait,' he added a second later. 'They're falling back!'

Yusuf looked back, incredulous. But it was true: the

bandits were slowing, letting them escape. Yusuf met John's eyes and they both grinned. Then, as their horse rounded a corner, the grin fell from John's face. '*Stop*!' he yelled, but it was too late.

The ground fell out from beneath them as they rode straight over the edge of a tall cliff. The horse tumbled head first down the steep, gravelly slope, sending both John and Yusuf flying. Yusuf hit the ground and went tumbling head over heels. To his left, he caught a glimpse of John lying flat on his stomach, his arms and legs extended as he slid down the face of the slope. Yusuf saw the sky flash by, then the floor of a valley far below rushing up to meet him, then the sky again. Next moment, his head slammed into a rock, and the world went black.

Yusuf awoke in a darkness so absolute that he could not see his hand in front of his face. He was stiff and shaking with cold. He stretched gingerly, flexing his arms and legs. He was covered in bruises and his head ached, but he did not appear have broken anything. He sat up and slammed his forehead into hard rock. He fell back, groaning.

'*Quiet*!' John hissed, his hand clapping over Yusuf's mouth. 'They'll hear you.'

Yusuf fell silent, and John removed his hand. 'Where are we?' Yusuf whispered.

'In a cave,' John replied, his voice so low that Yusuf could barely hear him. 'I carried you here after we fell. The bandits searched for us and then returned to their camp. It is not far from here. Come and see.' Yusuf felt

John tug on his arm, and he crawled forward after him, groping his way over the rocky floor. The passage narrowed until Yusuf was forced to squirm forward with his head sideways and his cheek pressed against the cold stone. On the other side of the narrow passage, the cave grew brighter. Yusuf could see John ahead, his finger to his lips. Yusuf joined him at the mouth of the cave. They were thirty feet up a steep slope, looking out over a rocky ravine.

'There,' John whispered, pointing to the right, where flickering firelight danced on the ravine walls. 'They are camped a hundred yards down the ravine. I think they are Franks; I overheard two of them speaking Latin.'

'Franks?' Yusuf looked at John. 'You could have gone to them.'

John shrugged. 'And leave you to die? You know me better than that, Brother.'

Yusuf placed his hand on his friend's shoulder. 'Saving me was not the act of a slave, John. From this moment, you are free.'

John turned away. When he looked back, his eyes shone with tears. 'Just my luck,' he whispered, forcing a smile. 'I gain my freedom just in time to die. We have one waterskin and no food. And with our guide dead, we have no idea how to get to Tell Bashir.'

'Are the English all so grim?' Yusuf said, clapping John on the back. 'You are free, and we are alive. Allah has saved us from the bandits for a reason. He will guide us to Tell Bashir.'

'How?'

'The stars.' Yusuf pointed to the heavens. 'That is

smiya, the north star. That means east is that way.' He
nodded across the ravine. 'If we head east then we will
meet the Sajur River, and it will lead us to Tell Bashir.
The moon will set within the hour, and we will go then,
under the cover of darkness. The further we are from
those bandits come morning, the better.'

'Christ's blood,' John cursed under his breath as he
trudged forward, his chest heaving and his feet sore after
jogging through the night. He stumbled to a stop as the
fiery red sun rose above the horizon, and the first rays of
sunlight hit him. Yusuf also stopped, and they looked
about at the world now visible around them. They had
left the hills behind and now stood on a rocky plain that
stretched away as far as John could see in every direction. The landscape was empty save for the occasional
twisted tree and scattered clusters of delicate, trumpet-
shaped flowers, golden on the inside and pale pink on
the outside.

'We'll be easy to spot out here,' John said, keeping his
voice low as if afraid to disturb the stillness around
them.

Yusuf nodded. 'We had best carry on.'

They walked towards the sun as it rose higher and
higher, burning away the cool night air and baking the
hard ground beneath their feet. Soon John's tunic was
soaked with sweat. They trudged on in silence, drinking
from the waterskin when the hot desert air became too
much to bear. In the afternoon, they stopped beside a
stunted, gnarled tree that cast a tiny pool of shade. Yusuf
took a swallow from the waterskin and then handed it to

John. He tipped it back and a tiny mouthful of water ran out, then nothing. He tossed the skin aside. 'We're out of water.' He gazed across the endless plain stretching out before them. The landscape wavered and shifted as heat rose from the ground. John licked his dry lips. 'Maybe we should rest here.'

'No, we cannot stop.' Yusuf pointed to the ground behind them. Their footprints in the dust stretched away into the distance. 'If the bandits decide to follow us, it will be easy enough.'

'We won't make it much further in this heat.'

'We have no choice. We'll stop when night falls. It will be harder to track us, then.'

They pushed on across the scorching desert. At first, John glanced back frequently, checking for signs of pursuit. He saw nothing, and after a few hours he ceased to care. His mouth grew so dry that he could not summon spit. His muscles burned and his thoughts slowed. He became dizzy, but he staggered on after Yusuf. Finally, the sun set behind them. Yusuf stopped. 'That is far enough.'

Groaning with relief, John lay down and stared up at the sky. Yusuf joined him, and they lay there without speaking while the world darkened around them. The fading light took the heat with it, and the air grew chill. John began to shiver in his sweat-soaked clothes and curled up on his side. He and Yusuf huddled together, back to back, and John could feel Yusuf shaking with cold. They lay awake, too miserable to sleep.

'Do you think we'll reach the river tomorrow?' John asked.

'I-inshallah,' Yusuf replied, teeth chattering. 'We w-won't make it through another day without water.'

Then John saw something in the dark – a pinprick of light. He sat up and squinted into the distance. 'I see something. Look, there.'

'A fire,' Yusuf said as he sat up.

'The bandits?'

'Or Bedouin.'

'They would have water,' John said, pushing himself to his feet. He began to stumble towards the light.

'John!' Yusuf called. 'If it is the bandits, then you are walking to your death.'

John turned to face Yusuf. 'What does it matter? Like you said, we'll die anyway without water.'

'You are right,' Yusuf said and rose. 'Let us go to meet our fate.'

Yusuf stood just beyond the reach of the firelight and peered into the camp. The flickering light played on the dark wool of three tents – large, rectangular structures with peaked roofs, which had been erected in a row to the right of the fire. The shadowy forms of camels were just visible in the darkness beyond the camp, and from behind them came the bleating of sheep. A piece of meat roasted over the fire, unattended. There was no movement anywhere.

'Are they Bedouin?' John whispered, leaning close to Yusuf.

Yusuf nodded. 'But something is wrong. Someone should be tending the fire.' He put his hand to his sword hilt and took a step forward into the ring of firelight.

'Waqqif!' a deep voice called from the darkness behind them – stop. Yusuf spun around to see four Bedouin step out of the night with bows drawn. A fifth man stepped past them, leaning on a long staff. As he approached, the fire lit his face which was leathery and tan, with a long, greying beard.

'Who are you?' the old man demanded in a gravelly voice.

'As-salaamu 'alaykum, sheikh. I am Yusuf ibn Ayub, emir of Tell Bashir.'

One of the archers laughed at this. He was tall with a short, black beard and teeth that flashed white in the night. 'You are far from your citadel, emir.'

The old man waved for him to be quiet. 'Wa 'alaykum as-salaam,' he said to Yusuf. 'I am Sabir ibn Taqqi, sheikh of this goum.' A goum was several related families, living together. 'And who is this?' Sabir pointed to John.

'My servant.'

'What brings you to our camp?'

'We were attacked by Frankish bandits. We have wandered far on foot. We need water and have come to beg your hospitality.'

Sabir looked into Yusuf's eyes, and Yusuf returned his gaze. After a moment the old man nodded. 'You are welcome in my tent.' He raised his voice. 'Wife! Prepare food for our guests.' A veiled woman stepped out of one of the tents and began to turn the spit of roasting meat.

The archers surrounding Yusuf shouldered their bows, and Sabir led the way towards the fire. 'Sit and warm yourselves,' he said, gesturing to a wool mat that had been laid out beside the fire. Yusuf and John sat, and the other Bedouin men joined them around the fire. 'Drink.'

One of the women handed Yusuf a waterskin. The cool water stung his cracked, dry lips, but he did not care. He took a long drink, then handed the skin to John. 'Shukran,' he said to Sabir, thanking his host.

Sabir nodded. 'This is my brother, Shaad,' he said, gesturing to the heavy-set man seated across from Yusuf. 'And this is my cousin, Saqr, his son Makin, and my own son, Umar.' Umar was the tall archer with the white teeth. In better light, Yusuf saw that he was a handsome man, with lean features and a prominent nose. He was fingering his dagger as he eyed John.

Suddenly Umar rose to his feet, dagger drawn. He stepped around the fire and tore the waterskin from John's hands, tossing it to the side. 'He has blue eyes,' he growled. 'He is a Frank!' Umar grabbed the front of John's tunic and held the dagger close to his face.

Yusuf sprang to his feet, his hand on his sword hilt. 'If you kill him, then you will die,' he said quietly.

'Put your dagger away, Umar!' Sabir barked.

'But he is one of them!' Umar protested.

'He is our guest. It would shame us to do him harm.'

Umar released John and stepped back, shaking his head. 'There would be no shame in it. I recognize him. He is one of the Franks who attacked us.'

'Forgive my son,' Sabir said as he pushed himself to his feet, leaning on his staff. 'We were attacked by Frankish raiders two days ago. They killed Umar's wife.'

'You did it!' Umar spat, pointing his dagger at John.

'My servant had nothing to do with this,' Yusuf said. 'Those same Franks attacked us. They killed ten of my men.'

'You lie!' Umar snarled.

'Silence!' Sabir roared. He examined John for a moment, then turned to Yusuf. 'You swear that this man is your servant, that he had nothing to do with the Franks who attacked us?'

Yusuf nodded. 'By Allah, I swear it.'

'You would accept the word of this stranger over that of your own son?' Umar demanded, red-faced. 'I tell you: I saw this ifranji kill my wife. He must die!'

Sabir looked from his son to John, and then back to Yusuf. 'There is only one way to prove that what you say is true, young emir. You will undergo the bisha'a.'

The blood drained from Yusuf's face, leaving him pale, but he nodded. 'I will.'

'Then let it be done.' Sabir drew a dagger from his belt and crouched down beside the fire. He plunged the dagger's blade into the glowing coals. Women and children came out of the tents and gathered around the fire.

John stepped close to Yusuf. 'What is going on?'

'Bisha'a is a trial by fire, an old Bedouin ritual. I will lick the hot blade of the dagger three times. Then the sheikh will examine me. If my tongue is burned, I lie. If it is not, then I tell the truth.'

'But that is ridiculous!'

'It is their way,' Yusuf said and turned back to face the fire.

Umar crouched down with a wet cloth in hand, and pulled the dagger from the fire. 'The blade is ready!' he declared, holding it up for all to see. The dagger's blade glowed red against the night sky.

Umar handed the dagger to Sabir, who brought it to Yusuf. The rest of the tribe pressed close as Sabir held the dagger out before Yusuf's face. Yusuf could feel the heat radiating from the blade. 'Now,' Sabir commanded.

'Allah protect me,' Yusuf whispered under his breath. He extended his tongue and pressed it briefly to the glowing blade. The searing pain was excruciating. He thought he could already feel his tongue beginning to blister, but he clenched his jaw, forcing himself to show no sign of his agony. If he showed pain, it would be clear his tongue was burned. John would die.

'Again,' Sabir told him.

Yusuf licked the blade a second time. It felt as if a hundred angry wasps were in his mouth, stinging at his tongue. Sweat began to bead on his forehead. He dug his fingernails into his palms. Yusuf met the eyes of Umar, who was watching him closely, and forced himself to smile. Then, before Sabir even prompted, he licked the blade a final time. He could taste blood in his mouth now and felt himself grow faint. Sabir took his arm, steadying him.

'Bring him water!' Sabir shouted.

A woman presented a cup, and Yusuf drank. The cold water only worsened the ache in his tongue. He drained the cup and forced a smile. 'Shukran,' he said to the woman who had given him the water.

Umar pressed forward. 'Examine him, Father. Let us see if he tells the truth.'

Sabir nodded. 'Back!' he shouted to the crowd. They retreated several feet, opening up a space around Yusuf and Sabir. Sabir turned to Yusuf. 'Open.'

'I do not lie,' Yusuf whispered to him, then opened his mouth.

Sabir peered inside for a moment, then nodded in satisfaction. 'He speaks the truth!'

'Impossible!' Umar protested, rushing forward.

'I have made my judgement, Son. Yusuf speaks the truth. You will apologize to him.'

Jaw clenched, Umar bowed slightly to Yusuf. 'Forgive me my error,' he spat, then turned and strode away into the darkness beyond the firelight.

'Forgive him,' Sabir said. 'The death of his wife has unbalanced him. Now come to my tent. You need food and water.'

Yusuf began to follow Sabir, when John grabbed his arm. 'I don't understand,' he whispered in Frankish. 'How did it not burn you?'

'It did,' Yusuf replied.

John looked to Sabir, who was standing at the entrance to his tent, beckoning for them to follow. 'Then why did he lie?'

'He is a wise man. He knew I told the truth.'

'Wake up! Wake up!'

John opened his eyes to see Sabir crouched over Yusuf, shaking his arm. The tent flap was open and morning sunlight streamed inside. 'What is it?' Yusuf mumbled, his burned and swollen tongue making it painful for him to speak.

'The Frankish bandits have followed you. You must go quickly. If they find you here, then we will suffer.'

Yusuf rose immediately. 'I understand.'

John and Yusuf followed Sabir outside. He pointed to the horizon, where a plume of dust rose high above the desert floor. 'There. They are only a few miles off.' He handed them each a full waterskin. 'Take these and head east.' He pointed in the opposite direction of the Franks, to where John could just make out a line of low hills on the horizon. 'The Sajur River is just over those hills. Once you reach it, Tell Bashir is not far. If you move fast, you may make it.'

'Thank you, sheikh,' Yusuf told him. 'You have saved our lives.'

'Not if you do not hurry. Go!'

Yusuf kissed Sabir on both cheeks, then slung the waterskin over his shoulder and loped out of camp. John joined him, jogging at his side. 'The Franks already have our gold. Why would they follow us?' John huffed between breaths.

'Perhaps it is not our gold that they are after.'

'What then?'

'Me. If they know who I am, then they know my father will pay for my ransom.'

John glanced back at the cloud of dust. It already seemed much closer. 'Then we had best hurry,' he said and picked up the pace.

They ran on in silence, conserving their breath. John's legs burned with fatigue after the previous day's march across the desert, and painful blisters had formed on his heels. He gritted his teeth and pressed on. The sun rose from behind the hills ahead, and John was soon soaked in sweat. When they finally reached the shade cast by the hills, they stopped to drink. As he tilted back his water-skin, John looked back to the cloud of dust thrown up by their pursuers.

''Sblood,' he cursed. 'They're close.'

'Only a few miles back,' Yusuf agreed. 'And closing fast.' He placed the stopper back in his waterskin. 'Come on.'

To save time, they avoided the twisting paths that ran at the base of the hills and headed straight east, slogging up and down hill after hill. Sweat ran down John's face, stinging his eyes, and his muscles screamed with agony. But he forced himself to keep going, trudging up the face of the hill before him. Yusuf ran ahead, seemingly tire-less. He was already halfway up the next hill, and when he reached the top, he let out a whoop of joy. John stag-gered up after him and stood bent over, hands on his knees. 'Thank God,' he managed between breaths.

Before them, the hill sloped down towards carefully tended fields that ran up to the edge of a broad river, its slow-moving waters sparkling silver. A road alongside the river snaked to the north, and there, rising high above the valley on a lone hill, was the fortress of Tell Bashir, with the houses of the town scattered around it. It was no more than a mile off.

Yusuf clapped John on the back. 'We made it!'

'Not yet.' John pointed behind them. The dust from the hooves of the bandits' horses was rising up from the hills just behind them.

'We'll have to run,' Yusuf said. 'Are you up to it?'

John grimaced, but nodded. 'Come on, then!' Yusuf sprinted down the hill, and John followed.

They reached the bottom of the slope and tore across a field of saffron, leaving a haze of yellow pollen hanging in the air behind them. They crashed through a spinach patch and out on to the road. Despite his burning lungs, John kept going, straining to keep up with Yusuf. As they raced down the road, the fortress loomed closer and closer. It was of Roman construction, its thick walls showing bands of red brick separated by a mixture of concrete and rough stone. John could see three soldiers standing above the gatehouse, bows in hand.

As they passed the first house on the outskirts of town, John began to slow. 'We're almost there!' Yusuf called back in encouragement, but John could go no further. He stumbled to a stop, bent over and vomited. Looking back, he saw the Frankish bandits sitting astride their horses atop the distant hills. The bandits thundered down the hill after them. With a groan, John straightened and ran on, stumbling down the main street. Houses were built close on either side, but nobody was out. The doors were all closed and the windows shuttered.

They reached the hill on which the fortress sat and John gritted his teeth, forcing himself up the sloping road after Yusuf. The two staggered to a stop before the closed gate and John fell to his knees, gasping for breath. Behind him, the bandits were galloping along the road towards them. They would reach the fortress in minutes.

Yusuf pounded on the closed gate. 'Open up! Open the gate!'

A grill slid open, revealing a man's face. His square jaw was clean-shaven, indicating that he was a mamluk, and he had dark, penetrating eyes. 'Who are you?' he demanded. 'What do you want?'

'I am Yusuf ibn Ayub. I have been sent by Nur ad-Din to take command of this fortress. Open the gate.'

The man frowned. 'And why should I do that?'

'I told you!' Yusuf shouted, exasperated. 'I have been sent by Nur ad-Din. I am your lord, and I command you to open the gate!' While Yusuf shouted, John glanced behind them. The bandits had now reached the outskirts of the town.

'Gumushtagin is my lord,' the man behind the gate replied. 'He commanded me to hold this fort until the Seljuks arrive. They are bringing us a fortune in gold.' He eyed Yusuf's ragged clothing. 'What do you bring?'

Yusuf's face was beginning to turn red, and John could tell he was on the point of exploding in rage. John placed a hand on his shoulder. 'Easy,' he whispered. 'We cannot afford to anger him.' He glanced back to the bandits, who were only two hundred yards away.

Yusuf nodded. 'What is your name, mamluk?' he asked in a more even voice.

'Baha' ad-Din Qaraqush.'

'I bring only myself, Qaraqush, but that is enough to make you rich.'

Qaraqush laughed. 'You are only a child.'

Yusuf's jaw clenched, but his voice remained calm. 'You are right. I am a child. I am no threat to you and your men. I humbly request your hospitality. Please let us into the citadel.' Qaraqush's brow creased, and he hesitated. To deny a traveller hospitality was a terrible breach of honour, and Yusuf in his dirty, torn tunic certainly did not look threatening. 'Please, man,' Yusuf insisted. 'We have walked for miles through the desert. I am tired, hungry and in no mood to argue. All I ask is shelter, food and drink. We will leave in the morning.' Qaraqush examined Yusuf for a moment longer, then the grill slammed shut.

''Sblood!' John cursed. The Frankish bandits were racing up the main street, bows in hand. One let fly, and an arrow hit the gate next to John with a thud. Then the gate behind them creaked open, just enough for Yusuf and John to slip through. They hurried inside, and the gate slammed shut behind them.

Qaraqush stood before them. He was short but powerfully built, with a thick neck and arms. 'Welcome,' he said, 'to Tell Bashir.'

Chapter 11

NOVEMBER 1152: TELL BASHIR

Yusuf sat on the dirt floor of the small cell, his knees drawn up to his chest in an attempt to ward off the evening chill. John was slumped against the opposite wall, his head hanging between his knees, his blond hair lit by a stream of light slanting in through the barred window. As soon as they had been admitted to the citadel, they had been marched to this cell. They had seen no one since.

John raised his head. 'What do you think they will do with us?'

'They will not kill us,' Yusuf replied, 'not after inviting us in. That would shame them.'

'What then?'

Yusuf shrugged. 'I do not know.' There was the rasp of metal on metal as the door's bolt slid back, and he got to his feet. The cell door swung open to reveal four mamluk soldiers in chainmail. One of them, a slender young man with a shaved head, stepped inside and held out his hand. 'Your weapons.' Yusuf hesitated. 'They will be returned to you,' the mamluk promised. Yusuf handed over his weapons, and John did the same. The young mamluk tucked Yusuf's sheathed sword and dagger into his belt and handed John's sword to one of the other men. 'Come with us,' he said. 'Qaraqush requests your presence at dinner.'

Yusuf and John followed the young mamluk out of the cell, and the other guards fell in behind them. They crossed the courtyard to the citadel's keep, a thick-walled, three-storey building. They stepped through the arched doorway and into a dimly lit entrance chamber. A staircase opposite led to the next floor. Yusuf and John headed for it, but one of the mamluks grabbed John's arm, stopping him.

'Your slave will eat in the kitchen,' the soldier said, gesturing to a door to the right.

'He is not a slave,' Yusuf replied.

'He is a Frank,' the bald mamluk spat.

Yusuf's brow furrowed. He opened his mouth to speak, but John put a hand on his shoulder. 'It is all right, Yusuf. Go ahead. I will be fine.'

'Very well,' Yusuf grumbled. The guards led John away, and Yusuf followed the young mamluk up the stairs and into a thickly carpeted room, well lit with candlelight. Opposite the door, Qaraqush sat on a cushion before a low table. He was dressed simply in a tunic of white cotton. He extended his hand, indicating that Yusuf should sit on the cushion opposite him.

'Thank you for your hospitality,' Yusuf said as he sat. 'You saved my life today. I am in your debt.'

Qaraqush waved away his thanks. 'The Prophet,

peace and blessing of Allah be upon him, commands us to welcome friend and enemy alike with open arms.'

'I hope you shall count me as a friend.'

Qaraqush frowned. He clapped his hands, and two servants entered carrying bowls of hot water and towels. When Yusuf had washed his hands, more servants entered, and a bowl of steaming lamb stew, a plate of fresh flatbread, and a dish of cool cucumber yoghurt were placed on the low table before Yusuf. His stomach rumbled loudly.

'You are hungry,' Qaraqush said. 'Eat.'

Yusuf eagerly tore off a piece of the soft flatbread and scooped up some of the lamb stew. 'In the name of Allah,' he murmured and ate, closing his eyes to savour the taste. He tore off another piece of bread.

'Eat well,' Qaraqush told him. 'Tomorrow morning you leave.'

Yusuf lowered the bread. 'You know that if you send us away, we will die. The Frankish raiders are waiting for us.'

'That is no concern of mine.'

'On the contrary. You know of my uncle, Shirkuh?'

Qaraqush's eyebrows shot up. 'Shirkuh?' His eyes narrowed as he examined Yusuf more closely. 'Of course I know of him. He is Nur ad-Din's greatest general.'

Yusuf met Qaraqush's eyes. 'If I am killed, my uncle will not rest until he sees you dead.'

Qaraqush thought for a moment, then shook his head. 'I am afraid you are wrong. Why should Shirkuh seek vengeance against me, when it is Frankish bandits who will have killed you?'

'I see,' Yusuf murmured.

'I am sorry, Yusuf, but it seems we are not destined to be friends. Tomorrow you will leave. What happens after that is in Allah's hands.' Qaraqush clapped, and servants entered with the next course.

Yusuf had lost his appetite, and he ate little for the remainder of the meal. Qaraqush was content to dine in silence. When the last course had been consumed, he bid Yusuf farewell. 'Ma'a as-salaama, Yusuf. The guards will show you out.'

The door opened and the bald mamluk guard entered. Yusuf rose to leave, but then stopped at the door. 'Wait,' he said, turning back to face Qaraqush. 'I have a proposition for you.'

'A proposition?'

'A challenge: I will fight your strongest man in hand-to-hand combat. If I win, we stay.'

'You against my strongest man?' Qaraqush chuckled. 'You are brave, Yusuf, but you are little more than a boy.'

'Then you should have no fear of my winning.'

'*Hmph*,' Qaraqush snorted. 'And why should I accept your challenge? What do I have to gain?'

'My dagger.' Yusuf gestured to the weapon tucked into the bald mamluk's belt. 'The man who defeats me will have it. And you, Qaraqush, shall have my sword.'

Qaraqush beckoned to the guard, who handed the two weapons over. Qaraqush took the dagger – the one that Shirkuh had given Yusuf – and whistled in appreciation as he fingered the eagle intricately carved into the hilt. Then he drew the sword and ran his finger along its curving blade. 'Damascus steel,' he noted. 'A fine piece of craftsmanship.' He sheathed the blade and smiled. 'I like you, boy. You have spirit. I accept your challenge, but your victory will not win your Frank's freedom.'

'John is my friend,' Yusuf protested. 'I will not leave without him.'

'Then he shall have to fight for himself. My men will enjoy watching him beaten.'

'I am sure,' Yusuf said, a trace of a smile on his lips. 'I accept.'

'Then we have a deal.' The two men clasped shoulders and kissed one another's cheeks to seal the agreement. 'But even if you win, you will only be postponing the inevitable,' Qaraqush warned Yusuf. 'The Seljuk Sultan's men will arrive in two weeks. My lord, Gumushtagin, has ordered me to turn the citadel over to them, and you will go with it. The sultan will pay good money for the nephew of Shirkuh, and I fear he will not treat you as generously as I have.'

'You will not turn the fortress over to the sultan.'

'No?' Qaraqush's eyebrows rose. 'And why is that?'

'Gumushtagin is no longer your lord. I am. Nur ad-Din has decreed it.'

'Yes, but Nur ad-Din is far away, and the Seljuk Sultan is paying us well for Tell Bashir – one thousand dinars.'

Yusuf looked Qaraqush in the eyes. 'I will give you two thousand.'

'And where will you find two thousand dinars?' Qaraqush scoffed.

'That is my concern, but I promise: you will have your money.'

Qaraqush frowned. 'I think you lie.'

'I do not expect you to believe me. But you have nothing to lose. If I am defeated by your champion tomorrow, then you will be rid of me. If I win, then you can hold me hostage until the sultan's men arrive. If I do not get you the money before then, you can sell me to the sultan. But if I do succeed, then you will swear loyalty to me and to Nur ad-Din.'

Qaraqush grinned. 'You are a bold one, Yusuf. You will make a great leader, if you do not die first.' He placed his hand on Yusuf's shoulder. 'If you defeat my champion and find the money, then I will gladly swear loyalty to you.'

'I have one more condition,' Yusuf warned. 'Until the sultan's men arrive, you and your men must do as I say. I will be in command here, as Nur ad-Din has decreed.'

Qaraqush burst out laughing, his head tilted back and his shoulders shaking. 'By Allah, you are brash. First win your fight. Then we shall see.'

'Wake up!' John jerked awake to find Yusuf shaking his shoulder. It was morning, and pale sunlight streamed through the cell window. John sat up. He could hear dozens of voices outside. Occasional snatches of conversation floated through the window. 'The little one won't last one minute—' 'The Frank either—' 'Al-Mashtub will fight. I saw him kill a man with one blow—'

'They started gathering after morning prayers,' Yusuf said. He smiled. 'One minute? They're in for a surprise.'

John shook his head. 'Just make sure you don't get yourself killed. Remember what I taught you.'

Outside, the crowd began to roar, and a moment later, John heard the rasp of the door's bolt. The door swung open, and he blinked against the sudden brightness. A mamluk stood in the doorway, silhouetted against the morning light.

'Come,' the guard said. 'It is time.'

John followed Yusuf out of the cell. The courtyard was crowded with dozens of mamluks, who stepped aside to create a narrow path. As John passed, they leaned close, spitting insults: 'Frankish bastard!' 'Son of a donkey!' 'Male whore!' 'Your mother is a slut!' John thought back to Acre, when, newly arrived in the Holy Land, he had fought the Saracen prisoner. Now he was the one being led to the slaughter. John shook the thought from his head. He would not die in this godforsaken frontier town, not if he could help it. He walked on stone-faced, following Yusuf into an impromptu ring that had been marked off in the dust of the fortress courtyard.

Qaraqush was waiting for them in the centre of the ring. He pointed to John. 'You first.'

John stripped off his tunic so that he wore only his breeches. 'Remember,' Yusuf told him, 'fight to the end. If you lose, you die.' John nodded. Yusuf clasped his arm. 'Good luck. Allah yasalmak.' God keep you safe. Yusuf stepped back to the edge of the ring, and John turned to await his opponent.

'Nazam!' Qaraqush called.

The crowd cheered as the young, bald-headed guard

from the night before stepped forward. He had already stripped to his waist, and his well-defined stomach and chest glistened with oil. That would make it hard for John to grab hold of him. John could hear men in the crowd placing bets over how long the fight would last. Then Yusuf shouted, 'I'll take the Frank to win! I will take all comers!' He was immediately crowded about by mamluks.

Qaraqush chuckled and turned to John. 'What is your name?'

'John.'

The mamluk commander frowned at the foreign-sounding name. He turned and gestured to John's opponent. 'I present to you Nazam!' he roared to the crowd. 'Our fiercest warrior, he has already killed six Franks. Today, he fights another: Juwan. They will fight until one of them is unconscious, or dead.' Qaraqush stepped out of the circle. 'Fight!'

Nazam circled left, his movement smooth and assured. John shadowed him, keeping the ring between them. The crowd was close behind him, yelling insults. Someone shoved John in the back, and he stumbled into the centre of the ring. Nazam attacked immediately, stepping forward and levelling a straight right at John's chin. John ducked the blow and slammed his shoulder into Nazam's gut. He tried to wrestle the mamluk to the ground but slid off his oiled skin. Nazam spun away and moved to the far side of the ring.

John turned to face him, careful now to keep distance between himself and the crowd. He edged towards Nazam. Suddenly the mamluk sprang forward and snapped off two quick jabs. John stumbled back, his right eye already swelling. Nazam grinned, and the crowd roared, calling for him to finish the Frank. Nazam pressed the attack, delivering another left jab that caught John on the chin. The mamluk put all his weight behind a straight right, but this time John knocked the blow aside with his left arm. He stepped inside Nazam's reach and threw a vicious uppercut that caught the mamluk in the jaw, snapping his head back. Nazam stood unsteadily, blood running down his chin from where he had bitten his tongue. Then his knees buckled and he collapsed. The crowd fell silent.

John rolled Nazam over and knelt on his chest. He raised his fist threateningly, but Nazam did not respond. He was already unconscious. John rose. The mamluk warriors around him were looking on wide-eyed. Qaraqush entered the ring, his brow knit. Then he grabbed John's right wrist and raised his arm high. 'The winner!' he shouted. Several of the men spat. John walked over to Yusuf amidst silence.

'You just made us ten dinars,' Yusuf told him, sliding a handful of coins into a pouch and handing it to John.

'Be careful,' John replied. 'My opponent was over-confident. Whoever you fight, he'll be ready for you.' Yusuf nodded and pulled off his tunic. He was thin, his ribs showing clearly, but John knew that he was stronger than he looked. 'Allah yasalmak,' John called as Yusuf stepped into the ring.

'Al-Mashtub!' Qaraqush yelled. 'You're next.'

The crowd parted, and a bear of a man stepped forward. He was easily a foot taller than Yusuf and perhaps twice as heavy. He had thickly muscled shoulders, a barrel chest, and his biceps were thicker than Yusuf's thighs. The giant grinned when he saw Yusuf, revealing a broad gap between his front teeth.

'Mary, Mother of Jesus,' John whispered.

'You said you wanted to face my best man,' Qaraqush told Yusuf. 'Allah save you.' He stepped out of the ring. 'Fight!'

The crowd roared. Al-Mashtub raised his huge fists – like twin mallets – and headed straight across the ring. Yusuf began to circle away, and Al-Mashtub charged, moving surprisingly quickly for his size. Yusuf just managed to jump aside, and the huge man went barrelling into the crowd, bowling over three men.

Yusuf waited in the centre of the ring while Al-Mashtub turned and lumbered back into the circle. The huge mamluk advanced more slowly this time. Yusuf tried to circle away, but Al-Mashtub shadowed him, keeping the smaller man in front of him. Yusuf was running out of space, and Al-Mashtub was almost on top of him.

'Move!' John shouted. 'Don't let him get a hold of you!'

Yusuf stepped forward and snapped off a jab, catching Al-Mashtub in the chin. Al-Mashtub swung, but Yusuf ducked and got off two more quick blows to his gut. It looked like he had punched the side of an ox. Al-Mashtub did not even wince. He tried to grab Yusuf, but the smaller man ducked away and sprinted past him.

'He's a slippery bastard,' the mamluk to John's

right spat as he handed a few coppers to the next man along. 'I was certain that runt wouldn't last a minute.'

Al-Mashtub moved in again, and Yusuf hit him with a quick combination – two left jabs to the chin and a right to the gut – before dancing away. The giant mamluk's lower lip was split and bleeding, but he kept bulling his way in, trying to get a hold of Yusuf. Yusuf continued jabbing and slipping away. As the fight wore on, John noticed that some in the crowd had started to cheer for Yusuf.

Al-Mashtub closed again, swinging in a wide arc for Yusuf's head. Yusuf ducked the blow and delivered an uppercut to the chin, then two quick blows to the gut. 'Get out!' John yelled, but it was too late. Yusuf stayed in close to deliver another right to the head. Al-Mashtub caught the blow in his huge hand. He jerked the smaller man towards him and then locked his arms behind Yusuf's back, hugging him to his chest and lifting him off the ground.

Yusuf's arms were pinned to his side, and he struggled in vain to break his opponent's grip. He kneed Al-Mashtub in the groin, and although the huge man's eyes widened, he did not release Yusuf. Yusuf smashed his forehead into Al-Mashtub's face, splattering blood as he crushed the giant man's nose. Al-Mashtub grinned despite the blood running down his face, and he squeezed Yusuf tighter, forcing the air from him. Yusuf's face shaded scarlet, then purple. He tried to head-butt Al-Mashtub again, but this time the mamluk pulled his head back out of the way. Yusuf thrashed wildly, desperate to escape. The veins on his forehead and neck bulged as he gasped for air.

Then Yusuf went still. Al-Mashtub grinned in triumph. Suddenly Yusuf opened his mouth wide and sank his teeth into the mamluk's thick neck. Al-Mashtub tried to jerk away, but Yusuf did not let go. Blood ran down the huge man's neck, and he roared out in pain. He released Yusuf and began trying to push him away. But Yusuf clung to him. When Al-Mashtub finally managed to throw Yusuf off, the boy fell back with a piece of flesh in his mouth. Al-Mashtub stood wide-eyed in the centre of the ring, his hand to the ragged wound in his neck, blood oozing between his fingers.

The crowd had fallen silent. Yusuf stood and spit out the piece of flesh. He snarled, showing teeth stained red with blood. Then he clenched his fists and went on the attack, pounding four quick blows into Al-Mashtub's stomach. Al-Mashtub swung at Yusuf's head, but he ducked the blow and threw a wicked uppercut, followed by two more straight rights to the head. He skipped back out of the way at the last second, avoiding another wild punch from the mamluk.

Al-Mashtub was staggering now, covered in his own blood. In one last effort, he roared and charged. Yusuf was ready. He jumped aside and punched Al-Mashtub hard in one of his kidneys. With a cry of pain, the huge man fell to his knees, and Yusuf sprang on him from behind, wrapping his arms around his opponent's throat. Al-Mashtub pawed feebly at Yusuf's arms, but he was too battered and weak to put up much of a fight. His lips tinged blue and his eyes bulged. Then the huge man collapsed, unconscious. Yusuf rose and stood unsteadily, his chest heaving.

John stepped forward and put his arm around Yusuf to keep him from falling. 'I can't believe you bit him. I have never seen you fight like that.'

'I did what I had to do to win.'

Qaraqush stepped into the ring. 'By the prophet, I can't believe it,' he murmured as he took Yusuf's hand and raised it. 'The winner!'

As the crowd of mamluks cheered, Qaraqush turned towards Yusuf. 'You're a tough one, all right, Yusuf. Nur ad-Din was no fool when he sent you here. I will follow you, at least until the Seljuk Sultan's men arrive.' There were murmurs of approval from the crowd. 'What is your first command?'

Yusuf gestured to Al-Mashtub. 'Bring a doctor for your man and see that he is looked after.' He wiped the back of his hand across his mouth, and it came away streaked with blood. 'I need a drink. I command you all to the tavern.' He took the pouch with his winnings back from John and held it up. 'I'm paying.'

Qaraqush slammed a cup down in front of Yusuf and filled it with wine from a clay jug. He slapped Yusuf on the back. 'Drink your fill!'

Yusuf raised the cup and peered at the murky, red contents. He had never tasted alcohol; it was forbidden by the Prophet. The moment he drank it, he would be unclean. Yusuf's grip tightened around the cup. He could hear Shirkuh's final words to him: if he wanted to lead his men, then he first had to be one of them. Yusuf tilted his head back and drained the cup of wine, grimacing at the bitter taste. The men cheered and emptied their cups. They began to pound the long table with their fists. 'More! More! More!'

'Another cup for our brave commander,' Qaraqush roared as he refilled Yusuf's cup, splashing wine on the table in the process. Yusuf took a deep breath and drank it. The taste was not so horrible this time. Perhaps alcohol was not as bad as he had feared.

An hour later, as he slammed down yet another drained cup, Yusuf felt the world spin around him. He began to slip off the bench, but Qaraqush reached out and held him upright. 'More!' the men roared. Yusuf fumbled in the pouch at his belt and pulled out his last two dinars. He tossed one of them on the table. 'Another round!' he shouted. The men cheered, and the tavern keeper – a pot-bellied, smiling man named Zarif – brought more jugs of wine to the table. He set one down before Yusuf.

John came forward from his place in the corner and whispered in Yusuf's ear. 'I think you have had enough.'

'Nonsense.' Yusuf stood, gripping the table to steady himself, and held his cup high. 'To my new men, the brave warriors of Tell Bashir. I shall lead you to riches and glory.' The men roared their approval and pounded on the table. 'From Tell Bashir, we shall conquer Damascus, Cairo—'

'Jerusalem!' one of the men suggested with a laugh.

'Jerusalem!' Yusuf agreed. 'I shall be king, and I shall make you all lords.' More pounding. 'To glory!'

'To glory!' the men chorused.

Yusuf drained his cup and sat down with a thud, almost falling backwards off the bench. His stomach grumbled ominously as he straightened. 'I do not feel well,' he murmured.

Qaraqush clapped him on the back. 'Nothing a woman cannot cure. Zarif! Let us have entertainment!'

'Of course, yâ sîdi.' Zarif clapped his hands. 'Dancers!'

Yusuf heard the sound of tambourines and turned his attention to a beaded curtain at the far end of the room. A tall, lithe Frankish woman emerged, a tambourine held high over her head. 'Faridah,' Qaraqush whispered. She had long auburn hair and creamy-white skin. Her large breasts and narrow hips were covered by strings of shining copper discs that showed flashes of curly pubic hair and pink nipples. A brilliant jewel hung from her gyrating belly-button. She was veiled, but her eyes were visible – bright green and highlighted with kohl. They locked immediately upon Yusuf.

Three more women followed, beauties all, but Yusuf could not take his eyes from Faridah. She slowly crossed the room, her hips swaying in time to the beat of her tambourine as she weaved between the crowded tables. She came tantalizingly close to some of the men, but when they reached out to grab her, she spun away and continued dancing. And always, her eyes came back to Yusuf.

'She's got her eye on you, boy,' Qaraqush winked.

Faridah reached Yusuf's table, and he turned to watch her. She stopped before him, her hips still rotating, the tambourine held high as she slowly turned. Qaraqush reached out to grab one of her perfectly shaped buttocks, and she slapped his hand away. She turned back to face Yusuf, placing a hand on his shoulder and sitting on his lap so that her breasts were only inches from his face.

Yusuf flushed as Faridah's eyes moved to the prominent bulge in his breeches. She leaned close and breathed in his ear, 'Come.' Then, she took his hand and led him from the table.

'Lucky bastard,' Qaraqush grumbled.

The rest of the men cheered as Yusuf followed Faridah through the curtain of beads and up a dark stairwell. He stumbled after her into a small room, where a single candle cast a flickering light over a wide bed. Faridah closed the door behind Yusuf and turned to face him. He did not move. He had no idea what to do next. She stepped close and pulled his tunic over his head. His breathing quickened as she proceeded to unlace his breeches. She gestured to the bed, and he sat. Faridah knelt before him and removed his boots. Then she took hold of his breeches and pulled them off. Her eyes widened when she saw his fully erect zib. Yusuf felt the room spin around him as the blood pounded in his temples.

Faridah stepped back and untied the string that held the dangling copper disks in place around her chest. It dropped to the floor, revealing her firm breasts. She untied the string around her waist and then removed her veil last of all. She was striking, her lips full and her cheeks soft curves. Her eyes had the faintest hint of wrinkles at the corners. She was older than Yusuf had expected, perhaps thirty.

She sat beside him. Yusuf's hand trembled as she took it and placed it on her warm, soft breast. She met his eyes. 'This is your first time?' He nodded, and she smiled. She gently pushed him back down on the bed and straddled him. She bent forward, and Yusuf gasped as she kissed his neck, her tongue flicking over his skin. He reached out tentatively and ran his hand down her side.

Faridah moved down, kissing his chest, his stomach. Yusuf closed his eyes, dizzy with pleasure and wine. Then there was an ominous grumbling from his stomach. Faridah pulled back as Yusuf rolled over and vomited over the side of the bed.

'I am sorry,' he mumbled as he rose and hurriedly dressed, pulling on his leather breeches and tunic without even bothering to tie them.

Faridah remained on the bed. She reached out and touched his arm. 'You do not have to go,' she said softly. Yusuf nodded and sat, his head in his hands. Faridah rubbed his back. 'You are not used to drink?'

'It is my first time,' Yusuf said without looking up.

'You are celebrating something?'

Yusuf shook his head. 'I am trying to earn my men's trust, to show that I am one of them.'

'You will do so with deeds better than with drink,' Faridah advised.

'What do you know of such things?' Yusuf snapped, pulling away and standing. 'You are only a whore.' He moved to leave.

'A whore yes, but not a fool. I know more than you would imagine. I know why the Franks are waiting for you outside town. I know why they want you dead.'

288

Yusuf froze, his hand on the door handle. He turned to face her. 'What do you mean?'

'The leader of the Franks sometimes sends a local man to fetch me to him. He has promised to buy me after you are dead. He said that before Gumushtagin left for Bizaa, he promised one thousand dinars for your head. The Franks wait for you even now in the hills beyond town. If you leave, you die.'

'Gumushtagin,' Yusuf whispered. He looked to Faridah. 'Why tell me this? You are a Frank.'

'I was, once, but that was long ago.'

Yusuf took the last dinar from his purse and held it out to her. 'Thank you.'

She shook her head. 'I have not earned it.'

'Please, take it.' Yusuf tossed the coin on the bed.

'No, my lord, keep your money.'

'I wish to give you something,' Yusuf insisted.

Faridah took the coin and rose. She pressed herself against him, wrapping one arm around his waist while with the other she dropped the coin back in the pouch at his belt. 'Send for me soon,' she whispered. 'You can pay me then.'

Yusuf nodded. He picked up his boots and left the room, stumbling down the stairs. As he passed through the beaded curtain, the men cheered.

'Wake up.'

Yusuf cracked open a bloodshot eye to see John standing over him. Outside, the muezzin was loudly calling the faithful to prayer. Yusuf grimaced as he put his hands over his ears. 'Leave me be.'

'The men will expect you at prayers,' John insisted. 'This is your first day as their emir. You must set an example.'

'Very well.' The world spun as Yusuf sat up, and he leaned forward, his head in his hands. 'I feel as if a blacksmith is hammering inside my head.'

'I told you not to drink so much.'

'No wonder the Prophet forbids alcohol. It is poison.'

Yusuf dressed and left the room he had been given in the keep. The guards in the courtyard nodded respectfully as he passed in the pre-dawn gloom. He headed out of the gate and down to the village mosque. After prayers, he emerged to find Qaraqush waiting for him. The mamluk commander fell in beside Yusuf as they walked back towards the citadel.

'I trust you slept well,' Qaraqush said with a wink. Yusuf gave him a hard look. 'I was wondering what you have planned for today. Nothing too onerous, I hope. The men are still recovering from yesterday's festivities.'

'They will have to rouse themselves,' Yusuf replied. 'Today, we shall get your money, two thousand dinars.'

'And where will we find this fortune?'

'In the hands of the Frankish bandits who attacked me. We shall take it from them.'

Qaraqush stopped. 'No. We will not.'

Yusuf turned to face him. 'Are you afraid, Qaraqush? They are only bandits.'

'I am not afraid,' the mamluk commander growled, 'but nor am I a fool. Why risk my men's lives when we can have the sultan's money for nothing?'

'They are *my* men, Qaraqush,' Yusuf said quietly.

'Not yet.'

'But they will be. I will not lead them to the slaughter. So long as you do as I say, there will be little danger to the men.'

Qaraqush's eyes narrowed as he examined Yusuf. 'Tell me what you propose. For your sake, I had best like it.'

The gate of the fortress of Tell Bashir slammed shut behind John and Yusuf. They carried only their swords and a single waterskin – no more than they had had when they arrived. It was raining a fine rain that showed no sign of letting up, and John's tunic was already soaked. He looked over at Yusuf. 'What have you got us into now?'

'Allah will protect us,' Yusuf replied. 'You will see.' He strode down the hill towards the town. John followed.

The rain had kept the townsfolk inside. They passed only one man, an elderly beggar propped up against the side of the tavern, a cup in his hand. Yusuf dropped his last dinar into the cup as he passed.

'Why did you do that?' John asked, his eyes wide.

'We won't need it any more, will we?'

They emerged from town on the road – now little better than a muddy track – and followed it alongside the winding Sajur River. After half a mile, John stopped at a side track that led between fields and towards the low hills on their right. 'Look,' he said, pointing out a single rider, who sat atop one of the hills. The rider watched them for a moment, then galloped out of sight over the far side of the hill. 'They have seen us.'

'Then let's not keep them waiting.'

They marched through the fields, the mud sucking at their boots. The track grew wetter and widened before cutting into the hills, running between two sheer slopes. John splashed ahead into the ravine, Yusuf close behind him. They had not gone far when John heard the sound of hooves echoing off the hills around them. He and Yusuf began to run. They rounded a curve, and the narrow trail suddenly opened up into a circular, gravel-strewn wash, surrounded by steep slopes. On the far side of the open area, a narrow passage led further into the hills. They were halfway across the wash when riders started pouring out of the narrow gap. They turned to run, but more riders were emptying out of the ravine behind them.

Two of the bandits rode forward to confront John and Yusuf. Both wore chainmail and helmets that hid their faces. 'What have we here? Two mice in our trap,' one of the riders said in Frankish. 'We've been waiting for you, Yusuf ibn Ayub,' he added as he removed his helmet.

'Reynald!' John growled.

The man's forehead creased as he examined John. 'Do I know you, Saracen?'

'I am no Saracen.' John pulled off his turban to reveal his blond hair.

Reynald shrugged. 'Whoever you are, I have never seen you before in my life.'

'I was your man, once,' John snarled. 'You betrayed

me, you bastard! You sent your man to kill me and left me for dead.'

'Saxon?' the other Frank said, removing his helmet to reveal the wide face of Ernaut. 'I thought I killed you.'

'Not yet,' John replied.

'We will remedy that soon enough,' Reynald said. 'Ernaut, finish him.'

Ernaut replaced his helmet, then drew his sword and spurred towards John, who backed away, drawing his weapon. Ernaut had just raised his sword when an arrow struck him in the neck. Wide-eyed, he looked down at the shaft protruding from him. He slumped from the saddle, and three more arrows sank into the ground around him. Another struck Reynald's horse, and it reared, throwing him. Reynald scrambled to his feet, looking about wildly.

Qaraqush and his men stood high above on the surrounding hills, firing arrows down on the Christians. Reynald turned to run, but more mamluks had filled both the exits from the wash, blocking all escape. Dozens of Frankish bandits were down and screaming in pain. Reynald turned to face Yusuf and John.

Yusuf raised his fist, and the arrows stopped. 'It seems that you are the one in a trap,' he said to Reynald in Frankish.

The Frank drew his sword. 'I will kill you both before I die,' he growled.

'No. You will do as I say, and you will live,' Yusuf said. Reynald paused, lowering his sword. 'Show me where you have hidden our gold, and you will be given a horse and enough supplies to reach Antioch.'

John grabbed Yusuf's shoulder and spun him around. 'What are you doing?' he demanded in Arabic. 'This man is the reason I was sold into slavery. He is a coward and a liar. He deserves to die!'

'I am sorry, friend. We need that money, and only Reynald can show us to it.'

John looked from Yusuf to Reynald. He had dreamed of killing this Norman bastard for so long that the hatred had become a part of him, but eventually he nodded. 'Very well.'

Yusuf turned back to Reynald. 'Do you accept my offer?'

'Why should I believe you, infidel?'

John stepped forward. 'I would be only too happy to see you die, Reynald. But I give you my word as a fellow Christian that if you do as he says, you will not be harmed.'

'Your word as a Christian?' Reynald spat. 'You're one of them now, another sand-devil!'

'I am a Christian and an Englishman, and I give you my word that you will not be harmed.'

Reynald hesitated a moment longer, then sheathed his sword. 'Very well, I will do as you ask.'

Yusuf watched as Reynald galloped away, then he turned back to the camp, which Qaraqush and his men were busy ransacking. Several men were rounding up the dozens of sheep that the bandits had stolen. Others were dragging rolls of fine silk from a tent. Two mamluks dragged the money chest to the centre of camp; Reynald had shown them where it had been buried, not far from his tent. Yusuf watched as a grinning warrior hacked the lock off the chest with his sword. The man threw back the lid and gold coins spilled out. The men cheered, and Yusuf smiled. He would not be sold as a hostage. He would be emir of Tell Bashir, and he would send the Seljuk Sultan's men back to their master. But if he were to be emir, then he would need a banner to fly above the gate of the citadel.

Yusuf strode into Reynald's tent. The floor was covered with sheepskins and a pile of weapons lay in one corner. In the other corner, Yusuf found the saddlebags that he had brought from Aleppo. He rooted through them and pulled out the banner that his father had given him, white with a golden eagle in the middle.

As Yusuf left the tent, Qaraqush approached and clapped him on the back. 'Well done, Yusuf! There is wealth enough here to put the Seljuk Sultan's offer to shame. You are a brave man, and you have Allah's favour.' He knelt at Yusuf's feet. 'I will follow wherever you lead. I am your man, Yusuf ibn Ayub.' The other mamluks gathered around and also knelt. John joined them.

Yusuf extended his hand and pulled Qaraqush to his feet. 'You will not regret your decision. This is just the beginning.'

That night, Yusuf stood at the window of his chamber in the keep of Tell Bashir and looked down on his men, their figures lit by a celebratory bonfire in the centre of the courtyard. Some drank, passing around wineskins and recounting their roles in the day's battle. Others had already spent their spoils on women, whom they pulled away towards the barracks. Still others were dancing around the bonfire while their fellows stood to the side with instruments in hand. Yusuf spied Qaraqush amongst these last, smiling as he beat out a rapid tattoo on his drum. Al-Mashtub, the giant of a man that Yusuf had fought less than two days ago, stood beside him, his flute toylike in his massive hands. The tune they were playing floated up to Yusuf. It was an old Turkish folk-song, the drums quick under the plaintive notes of the flute.

On the far side of the courtyard the gate opened, and Yusuf saw John enter, his chainmail glimmering red in the firelight. He was followed by a figure whose face was hidden in the shadows of a black cloak. They crossed the courtyard towards the keep, and the mamluks stepped aside to let them pass. A moment later there was a knock on Yusuf's door.

'Enter,' he called, turning from the window. John opened the door and stood aside to allow his companion to enter. She pushed aside her hood. It was Faridah.

'Good evening, my lord,' she said and bowed.

Yusuf nodded to her, then turned to John. 'Go and join the men. Celebrate. You have earned it.' John left, closing the door behind him.

'I am honoured that you sent for me, my lord,' Faridah said as she untied her cloak and allowed it to drop to the floor. She was wearing a tight-fitting caftan of red silk. It complemented her hair, which cascaded loose around her shoulders. Her green eyes, ringed with kohl, fixed on Yusuf. His heart began to pound.

'We defeated the Frankish raiders,' he told her. 'They were waiting for me as you said.'

'And their leader, Reynald? He is dead?'

'I let him go.'

'Why?' Faridah demanded. 'He deserved to die.'

Yusuf went to her and touched her arm. Up close, she smelled of jasmine. 'I had to free him,' he told her. 'I gave him my word.' Faridah frowned. 'Why do you hate him?'

'It is nothing,' Faridah murmured. She reached out and pushed a strand of hair back from Yusuf's face, then pressed her body against his. Yusuf put his arms around her waist and tentatively kissed her. Her lips were soft and warm. She opened her mouth and kissed him back passionately. Her mouth tasted sweet, like melon.

Faridah smiled. 'Help me with my caftan,' she whispered.

Yusuf undid the first button, then the second and third. The caftan spread open to reveal the gentle curves of her breasts. Yusuf's hands began to tremble as he fumbled with the fourth button.

'Let me,' Faridah told him. She quickly unfastened the rest of the buttons and shrugged off the caftan to stand naked before Yusuf. 'Now, it is your turn, my lord.' She unfastened Yusuf's belt, then pulled his tunic over his head. She knelt down as she lowered his loose cotton pants. Yusuf gasped as she took his zib in her mouth.

'By the Prophet!'

Faridah looked up at him. 'Do you wish me to stop, my lord?'

'N-no,' he managed. 'Do not stop.'

Yusuf awoke when he felt Faridah stir in the bed beside him. She kissed his cheek, and he smiled sleepily. He had never before tasted such pleasure as she had shown him, and he was still glowing from the experience. He reached out and pulled her towards him.

'I must go, my lord,' she whispered in his ear and pulled away. She rose and began to dress. 'My master will be angry if I do not return soon.'

Yusuf sat up in bed. 'Your master?'

'Zarif, the tavern owner. I am his slave.'

'Not any more. You are free.'

'Do not jest of such things,' Faridah scowled.

'I do not jest.'

Faridah shook her head. 'And what would I do with freedom? I have no family. No man will have me.' She turned her back to him as her eyes grew moist. 'Zarif is good to me, better than most.'

Yusuf approached her from behind and put his arms around her waist. 'I will protect you now,' he whispered in her ear. 'If you must serve a master, then let it be me.'

Faridah turned to face him. 'You do not want me, my lord,' she protested, tears in her eyes. 'I will never bear you children. I cannot.'

Yusuf wiped a tear from her cheek. 'I do want you. And you may call me Yusuf.'

Faridah smiled. 'Very well, Yusuf.'

'Now, I wish to know more about the woman who will share my bed. Where are you from?'

Faridah pulled away. 'I do not wish to speak of it. I am here now. That is all that matters.'

Yusuf gently touched her arm. 'If I am to take a

Frankish concubine, then I must know everything about you.'

Faridah nodded, then went to the window and looked out into the darkness. 'I grew up in Edessa,' she said. 'My father was a Frankish lord and my mother an Armenian Christian. They died when the city fell to Nur ad-Din's father, Zengi. My father was killed at the walls. My mother—' she looked away. 'My mother was raped and murdered. I was sold as a slave.'

'And?'

'And I would rather not speak of it. Those days are past.'

Yusuf went to her and held her close, stroking her hair. 'I am sorry,' he murmured. 'You must hate my people.'

'No. I grew up amongst Saracens in Edessa. I wore the same clothes, spoke the same language, ate the same food. I never knew I was different until the city fell.'

'And afterwards, surely you must have thought of revenge?'

Faridah shook her head sadly. 'Where would my dreams of revenge get me? Women exercise power through love, Yusuf, not hate. We leave that to men.'

Chapter 12

John stood on the wall of the citadel of Tell Bashir and watched the men gathered in the courtyard below. Six mamluks stood in a line, each with a bow in hand and a quiver slung over his shoulder. Yusuf was thirty paces away, hanging a small, round shield from the inside of the citadel wall. When the shield was in place, he turned to face the archers and the men crowded behind them. 'You know the rules,' he called out as he walked towards the line of archers. 'Each archer will fire one arrow. The two men who come closest to the centre of the shield will then compete for the prize: six dinars.' The crowd of mamluks cheered. Some of the archers smiled, thinking what they would do with the money – two month's pay. Others glanced at their competition. One man – the bald warrior, Nazam – checked the tautness of his bowstring.

Yusuf had been holding these contests every Sunday since he and John had come to Tell Bashir, over a year ago. One week it was archery, the next horsemanship, the next swordplay. The men's skills had improved dramatically as they sought to win the weekly prize.

300

John watched the games each week, but he never participated. As the commander of Yusuf's khaskiya – his private guard – John had earned the respect of the men, but he would never be one of them. To them he would always be al-ifranji, the Frank, a man apart. He had a different past, different memories. John thought of the brilliant green fields of England and then of Zimat. He frowned. She would be married by now, and as unreachable as his home country.

'Ready!' Yusuf called, drawing John's attention back to the courtyard. Yusuf had stepped behind the line of archers, each of whom now reached back and, in a fluid motion, drew an arrow from his quiver and nocked it to his bow. The crowd quieted in anticipation, and John could hear the bows creak as the archers drew them taught. 'Rama!' Yusuf shouted, and the men let fly. The arrows hissed through the air, and all six found their target, thudding into the leather shield.

Yusuf took the shield from the wall, and as he walked back towards the archers, he pulled out the arrows, starting with the ones furthest from the centre. 'Manzur!' he called after examining the colours painted on the shaft of the arrow. He tossed the shaft aside. 'Rakin! Akhtar! Liaqat!' He dropped the last arrow as he came to a stop before the archers. 'Your aim was true, but not true enough. The Frankish armour is thick. It is not enough to hit them, for if you hit their chest, your arrows are wasted. You must strike their neck where the armour is thin.' He wrested the remaining two arrows from the shield. 'Nazam and Uwais, you have come closest to the mark. Ready yourselves.'

The two men grinned, and their fellows clapped them on their backs as they stepped forward. Each man notched an arrow to his bow. John could hear some in the crowd placing bets as to who would win. 'In battle,' Yusuf told them, 'you must hit a moving target. Let us see how skilled you truly are.' He tossed the shield high into the air.

Immediately, Nazam pulled back and let fly. His arrow thudded into the shield before it had even reached its apex. Uwais waited until the shield was frozen at its highest point before shooting, his arrow slamming into the shield. The shield had just begun to fall when Nazam hit it with another arrow. He quickly nocked another and managed to strike the shield once more before it hit the ground. The men cheered his feat, and John gave a low whistle of appreciation.

Yusuf went to the shield and raised it high. Uwais's arrow – the shaft decorated in black and blue – protruded from the centre of the shield. Nazam's three arrows were scattered around it. 'The winner is Uwais!' Yusuf declared. He took a coin pouch from his belt and tossed it towards the victorious archer.

Nazam snapped the pouch out of the air before it reached its intended target. 'It is not right! I struck the shield three times, and Uwais hit it only once.'

The mamluks in the courtyard went quiet. Even from high on the wall, John could see the change in Yusuf's bearing – his back straighter, his shoulders back. He stepped close to Nazam and placed a hand on the mamluk's shoulder. 'It is not he who strikes most, but he whose strike is the most telling who wins, Nazam.'

'But—'

'I have spoken!' Yusuf snapped.

Nazam lowered his head. 'Yes, qadi.' He handed the pouch to Uwais.

John turned away from the scene to gaze out beyond the castle walls. His eyes wandered across the town to the glittering waters of the Sajur River. Two miles off, he saw a cloud of dust rising above the road beside the river. John could just make out the shapes of riders amidst the dust.

The lookout spotted the men at the same time. 'Riders approaching!' he shouted down to Yusuf. 'Three of them.'

Yusuf hurried up the stairs to join John atop the wall. The riders were closer now, just entering the outskirts of the town. John could see that two were older warriors, well-muscled and tanned, with full beards. The third was a young man, still beardless. Yusuf squinted as the riders drew closer. 'The young one, I know him.' He grinned and slapped John on the back. 'Come!'

John followed Yusuf as he hurried down from the wall. 'Open the gate!' Yusuf shouted. The gate swung open just as the riders were coming up the ramp towards the citadel. When he saw Yusuf, the young rider slid from the saddle and sprinted forward. The two men embraced and exchanged kisses.

'As-salaamu 'alaykum, Brother!' the young man exclaimed.

'Wa 'alaykum as-salaam, Selim.'

Selim? John's eyebrows rose as he looked more closely. Yusuf's younger brother had added several inches since John last saw him, and his round, boyish face was now lean.

'You are a man, now,' Yusuf said, gripping his brother's shoulder. 'What brings you to Tell Bashir?'

'Shirkuh has sent me. Nur ad-Din has need of you and your men. He is marching on Damascus.'

APRIL 1154: ON THE ROAD TO DAMASCUS

Yusuf smelled Nur ad-Din's camp long before he saw it. The breeze brought him the pungent odours of wood smoke and manure mixed with the musky scent of the thousands of horses, camels and sheep that accompanied the army. As Yusuf neared the top of a low hill, he could hear the snorting and harrumphing of the camels and the bleating of sheep. Then he crested the rise, and the camp lay before him, stretching for a mile along the Orontes River, which blazed red under the setting sun. Thousands of animals grazed at the edge of the camp. Beyond them rose a maze of tents, the sprawling structures of the Bedouin interspersed with the neat, wool triangles of the mamluks. In the centre was Nur ad-Din's grand pavilion, his banner flying from the top.

'Qaraqush!' Yusuf called, and the mamluk commander left the column of Yusuf's warriors – fifty men in all – and rode up beside him. 'See that the men are quartered. Make sure to camp upwind of the livestock.'

'Yes, my lord.'

'Selim and John, come with me,' Yusuf continued. He

looked behind him to where Faridah sat on a camel, her face veiled. 'You too, Faridah.'

Yusuf rode down the hill, and Selim and John followed, riding on either side of Faridah. They passed through a herd of camels chewing impassively at their cuds. At the edge of the tents, two mamluk sentries were waiting for them. 'Halt, friend,' one of them called. 'Where are you going?'

'I am Yusuf ibn Ayub, emir of Tell Bashir,' Yusuf replied as he and the others dismounted. 'I have come at Nur ad-Din's request.' He handed his reins to one of the sentries. 'Take care of our horses,' he said and walked past.

'Yes, my lord,' the sentry called after him.

Yusuf led the way between the Bedouin's ramshackle tents – sprawling structures that held entire clans. Hard-faced men in patchwork leather armour lounged outside, chatting or tending their cooking fires. The Bedouin's bravery was legendary, as was their greed. They had been known to put down their arms in the midst of battle in order to strip the bodies of the dead, friend and foe alike.

Past the Bedouin, Yusuf entered amongst the tents of the vassal lords who served Nur ad-Din. These tents were more luxurious: tall, round structures with several rooms, each surrounded by the tents of the emir's men. Yusuf spotted Shirkuh's standard fluttering in the distance, but lost sight of it as he wove his way through the maze of tents. He stopped when he came to a fire surrounded by a dozen men who he recognized as Shirkuh's soldiers. They were eating, scooping boiled wheat out of a common pot.

'I am looking for Shirkuh,' Yusuf said to them. 'Where is he?'

The men looked up from their food. One of them, a tall, muscle-bound man, grinned. It was Qadir, the man who had confronted Yusuf all those years ago on the practice grounds of Aleppo.

'Look here, boys,' Qadir said. 'It's the little bugger himself, all grown up.'

Yusuf raised an eyebrow. 'What did you say?'

Qadir rose, towering over Yusuf. 'You heard me, bugger.'

Yusuf smiled, then turned his back on the man. 'John,' he called.

Without a word, John stepped forward and punched Qadir hard in the groin. The huge mamluk grabbed his crotch and fell to his knees, eyes bulging. John hit him with an uppercut that snapped his head back, then a hard right to the chin. Qadir toppled into the dust, unconscious. John wiped his hands and stepped away.

Yusuf noticed that Selim was watching him wide-eyed. He winked at his brother, then turned back to the men around the fire. 'Let us try again. Where is my uncle?'

A grey-haired man rose. 'I will take you to him, my lord.'

Yusuf was approaching Shirkuh's tent when Turan stormed out, scowling. He stopped short when he saw Yusuf and the others.

'As-salaamu 'alaykum, Brother,' Yusuf called as he approached. He embraced Turan stiffly, and the two exchanged kisses.

'Wa 'alaykum as-salaam,' Turan replied. His eyebrows rose as he noticed Faridah. 'What's this you've brought with you, Brother? She is delicious.'

Yusuf's hand went to the eagle-hilt dagger that he always wore at his belt. 'If you touch her, I will kill you.'

Turan's smile faded. 'I see you have not changed, Yusuf.'

'Nor have you, Turan.' The two brothers locked gazes.

'Is that Yusuf I hear?' Behind Turan, the tent flaps parted and Shirkuh emerged. He stepped past Turan and embraced Yusuf. 'Welcome, young eagle!' he said, and they exchanged kisses.

'Salaam, Uncle.'

Shirkuh turned to Selim and again exchanged kisses. 'I am glad to see you returned safely.' He looked to Turan. 'What are you still doing here? I gave you an order.'

'Yes, Uncle.' Turan strode away.

Shirkuh turned back to Yusuf. 'We have much to discuss, nephew. Selim, see that his servants are taken care of. Now come.' He placed his arm around Yusuf's shoulders. 'Let us walk.'

Shirkuh did not speak as he led Yusuf past a few tents and up the gentle rise that bordered the river. He stopped at the top and looked out over the waters, which ran dark silver now that the sun had set. 'I have heard good things of you, Yusuf,' he began. 'The caravans move without fear through your lands, and you have increased your tribute.'

'The land is rich, and I have good men.'

'If they are good, it is because you have made them so. When Nur ad-Din sent you to Tell Bashir, I feared the worst.' Shirkuh lowered his voice. 'I received your letter about Gumushtagin. You say he hired Franks to kill you.' Yusuf nodded. 'You should not trust such things to paper, Yusuf. Messengers too often go missing.'

Yusuf lowered his head. 'I thought it important that you know, Uncle.'

'*Hmph*,' Shirkuh grunted. 'That is the least of Gumushtagin's crimes. He is cunning, that one. And now he has our lord's ear.'

'But I thought Gumushtagin had been sent to Bizaa in disgrace.'

'He was, but he has since earned Nur ad-Din's trust. As a eunuch, Gumushtagin has access to the harem. He discovered an emir sleeping with one of Nur ad-Din's concubines. Our lord was very grateful, but I am not so sure that Gumushtagin did not encourage the emir, only to betray him.'

'What happened to the man?' Yusuf asked.

'He was bound, and his privates cut off and stuffed in his mouth. Then Nur ad-Din took a rod and beat him to death.' Shirkuh sighed. 'The emir was a good man.'

'But he betrayed our lord.'

'Yes, he did.' Shirkuh turned to face Yusuf. 'There is something we must discuss before you go to Nur ad-Din's tent. I have heard that you have begun to frequent a Frankish whore.'

Yusuf flushed red. 'Faridah? She is no whore. She is my concubine. I freed her.'

'Once a whore, always a whore,' Shirkuh grumbled.

Yusuf met his uncle's eyes. 'I am not concerned with her past. I – I love her.'

Shirkuh sighed. 'Sit beside me, boy.' They sat on the sandy dune, facing back towards the camp. 'Look at all of this.' Shirkuh waved to the thousands of tents before them. 'As Nur ad-Din's atabek, I have thousands of warriors at my command. And do you know why Nur ad-Din trusts me? Because I have learned to control my passions, because I know that if I give in to them, all of this—' he gestured towards the camp '—could be gone in a night.'

'I do not understand.'

'Before you were born, your father and I lived in Tikrit. Ayub was governor of the city. Did he ever tell you why we left?' Yusuf shook his head. Shirkuh sighed. 'It was my fault. I was eighteen, only a little older than you are now. I fell for the wife of the commander of the castle gate. Her husband found out and beat her to death. I was furious. I confronted the man and killed him.'

'And you were right to do so.'

'No. I should have gone to your father. He was the governor. He would have had the man brought to justice. But I loved her, and so I did not think. I killed him.' Shirkuh lowered his head. 'The man was a nephew of the sultan. Your father and I were cast out of Tikrit as exiles. We lost everything. We were lucky that Nur ad-Din's father took us on. Otherwise, we would have died in the desert.' Shirkuh met Yusuf's eyes. 'Do not let your passions blind you as I did, Yusuf. You must govern your heart if you wish to rule men.'

'I understand.'

'Good. Now go. You should greet our lord, Nur ad-Din.'

John held aside the flap of Yusuf's tent and gestured for Faridah to enter. She ducked inside, and he followed. Several lamps hung from the ceiling, shedding a dim light. Carpets had been spread over the grassy ground and cushions were scattered about. A low table held Yusuf's writing implements. Faridah strode to the centre of the tent and removed her veil and head covering. With a sigh of relief, she shook out her long, auburn hair.

'Do you need anything?' John asked.

Faridah shook her head, and John began to leave. 'John, wait,' she called. 'I wish to speak with you.'

John turned and met her dark eyes for a second, then looked away. 'I should not stay,' he mumbled and headed towards the tent flap.

'I do not understand you,' Faridah said. John paused. 'You are a free man, now. Why do you still serve Yusuf?'

John looked back at her. 'Why do you?'

'I am a woman. I am nothing without Yusuf – worse than nothing, a whore. But you are a man, a warrior. You could have a place of honour amongst the Franks.'

John shrugged. 'Yusuf is my friend.'

'He is a good man, but that does not change things. You will always be an ifranji to them. You will never be truly accepted here.'

'I was not accepted amongst the Normans, either,' John said bitterly. 'I have no place amongst the Franks.'

She met his eyes. 'And do you not wish for a woman? A wife?'

John held her gaze. 'What are you asking me?'

'We are the same, you and I,' she whispered. 'We could comfort one another.'

John felt his heart beat faster. It had been long since he held a woman. He found himself staring at the curve of Faridah's large breasts beneath her tight caftan. He took a deep breath and shook his head. 'He loves you, Faridah. I will pretend that I did not hear what you have just said.'

Faridah looked away, her cheeks reddening. 'I only wanted you to know that I understand what it means to be a stranger in this land. If you need a friend, I am here.'

John nodded and left the tent.

Yusuf stepped into Nur ad-Din's spacious tent to find the emir seated on the thickly carpeted floor, a map of Damascus laid out before him. Yusuf was surprised to see the emir's wife, Asimat, seated to his left. A bald, fat-faced man in an elaborate caftan of scarlet silk sat to his right.

Nur ad-Din looked up and smiled. 'Yusuf! I am glad that you have come. I can use your keen mind. Sit.' He waved to a place opposite him. 'You know my wife, Asimat. She insisted on returning with me to her child-hood home, and to tell the truth, I am happy to have her. She knows Damascus better than any of us.'

'My lady,' Yusuf murmured with a nod in her direction.

'And I believe you have not yet met the Emir of Bizaa,' Nur ad-Din continued, gesturing to the portly man beside him. 'Yusuf ibn Ayub, this is Gumushtagin.'

'I am honoured to meet you.' Yusuf met the eunuch's eyes. 'I have heard so much about you.'

'And I you,' Gumushtagin replied, his voice high-pitched. 'I have long desired to meet my successor in Tell Bashir. I hope that you did not encounter too much trouble when you arrived.'

'A few Frankish bandits, that is all. I captured their leader easily enough.'

Gumushtagin's eyes widened. 'You spoke to him?'

'He had an interesting story to tell.' Yusuf turned back towards Nur ad-Din. 'Where is my father? I expected to find him with you.'

Gumushtagin answered for Nur ad-Din. 'He is in Damascus, at the court of Emir Mujir ad-Din.'

'On my orders,' Nur ad-Din added.

'Yes, of course,' Gumushtagin agreed. 'But we have not heard from him in weeks. Only Allah knows what has become of him.'

Yusuf swallowed hard. 'Do you think he is dead?'

'Or a traitor,' Gumushtagin said evenly, his green eyes fixed on Yusuf.

'You dare insult my family's honour?' Yusuf reached for his dagger, but then realized that it had been removed by the guard outside.

'Peace, Yusuf,' Nur ad-Din said. 'We are here to punish Mujir ad-Din for his refusal to join in the fight against the Christians. We should not waste our energy squabbling amongst ourselves.' He turned to Gumushtagin. 'There is no man I trust more than Yusuf's father. Apologize.'

'My apologies,' Gumushtagin said with an insincere smile.

'Good,' Nur ad-Din said. 'Now, let us turn back to the business at hand. My clever wife, Asimat, says that we should establish ourselves in the orchards to the west of the city.' He pointed to their location on the map. 'I agree. This is where we shall conduct our siege.'

APRIL 1154: DAMASCUS

John rode beside Yusuf at the head of a column of men that stretched for miles over the arid, rolling hills. Ahead, spread out below them, was the city of Damascus, its thick walls rising up from the verdant orchards and gardens that surrounded it. Squinting, John could make out men atop the walls, their chainmail and iron helmets glinting in the sunshine. His hands tightened on the reins as he thought back to his first trip to Damascus, as part of the doomed crusade.

'She is beautiful, is she not?' Yusuf said, pointing to the city.

'You will find the view less inspiring when you stand in the shadow of her walls,' John replied. 'Damascus is not an easy prize.'

'But with the army Nur ad-Din has assembled, how can she resist?'

John's forehead creased. 'That is what the crusaders thought.'

They rode on in silence, following Nur ad-Din and Shirkuh. Turan rode beside them, but kept his distance from Yusuf. At the foot of the hill Nur ad-Din reined in his horse. 'We will divide the army into columns and seize the orchards,' he told them. 'Tonight, we will camp before the walls.'

As the army trooped down the hill, the men were separated into columns, lined up before the many paths into the orchards. Shirkuh and Turan each rode off to take the lead of a column, but Yusuf's men were selected to ride with Nur ad-Din. As John watched them form into a column four across, a memory flashed into his mind: One-Eye, the Frank, eating a mango when a spear burst from his chest.

'I do not like this,' John told Yusuf. 'Those orchards are a deathtrap. In the crusade, we lost a quarter of our men taking them.'

'We have no choice. We will follow orders and trust in Allah to lead us through.'

The column of men moved forward with Nur ad-Din riding at its head, and Yusuf and John just behind. John rode with his hand on his sword hilt, his eyes searching the low mud walls to either side for signs of warriors hidden behind them. He saw only the fronds of date trees shimmering in the breeze, and heard only the chirruping of birds over the rumble of the horses' hooves. 'Something is not right,' he whispered. 'Where are Mujir ad-Din's men?

'Perhaps he has kept them within the walls to better defend the city,' Yusuf suggested.

Ahead, the walls of Damascus loomed larger and larger. They were headed for the Bab al-Faradis, or Gate of Paradise, which led into the city from the orchards.

It was a massive structure, twice as high as the walls around it. Many of the men crowded atop the gate had bows in hand. John nervously fingered the hilt of his sword as Nur ad-Din led them on. In only a few more feet, they would be within bow shot of the walls.

'What is Nur ad-Din doing?' John grumbled. 'He's going to get us killed.'

'Emir Mujir ad-Din would not dare let his men shoot at Nur ad-Din,' Yusuf said. 'They will speak, first. Then we will fight.'

Nur ad-Din finally reined in his horse only thirty feet from the gate. 'People of Damascus!' he called loudly. 'Your emir has betrayed you. He has refused to join me in my fight against the Christians. He has betrayed his oath to me in order to make peace with the Franks. He does not deserve your service.' He paused, gathering breath, then roared: 'Open the gates to me! I have come for Damascus!'

There was silence, broken only by the nickering of horses and the distant call of birds. None of the men on the wall moved. Then the gate opened inward, groaning on its hinges. A man rode out, unarmed and dressed in a ceremonial silk caftan. As he came closer, John recognized him as Yusuf's father, Ayub. Behind him came four armed men on foot, leading a prisoner in chains. The prisoner was a young man, with fat cheeks and a carefully trimmed beard. The procession stopped before Nur ad-Din.

'Greetings, my lord,' Ayub said and bowed in the saddle. 'The city is yours. The leading nobles of Damascus have come to pay homage to you.' He gestured to the man in chains. 'And they have brought the emir, Mujir ad-Din.'

'Bring him to me,' Nur ad-Din said. Ayub waved, and the emir was pulled forward.

'Allah bless you, my lord,' Mujir ad-Din said, bowing awkwardly due to the chains about his wrists. He straightened, licking his lips nervously. 'You are welcome in my city.'

'It is not your city any more.'

'Yes, my lord.'

'You were wrong to oppose me,' Nur ad-Din told him. 'But I am a generous man. You shall have Homs and its lands to rule as emir, and you shall join me in my war against the Franks.'

Mujir ad-Din bowed again. 'Thank you, my lord.'

'Release him,' Nur ad-Din commanded, and the noble removed the emir's chains. 'Now, let us enter my city.' He spurred forward, riding towards the open gate. Ayub fell in beside him, while Yusuf and John trailed behind. Atop the wall, the people began to cheer, and white rose petals were cast from the top of the gate.

'The nobles of Damascus expect to be paid from the treasury for betraying their lord,' Ayub said to Nur ad-Din. 'And it would be wise to distribute money to the mamluk troops to ensure their loyalty.'

Nur ad-Din nodded. 'You have done well, my friend. You shall be my governor, wali of Damascus.'

'Thank you, Malik.'

'Malik? I am no king, Ayub, only a servant of Allah.' Despite his modest words, John saw that Nur ad-Din

316

wore a smile as he passed through the gentle shower of rose petals and into the city.

That evening Yusuf attended a celebratory feast in the domed chamber at the heart of the palace of Damascus. He had last visited the palace as a child, during the Franks' failed siege. Now, as then, he and Turan sat together, just to the left of the emir's dais. Yusuf had been in awe of the emir then. Now, his father sat on the dais, nodding at Nur ad-Din's lords and generals as they entered and took their seats around the edge of the circular chamber.

Nur ad-Din entered last of all, and all the men stood. As he strode into the open circle at the centre of the room, Nur ad-Din gestured to Ayub. 'Please, friend, remain seated. You have earned it.'

'I am honoured, my lord,' Ayub said as he sat. Nur ad-Din joined him on the dais. He waved to his vassals, who also sat.

Yusuf frowned. His father had opened the city through treachery and bribes. Such tactics hardly deserved praise. He caught Ayub watching him and turned away.

The feast lasted for hours and featured dozens of courses. Yusuf and Turan ate in silence, each avoiding the other's gaze. As the meal drew to a close, Ayub stood, holding up his hands for silence. 'Friends, I welcome you all, and especially our lord Nur ad-Din, emir of the great cities of Aleppo, Edessa and Damascus, a kingdom greater than that of the Seljuk Sultan himself. He has accomplished his father's dream. He has unified our lands, and today I greet him as malik, emir amongst

317

emirs, King of Syria. May Allah continue to bless him!' The men showed their approval, slapping the floor with their palms and shouting 'Malik! Malik! Malik!'

Nur ad-Din gestured for quiet and then rose. All present stood as he descended the dais and walked to the centre of the circular chamber, where he turned, looking at the men around him. 'Malik,' he said and smiled. 'So be it. But it is not I who deserves this praise, but Allah. For surely it is Allah's will that all Muslims be united against the Franks. Ayub, my faithful servant, has delivered Damascus to me without shedding a drop of blood. Could he have performed such a miracle without the blessing of Allah? And why, my friends, has Allah helped us? For one reason alone: He wishes us to free the holy city of Jerusalem and to drive the Frankish invaders into the sea. My father began this task when he conquered the Christians' kingdom of Edessa. Now that we are united, I shall complete his work!'

The men stomped the floor with their feet, and Nur ad-Din smiled. 'As ever, you have my thanks for your service, and you shall each be rewarded from the treasury of Damascus. Now go. Take your men back to their lands. But be ready for my call. For I promise you that soon enough, we shall drive the Christians from our shores!'

Nur ad-Din gestured for quiet as he rose. The emirs began to file out after him, but as Yusuf headed for the door, his father called to him. 'Come with me, Yusuf. I wish to speak.'

Yusuf followed his father out of the back of the chamber and into a small, square room bare of furniture. Through the single window Yusuf could see the great mosque of Damascus, its towering minarets and great dome shining silvery under the light of the moon.

Ayub turned to face Yusuf. 'You are displeased with me, my son?'

Yusuf lowered his eyes. 'No, Father.'

'Yes, you are. You think I have acted dishonourably in turning Mujir ad-Din's people against him and negotiating his surrender. You would have preferred a contest of arms?'

'Yes!' Yusuf met his father's gaze and held it. 'Where is the glory in bribing men to turn against their ruler? I hear that you even spread a rumour that Mujir ad-Din had slept with another man.'

'He did.'

'How could you know such things?'

'Because I paid the man, an Egyptian prostitute, to sleep with him.'

Yusuf's face wrinkled in disgust. 'I do not understand why our lord Nur ad-Din honours you so,' he said. 'You disgust me.'

Ayub raised his hand as if to slap Yusuf, but then lowered it. He sighed. 'You are young, Yusuf, so I will forgive you your anger. And you are right: intrigue is distasteful. Do not think that I enjoy it. But shedding the blood of our Muslim brothers is still more distasteful. You heard Nur ad-Din. He wishes to drive the Franks from our lands. He will need all our people to do so.' Ayub placed a hand on Yusuf's shoulder. 'We will speak no more of it. I have a place for you here in Damascus,

319

my son. I need someone that I trust to serve as my deputy.'

Yusuf shook his head. 'I must return to govern my lands and to train my men. When Nur ad-Din marches on the Franks, I must be ready to join him.'

'Then go to him when he calls. Until then, your place is here with me.'

'And what of Turan?' Yusuf asked. 'He is the oldest.'

'Your brother will return with Nur ad-Din to Aleppo. He hopes to be made emir of Baalbek.' Ayub sighed. 'Turan is brave, but he does not have your wisdom. Shirkuh told me how you handled Tell Bashir. I need you to do the same here. Mujir ad-Din's family has ruled Damascus for decades. Many of the men here are still loyal to him.'

'I am sure you can pay them,' Yusuf sneered. 'You seem to be good at that.'

Ayub slapped him. 'I am your father! You will show me respect.'

'You are my father, but you are not my lord.' Yusuf glared at him. 'I will go to my lands until Nur ad-Din calls for me.' He began to leave, but Ayub grabbed his arm.

'You are my son, Yusuf. If you stay in Damascus, then the city will be yours to govern when I die. Think on that.'

Yusuf shrugged off his father's hand. 'I wish for more than to govern Damascus, Father. I will be more than a mere wali.'

Ayub's eyebrows rose. 'What then? You would dare challenge our lord?'

'No, but there are other kingdoms, Father. Cilicia. Egypt.'

'Ha! You are no pharaoh, my son. You are a Kurd. Do not forget your place. I am lucky to have risen so high. We owe everything to Nur ad-Din.'

'I do not owe him my honour, and I will not stay in Damascus if it means that I must serve you.' Yusuf locked eyes with his father, and the two faced one another in silence. Finally, Ayub looked away.

'Very well,' he sighed. 'Return to your lands. Perhaps it is for the best.'

Chapter 13

Yusuf's breath hung in the air as he rode across white fields towards Aleppo, its distant walls dusted with snow that shone pink under the morning sun. Yusuf had spent the past year and more in Tell Bashir, collecting tribute and training his men. Now, Nur ad-Din had called for him. The malik was gathering his emirs in preparation for war. Eager to arrive for the campaign season, Yusuf had left as soon as the first tender green shoots had appeared in the wheat fields. He had ridden fast, keeping only John, Qaraqush and Al-Mashtub for company and leaving the rest of his mamluks and Faridah to follow at a slower pace. The snows had hit them on their first day out of Tell Bashir.

'This weather does not bode well,' Qaraqush murmured. 'A bad harvest will mean little money for the campaign season.'

'It's only a dusting,' Yusuf replied. 'Inshallah, the crops will not suffer.' He glanced at John, who rode with his eyes fixed on the distant walls. He had been quiet throughout the trip from Tell Bashir. 'Come,'

Yusuf said. 'The sooner we're inside and before a fire, the better.' He spurred his horse to a trot, and the others followed.

Yusuf nodded to the guards as they passed through the Jew's Gate and into the narrow streets. The city was quiet, and Yusuf could clearly hear the crunch of their horses' hooves in the snow. They crossed the deserted square at the heart of the city and clattered across the drawbridge that spanned the moat at the base of the citadel. They rode up the steep causeway, and as they approached the gate, the guards stepped aside for Yusuf.

The oval field that lay at the centre of the citadel grounds was crowded with mamluks on horseback, training on a course that had been set up near the periphery of the turf. Yusuf watched one of the riders gallop past, bow in hand. The rider jumped a low wooden barrier and, without slowing, drew an arrow from the quiver on his back and fired it at a suit of stuffed chainmail, complete with false head and helmet. The arrow hit the mannequin in the shoulder, and the mamluk galloped past, whooping victoriously.

'Not bad,' John said.

'*Hmph*,' Qaraqush snorted. 'I never saw an enemy killed by a blow to the shoulder.'

As Yusuf spurred his horse past the crowd of mamluks, he noticed that one of them was staring at him. The man was lean, his black hair and beard worn short. Yusuf looked more closely and blinked in recognition. 'Khaldun!'

'Yusuf!' Khaldun rode over Yusuf and clasped his arm. 'It has been too long, old friend.'

'Too long, indeed. You look well.'

Khaldun grinned. 'And I am the newly appointed Emir of Baalbek.' His smile faded suddenly. 'I am sorry, Yusuf. I know that Turan wanted the post.'

'It is no less than you deserve.'

Khaldun placed his right hand over his heart and bowed slightly to signal his thanks for the compliment. Then he gestured towards John. 'This is the ifranji who leads your personal guard, the one they call Yusuf's shadow?'

Yusuf nodded. 'His name is John.'

Khaldun rode forward and clasped John's arm. 'I have heard much about you.'

'We met once before,' John said quietly. 'In Baalbek.' Khaldun's forehead creased; he clearly did not remember. 'There is no reason for you to remember me. I was a slave then.'

'Tell me about your wife,' Yusuf said to Khaldun. 'How is my sister?'

'Zimat is here in Aleppo, and she is well,' Khaldun replied, then scowled. 'She has borne me two girls.'

'Then surely a boy will be next.'

'Inshallah,' Khaldun said. 'You must come to visit her. I have invited Nur ad-Din to my home tomorrow night to thank him for granting me Baalbek. Turan will be there, too. You should come. It will be just like old times.'

Yusuf smiled. 'I will be there.'

The sun was just setting the next day when Yusuf left the citadel, John riding at his side. Khaldun had sent a mamluk for them, and they followed the man down the long causeway and out into Aleppo's main square, which was dotted here and there with farmers packing up their carts. They left the square on a street that dead-ended after a hundred yards. The mamluk headed right, into a narrow alleyway with tall walls rising on either side. As Yusuf and John entered, the gate that protected the homes in the alleyway from thieves swung shut behind them. They rode past several wooden gates before coming to one that was open. The mamluk led them through into a courtyard with a fountain at the centre and tall palms growing around the edges. Turan had entered ahead of them and was dismounting his horse.

'Greetings, Turan,' Yusuf said as he slid from the saddle.

Turan nodded back. 'Brother.'

Their mamluk guide gestured to a room built against the outer wall of the villa. 'Your servant can wait there.' John nodded and headed that way.

Yusuf and Turan followed the mamluk across the courtyard and into Khaldun's home. They found themselves in a large, thickly carpeted room lit by braziers burning in the corners. Nur ad-Din was already there, seated on cushions across from the doorway. To his left sat Khaldun and a man that Yusuf did not recognize. The man had handsome features: a strong jaw, dark eyes, a smallish nose, and a carefully groomed brown beard. To Nur ad-Din's left sat Asimat, and beside her Zimat and another woman, short and plump with broad hips, large breasts and brown skin the colour of desert sands after rain.

'Yusuf!' Zimat exclaimed when she saw her brother. She rose and crossed the room to embrace him. There were tears in her eyes.

'Greetings, Sister. You are well?'

'I am glad to see you. That is all.'

Yusuf gently extricated himself from her embrace. He bowed to Nur ad-Din. 'Malik,' he said, then turned to Khaldun. 'Thank you for inviting me, my friend.'

'Malik,' Turan murmured, also bowing to Nur ad-Din.

'Yusuf, this is Usama bin Munqidh, the emir of Shaizar,' Khaldun said, gesturing to the man beside him.

'A pleasure to meet you,' Yusuf said.

'And you,' Usama replied. 'I have heard much about you.'

'And this,' Khaldun gestured to the woman beside Zimat, 'is my second wife, Nadhira.'

'My lord,' she whispered, nodding in Yusuf's direction.

'Now, please sit,' Khaldun said, waving them to their places. Yusuf sat across from Nur ad-Din, beside Usama. Turan sat to his left, beside Nadhira.

Servants entered and placed steaming bread and a dip of roasted eggplant and ground walnuts on the small tables next to each guest. 'In the name of Allah,' the diners murmured as they each tore off a piece of bread and began to eat. As he dipped his bread, Yusuf stole a sidelong glance at Asimat. Their eyes met, and he looked quickly away. He glanced at Turan, who was talking to Nadhira in hushed tones. Yusuf looked away as Nur ad-Din began to speak.

'Usama has recently returned from a trip to the Frankish court in Jerusalem,' he said.

'What was it like?' Yusuf asked.

'A nest of vipers,' Usama replied. 'King Baldwin's mother seeks to rule despite her son. A few years ago, he had to lead an army against Jerusalem to reclaim his throne from her. Still, her faction intrigues. And that is just within the king's family. The Templars and the Hospitallers, Tripoli, Antioch and Jerusalem, all are at odds with one another. King Baldwin is at his wit's end, and in his case, he did not have very far to go to get there. His brother Amalric has all the brains, but the man is cursed with a stutter and fits of laughter.'

'We should move against them,' Turan said. 'They are divided and weak.'

'But we have a treaty with the Frankish king, Baldwin,' Yusuf noted.

Nur ad-Din frowned. 'Yes, and I will honour my word. But the Franks, if all goes well, will not honour theirs. That is why Usama visited Jerusalem. One of the reasons,' he concluded with a wink.

Usama spread his hands. 'I have no idea what you mean. I visited Jerusalem only to serve you, my lord.'

Nur ad-Din laughed. 'Me and the ladies of Jerusalem. I know you too well, Usama. I'll wager that there's more than one Frank in Jerusalem who will be expecting a suspiciously dark-skinned child.'

All eyes turned to Usama. 'How can I help it,' he asked, 'when their women are so obliging, and their men so lacking in honour?'

'Ah ha, you see!' Nur ad-Din exclaimed. 'You are a scoundrel.'

'Do tell,' Asimat said, her eyebrows raised.

'If you insist, my lady,' Usama said with a smile. 'Just a few days ago, on my way back from Jerusalem, I passed through the valley of the Kadisha, where I found myself in the bed of a kind Frankish lady, the wife of a wine merchant.' He paused as the servants entered with two more dishes – fragrant, roasted lamb with chickpeas and onions, and a dish of oranges and figs.

'And how did you happen to find yourself in her bed?' Khaldun asked.

'It was an arduous journey,' Usama said with a wink. 'I was tired, which is what I told her husband when he returned and found us together. "What are you doing with my wife?" he demanded. I told him that I had come in to rest. I found the bed made up, so I lay down to sleep. "And my wife slept with you?" he asked. "The bed is hers," I replied. "How could I prevent her from getting into her own bed?" The wine merchant, as you might imagine, grew quite upset at this. His face turned red and he shook his fist at me. And do you know what he said?'

'I'll kill you here and now?' Yusuf offered. Usama shook his head.

'I'll have your balls for this, you Saracen bastard?' Nur ad-Din suggested.

'Not even close.' Usama grinned as he anticipated the punch line.

'Did he beat his wife for her infidelity?' Khaldun asked.

'No,' Usama said. 'He shook his fist and roared, "By God, if you do it again I will take you to court!"'

There was a moment of silence, and then Nur ad-Din began to roar with laughter. One by one, the others joined him, all except Turan and Nadhira. Yusuf examined his brother, who looked away and forced an unconvincing laugh.

'But surely not all Franks are so permissive,' Asimat said when the hilarity had subsided. 'There must be some with a sense of honour.'

Usama nodded. 'I have a theory regarding this. The longer the Franks remain in our lands, the more they adopt our ways. Eventually, they may even become civilized.'

'Ridiculous,' Turan snorted. 'They will always be savages. It is in their nature.'

'I am not so sure,' Yusuf said. 'I have a Frank amongst my men, a former slave. When I bought him, he was as dirty and savage as the rest of his kind. Now he dresses as we do. He reads and speaks Arabic. He is as civilized as any of us.'

'You see!' Usama declared.

Asimat turned her dark eyes upon Yusuf. 'I should like to meet this Frank of yours.'

'Of course.'

'But is he a jealous man?' Khaldun asked.

'I do not know,' Yusuf said. 'I have never seen him with a woman.'

'This is no man. He is a saint,' Nur ad-Din declared. 'Or a eunuch!' He chuckled at his own joke.

'And he proves nothing,' Asimat added. 'He may be

civilized, but we know nothing of his sense of honour.'
She paused, glancing at Nur ad-Din. 'Perhaps the Franks
are not wrong to give their women more freedom.'

Nur ad-Din's eyebrows shot up. 'Freedom for what,
Wife?' he demanded, his voice rising. 'To be prostitutes
and whores? To bear other men's children? No, women
must be protected. Their place is in the home.' He met
Asimat's eyes. 'The good wife is the one who bears many
sons. You do not need freedom to do that.'

'Well said,' Khaldun agreed, slapping the floor for
emphasis.

Asimat flushed red. 'I see,' she said tersely. 'I am not
feeling well, Husband. Please excuse me.' Nur ad-Din
nodded, and Asimat rose.

'Makin!' Nur ad-Din called, and a mamluk stepped
into the room. 'Escort Asimat back to the palace.' Asimat
pulled her veil over her face and followed the mamluk
out into the courtyard.

'May Nadhira and I also be excused, Husband?'
Zimat asked Khaldun. He nodded, and the two women
rose. 'We will leave you men to your talk. Good-night,
brothers,' Zimat said. She gave a small bow, and they
left.

'I fear I will have no peace tonight,' Nur ad-Din said
with a sigh when they had gone. 'I have made Asimat
unhappy.' He cocked his head as a thought came to him.
'She seems to like you well enough, Yusuf. Perhaps you
can amuse her. You will visit her, tomorrow.'

Yusuf's eyes went wide. 'Are you sure, my lord?'

Nur ad-Din smiled. 'You are an honourable man. I
am sure I can trust you. But remember this,' he added,

and his smile faded. 'I am no Frankish wine merchant. If you touch my wife, I will have your head.'

John shivered in the chill night air as he stepped out into the courtyard, leaving the mamluks behind him in the gatehouse. The men were laughing and joking as they played at dice, but John had no stomach for their good spirits. He walked to the fountain at the centre of the courtyard and stood staring at the main door into the villa, light peaking out around its edges. Zimat was there, just beyond that door. How long had it been since he last saw her? Three years? And now she was married with children. John doubted if she would even remember him. He sighed and looked up at the bright stars above.

The door to the house opened, spilling bright light into the courtyard. A mamluk stepped out, followed by a veiled woman. John's heart quickened. He examined her closely, and their eyes met as she passed around the far side of the fountain. The woman looked quickly away. She was not Zimat. John watched as she stepped into a litter. As the gate swung open, four burly mamluks emerged from the gatehouse and carried the litter away. The gate was just swinging closed when John heard a creaking sound behind him. He turned to see a veiled woman standing in a shadowy doorway that opened into the courtyard from the side.

'Zimat?' John breathed.

'John,' the woman whispered. 'Come quickly.'

John stepped through the door, and the woman closed it behind him. She took his hand and led him down a dimly lit hallway and into a bedroom on the right. She shut the door and removed her veil as she turned to face him. It was Zimat. Her face was thinner and her features sharper than when John had last seen her, but she had the same enchanting, dark eyes. John opened his mouth to speak, but no words came. His mouth felt dry and his heart pounded. He had played this moment out a million times in his mind, but now that it had come, he felt awkward and confused.

Zimat stepped close. 'I thought you would be happy to see me, John. Surely you have not forgotten me.'

'Of course not.' He embraced her, and she pressed her head against his chest. Her hair had been oiled and smelled of jasmine, as he remembered. After a moment she began to sob quietly, her shoulders shaking. 'What is wrong?' John asked. 'What has happened?'

'Do you still love me?' Zimat asked.

'You know I do,' John whispered and kissed her. Her lips were soft, and her mouth, when she opened it to him, tasted of honey. But after a moment she pulled away to once more bury her face in his chest.

'I never stopped loving you,' she murmured, 'even when I was in the arms of my husband.'

'Your husband—' John's brow furrowed, and he gently pushed Zimat away. 'I should go. Khaldun will be missing you.'

'No, he is more interested in his new wife, Nadhira. He has not visited my bed in weeks.'

'Why? Surely he is pleased with you.'

Zimat lowered her head. 'I have borne him two

332

daughters, but no sons. It is not my fault. None of Khaldun's concubines has produced a male child.'

'I see. So now you come to me for comfort,' John said, his voice hardening. 'And I was fool enough to believe you loved me.' He stepped past her and put his hand on the door. 'I will not be your toy, Zimat. And I will not put both our lives at risk just so you may spite your husband.'

Zimat grabbed his arm. 'Wait! There is more that I must tell you.' John lowered his hand. 'Khaldun's new wife is not faithful to him. She sleeps with another, hoping he will give her a son.'

'Why tell me this, not your husband?'

'Because he would not believe me, and because Yusuf will want to know. The man that Nadhira lays with is Turan.'

John's eyes widened. 'Are you sure?'

Zimat nodded. 'I have seen them together.'

'You were right to tell me,' John said.

'You will tell Yusuf?'

'Yes.'

'Thank you.' Zimat stepped closer to John and placed a hand on his chest. She looked up at him with her dark eyes. 'I have missed you, John. May I see you again?'

John hesitated. He knew he should say 'no', but as he looked into her eyes, he felt his resistance crumble. 'Yes,' he said at last, 'but how?'

'Come to my chambers at night.'

'I cannot. It will cost both of us our lives if I am seen.'

Zimat flashed a brilliant smile. 'You won't be. I will tell you how.'

The next morning Yusuf presented himself at the door to the harem, which occupied its own wing of the palace. He was met by the tawashi – the chief eunuch in the service of Nur ad-Din's wives. 'You are expected,' he said, and led Yusuf to Asimat's chambers. At the door, he paused and turned to Yusuf. 'I will be watching,' he said. Then he knocked and pushed the door open. Sunlight from a row of broad windows on the far wall spilled into the room, illuminating the saffron-yellow carpet, a canopied bed in the corner and a large loom at which two servant girls sat, passing a pair of shuttles back and forth as they wove red and gold threads into a weft of tautly stretched, white wool fibres. The only other furniture was a washbasin. Asimat sat in one of the windows, reading. She looked up from her book and frowned.

'Forgive me for disturbing you, my lady,' the tawashi said with a bow. 'May I present Yusuf ibn Ayub. He has come at the request of lord Nur ad-Din.' The eunuch bowed again and backed out, closing the door behind him.

The girls at the loom kept working, ignoring Yusuf. Asimat stared at him fixedly. The soft morning light illuminated her from behind, outlining her form underneath a thin caftan of green silk. Yusuf shifted awkwardly and looked away, then looked back. 'Well?' Asimat demanded.

'Nur ad-Din—'

'My husband has sent you to cheer me,' Asimat said, cutting him off. 'I do not need cheering. You may go.' She returned to her book. Yusuf did not move, and after a moment, Asimat looked up. 'Why are you still here?'

'I am sorry, Khatun, but you are misinformed. You husband did indeed send me to cheer you, but that is not why I am here. I have come because I wish to speak with you.'

Asimat's eyebrows rose. 'That is unfortunate, because I do not wish to speak with you.'

Yusuf felt himself flush, but he held his ground. 'In that case, my lady, I will do the talking.'

Asimat sighed in exasperation. 'Since it seems I cannot get rid of you, what did you wish to discuss?'

'Damascus. You visited the city when Nur ad-Din took it.'

Asimat stared at him for a moment. 'Very well,' she said, rising from her seat in the window. 'Come, we will speak in the gardens. Kaniz, bring me my veil.' One of the servants left the room and came back with a white silk veil, which Asimat pulled over her face. She opened the door to find the tawashi waiting just outside. 'I wish to visit the gardens,' she told him.

'Of course, Khatun,' the eunuch said. He clapped loudly, and a moment later a dozen eunuch guards marched into the hallway. They surrounded Yusuf and Asimat as they left the palace, heading across the broad open space within the citadel towards the gardens on the far side. Asimat walked ahead of Yusuf and did not speak. She did not turn to look as they passed the mamluks training in the middle of the field. Finally they came to the gardens. Asimat took a gravel path that passed through an orange grove and into a large rose garden containing dozens of varieties in shades of red, white, yellow, pink and orange. The eunuch guards waited outside the garden.

Asimat stopped before a rose bush covered in loose, pink blossoms. She picked a flower and smelled it. 'A damask rose. They were first cultivated in Damascus. They always remind me of my childhood.'

'I, too, spent much of my childhood in Damascus,' Yusuf said. 'My family lived in Baalbek, but we had a home in the city, not far from the great mosque.'

'I know it well,' Asimat said. 'I was rarely allowed outside the palace. Most of what I know of the city, I saw from the windows of my room. It faced the mosque. I used to watch the people in the market square behind the mosque and wonder what it would be like to be one of them.'

'Surely you do not regret your place in life. You are married to the greatest ruler in all of the East, perhaps in the world.'

Asimat sighed and dropped the rose. 'No, I do not regret my place,' she said as she resumed walking. 'But I remember once visiting the orchards of Damascus to pick mangos. I must have been five or six. As I was carried to the orchards in a litter, I saw two children my age playing in one of the gardens beside the road. They seemed so happy.'

'I too visited those orchards,' Yusuf said. 'They are beautiful, a paradise. But the people there are not so happy. They lead a hard life.'

Asimat nodded. 'I miss Damascus. Seeing it again after all these years was hard. I had not visited it since my marriage. That was long ago, just before the Christian siege.'

'How old were you?'

'Fourteen, barely a woman. Nur ad-Din was more than twice my age. I was terrified of him. I begged my father not to send me away, but it was an important alliance. It could not wait.' She smiled. 'I was wrong to be afraid. Nur ad-Din is a kind man.'

'And yet he says you are unhappy.'

'I have not given him a son,' Asimat explained. 'You heard Nur ad-Din last night. That is my one duty as a wife, and I have failed.'

'You are young still.'

Asimat shook her head. 'After eight years, what hope do I have? I have donated to the mosques and prayed to Allah, but my prayers have not been answered. I fear they never will be.' They walked on in silence, their feet crunching on the gravel, until they reached the end of the path. 'What of you?' Asimat asked. 'Do you have a wife?'

'Not yet.'

'You should.' Asimat turned and began to retrace their path through the garden. 'A man needs sons to carry on his legacy.'

'I have no legacy, not yet.'

'But you are Emir of Tell Bashir and a trusted councillor of Nur ad-Din.'

Yusuf shook his head. 'I have accomplished nothing. My father and uncle started with no lands and no name. Shirkuh has become atabek of Nur ad-Din's armies, and my father is wali of Damascus. I shall surpass them both.'

'I do not doubt it. Nur ad-Din is right to expect great things from you. I see much of him in you.'

Yusuf met her eyes. 'Do you?'

'You have the same confidence, the same thirst for greatness. And you will have your chance in the years to come. We will go to war with the Franks. If you survive, you will rise to great heights.'

Yusuf grinned. 'I do not plan on dying.'

'I thought not,' Asimat said, smiling back. They had reached the end of the path leading from the rose garden, and the eunuch guards stood nearby. Asimat stopped and turned to face Yusuf. 'I must apologize for my rudeness earlier. I have enjoyed our talk, Yusuf. We shall speak again soon, I hope?'

'If Nur ad-Din wills it, my lady.'

'Until then.' Asimat gestured to the guards, and they surrounded her as she headed towards the palace.

Yusuf picked a rose bloom and absent-mindedly plucked its petals as he watched her walk away. She was halfway back to the palace when she glanced back over her shoulder towards him. Yusuf smiled. He held the rose to his nose and inhaled. 'Asimat,' he whispered.

Yusuf was still smiling when he returned to his chamber. He found Faridah waiting for him. She stood at the window, looking out towards the grounds of the citadel. She was wearing a thin cotton robe, through which Yusuf could see the curve of her back and buttocks. 'I saw the two of you from here,' she said, her back still to him.

Yusuf crossed the room and placed his hands around

her waist. He kissed her neck. 'Surely you are not jealous of Asimat.'

'Of course not.' Faridah pulled away and went to sit on the bed. 'I owe you my life, and I ask for nothing more. I know that there will be other women.' She met Yusuf's eyes. 'But Asimat is the wife of your lord.'

Yusuf came over and sat beside her. 'I am not a fool,' he said.

Faridah touched his shoulder. 'And I am not blind. I have seen Asimat. She is beautiful, and she is young.'

Yusuf reached beneath Faridah's robe and ran his hand up her side to caress her breast. 'You are hardly old.'

'But I cannot bear children, and soon you will want a son.' She looked away. 'You will want someone younger.'

Yusuf touched her cheek and turned her face towards him. There were tears in her eyes. He brushed them away and kissed her. 'You will always have a place in my household, Faridah.'

'And in your heart?' Faridah whispered. Yusuf nodded. 'Then that is all I ask.' She kissed him, sliding her arms around his back and pulling him down on top of her. He pulled her robe aside and began to kiss her breast.

There was a loud knock at the door, and Yusuf pulled away. Faridah sat up, pulling her robe back around her. 'What is it?' Yusuf demanded.

The door opened, and John entered. 'Excuse me, Yusuf. I must speak with you.' He glanced at Faridah. 'In private.'

'I have no secrets from Faridah,' Yusuf replied, rising. 'What is it?'

'Your brother, Turan. He has committed adultery with Khaldun's new wife, Nadhira.'

'Zimat's husband,' Yusuf whispered, his jaw tight. He went to the window and gripped the sill as he looked out. Turan again. Always Turan. The fool would be the ruin of their family. Yusuf wondered if he truly loved Nadhira or if he were using her to get revenge against Khaldun for winning Baalbek. It hardly mattered. Yusuf turned back to John. 'How do you know this?'

John refused to meet his gaze. 'I cannot say.'

'Cannot say? I am your lord!' Yusuf snapped. 'You will tell me.'

'I am a free man,' John replied quietly. 'I will not tell you.'

Yusuf's eyes narrowed. 'Was it Zimat?' John said nothing, and Yusuf crossed the room to him. 'I will say this only once: Zimat is my sister. If you stain her honour, I will kill you myself.'

'I understand.'

Yusuf nodded, then turned away to pace the room. 'Send for Turan,' he told John. 'I will know the truth of this from him.'

'He is not in the citadel. I saw him leave for town earlier today.'

Yusuf stopped pacing. 'Do you think he went to—?' John nodded. 'Saddle my horse. I will go to Khaldun's home.'

'I will meet you at the stables,' John said and left.

Faridah rose and went to Yusuf, putting her arms around him from behind. 'What will you do?' she asked.

Yusuf picked up his sword belt and pulled it tight around his waist. 'I do not know.'

'Open up!' Yusuf shouted as he pounded on the gate of Khaldun's villa. John stood behind him, holding the reins of their horses. 'I am Yusuf ibn Ayub, come to see Khaldun. Open this gate!'

The gate creaked open a few feet to reveal two eunuch guards. 'Our lord is not here,' one of them said in a high voice. 'He left for Baalbek this morning.'

'Then I will see my sister, Zimat.' Yusuf tried to push past the guards, but they grabbed his arms, stopping him.

'You cannot enter,' the first guard said. 'Khaldun has told us to admit no guests while he is absent.'

'Not even my brother, Turan,' Yusuf growled. The two guards exchanged a nervous glance. 'Shall I tell Khaldun what you have allowed to take place in his absence?'

The second guard paled. 'I will take you to your sister. Come.'

Yusuf turned to John. 'Make sure no one leaves or goes to warn Turan.' John nodded, and Yusuf followed the eunuch guard inside. They crossed the villa court-yard and entered the carpeted room where Yusuf had feasted the night before. They passed through into a cor-ridor on the right, then turned sharply right again into a long hallway with rooms opening off to either side. The guard knocked at one of the doors.

'Enter,' Zimat called from inside, and the guard pushed the door open. Zimat, dressed in a simple white caftan, stood at the centre of the room. 'Brother!' she exclaimed. 'Thank Allah you have come.' She went to Yusuf and embraced him.

Yusuf gently pushed her away. 'Is it true?' Zimat nodded. 'Why did you tell John and not me?'

'I wanted to tell you, but I did not know how. Khaldun was there, and he would never believe me.' Her face twisted into a scowl. 'That slut Nadhira has blinded him.'

'You should not have spoken to John,' Yusuf told her. 'He is a man and a Frank. You could be whipped for seeing him alone.'

Zimat lowered her head. 'I did not know what else to do. Someone had to know.'

'Very well. But you are never to see John again. You must promise me.'

Zimat looked away. 'I promise.'

'Now tell me, do you have proof of what you say about Turan?'

'You will see for yourself.' Zimat led him down the hallway to another door. 'This is Nadhira's room,' she whispered.

Yusuf tried the handle. The door was locked. He reared back and kicked the door, splintering the wood around the lock. The door swung open to reveal a room dominated by a large bed. Nadhira was on the bed, her legs wrapped around Turan, who lay naked on top of her.

'I said we were not to be disturbed!' Turan roared as

he turned towards the door. His eyes widened when he saw Yusuf. 'Brother!' he gasped.

'What have you done?' Yusuf roared, drawing his sword. Turan scrambled from the bed and backed into the far corner, his hands over his crotch. Nadhira screamed and pulled a silk sheet over herself. 'You have dishonoured our family,' Yusuf growled.

'The whore seduced me!' Turan protested.

'He lies,' Nadhira sobbed. 'He forced himself upon me. He made me.'

Yusuf looked from one to the other. His lips curled back in a snarl as he felt rage build within him. He stepped around the bed towards Turan, who cowered in the corner. Yusuf raised his sword, but then stopped. Shirkuh had told him that he must not allow his passions to rule him. Yusuf closed his eyes and forced himself to breath deeply. When he opened his eyes, his features had calmed, his mouth setting in a hard line. He picked up Turan's caftan and tossed it to him. 'Get dressed.'

'What will you do to me, Brother?' Turan asked as he pulled on his caftan.

'Nothing.' Yusuf turned away.

Zimat grabbed his arm. 'What are you doing?' she demanded. 'He has shamed the family! Father would have him beaten!'

Yusuf pulled away from her. 'I am not Father.'

'Then I will not be punished?' Turan asked.

Yusuf looked back to him. 'You will come with me to witness Nadhira's fate. That will be your punishment.'

Nadhira left the bed and approached Yusuf. 'And

343

what will happen to me?' she asked, her hands trembling and her eyes wide with fright.

'I do not know,' Yusuf replied. 'That is for your husband to decide.'

Yusuf stood with Turan and John in the central market square of Aleppo on a warm spring morning, the air heavy with the scent of oranges from the trees that ringed the square. The space was crowded as usual, but today the people had not come for the market. Veiled women stood whispering at the edge of the crowd, their children playing around them. At the centre of the square, grim-faced men stood silently in groups of threes and fours, their eyes on the street that led from Khaldun's home. In their hands, the men held fist-sized rocks.

A murmur of anticipation ran through the crowd as they caught sight of Khaldun approaching on foot, his hand clamped around Nadhira's arm as he pulled her along beside him. He had returned yesterday after a week in Baalbek, and Yusuf had gone immediately to tell him of Nadhira and Turan. Khaldun had not questioned Yusuf's word. He had simply nodded and told Yusuf to meet him in the square after morning prayers. Yusuf noticed that Khaldun, too, carried a white stone in his hand.

'Do we have to be here?' John asked.

Yusuf nodded. 'It is my duty. I am the witness to the crime.'

The crowd parted as Khaldun dragged Nadhira to the centre of the square. She was dressed in a white cotton caftan, with no veil, and her eyes were red from weeping.

The crowd closed around her. Yusuf pushed his way to the front, pulling Turan after him. Khaldun released Nadhira and left her standing alone as he turned to face Yusuf.

'This woman has been accused of adultery,' Khaldun said, speaking loudly so that the crowd could hear. 'Yusuf ibn Ayub, you witnessed her crime. Do you swear by Allah that she is guilty?'

The square fell silent. The men in the crowd seemed to be holding their breath as they waited for Yusuf to speak. He looked at Nadhira, who shook so strongly with fear that she was barely able to stand. Yusuf suddenly felt sick. He looked away from Nadhira and said softly, 'I swear it.'

'The punishment for her crime is death by stoning,' Khaldun said. He moved to stand across from Yusuf and raised the stone he held. As the wronged party, it was his duty to cast the first stone.

Nadhira took a step towards Khaldun. 'Please, Husband—' she sobbed. 'Forgive me.'

Khaldun said nothing, but his face contorted in a grimace as he hurled the rock at her. Nadhira cried out in pain as it caught her in the shoulder, spinning her around. Her screaming was cut short as another rock smashed into her mouth, breaking her jaw and spattering blood across Yusuf and Turan. Turan looked away, his face pale. Yusuf grabbed his jaw and turned his head, forcing him to watch. Nadhira lay curled on the ground, moaning as rock after rock slammed into her with a sickening crunch. Her eyes fixed on Turan, then a rock hit her in the face, crushing her right eye and knocking her unconscious. The stones continued to fall until her broken, bloodied body was barely recognizable as human.

Yusuf turned and pushed his way through to the edge of the crowd, where he bent over and vomited. He wiped his mouth with the back of his hand and rose to find that the crowd was already dispersing, the men hurrying away as if ashamed of what they had done. John and Turan remained standing near Khaldun, who knelt in the centre of the square, cradling the wrecked body of his wife in his arms.

Turan went to Khaldun and placed his hand on his shoulder. 'Forgive me,' he pleaded, his voice shaking.

Khaldun looked up, his eyes wet with tears. 'Leave me,' his said, his voice breaking. His lips curled back into a snarl. 'Get out of my sight, you bastard!'

Turan backed away, and Yusuf grabbed his arm, pulling him towards the citadel. When they reached the moat, Turan stopped and turned to Yusuf, who was surprised to see tears rolling down his brother's cheeks. He had never seen Turan cry.

'I – I loved her, Brother,' Turan said. 'And she is dead because of me. I cannot live with her blood on my hands.'

'You must make amends,' Yusuf told him.

'How? I will do whatever you ask.'

'I need capable men. Will you serve as my second in command?'

Turan hesitated. His hands clenched into fists, and Yusuf half expected his brother to refuse, to explode in a rage. But his hands relaxed and Turan nodded. 'You could have killed me. I owe you my life.'

'Good.' Yusuf put his hand on his brother's shoulder. 'But that is not enough, Turan. It is not in my power to forgive you for what you have done to the two of them.' He nodded towards the square. Khaldun was still there alone, Nadhira clasped to his chest. 'For that, you must look to Allah.'

That night John sat on the bed in his room in the citadel palace, staring at the candle flickering on the table before him and fiddling with a copper fal. His hair was still wet from washing, and he wore a fresh white caftan. He glanced out of the window to where the crescent moon was rising above the horizon. He crossed himself and rose. Yusuf was dining with Nur ad-Din, and John knew that Khaldun was with them. Nur ad-Din was seeking to cheer him after his wife's betrayal, and so they would dine late into the night, which meant that John had more than enough time. He ran a hand through his long blond hair, then picked up his sword and pulled it part way from the scabbard, checking his reflection in the blade. The lines of his face were harder than they had once been, and his short blond beard fuller. He sheathed the sword and buckled it around his waist. Then he blew out the candle and left.

The gate leading out of the citadel was guarded by four men, lit by torches burning in brackets. John recognized al-Mashtub amongst the men and nodded. The huge mamluk winked back.

'What are you doing leaving so late?' he asked. 'Off to see a woman?'

'I am going to church, to pray,' John replied as he

strode past and headed down the ramp leading to the moat.

'Give her my regards,' al-Mashtub called out behind him, and there was laughter in the gatehouse.

John headed across the moat and out into the city. The cobbled surface of the main square stretched away before him, empty save for a single homeless beggar, slumped in the middle and calling out for alms. John passed by the man and turned left, walking to the end of a wide avenue. A narrow alley, barred by an iron gate, opened off to his right. John looked both ways, then quickly scaled the gate, avoiding the sharp spikes at the top, and dropped over the far side. The alleyway was so dark that John could hardly see his outstretched hand before him. A dozen feet ahead, he tripped over a sleeping figure, who cursed him loudly before rolling over and dropping back to sleep. John continued on his way, counting his steps. After thirty-two paces he stopped. He felt the wooden gate to his left. Unless he was mistaken, this was the home of Khaldun, and Zimat.

John could see the top of the wall above him, silver in the moonlight. It was at least ten feet high. Luckily, the alleyway was no more than four feet across, and putting his feet against one wall and his hands against the other, he was able to slowly walk his way upward until he grasped the edge of the roof. Gripping it tight, he kicked off from the wall behind him and scrambled on to the flat roof of Khaldun's villa. He crawled to the opposite side and looked down into the courtyard. The fountain burbled in the darkness, but he saw no movement. John took a deep breath and then dropped off the roof. His boots sounded loudly as he landed, and he scrambled back and crouched in a shadowy corner, his heart pounding.

A door in the gatehouse opened, shedding soft candle-light into the courtyard and illuminating the low fountain. A guard in chainmail, sword in hand, stepped into the courtyard just to John's left and walked away along the periphery of the garden. He reached the far side and turned. John held his breath as the guard approached and then walked past, close enough that John could have reached out and touched him. The guard did not stop. He finished his tour of the garden and, satisfied, re-entered the gatehouse.

John exhaled in relief and stood. The door that Zimat had shown him through was on the far side of the garden, lit by the bright moon above and in clear view of the gatehouse. John whispered a prayer to the Virgin, then slipped from the shadows and hurried to the door. It was locked. Cursing under his breath, he turned and went to the main door of the villa. He tried the handle, and breathed a sigh of relief. It was open. He slipped inside and closed the door quietly behind him. Then he waited with his ear to the door. They were no sounds of alarm.

John turned away from the door to find himself in a large, carpeted entrance room with passages leading off to the left and right. He took the dark hallway to the right and crept down it. After only a few feet the passage turned to the right. John rounded the corner just as one of the doors further down the hallway opened. John quickly stepped back behind the corner.

'Yes, my lady,' he heard a female voice saying,

then the slap of sandals on stone as someone headed his way.

John retreated into the entrance room and slipped into a corner, pressing himself against the wall. A moment later, a maidservant entered. She crossed the room without even a glance to the side, and exited through the passage on the far side. As soon as she was gone, John hurried back down the hall to the door of the room she had left. 'Mother Mary, let this be the right one,' he whispered and then pushed the door open.

The room was dark, but John could make out the dim outlines of a bed with a woman lying in it. She sat up. 'Who is there?' she asked. It was Zimat's voice. 'Khaldun?'

John stepped into the room and closed the door behind him. 'It is me, John.'

'John!' Zimat rose from the bed and rushed to him, throwing herself into his arms. 'Praise Allah, you have come.' She looked up and her mouth opened as she kissed him. She took his hand and placed it on her breast.

John pulled away. 'I did not come for that, but only because I promised I would, and to tell you that we must not meet again. You know what happened to Nadhira. The same will happen to you if we are caught.'

Zimat lowered her head. 'I was there,' she whispered. 'I did not think that Khaldun would kill her. I did not wish that for her.'

'But you are your husband's first wife again,' John said gruffly. 'Isn't that what you wanted?'

'No, what I want is you, John.' She met his eyes. 'I am

property to Khaldun, no good unless I bear him a son. But you love me.'

John frowned. 'I cannot betray Yusuf, not again. We were young and foolish before, Zimat. We should not make the same mistake twice.'

'You think it a mistake?' Zimat turned away. 'Then go. You do not love me.'

John touched her shoulder. 'You know I do.'

'Then choose: you betray Yusuf, or you betray our love.' Zimat turned and put her head against his chest. 'You left me once, John. Do not leave me again.'

John hesitated, then put his arms around her. They stood silently for a moment while he stroked her hair, and then she began to untie his cloak. John took her hands, stopping her. 'But if we are discovered?'

'Then we will die together. It is a chance that I am willing to take. Are you?'

An image of Nadhira's broken body rose in John's mind, but he shook his head, dispelling the thought. How many nights had he dreamed of holding Zimat? She was right: it was a chance worth taking. He stepped forward and took her in his arms, kissing her soft lips.

Chapter 14

Yusuf stood before a bronze mirror in his palace chamber and examined his reflection. He had been to the baths, where a barber had trimmed his beard short and smoothed back his hair with sweet-smelling oil. Upon his return, he had dressed in a red satin caftan decorated with swirling patterns in silver thread. Yusuf straightened his collar, then leaned closer to the mirror and frowned at the patchiness of his beard. He went to a trunk and took out a small wooden box. He opened it, scooped out a handful of kohl – a mixture of ash and ghee – and rubbed it into his beard. He went back to the mirror and nodded in satisfaction.

'Are you ready yet?' John grumbled as he entered the room.

Yusuf quickly turned away from the mirror. 'Yes. Let's not keep her waiting.'

Yusuf led them across the palace to the harem entrance. They were expected, and the tawashi escorted them to Asimat's room. He knocked, and a moment later one of Asimat's female servants opened the door. Yusuf and John followed the tawashi into the room.

'My lady,' the eunuch declared. 'Your guests.' He withdrew, shutting the door behind him. The servant went back to the loom in the corner.

Asimat sat cross-legged, a writing table on her lap and her quill poised above the paper. She looked up and smiled. 'Yusuf! And who is this you have brought with you?'

'My friend, John,' Yusuf said with a small bow. 'You sent for us.'

'Ah yes, the civilized Frank who, you say, is immune to the charms of women,' Asimat teased. John's cheeks reddened. 'Come, sit,' Asimat continued. 'I am glad you came. I wished to see you before you departed.'

Yusuf frowned as he and John sat across from Asimat. 'Departed? I have no plans to leave Aleppo.'

'Nevertheless, you shall leave soon enough.'

'For where?'

'Frankish lands. Nur ad-Din will tell you at the council meeting tomorrow.'

'You are better informed than I, Khatun.'

'Of course. I am Nur ad-Din's wife. You see him only during council meetings or hunts. The rest of the time, he is mine,' Asimat concluded with a wink.

'Perhaps you could tell me, then, what I will be doing amongst the Franks.'

'I have told you enough already. You will find out the rest tomorrow.' Asimat turned her gaze to John. 'Is it true that you have not yet taken a woman?'

John flinched noticeably. 'It is true.'

'Is it because of your religion?'

'No, Khatun.'

'You do not like women then?'

'No – I mean yes,' John said, flustered. 'I like them.'

'I see,' Asimat mused, her head tilted to the side. 'And if you did have a woman, what would you do if you found her with another man?'

John looked away. 'I do not know.'

'Would you kill her?'

'No, my lady,' John said softly.

'What then? Imagine the woman you love in the arms of another man. What would you do?'

John's brow knit and he clenched his jaw. 'I – I do not know.'

'I see my questioning has made you uncomfortable,' Asimat said. 'You may go.'

'Thank you, Khatun.'

Asimat watched John leave, and then her eyes turned to Yusuf. 'Usama was wrong. It seems your friend remains a Frank at heart. He does not have our sense of honour.'

'Perhaps John is right.'

Asimat arched an eyebrow. 'What do you mean?'

'You have heard what happened to Emir Khaldun's wife, Nadhira?'

'The girl who was stoned.'

'It was my doing,' Yusuf said bitterly. 'There was no honour in that.'

'You should not blame yourself, Yusuf. It is our law.'

Yusuf's cheek twitched as an image of Nadhira's mangled face flashed through his mind. 'Have you ever seen a woman stoned?'

'Yes,' Asimat said quietly. They sat in silence for a moment, then her face brightened. 'But let us talk of other things. I asked you here to tell you my good news: Allah has blessed me. I am with child.'

Yusuf was surprised to find that he was disappointed, jealous of Nur ad-Din. He lowered his gaze as he struggled to compose his features. 'Praise be to Allah,' he murmured, forcing a smile.

Asimat seemed not to notice his lack of enthusiasm. 'Nur ad-Din is pleased. He will hardly let me out of his sight. He has three doctors attending to me, including a Jew who says he knows you. Ibn Jumay he is called.'

'I have known him since I was a child. I would trust my life to him before any other.'

'He tells me I must not drink wine while pregnant,' Asimat pouted, then smiled. 'But what of you? Have you found a bride yet?' Yusuf shook his head. 'You should be married soon, Yusuf. Shall I find a girl for you?'

Yusuf looked away. 'That would be most kind, Khatun,' he forced himself to say.

'It is settled, then,' Asimat said brightly. 'I will speak to Nur ad-Din. By the time you return to Aleppo, I shall have found you a wife.'

'As-salaamu 'alaykum,' Yusuf said, looking over his right shoulder while kneeling on the floor of his room. 'As-salaamu 'alaykum,' he repeated as he looked left. His morning prayers finished, he rolled up his prayer mat and went to the window. The sun was just rising over the horizon. It was time for the council meeting. He left his room, heading for the council chamber, which

355

sat atop the palace's tallest tower. Nur ad-Din said it was the only place where he could be sure they would not be overheard.

Two mamluks stood at the entrance to the narrow, spiralling staircase that wound up to the council room. They searched Yusuf for weapons, then waved him through. He hurried up the stairs, glancing through the window slits as he passed. The hill on which the citadel sat fell away steeply below the tower, and the buildings of the town appeared tiny at this height. The stairs ended at a thick wooden door, guarded by another mamluk. The guard nodded to Yusuf and pulled the door open.

The council chamber was round and twenty feet across, with arched windows on all sides. Cushions had been placed along the wall, but the half-dozen emirs present were not sitting. Yusuf recognized Usama speaking with the fat-faced eunuch, Gumushtagin. Khaldun stood just apart from them, scowling grimly. There were black rings under his eyes. Yusuf crossed over to him. 'Salaam, Khaldun. I have not seen you for many days. You have been well?'

'Well enough.'

'I am sorry about Nadhira.'

Khaldun's face twisted into a grimace. 'Sorry? For what?'

Across the room, the door opened and Nur ad-Din entered, followed by Shirkuh. The emirs fell silent. 'Welcome, my friends,' Nur ad-Din said as he crossed the room and took a seat against the wall. 'Please, be seated.'

The emirs sat in a circle in order of their seniority. Usama and Shirkuh sat to Nur ad-Din's left and right.

Yusuf found himself directly across from the king. 'I have called you here because I have received important news from the Frankish court,' Nur ad-Din said and looked to Usama.

'While last in Jerusalem,' Usama began, 'I learned that the Frankish king, Baldwin, is secretly gathering troops in the Kadisha. On my way home, I passed through Tripoli, where I saw many Frankish knights arriving from overseas. And I heard rumours of raids against the Bedouin who live on the borders of the Frankish kingdom.'

'Raids?' Gumushtagin asked. 'That would violate our treaty with Baldwin.'

Nur ad-Din nodded. 'War is coming at last. I will send word to the emirs and sheikhs telling them to gather their men. We must prepare to strike!' The assembled men nodded their agreement.

'Where will we attack?' Yusuf asked.

'Acre,' Nur ad-Din said. 'We shall take the Franks' main port, cutting their lands in half and dividing Jerusalem from Tripoli and Antioch in the north. With Acre in our power, we can then turn south to take Jerusalem. Their kingdom will fall.'

'Inshallah,' several of the emirs murmured. Others slapped the floor to show their approval. Yusuf cleared his throat. 'Excuse me, Malik, but if we strike at Acre, will this not leave Aleppo exposed?'

The emirs glared at Yusuf, but Nur ad-Din nodded. 'You are correct, Yusuf.' He turned to Shirkuh. 'Tell them our plan.'

'We will divide our army in two,' Shirkuh explained.

'I will command a force in Aleppo while Nur ad-Din will lead a larger army from Damascus. My men will march through the Kadisha valley towards Tripoli, in order to distract the Franks and block them from attacking Aleppo. When the Frankish forces move against us, then Nur ad-Din will move on Acre, taking the castle of Banyas along the way.'

Nur ad-Din grinned. 'The Frankish army will no doubt leave the Kadisha and march to relieve Acre. When they reach the city, my forces will engage them, and Shirkuh's army will then attack them from behind.' He clapped his hands together. 'They will be crushed between us.'

'A brilliant plan, Malik,' the eunuch Gumushtagin said.

'We will be rid of the Franks once and for all,' Usama agreed.

Yusuf frowned. 'But we cannot violate our treaty with the Frankish king based on rumours alone.'

'No, Yusuf,' Nur ad-Din agreed. 'We need more than rumours. That is why I am sending you to Frankish lands to find the truth of the matter. You will leave tomorrow.'

Yusuf bowed at the waist. 'I am honoured to serve you, Malik. With your permission, I will go now to prepare my men.'

'Take no more than a dozen mamluks, not enough to attract attention,' Nur ad-Din told him. 'And do not take the Frank, Juwan.'

'But he is captain of my khaskiya. It is his duty to protect me at all times.'

Nur ad-Din frowned. 'I know you think him loyal,

but he is an ifranji. He will cut your throat and run to the Franks at the first opportunity.' Several of the emirs nodded their agreement.

Yusuf met Nur ad-Din's eyes. 'Forgive me, my lord, but you do not know John as I do. I trust him with my life. He will come with me.'

Nur ad-Din said nothing. His golden eyes bore into Yusuf. Finally, the malik nodded. 'Very well, but watch him close. You may go.' Yusuf rose and opened the door. 'Wait,' Nur ad-Din called, and Yusuf turned to face him. 'Do not fail me, Yusuf. Bring me my war.'

NOVEMBER 1156: ON THE BORDER OF THE KINGDOM OF JERUSALEM

John rode beside Yusuf and Turan, their horses' hooves kicking up dust from the dry road. Behind them trailed two dozen mounted mamluks, Qaraqush at their head. They rode alongside the Orontes River, which marked the boundary between the Frankish kingdom of Jerusalem and Nur ad-Din's lands. On the eastern side were the Muslim strongholds of Shaizar, Hama and Homs. Some way off, on the opposite side of the river, stood the crusader castles of Montferrand and Krak des Chevaliers. In between was a no-man's-land roamed only by the Bedouin, who knew no lords, neither Frankish nor Muslim. Across the river and near the horizon, John spied a group of Bedouin on foot, driving a flock of sheep towards the water. He pointed to them. 'Perhaps they will know something.'

'Perhaps,' Yusuf agreed. After nearly three months of riding up and down the border from Shaizar to as far south as Banyas, they had still found no sign of Frankish troops or raiders. Yusuf looked to Turan. 'Wait here with the men. John and I will speak with the Bedouin.'

Turan frowned. 'I should come with you, not the ifranji.' Yusuf's jaw set. He locked eyes with his brother, and eventually Turan lowered his gaze. 'Let it be as you say, Brother,' he murmured. John could hardly believe his ears.

Yusuf turned to John. 'Come.' He turned into the river, and John followed, his horse's hooves kicking up a spray that sparkled in the bright sunshine. The river was deep here, and soon their horses were swimming, the cold water coming up to John's waist. They crossed to the far side without incident, and their mounts climbed up the bank, water streaming off them. Yusuf looked over to John and grinned. 'I'll race you,' he said and kicked at his horse's sides, sending it galloping over the hard-baked earth towards the Bedouin.

John spurred after him, standing in the stirrups and leaning forward, his head low against his horse's neck. He came up alongside Yusuf, grinned at him, and then shot past. He pulled up in a cloud of dust upon reaching the shepherds. Yusuf joined him a moment later. The Bedouin's sheikh – a wrinkled old man with a shepherd's crook in his hand – stepped forward and stared at them impassively. Behind him, several of the shepherds had taken bows from their backs and were stringing them. John blinked in surprise. He had seen the sheikh before.

'Sabir ibn Taqqi!' Yusuf exclaimed. It was the same

sheikh who had given them food and water years ago during their harrowing trip to Tell Bashir. 'As-salaamu 'alaykum.'

'Wa 'alaykum as-salaam, Yusuf son of Ayub,' Sabir replied. 'When I saw you last, I did not number your days long in this world. And now I find you again in great danger. There is a Frankish fortress not far from here.' He pointed towards the horizon. 'Qal'at al-Hisn – Krak des Chevaliers, the Franks call it. We passed through its shadow yesterday.'

'Did you notice anything unusual? More men? Preparations for war?'

'We kept our distance. I saw nothing.'

'Have you heard of Frankish raids against the Bedouin?'

The sheikh shook his head. 'I hear little. We have been travelling the desert from oasis to oasis. We have not visited a town in months.'

'Thank you for your help, sheikh.' Yusuf untied his purse from his belt and tossed it to Sabir. The Bedouin sheikh looked inside and whistled in appreciation.

'What is this for?'

'You saved my life. It is yours.'

Sabir shook his head. 'I only gave you hospitality as our laws dictate.' He pocketed a silver dirham and tossed the pouch back to Yusuf.

'You will always be welcome at my home,' Yusuf told the man.

Sabir nodded, then turned back towards the other Bedouin and made a clicking noise. The tribe moved on, herding their sheep past John and Yusuf.

Yusuf shook his head. 'We are wasting our time out here,' he muttered.

'We could find out more in the Frankish towns,' John suggested.

'I cannot enter uninvited. It would violate the treaty.'

John smiled. 'You cannot, but I can.'

NOVEMBER 1156: TRIPOLI

John pulled a fold of his turban down around his mouth and nose to keep out the dust as he walked behind a long line of heavily laden camels. Outside Akkar, he had joined a caravan of dusky Indians bringing spices from the East. He had followed them as they marched alongside the Kadisha River, winding their way through green fields dotted here and there with distant villages or farmhouses. The local peasants – a mix of native Christians and Saracens – were outside, preparing the soil for the spring planting. Beside the river to John's left, a peasant yelled encouragement to a bony ox as it pulled a plough through the rich earth.

'Tripoli!' one of the Indians ahead in the caravan shouted, and John squinted into the distance, trying to pick out the city. On the horizon, he could make out the sea, golden under the late-afternoon sun. The walls of the city were just visible as a dark smudge against the glittering water. As they drew closer, the city began to take on a definite shape. A massive castle stood at the eastern end of the city wall, which stretched for a mile to the west, where it was anchored by a squat, round tower.

Behind the wall lay Tripoli, built on a peninsula that curved out into the Mediterranean. John could make out the peaked roof of a church and two soaring minarets – now converted into bell towers.

The caravan entered the shadow of the white stone walls and headed for a wide gate flanked by guards wearing the distinctive black surcoats with white crosses that distinguished the Knights Hospitaller. The Indian merchant at the head of the camel train handed one of the guards a silver piece, and the caravan passed through with no interference. John stayed close to the last of the heavily laden camels, but as he entered the shadow of the gatehouse one of the guards stepped forward to block his way.

'You, Saracen!' the guard barked. 'What's your business here?'

John unwrapped his turban to reveal his blond hair and beard. He turned his blue eyes on the guard. 'I'm no Saracen, friend. As for my business, I am a slave merchant, here for the market.'

The guard studied him for a moment, then nodded. 'Go on then.'

John strode into the densely packed city, a network of narrow alleyways running between tall buildings huddled one on top of the other inside the tight space within the walls. He headed right into a dark alleyway, his boots squishing in the muck, a nauseous mixture of emptied chamberpots and refuse, all slowly draining away to the sea. It was a far cry from the cleanliness of Aleppo. He passed a doorway where an emaciated man with glazed eyes stood staring vacantly out into the alleyway – an opium addict. Ahead, the alleyway divided, running either side of a narrow building. A young prostitute, wearing a gauzy robe that revealed her budding breasts stood at the crossroads. 'Fancy a good time?' she asked in Frankish, then Latin and Arabic. John stopped, and her reddened lips stretched back in a leer.

John held up a copper. 'Which way to the port?'

The prostitute frowned. 'That way,' she said, pointing to her right.

John flipped her the coin and continued, following the narrow, twisting street in the direction she had indicated. As he neared the port, he heard the cries of seagulls wheeling overhead. The street broadened, and the houses lining it grew more luxurious, tall buildings of white stone replacing the wood and mud constructions nearer the walls. John entered a square and found himself facing a massive, domed church. He skirted the building and came to a broad street that ran down towards the gate that led out to the port. Carts were crowded around the gate, and merchants were loudly hawking their wares, preying on new arrivals to the Holy Land. John saw wine for sale, swords of Damascus steel and a collection of half-starved Saracen slaves. He strode passed and out into the port.

John headed left down the harbour, breathing deeply of the tangy ocean air to rid his nose of the rank smell of the city. To his right, ships were tied up along the pier, which curved out into the glittering blue sea, forming a natural breakwater that sheltered the port. Just ahead, a dozen wide-eyed, filthy pilgrims, their possessions slung over their shoulders in cloth bags, were stepping off one of the ships. John paused to watch them, thinking back to his arrival in the Holy Land.

'You there!' a sailor called to John from the deck of the ship. 'Do you seek passage? We sail for Cherbourg at week's end. A silver piece will see you on board.'

John hesitated for only a moment, then shook his head. 'I have business here,' he told the sailor and continued on down the harbour. To his left, a series of warehouses and taverns had been built against the city wall. He headed for the first tavern he saw, a rickety, two-storey building that leaned into the structure next to it. Over the door hung a sign depicting a fighting cock standing over a tankard of beer. From inside, John could hear a steady din of loud voices, overlaid occasionally by shouted curses or loud laughter.

He opened the door and stepped into the dim interior. Two long tables with benches on either side ran the length of the narrow, deep room. The table to the left was crowded with sailors, Italians mostly, judging by their speech. Men in chainmail were seated at the other table. At the far end, a group of Germans were singing loudly. Closer to him, four Hospitallers were playing cards and arguing in Frankish. Nearby, someone with a telltale accent called for another tankard. The man was middle-aged and thickset, with fair skin and dark hair. He wore chainmail and a sword, and a wool bag sat between his feet. One of the serving girls delivered him a tankard, and the man took a long swallow. John sat down opposite him.

'How goes it, friend?' John asked in English.

The man lowered his tankard, his eyes wide. 'By God,

a fellow Saxon!' he roared. He grabbed the arm of a passing serving girl. 'Another beer for my friend here.'

'My thanks,' John said. He held out his hand. 'I am Iain.'

'Aestan,' the man replied, grasping John's arm. 'It's good to hear the mother tongue again. Nothing but bloody Normans around here.' He nodded towards the Hospitallers down the table, then took another swallow from his tankard and turned back to John. 'What brings you to Tripoli, friend?'

'I am a merchant, here to purchase slaves.'

Aestan put his beer down and squinted at John. 'You look like a soldier to me.'

'Used to be, I gave it up for more profitable pursuits.'

'*Hmph*,' Aestan grunted. 'I have no skill for such things.' He patted the sword at his side. 'My talents lie elsewhere. But there's not much need for a Saxon with a sword in England these days.' He spat to the side of the table. 'The Normans run things now. I came here to make my way.'

'When did you arrive?'

'A few days ago. I'll make the pilgrimage to Jerusalem, and after that I plan to join the service of whoever will have me. I hear there's good money to be made in fighting the Saracens.'

John nodded. His tankard arrived, and he took a sip, grimacing at the taste of the stale beer. 'Any leads on who is taking on men? Armies always need slaves; maybe I can turn a profit.'

'They say the Prince of Antioch is recruiting. Reynald's the name.'

John put his tankard down. 'Reynald de Chatillon?'

'That's the one. Know him?'

'I fought for him. Back then, he was a minor noble.'

'Not any more. No one seems to know how, but he has become rich as a Jew. He seduced the Crown Princess of Antioch, dazzling her with fine gifts. Now they are married and he is a prince. And a right bastard he is, too, from what I hear.'

'Sounds like the Reynald I knew,' John murmured.

Aestan took another drink. 'Still, I'd fight for the devil himself, so long as he pays.'

John smiled. 'I'll drink to that.' He had lifted his tankard to his lips when someone roughly grabbed his shoulder, causing him to spill his drink.

One of the Hospitallers, a bearded, red-faced man, leaned over the table next to him. His breath stank of cheap wine. 'What are you two Saxon dogs scheming about?' the Hospitaller demanded in Frankish.

'Bite your tongue, Norman swine,' Aestan growled in English. He began to stand, but John reached across the table and placed a hand on his shoulder. He rose and turned towards the Hospitaller, who was backed by three more knights. They were all armed. John wished that he had not left his sword back in Yusuf's camp.

'I am a slave merchant,' John said in Frankish. 'We were discussing business.'

'A merchant, eh?' the knight slurred. His eyes went to John's purse. 'There's a tax on merchants operating in the port.' He held out a hand. 'I'm collecting.' John did not want to make a scene. He reached into his purse and handed the knight a silver dirham. The knight held it up to examine it. Nur ad-Din's likeness was printed on one side. 'Saracen money,' the knight said. 'This is no good here. What else have you got?'

'That is all I have.'

The knight looked to his friends and grinned. 'Well, then, it's the stocks for you.' He placed a meaty hand on John's shoulder.

John sighed. It seemed the knight was determined to make trouble. 'Wait,' John said. 'I may have a Frankish gold piece.' The knight's eyes went wide with greed, and he released John's shoulder. John placed his hand in his purse, then pulled it out in a fist, which he slammed into the Hospitaller's face, knocking him sprawling backwards into one of his friends. The other two knights raised their fists.

'You'll pay for that, Saxon dog,' one of them said. He started to throw a punch when Aestan leapt over the table and slammed into the knight, bowling him over.

'Norman pig!' Aestan roared, his face flushed red and his fists flying.

The tavern owner – a beefy, native Christian – waded into the melee, separating John from the fourth Hospitaller. 'That's enough,' he roared as he reached down to pull Aestan off the fallen knight. He received a punch in the back from the fourth Hospitaller for his efforts. A moment later, a serving girl slammed a tankard over the knight's head, dropping him. John took advantage of the chaos to slip outside.

He set out immediately from the city, the sun setting behind him as he strode along the road beside the Kadisha River. Eventually, he left the river behind, and it was long since dark when he reached the banks of the Orontes. He headed upstream and then waded across the river and into Yusuf's camp. Yusuf came out to meet him.

'Did you find anything?' he asked.

John nodded. 'The Franks are gathering troops to the north, in Antioch.'

NOVEMBER 1156: ON THE BORDER OF THE KINGDOM OF JERUSALEM

They broke camp that night, and Yusuf led them north along the Orontes River, past the castle of Shaizar and into the lands of the principality of Antioch. This was Frankish territory, and they gave wide birth to the Frankish castles in their path – Apamea, Sarminiqa, Inab and Arzghan. During the day they camped out of sight in the hills that bordered the river. On the third day, as they were making camp in the hills, John pointed out a far-off band of Frankish knights heading east, their helmets glinting under the morning sun. 'Where do you think they are headed?'

Yusuf shrugged. 'There are not enough to attack a castle. They must be raiders.'

'If they are raiding into Muslim lands, then that would violate the treaty.'

Yusuf nodded. 'When night falls, we will follow their tracks.'

They broke camp as the sun was setting, and rode down from the hills. The Franks had left a wide trail, and Yusuf found their tracks easily, even in the dim twilight. They followed the tracks east as the light faded from the sky, and stars emerged above them. They had been riding for several hours when Yusuf saw something in the distance. It looked like a disembodied, turbaned head, floating in the darkness. Yusuf blinked, but the head remained.

''Sblood,' John muttered beside him. 'What sort of devilry is this?' They rode on, and more floating heads appeared. Yusuf's horse whinnied nervously.

'We should turn back,' Turan said, reining in.

Yusuf shook his head and spurred forward. As he reached the first head, he saw that it was impaled on a spear that had been planted in the ground. The head had belonged to an older man, with a long, greying beard. His mouth was stretched open in anguish, and his eyes had already been pecked out by birds, leaving black holes. Still, Yusuf recognized him.

'Sabir ibn Taqqi,' he whispered.

'Why would anybody do such a thing?' John asked as he rode up beside Yusuf.

'It is meant to send a message.'

'Of what?'

'Of war.'

They rode through the forest of heads and came to the bodies. Most were gathered close together where they had fallen, bows and shepherd's crooks still clutched in their hands. Hyenas moved amongst them, gorging on the dead. They ran off howling as Yusuf and his men approached. Yusuf reined in and sat staring at carnage. Then he saw movement amongst the bodies. 'I think one of them is alive!' he cried as he slid from his saddle.

Yusuf approached a pile of bodies, pulling a fold of his turban over his mouth and nose to keep out the foul smell. From under three dead Bedouin, he saw two eyes staring out at him. It was a boy, a knife clutched in his hand. 'D-don't come any closer!' he cried out.

'I am a friend,' Yusuf said, kneeling a few feet away. He looked over his shoulder towards his men and shouted: 'Quick, bring water and food!' John handed him a waterskin, and Yusuf held it out towards the boy.

Slowly, carefully, the boy crawled out from under the dead. He was thin and dark, with wide eyes and short black hair. His face was covered with dried blood. The boy reached out and snatched the waterskin. He drank greedily. Then he dropped the waterskin and held out his knife. 'You're one of them!' he hissed at John.

'Easy, boy,' Yusuf said. 'One of who?'

'The Franks. They came for our herds.' The boy began to cry. 'They killed my family – they killed everybody.'

'You will have a new family now,' Yusuf told him. 'You will come with us to Aleppo, as a mamluk. You will learn to fight, and someday you will have your revenge against the Franks.' Yusuf rose and turned towards John.

'If the Franks did this,' John said. 'Then the treaty is broken, and that means—'

'War,' Yusuf finished for him.

'There's more,' the boy said from behind them. Yusuf turned. The boy had dried his tears and once more gripped his knife in his hand. 'I heard the name of their leader.' He spat into the dust. 'Reynald.'

Chapter 15

John jerked upright in bed, his heart pounding. The room was dark and the house quiet. He looked over at Zimat, who lay beside him. She stirred, blinking away sleep. 'What is it?' She yawned. 'Another nightmare?'

John nodded. 'I dreamt you were being stoned.'

'It was only a dream,' Zimat murmured, gently stroking his arm. 'I am safe, here with you.'

John pulled away and moved to sit at the edge of the bed, his head in his hands. 'In my dream, Yusuf cast the first stone.' He turned to look at her. 'Your brother trusts me. Every time I come to you, I betray him.'

Zimat's lips pressed together in a hard line. 'I do not wish to have this discussion again. Either we betray my brother, or we betray our love. We have made our choice.'

'It is not that simple,' John muttered. He rose and began to dress.

Behind him, Zimat sat up in bed. 'Do not go, not yet.'

'It will be dawn soon,' John replied as he laced up his

372

boots. 'The army leaves just after sunrise. I must help Yusuf organize the men.'

'Yusuf's shadow,' Zimat said bitterly. She turned away from him. 'You love him more than me.'

John sat beside her. 'I owe Yusuf my life.' He reached out and pushed her hair back from her face. 'But you are the reason that I remain in the East. In Tripoli, I could have taken a ship for England. I stayed because of you. I love you, Zimat.'

'I know.' She turned to John, and he kissed her, pulling her close to him. Finally she pulled away. 'When will I see you again?'

'I do not know when we will return.'

Zimat looked away, blinking back tears. John kissed her forehead, then rose. He went to the door and put his head against it, listening to make sure the hallway was empty before cracking the door open.

'John,' Zimat called softly. He turned. 'Come back to me.'

'I will,' John whispered, and left.

MAY 1157: NEAR BAALBEK

'O Allah, have mercy upon me,' Yusuf murmured. He knelt on his prayer rug, which he had laid out on the sand beside the Orontes River, facing south-east towards Mecca. Men knelt all around him. As Yusuf prostrated himself, touching his forehead to the ground, he glanced out of the corner of his eye at Nur ad-Din, who knelt a few feet to his left. Beyond the malik were thousands

373

more men, stretching for over a mile along the banks of the river, all facing Mecca and all with their foreheads to the ground. Only John stood out. He was kneeling nearby under a tree on the riverbank, praying in his own way.

Yusuf sat back on his heels, and as he spoke the final words of the maghrib – the evening prayer – he looked across the river at the green fields, which stretched away to craggy mountains, their peaks lit golden red by the setting sun. The last time Yusuf had visited those mountains, he and John had tracked and killed the panther that Yusuf now wore as a winter cloak. That seemed so long ago. They had left Aleppo over a week ago, and tomorrow they would pass through Baalbek on the way south to the Frankish stronghold of Banyas. And then the war against the Franks would begin.

Yusuf finished his prayers and began to roll up his mat. All around him men were heading up the gentle rise that separated the riverbank from their camp. Yusuf stood and began to follow them.

'Yusuf!' It was Nur ad-Din. A servant had taken his prayer mat, and he was standing alone beside the river, his shoulders slumped. 'Come here.' Yusuf walked over, his boots crunching softly on the wet sand. Nur ad-Din turned to face him. 'We will reach Banyas soon. Do you think the men ready?'

'Yes, Malik.'

'Good, good,' Nur ad-Din murmured. He sighed and turned to look out over the river. The glow had left the distant mountains, and the fields beneath them were now grey in the darkness. A single locust in one of the trees along the riverbank began its song, and a moment later the evening was full of their sound. Yusuf noticed that Nur ad-Din had closed his eyes. Yusuf opened his mouth to speak, but Nur ad-Din spoke first. 'Asimat miscarried last night. It was a boy. I should not have brought her with me on this campaign.'

'Is she well?'

Nur ad-Din glanced at him sharply, then nodded. 'She is alone in her tent. She has sent away the doctors, the midwife, even her servants.'

Yusuf placed his right hand on Nur ad-Din's shoulder. 'It is not your fault, Malik. Such matters are in the hands of Allah.'

Nur ad-Din shrugged off Yusuf's hand. 'Then why has Allah cursed me?' he demanded, his voice rising. 'I have built mosques to glorify Him. I have given to the poor. I have launched this campaign against the Franks in His name. What more must I do before He gives me a son?' He glared at Yusuf, who shifted uncomfortably, uncertain of what to say. Nur ad-Din sighed and turned back to the river. When he spoke again his voice was soft. 'Perhaps when I have driven the Franks from our lands, then Allah will bless me. Inshallah.'

'Inshallah,' Yusuf echoed.

They stood in silence, listening to the locusts and the gentle burble of the river. Finally, Nur ad-Din turned to face Yusuf. 'I did not call you here to burden you with my troubles. I want you to go to Asimat. She refuses to speak with me, and besides, I have little talent for gentle words.' He placed a hand on Yusuf's shoulder. 'She likes you. Make sure she is well. Comfort her for me, if you are able.'

'Yes, Malik.'

'Good.' Nur ad-Din released Yusuf and straightened, all sign of weakness suddenly gone. He nodded curtly. 'Now go. Her guards will be expecting you.'

Yusuf walked up the sandy hill that bordered the river. At the top, he looked back. Nur ad-Din was still standing alone on the riverbank. Yusuf turned and headed down the far side of the hill. Before him, the plain was dotted with hundreds of white tents, like flowers after a rain. He headed for Nur ad-Din's huge tent, which was easy to find. Asimat's smaller tent sat beside it, guarded by a dozen eunuch soldiers. As Yusuf approached, their captain gestured for him to enter and then followed, taking up a position just inside the door.

The tent's interior was brightly lit by two oil lamps that hung from the ceiling. Thick carpets covered the floor, and a screen of thin cloth divided the tent in half. Beyond the screen, Yusuf could make out the dark outline of a hammock slung between two tent posts, and standing beside the hammock, the form of Asimat. She moved to the flap in the middle of the screen and passed through. Her eyes were red and her face pale, but she managed to smile when she saw Yusuf.

'Salaam, Yusuf. I am glad that you came. Sit.' She took a seat amidst silk cushions, and Yusuf sat across from her. 'I have news for you. I have found you a wife.'

Yusuf's eyebrows shot up. He had not expected this. 'A wife?'

'As I promised. She is Usama's daughter – a good match. She is beautiful, and healthy. She will bear—' Asimat faltered, looking away to hide her tears. 'She will bear you many children.'

'Are you well, Khatun?' Yusuf asked softly. 'Your child—'

'I do not wish to speak of it,' Asimat snapped and angrily wiped away her tears. 'I am fine, as well as can be expected while travelling with an army.'

'You did not wish to come?'

'No. I do not like war. I have never understood this eagerness of men to kill one another.'

'But the Franks have broken their treaty with us. They have slaughtered innocent Bedouin.'

'So we shall slaughter them in turn?'

'We only return in kind the suffering that they visited upon us when they took our lands. They do not belong here.'

'They do not belong?' Asimat laughed, a hollow sound with no merriment in it. 'Tell me, Yusuf. Do you remember a time when the Franks were not here?'

'No, my lady. They arrived before I was born.'

'And your father?' Yusuf shook his head. 'If the Franks have held their kingdom for longer than you or your father have been alive, then what gives you more of a right to the land than they? The Romans held these lands before us. Perhaps the Franks feel that they, too, have merely reclaimed lands that were once theirs.'

Yusuf frowned. 'But it is our duty to fight them.'

'Perhaps,' Asimat murmured. 'But I have had enough of death.' She looked away, her hand on her stomach.

Yusuf reached out to comfort her, then glanced at the eunuch guard still standing in the doorway and thought better of it. 'What happened to your child is different,' he said gently.

Asimat looked back to him, and her eyes glistened with tears. 'Death is death. Each ifranji you kill has a mother, too.'

'But they are men who can defend themselves. Your child—'

'My child never had a chance to defend himself,' she said bitterly. 'Allah took him.' She began to sob. 'What did I do to anger him?'

'It is not your fault,' Yusuf soothed. 'It is Allah's will.'

'Then I curse Allah!'

Yusuf's eyes went wide. 'Do not say such things.'

'Why? Allah has taken my child from me after all these years of waiting. What more can He do to me? What could be more cruel than that?'

'You are right,' Yusuf said. 'Allah was cruel to take your child. If you wish to hate Him, then that is your right. But you are not weak, Asimat. If Allah has wronged you, then spit in His face. Do not spend your days crying. Have another child.'

Asimat said nothing, but after a moment she wiped away her tears and straightened. 'You are right. Thank you.'

Yusuf nodded. 'Allah only tests you. He would not curse one as beautiful as you.'

Asimat flinched. 'Be careful what you say, Yusuf. Nur ad-Din is a kind man, but he will defend his honour. He will have you killed at the slightest suspicion.'

'I am sorry if I offended you, my lady.' Yusuf glanced at the eunuch guard. 'It was not my intention.'

She waved away his concern. 'It is nothing. I am not my self since—' Asimat broke off and took a deep breath. 'I am not myself.'

'I will go and let you rest.' Yusuf stood and bowed. 'I am sorry for your loss, Khatun.' He headed for the tent flap.

'Yusuf,' Asimat called, and he turned. She was staring at him, her head tilted to the side. Her eyes met his, and there was something in her gaze that both excited and unnerved him. He forced himself to look away. 'I am returning to Aleppo tomorrow,' she said. 'I hope to see you again when you return.'

May 1157: Banyas

John stood at the edge of a broad ledge high up on the slopes of Mount Hermon. Yusuf was beside him, and past him, Nur ad-Din stood surrounded by emirs and advisors. A spring gushed from a cave behind them and flowed over the cliff face to John's left, plunging down to the valley floor far below, where it formed a silver ribbon that flowed through the walled town of Banyas and past its castle. The castle was an imposing structure with towering walls of white limestone rising straight from the hillside on which it sat. There was only one possible path of attack: a road that ran up the spine of the hill. The road passed through a series of gated, walled courtyards, each of which would have to be conquered before reaching the thick-walled, central keep. And before attacking the fortress, they would have to take the town. Squinting, John could just make out the tiny figures of townspeople leaving through the town gate.

'The Franks are taking shelter in the keep,' he said, speaking loudly over the roar of the waterfall. 'They know we are here.'

Yusuf nodded. 'The castle will not be easy to take.'

'Nevertheless, it will fall,' Nur ad-Din said confidently. 'The Frankish army has been drawn north by Shirkuh's approach. There is no one to help Banyas.' He turned to Yusuf. 'Take your men and seize the town. Your men will have until noon to loot as they wish.'

'Thank you, Malik.' Yusuf nodded to John. 'Let's go.'

They went to their horses and mounted. John followed Yusuf down the narrow track that led from the ledge in a series of cutbacks. The trail was wet with spray from the waterfall, and it was a perilous ride. John kept his eyes on the track before him, but his mind was elsewhere. He thought of the townspeople he had seen leaving Banyas. As a crusader, he had sworn to protect such people from the Saracens and to help his fellow Christian knights when they were in need. If he helped Yusuf take the town, then he would be violating his crusader's oath. He would be putting yet more blood on his head.

John looked up as they reached the valley floor, where the army waited in the shadow of the mountain, hidden from the city by low hills. Yusuf's troops were gathered beside the stream, watering their horses. Yusuf rode straight to Turan, who stood on the sands of the riverbank, sharpening the grey steel of his sword.

'We have been ordered to take the town,' Yusuf told him. 'Ready the men, and provide a dozen of them with torches.'

'Yes, Brother.' Turan turned and roared to the men. 'Saddle up and get in formation! There's fighting to be done!'

'Yusuf,' John said to his friend in a low voice. 'Do you think it wise to have brought Turan? Perhaps he should be left behind when you attack Banyas?'

'No, he will ride with us. He is a changed man since the death of Nadhira. And besides, I like to keep an eye on him.'

'There is something else.' John took a deep breath. 'I cannot fight against my fellow Christians. I swore an oath.'

Yusuf examined him for a moment, then nodded. 'You may remain in camp, friend. I do not expect you to fight your own kind.'

John frowned. 'But I am the commander of your khaskiya. I cannot let you ride into battle alone.' He had already betrayed Yusuf with Zimat, he would not fail him here as well. The creases on John's forehead melted away as he reached a decision. 'I will not fight to take Banyas, but I will kill to protect you, if I must.'

Yusuf grasped John's shoulder. 'Thank you, friend.'

The men had mounted and formed ranks three deep along the riverbank. Yusuf commanded his own mamluks from Tell Bashir, as well as the men his father had sent from Damascus – over three hundred warriors in all. They wore chainmail and each carried a small, circular shield along with three weapons: a curving, compact bow; a light spear; and a sword.

Yusuf rose in his stirrups to address them. 'We have been ordered to clear the town. We will attack from the east, where the river enters the city and the wall is weakest. Qaraqush, you will take the Tell Bashir men and set fire to the eastern gate to distract the Christians. Once Qaraqush has attacked, Turan will lead forty Damascus men to the right of the gate, where they will scale the wall. I will lead my personal guard to the left where the river passes under the wall. We will enter there. The rest will wait in reserve with Al-Mashtub, ready to charge when the gate opens. Understood?' There was murmured assent from the ranks.

'For Allah!' Yusuf shouted, and the men roared back, 'For Allah!' John said nothing. He turned his horse and followed Yusuf along the river, with Yusuf's guard following in a column three wide. Qaraqush and his men came next, their burning torches leaving a trail of black smoke. They followed the river through low hills, and as they rounded a last bend, the town of Banyas came into view, its pale stone houses huddled behind eight-foot-high limestone walls. 'Keep together!' Yusuf shouted back to the men. 'Wait for my signal.'

They rode closer and closer, until John could see the faces of men peering over the walls. An arrow fell from the sky and shattered against the hard ground to John's right. He heard a scream and turned to see a mamluk with an arrow in his gut drop his torch and slump from the saddle. John raised his shield, just before an arrow thumped into it.

'Qaraqush, charge!' Yusuf roared.

Qaraqush and his men galloped towards the city. One of the mamluks fell, then another, but the rest arrived to throw their torches at the base of the gate. They wheeled away, as the wood began to smoke. Two Franks appeared atop the gate with a cauldron of water and poured it over the side, dousing the flames. Qaraqush led his men galloping back, firing arrows that dropped the two men.

'Turan, now!' Yusuf yelled, and with a roar, Turan led his men away to the right. 'My men, follow me!' Yusuf cried and spurred to the left.

John followed close behind Yusuf. Arrows whizzed past as they streaked along the wall towards the mountain stream, which narrowed into a deep channel as it approached the town. As they neared the water, Yusuf dismounted, and John also slid from the saddle. They ran to where the water flowed under the wall. Yusuf was about to jump in when John grabbed his arm. 'What if the passage under the wall is barred?'

'Uwais!' Yusuf called, and a mamluk ran forward. 'Go!' The mamluk plunged into the stream and disappeared under the water. John counted to a hundred; Uwais did not reappear. He glanced at Yusuf.

'He must have made it,' Yusuf said.

'Are you sure?'

'There's only one way to find out.' Yusuf plunged into the water.

John took a deep breath and jumped in after him. His

armour pulled him down in the cold water. The current was pushing him towards the wall. He could see Yusuf just ahead. Then John passed under the wall and everything went black. As the current pulled him along, he reached out and felt the slick side of an algae-covered stone tunnel. The next moment he slammed into something, knocking some of the precious air from his lungs. He reached out in the darkness and felt crisscrossed lengths of iron; a grate was blocking the tunnel. John's hands moved along the grate until he came to a limp, unmoving form – Uwais, or Yusuf. Someone grabbed John and began to pull him back against the current. Suddenly a mamluk slammed into them both, knocking them on to the grate. Another mamluk piled into them, then another. John was growing short of air. He tried to scramble past the mamluks when he felt an elbow slam into his jaw, then a foot hit him in the stomach. In their panic to escape the tunnel, the men were only getting in each other's way. More mamluks came down the tunnel, making matters worse. There was no going back.

Desperate, his lungs burning, John twisted around and pulled his dagger from his belt. He began to chisel frantically at the mortar that held the grate in place. He felt a small piece of mortar float loose, and redoubled his efforts. He could see spots floating before his eyes in the darkness now, and it was all he could do not to open his mouth and breathe in the water. A chunk of mortar came free. Then another mamluk slammed into John, pinning him to the grate and knocking his dagger from his hand. John felt for it in the darkness, but the dagger was lost. His temples were pounding, and he could hold his breath no more. He started to open his mouth. But then several more mamluks slammed into the mass of men and the grate gave way.

John tumbled through the black tunnel, pushed ahead by the current, then he saw daylight above him. He managed to crawl up the side of the channel and broke the surface, gasping for breath. He pulled himself from the water and lay on his back, his chest heaving and blood pounding in his ears. Yusuf's face appeared over him.

'This is not the time to rest, John.' He held out a hand and pulled John to his feet.

'You're not even breathing hard,' John gasped, his hands on his knees.

'I'm used to holding my breath,' Yusuf replied as he went to help pull another mamluk from the water.

John looked about him. The wall stretched away in either direction, with a twenty-foot space of hard-packed earth separating it from the houses of the town. A dozen mamluks had already dragged themselves from the river and were helping to pull out their comrades. John could hear the shouts of men fighting in the distance.

'Follow me, men!' Yusuf shouted.

John drew his sword and followed Yusuf as he ran up the steps to the top of the wall and then sprinted along it. They rounded a corner, and the city gate came into view. There was no sign of Turan, but outside the gate, Qaraqush and his men were still fighting. Inside, there were at least a hundred Franks, some standing on the wall and firing arrows, others massed behind the gate. They were focused on Qaraqush's men beyond the wall.

'*Allah*! *Allah*! *Allah*!' Yusuf cried as he neared the Christians.

Behind him, John heard the mamluks take up the cry. The Frankish defenders on the wall looked over in alarm. The nearest archer turned and fired, but the arrow flew high. Yusuf impaled the man with his sword and shoved him aside. The next defender had drawn his sword. He slashed at Yusuf, who ducked the blow and came up under it, slamming his shoulder into the man's chest and knocking him off the wall. Further along the wall, the remaining defenders were grouping behind a wall of shields, blocking off the stairs that ran down to the gate.

'We must open the gate!' Yusuf cried and jumped from the wall, straight into the Frankish knights massed below. He landed on top of a knight, and both of them fell sprawling. As Yusuf plunged his sword into the fallen man's chest, another knight behind Yusuf raised his blade to finish him.

'Crazy bastard,' John muttered and leapt from the wall. He landed on top of the knight behind Yusuf, tackling him. John rolled off the man, but before he could get to his feet, he saw a sword flashing down towards his head. It was stopped at the last second by Yusuf's blade. John stabbed out, dropping the attacker. 'God forgive me,' John whispered, but he had no time to dwell on what he had done. He sprang to his feet and stood back to back with Yusuf as more Franks closed in. John parried and lashed out, fighting desperately to keep the men at bay. He glanced to the wall above, where the mamluks were blocked by the Franks. John saw one mamluk try to jump down, but the knights

386

below were ready now. The mamluk landed on the point of a Frankish sword.

'We've got to get to the gate!' John shouted.

'Right!'

Inch by inch, they made their way forward, fighting in perfect tandem, each blocking when the other was exposed. Finally, they reached the gate, pressing their backs against it. 'What now?' John asked. He dodged an axe blow, and the weapon embedded itself in the wood beside his head. John thrust his sword into the man's chest, dropping him, but another knight took his place. His sword sneaked through and glanced off the chain-mail on John's side. Another knight slashed John's leg, and he gritted his teeth in pain. 'We can't hold out much longer!'

'We won't have to,' Yusuf shouted.

A loud cry of '*Allah*! *Allah*! *Allah*!' went up behind the knights, and a moment later Turan and his men slammed into the Franks, who turned away to face the new threat. John struck down the man before him and found himself with no one to fight.

Yusuf grabbed his arm. 'Help me remove the bar!' John nodded and put his shoulder to the heavy oak log that held the gate shut. Gritting his teeth against the pain in his leg, he heaved. The two men barely managed to raise the bar out of its brackets, then dropped it on the ground with a thud. A second later, the gate ground inward as Qaraqush pushed his way in, followed by the rest of the mamluks. The Franks began to retreat. John stood aside as the mamluks flooded through the gate and pursued them down the main street of the town.

When all the mamluks had poured past, Yusuf walked over to John and clapped him on the back. 'We did it!'

John looked about him at the men he had killed and shook his head. 'The crusader's oath I swore had three parts,' he muttered. 'I was to make pilgrimage to the Holy Sepulchre in Jerusalem, to protect the people of the kingdom from the Saracens, and to aid my fellow Crusaders. I failed to reach Jerusalem, and now I have betrayed my oath twice over.'

Yusuf frowned. 'I am sorry, John.'

'It was them or you. I made my choice long ago.' John wiped the blood from his sword. 'The priests say those who die fighting the Saracens will go straight to heaven. Where shall I go when I die?'

Yusuf stood in the dusty central street of Banyas and watched as a dozen men with axes hacked at the beams of a wooden house and then pulled them loose. Nur ad-Din had sent the men, who would use the wood to build the first of the catapults necessary for besieging the citadel. John sat nearby, leaning against a wall in the shade as he rested his bandaged leg. The rest of Yusuf's men had spread out through the town. Nur ad-Din had given them until midday to loot before the rest of the army entered. Yusuf looked to the sky. Their time was almost up.

Turan approached from a side alley, his face set in a grim line. 'We have found little, Brother. The Christians left nothing of value when they fled.'

'Then we shall have all the more riches when we take the castle,' Yusuf replied.

A high-pitched cry, cut suddenly short, came from their right. It sounded like a child's voice. 'What was that?' John asked, rising.

'Sounds like the men have found something,' Turan said.

John was already heading in that direction, his hand on his sword. Yusuf followed. They passed through an alley and out into another street. From a house across from them, Yusuf could hear a woman cursing in Frankish, and then the loud wailing of a child. John rushed to the house, and Yusuf followed.

In the centre of the home's single room three mamluks were crouched over a red-haired Frankish woman. Her dress was torn, exposing one of her pale white breasts. Her eyes were wild, and she screamed and thrashed, trying to pull free of the two mamluks who were holding her down. The third mamluk was loosening the belt of his breeches. A blonde girl stood to the side, wide-eyed and sobbing. The mamluks ignored her, their eyes fixed on the Frankish woman.

John began to draw his sword, but Yusuf reached out to stop him. 'I will handle this.' He raised his voice. 'What have we here, men?'

The mamluks looked up and released the woman. She scrambled over to her child and clutched the girl to her breast. The men turned to face Yusuf. He recognized Nazam – the bald-headed mamluk John had fought long ago, when they first arrived at Tell Bashir.

'We've found no gold,' Nazam said. 'But we did find this prize. She'll fetch a fine price on the slave market, if we don't keep her for ourselves.'

Yusuf walked over to the woman, who shrank back in fear. He bent down and grabbed her jaw, turning her head towards him. She spat in his face. As Yusuf backed away, wiping the spit from his cheek, one of the mamluks stepped over and back-handed the woman, knocking her down. She pushed herself up, blood dripping from her lip, and the mamluk raised his fist to strike again.

'That is enough,' Yusuf said. 'Leave her to me. You shall each have a dinar to compensate you.'

'Thank you, my lord,' Nazam said.

'Now leave us,' Yusuf ordered. 'Report to Turan.'

'Yes, my lord. Enjoy yourself.' Nazam winked at Yusuf, and the men trooped out, chuckling.

When they were gone, the woman turned to John. 'You are not one of them. Kill me. Do not let him defile me. Don't let him sell my child.'

'I will not hurt you,' Yusuf said in Frankish. The woman's eyes went wide. 'You are free. I will escort you and your daughter to the citadel.'

'Thank you,' the woman sobbed in relief. She knelt before him and kissed his hand. 'Thank you, my lord.'

'We haven't much time,' Yusuf said, taking her hand and raising her up. He stepped outside, and the woman followed, holding her daughter. John brought up the rear. They reached the gate leading out towards the citadel without incident. It was open.

'Go,' Yusuf said. The woman lifted her daughter and ran up the slope towards the citadel.

'Thank you,' John said from behind Yusuf. 'You did not have to do that.'

'I did not do it for you,' Yusuf said, his eyes still on the woman. She reached the citadel gate, and it opened just enough for her to slip through. Yusuf turned to John. 'The Franks raped my mother when she was young. Now come. We must see to the building of the catapults.'

The next morning Yusuf stood atop the wall surrounding Banyas and looked out towards the citadel, rising high above on its hilltop. At the foot of the hill were the three enormous catapults that Nur ad-Din's engineers had constructed. Yusuf watched as one of the catapults fired. The heavy counterweight – stones and dirt gathered in a wooden bin – fell, and the long arm of the catapult rose into the air. Trailing from the far end of the arm was a leather sling, which now snapped upwards, hurling a three-hundred-pound boulder. The stone arced through the air and then shattered against the wall in a cloud of dust. When the dust cleared, the wall still stood, apparently undamaged. Then a few stones fell away and went tumbling down the hillside. A cheer went up from the Muslim camp, which was spread in a circle all around the hill on which the citadel stood. Yusuf smiled. The walls were strong, but they would fall.

From the corner of his eye Yusuf noticed movement, and he looked away from the citadel to the north. Beyond the tents of the camp, he saw a plume of dust rising into the sky. Squinting, he could make out a horse charging towards the town – a messenger. From the way he was pressing his mount, Yusuf guessed he had important news.

Yusuf left the wall and hurried to the two-storey merchant's home in town where Nur ad-Din had established himself. Yusuf arrived just as Nur ad-Din stepped out of the house.

'Who could this be?' Nur ad-Din asked, looking up the street to the distant rider.

Yusuf squinted. 'Khaldun,' he said, recognizing his brother-in-law through the dust that covered him.

'Salaam, Khaldun!' Nur ad-Din hailed as the rider reined to a stop.

Khaldun dismounted and bowed before Nur ad-Din. 'Salaam, Malik.'

'You bring news from Shirkuh?' Nur ad-Din asked.

Khaldun nodded. 'The Christians sent only a small force to confront Shirkuh. The main army is marching for Banyas. They will be here tomorrow.'

'So soon,' Yusuf whispered.

'When will Shirkuh arrive with the rest of my men?' Nur ad-Din asked.

'A week, my lord.'

Yusuf looked to Nur ad-Din. 'What shall we do? The Franks will outnumber us two to one.'

'We do what the Christians expect us to do: retreat.'

MAY 1157: JACOB'S FORD

John stood on the ridge of a long line of dusty, brown hills and looked down upon the Christian army as it moved through the narrow valley below, heading south alongside the silvery ribbon of the Jordan River. The Franks marched in a square formation, with foot-soldiers on the periphery providing protection for the horses of the mounted knights at the centre. But the ranks were loose. A constant stream of men left their places to go to the river and refill their skins. Most of the men marched with their helmets off and their shields strapped to their backs. A few had even removed their armour to better enjoy the beautiful spring day. Multicoloured pennants flapped gaily overhead in a cool breeze, giving the army a festive appearance. They had reason to celebrate, only three days before they had driven the Saracens from Banyas.

John turned his back on the Frankish army to look down the opposite side of the ridge, where thousands of mounted Saracen warriors were gathered out of sight of the Christians. John knew that Nur ad-Din was waiting with an equal number of men behind the hills on the other side of the valley. After leaving Banyas, Nur ad-Din had only pretended to retreat before turning south to shadow the Christians. Yesterday, he had driven his army through the night in order to lay a trap for the Franks.

John picked out Yusuf's eagle standard amongst the men below. He would not ride with his friend today. Since taking the town of Banyas, John had been troubled by bloody nightmares. Fighting Reynald's bandits was one thing; Reynald was a savage who had betrayed him. But John knew that he had put his soul in jeopardy by killing his fellow Christians. He did not wish to die in battle before he had received absolution.

'The Franks have reached the ford,' Imad ad-Din noted. He and a dozen other scribes had joined John atop the ridge, ready to record the coming battle for posterity. They sat on the ground around him, their writing tables across their laps, quills ready.

John turned back towards the Frankish army. They had reached the shallow waters of Jacob's Ford, the safest crossing point over the Jordan River. The first foot-soldiers were already wading across, the water reaching up to their waists at the deepest point. Behind them, the army had broken its square formation, forming a column in order to cross the narrow ford. John's stomach tightened with nervous tension. When half the foot-soldiers had reached the far bank, the first of the mounted knights entered the water, the standard of the King of Jerusalem flying above them. They were halfway across when a horn sounded from the hills on the far side of the river. As the low, mournful cry of the horn faded, the Christian army stopped, knights and foot-soldiers looking about nervously. In the silence, John could hear the distant Frankish horses, their anxious whinnies borne to him on the wind.

The blast of another horn sounded behind John, drowning out the sounds of the Frankish army. He turned to see the Saracen army on the move, Yusuf's eagle standard flying at their head. They headed for a gap in the hills that led out to the valley.

'Look!' Imad ad-Din cried.

John turned to see the other half of the Saracen army pouring from the hills on the far side of the river, the sound of the pounding horses' hooves rolling like thunder across the plain. There was disorder in the Christian ranks as the mounted knights hurried to cross the river to meet the threat. But the narrow ford slowed their efforts. Some entered the river south of the ford to avoid the bottleneck and were swept away by the current. Meanwhile, the foot-soldiers hurriedly formed a line, pikes out.

The horsemen led by Nur ad-Din split in two as they reached the foot-soldiers, riding parallel to the Christian lines and shooting arrows into their enemies. Christians fell by the dozen, but the line did not break. Behind the foot-soldiers, the last of the mounted knights were crossing the river to group around the standard of the Frankish king. A horn blast sounded out from the Christian ranks as the knights prepared to charge. Then, behind them, the other half of the Saracen army galloped forth from the hills, Yusuf's banner at their head. Shooting arrows as they rode, they cut through the Frankish foot-soldiers who had not yet crossed the river and then splashed across the ford to attack the Christian knights from behind. Trapped between the two halves of the Saracen army, the Franks panicked. Individual knights attempted to ride to safety, but their horses were shot out from under them. The line of foot-soldiers dissolved as men fled, only to be ridden down from behind. Hundreds of Franks stripped off their armour and leapt into the river, swimming downstream to safety.

A piercing horn sounded again and again as the Frankish king sought to rally his men. Only two hundred or so knights remained, encircled by the Saracen army, which closed in to finish them. John spotted Yusuf's standard at the heart of the fighting, pushing towards Baldwin's banner. If the king fell, the battle would be over. And then, after a final, long blast of the horn, the

Frankish knights charged, heading straight towards Yusuf. Nothing could stand in the way of the Franks' plate armour and strong horses. They crashed through the Saracen ranks, spearing men off horses with their long lances and then crushing them underfoot. For a moment Yusuf's standard stayed aloft as he and a handful of mamluks held their ground. John thought he spotted Yusuf at the head of the mamluks, his sword flashing in the sunlight. And then the mamluks were swept away and Yusuf's standard fell. Yusuf was nowhere to be seen.

'*Allah*! *Allah*! *Allah*!' Yusuf stood in the saddle, screaming as he slashed out at the Frankish knights streaming past. Then a knight's lance hit Yusuf's horse directly in the chest, killing it instantly. Yusuf managed to jump free of the saddle as his horse collapsed. He landed in the path of a charging warhorse and rolled to the side. Another horse was bearing down, and Yusuf curled into a ball as the horse galloped straight over him. He sprang to his feet and jumped to his right to avoid a knight's lance. As the Frank rode past, Yusuf knelt and slashed out, slicing through the girth that held the knight's saddle in place. The saddle slid off and the knight crashed to the ground, to be trampled. Yusuf ran after the horse, which had slowed to a walk. He grabbed its mane and swung himself on to its back. The last of the Christian knights were now flying past, and Yusuf kicked his mount's sides, urging it after them.

Yusuf's horse kicked up plumes of sand as it raced alongside the river. Two banners flew over the fleeing

Franks: one a gold cross with four smaller crosses on a white background, the other royal blue and scarlet. Four knights rode under the blue and scarlet flag, surrounding a tall man in chainmail and a steel breastplate. That had to be King Baldwin.

'*Yalla*!' Yusuf cried, urging his horse forward. He pulled alongside the rearmost knight. The knight slashed at Yusuf, who veered away to avoid the blow. Yusuf urged his horse back towards the knight and thrust out, stabbing the Frank in the side. With a cry of pain, the man slid from the saddle, taking Yusuf's sword with him.

Yusuf rode on. The king was just ahead now, with two knights flanking him. '*Yalla*! *Yalla*!' Yusuf cried as he surged forward into the narrow gap between the king and the knight on his right. The knight swung for Yusuf's head, but Yusuf ducked the blow. He jumped from his horse, throwing himself at the king and dragging him from the saddle. Yusuf rolled as he hit the ground and sprang to his feet. A few feet away, the king lay on his back with sword in hand, struggling to rise in his heavy armour. The other Frankish knights were galloping away along the Jordan. None turned to come back for their fallen comrade.

Yusuf drew his eagle-hilt dagger and approached the king. The Frank swung at him, but Yusuf jumped the blow. He stepped on the king's sword arm, pinning it, then kicked the weapon away. Yusuf knelt on the man's chest and raised his dagger. 'I yield!' the knight roared and pulled off his helmet. Yusuf blinked in surprise. It was not the Frankish king. It was Reynald.

'You,' Yusuf whispered. He raised his dagger to strike.

'Do not kill me!' Reynald begged. 'I am the Prince of Antioch. My ransom will be worth a fortune.'

'I do not want your gold,' Yusuf growled as he put his dagger against Reynald's throat. 'Only justice for my friend.'

'What have we here, Yusuf?' a voice called, and Yusuf froze. He looked up to see Nur ad-Din approaching on horseback.

'I am the Prince of Antioch!' Reynald cried. 'I am your prisoner. I beg your mercy.'

Nur ad-Din nodded. 'Let him be, Yusuf.' Reluctantly, Yusuf stepped away and sheathed his dagger. Two mamluks came forward and pulled Reynald to his feet. 'You shall be our guest in Aleppo until you are ransomed,' Nur ad-Din told him. 'Take him away.' The mamluks marched Reynald off to join the other Frankish prisoners. Nur ad-Din turned to Yusuf. 'You led your men well, Yusuf, and Reynald will be worth his weight in gold.'

'I had hoped to capture King Baldwin.'

'In good time, Yusuf. The Frankish army is broken. Baldwin will beg for peace, but I will not grant it. I will drive him and his people into the sea!'

MAY 1157: NEAR ACRE

Two days later, Yusuf was riding beside Nur ad-Din at the head of the army when the walls of Acre came into sight, the city's citadel rising high above them on its rocky perch. Nur ad-Din reined to a stop. 'Acre, our first prize, Yusuf: it is the key that will unlock the Frankish kingdom.'

Yusuf grinned, but then his smile faded. Looking past Nur ad-Din, he saw a column of dust rising from the horizon to the north. He pointed. 'Look! Do you think it is the Franks? Could they have regrouped so fast?'

Nur ad-Din shook his head. 'No, and besides, they fled south. This must be Shirkuh and his men. They have joined us at the perfect time. We will pause here and wait for them.'

Shirkuh arrived shortly, galloping up ahead of his men. He looked to have ridden far without stopping. He was covered in dust, and his horse was wet with sweat. 'My lord,' he said, bowing in the saddle.

'Well met, Shirkuh!' Nur ad-Din called, riding over and grasping his friend's arm. He glanced at Shirkuh's horse. 'Your horse can hardly carry you. What have you done to it?'

'We rode day and night to reach you. I fear I bring bad news. Manuel, the Roman emperor, is on the march from Constantinople.'

Nur ad-Din's brow creased. 'How many men does he bring?'

'Twenty thousand.'

'Are you certain?'

'I saw his army with my own eyes. They are only a day behind me.'

'*Yaha*!' Nur ad-Din cursed. 'I was so close.' He rode a short distance away and sat staring at Acre. Finally he looked away. 'Yusuf, tell the men to turn around. We are returning to Aleppo.'

'But why? We can defeat the Romans, too, as we defeated the Franks.'

Nur ad-Din shook his head. 'The Franks will rally now that the Romans are on the march. We cannot fight them both. If we lose, then Aleppo and Damascus will be theirs for the taking. We must make peace.'

'But the Franks are crushed!' Yusuf protested. 'We must strike now.'

'No, this campaign is over. But never fear, Yusuf. My peace will be with King Baldwin, and he will not live forever.'

Chapter 16

Rose petals, luminous in the spring sunshine, show-
ered down upon John as he rode through the
cheering crowd that filled the central square of Aleppo,
pressing close to the long line of riders headed towards
the citadel. Nur ad-Din rode at the head of the army, and
as he passed the crowd roared '*Malik, jazak Allahu khair!
Jazak Allahu khair!*' – great king, may Allah reward you.

But not all in the crowd cheered. John rode beside
Reynald, who still wore his chainmail and distinctive
breastplate, although his hands were now tied before
him. Some in the crowd hissed as Reynald rode past.
Others made the sign of the evil eye – bringing the forefinger and thumb together in a circle and shaking their
hands. Reynald ignored them, riding with his head held
high and his eyes fixed straight ahead.

John reached the far side of the square and rode into
the shade of the citadel. The crowd was thickest around
the bridge that led across the moat. Mamluk guards
struggled to hold the masses back, but as John watched,
the people surged towards Nur ad-Din, eager to touch

him. After a moment the guards pushed them back, and the convoy continued. John was almost to the bridge when the crowd again surged forward. Turbaned men pressed all around him, shouting insults at Reynald. The guards had begun to push the crowd back when a grey-bearded man, his mouth empty of teeth, stepped past them and spit at Reynald, catching him in the face. Reynald grimaced in disgust and raised his tied hands to wipe away the spittle. 'Savages,' he muttered and turned towards John. 'How can you fight for these infidels? You have betrayed your crusader's oath. You will burn in hell.'

'Then I shall have you there for company,' John muttered and urged his horse ahead of Reynald's and across the wooden drawbridge. They rode up the paved causeway and into the citadel grounds. The rest of the convoy had begun to gather around Nur ad-Din, who was addressing his men, inviting the emirs and sheikhs to a feast at his palace. John led Reynald to the right, towards the prison house.

John had not ridden far when Nur ad-Din hailed him. 'Where are you taking my prisoner?' he asked as he rode out from the crowd.

'To his cell, Malik.'

'No, bring him to the feast. And you come, too. You can translate for your countryman.'

'He is no countryman of mine,' John grumbled under his breath, but to Nur ad-Din, he nodded and said, 'Very well, Malik.'

'What did he say?' Reynald asked as Nur ad-Din rode away.

'He has invited you to tonight's feast.'

'I have no wish to dine with that infidel,' Reynald sneered.

'You have no choice.' As John rode past, he grabbed the reins of Reynald's horse and pulled it after him towards the barracks.

'Where are we going now?' Reynald asked.

'To the baths.'

Reynald's nose wrinkled in disgust. 'A bath? Do you wish to kill me?'

John gave Reynald a hard look. 'You smell like a pig. I will be sitting beside you, and I wish to enjoy my food. Come.'

The feast was held in the palace's great hall, a long, rectangular room with a high ceiling held up by two rows of stone columns. The guests — fifty in all — were seated cross-legged on cushions around a long, low table, with Nur ad-Din at its centre. Nur ad-Din had Reynald seated across from him, and John sat to Reynald's right, across from Yusuf.

When all the guests were seated, the servants entered. One stood behind each of the guests, and in a simultaneous movement they bent forward and placed a dish before each diner. John's mouth watered as he breathed in the aroma of the tharîdah — pieces of chicken on the bone in an aromatic sauce of chickpeas, onions, eggs, pounded almonds and cinnamon. He took up his knife and two-pronged fork and carved off a piece of the tender chicken. As he did so, he glanced at Reynald. The Prince of Antioch had picked up a drumstick with his hands and was gnawing the meat straight off the bone as fat dribbled into his beard.

'You are meant to use the fork,' John whispered, pointing to the piece of cutlery.

Reynald sucked a last piece of flesh from the drumstick and tossed it on the table. 'Why should I use a fork when God gave me two hands?' he asked, wiping his fingers on his caftan and leaving greasy streaks on the white cotton.

'What are the two of you discussing?' Nur ad-Din asked, leaning towards John.

'The Prince of Antioch was marvelling at your use of the fork,' John explained. 'He says that he prefers to use the hands that God gave him.'

'God gave him feet, too,' Nur ad-Din said. 'Perhaps he wishes to eat with those.' He chuckled at this pleasantry and was joined by the other men at the table.

Reynald flushed red and turned towards John. 'What did he say? Why is he laughing?'

'He said that God also gave you feet and suggested that you eat with those.'

Reynald's jaw clenched. 'Who is this infidel to mock me? Ask him what sort of people scorn pork and wine?'

John translated, and the laughter at the table died away. 'The Prophet, peace and blessings of Allah be upon him, has told us to avoid these things,' Nur ad-Din said sternly, his voice loud in the silence. 'If your Pope told you to forgo wine, would you not do so?'

'Fat chance of that,' Reynald snorted when he had heard John's translation. 'The Pope drinks like a fish.'

John turned to Nur ad-Din. 'He says, "no".'

'Do you not respect the words of your prophets, then?' Nur ad-Din asked. All eyes turned to Reynald.

'What are priests good for?' Reynald asked, picking up the drumstick and waving it to emphasize his point. 'They sit in their churches with their gold and their wine while the real men do the fighting.'

'Do your priests not pray for you, like our sûfis?'

'*Hmph*, I have no need of their prayers, so long as they give me money when I ask. And if they do not—' he snapped the chicken bone in half '—then I take it.'

When John translated, Nur ad-Din's eyebrows shot up. 'You do violence to your Holy Men? Kill them, even?'

'It is forbidden to kill a man of God, and I am no savage.' Reynald paused. 'But I have other ways of persuading priests to do as I ask. When the Patriarch of Antioch refused to fund my expedition against Cyprus, I had him stripped naked, covered in honey and tied down on the roof of the citadel. After four hours in the sun, with ants and bees crawling all over him, he became more amenable to reason.'

Nur ad-Din turned towards John. 'And this patriarch is like an imam?'

'Yes, only more powerful, almost like a caliph.' The emirs grumbled at this.

'Do you not fear the wrath of God?' Nur ad-Din asked Reynald.

'I have taken up the cross and fought to keep the Saracens at bay. It is because of men like me that Jerusalem is Christian, its churches filled with priests instead of infidels. I do not fear God. He has need of me.'

Nur ad-Din's face wrinkled in disgust. 'Men like this are why we must drive the Franks from our lands,' he declared loudly enough for all at the long table to hear. The emirs and sheikhs nodded and thumped the table to show their approval. 'Take him away. He is spoiling my appetite.'

John rose and pulled Reynald up beside him. 'Shall I place him in the prison?'

'No,' Nur ad-Din said. 'We are not savages like him. Give him a house in town and slaves to serve him as befits his station. The sooner he is ransomed, the better. I do not wish to see him again.'

'Yes, Malik.' John grabbed Reynald's arm and guided him from the room.

'What did he say?' Reynald asked as they passed through the palace entrance hall and out to the citadel grounds.

'You will be given your own house and slaves until you are ransomed. And he remarked that your customs are very different from theirs.'

'Damn right. I have nothing in common with those heathen savages.'

'Indeed,' John murmured.

The next day Yusuf stood before the mirror in his chamber, dressed in his finest caftan of red silk. He smiled and leaned close to the mirror to be certain there was nothing caught between his teeth. He straightened his caftan one final time, and satisfied, left his room and headed to the harem. The entrance was framed by two eunuch guards. 'I have come to see Asimat,' Yusuf said.

'You are expected,' one of the eunuchs replied. He led Yusuf down a long hallway, dimly lit by burning tapers. As they approached the door to Asimat's chambers, Yusuf was surprised to see Gumushtagin exit her rooms. When the bald eunuch saw Yusuf, he smiled ingratiatingly.

'Salaam, Yusuf.'

'Salaam, Gumushtagin. What brings you to the harem?'

'One of the few advantages of being a eunuch: I have free access to Nur ad-Din's apartments.' Gumushtagin gave Yusuf a hard look. 'But you are not a eunuch.'

'I am here to visit Asimat.'

'You spend a great deal of time with Nur ad-Din's wife.'

'At his bidding.'

Gumushtagin's eyes narrowed. 'Yes, of course. Ma'a as-salaama, Yusuf.' Gumushtagin gave a small bow and stepped past him.

'Allah yasalmak,' Yusuf replied to the retreating figure, then turned and waited while one of the eunuch guards entered Asimat's chamber and announced him.

'You may enter,' the guard told Yusuf.

Yusuf stepped into the room to find Asimat seated in one of the windows, half a melon in one hand and a spoon in the other. She was wearing a simple, white cotton caftan. One of her maidservants sat on a cushion at her feet, reading from a book. The servant stopped reading when Yusuf entered.

'My lady,' Yusuf said and bowed.

Asimat whispered something to the servant and then rose. 'Salaam, Yusuf,' she said. 'Come, sit.' She gestured towards the centre of the room, where silk cushions sat on the thick carpet. Yusuf waited for her to sit and then sat across from her. The maidservant closed the book and went to the loom.

'Would you like some refreshment?' Asimat asked, holding up the melon in her hand. Yusuf nodded. 'Kaniz!' Asimat called, and a moment later a female servant appeared carrying half a melon. She handed it and a spoon to Yusuf. The pulp of the melon had been mashed and mixed with crushed ice. Yusuf spooned out some of the mixture, which trailed wisps of cold air.

'Ice in the summer; how is it possible?' he asked.

'In winter it is brought from the mountains near Baalbek and stored under straw in a cellar beneath the palace. It is a rare luxury.'

Yusuf swallowed the spoonful of chilled melon and closed his eyes to savour the cool sweetness. 'Delicious.'

'I am glad you enjoy it, and I am glad that you have returned to Aleppo alive, if only so that I could see you again.'

The woman at the loom stopped her work and looked over. Yusuf paled. 'Careful what you say, Khatun.' There was an awkward moment of silence, during which Yusuf fingered his golden belt. 'You have been well since I last saw you?' he finally asked.

'Better. You were right: tears will not help me. If I wish to have a son, I must take my future in my own hands.' She met Yusuf's eyes and did not look away.

Yusuf cleared his throat and glanced towards the loom. 'I am sure that Nur ad-Din will be happy to hear that you are eager to try again.'

Asimat frowned. 'He has taken yet another favourite, who he hopes will give him an heir. I fear I will never have a son by him.'

'But you said—'

'It is best not to speak of it,' Asimat said, cutting him off.

'What shall we talk of, then?'

'I hear that you fought bravely at the battle at Jacob's Ford. Tell me about it.'

'It was glorious,' Yusuf said with a grin. He went on to describe the battle in detail, gesturing with his hands to indicate the position of the two armies. Asimat followed him closely, nodding with interest. 'We crushed them,' Yusuf concluded. 'Hundreds of Franks were killed and thousands more taken prisoner. Their king was lucky to escape.'

Asimat's forehead creased. 'And after all that, you let them go? You did not pursue them?'

'We could not. The Roman Emperor was leading an army from the north. We had to make peace.'

'I see. And did it strike you as strange that Nur ad-Din did not learn that the emperor was on the march until just after he defeated the Franks?'

'What do you mean?'

'An army as large as the emperor's would be hard to conceal.' Asimat lowered her voice. 'Sometimes I think that Nur ad-Din does not wish to conquer the Christians.'

'That is mad!' Yusuf spluttered. 'He speaks of nothing but driving them from our lands.'

'Yes, and the emirs and sheikhs follow him because of this. The people gladly pay their taxes to support his wars. But with the Franks gone, there will be nothing left to unite our people. I think Nur ad-Din fears that if he defeats the Franks, then he will lose his kingdom.'

Yusuf's forehead creased. He had never even considered such things. 'Nur ad-Din will crush the Franks,' he insisted. 'Usama is making peace with the Roman Emperor now. We will have no more to fear from him. Then, once King Baldwin is dead, we will strike again.'

'Perhaps you are right. But if Nur ad-Din does not move against them?'

'Then someone will.'

'You?'

Yusuf shook his head. 'I am only the Emir of Tell Bashir.'

'Yes, but your ambition burns bright, Yusuf.' He opened his mouth to speak, but Asimat held up a hand, stopping him. 'Do not deny it. I have seen the same flame burning in Nur ad-Din. But if you want to be great, then you must seize your destiny.'

'Be careful what you say, Khatun,' Yusuf said stiffly. 'I am a man of honour, and Nur ad-Din is my lord.'

'Nur ad-Din had a lord once, too.' Asimat glanced towards her maidservants and then continued in a whisper. 'His father, Zengi, was found murdered in his own bed.' Again, her dark eyes found his. 'Sometimes you must seize what you want, Yusuf.'

Yusuf forced himself to look away. 'Why are you telling me this? Do you think me a traitor?'

Asimat smiled. 'No, of course not. But not all of Nur ad-Din's subjects are so loyal. If you do not act, then someone will. Gumushtagin, for instance.'

'Is that what he was here for? To plot against Nur ad-Din?'

'Gumushtagin is far too clever to discuss his plans with me, and I would never support him. But you . . .' Asimat met his eyes and lowered her voice still further. 'I will help you, if you help me, Yusuf. We can take both our destinies in hand.'

Yusuf's eyebrows rose. 'Surely you do not mean—?'

Asimat held his gaze for a moment longer, then looked away. 'No,' she said brusquely. 'Forget I spoke. You should go.'

'But—'

'Go!' Asimat said with finality.

His brow knit, Yusuf rose and left the room, the unspoken words churning in his head.

Yusuf returned to his chambers to find Faridah lounging on his bed in a satin robe. 'You look very handsome, my lord,' she said.

Yusuf looked away, embarrassed. 'What do you mean?' he asked gruffly.

Faridah smiled. 'You have no secrets from me, Yusuf.' She crossed the room to him. 'You have been to see Asimat. You would never take such care for me.' She untied the belt of his caftan. 'Be careful of her, my lord. Nur ad-Din favours you. Do not throw away his generosity.'

'I have Nur ad-Din's permission to visit Asimat.'

'All the more reason to be careful.'

Yusuf turned away from her. He shrugged off his

411

caftan and dropped it on the floor. 'Do not lecture me, woman. I know what I am doing.'

Faridah moved close behind him and put her arms around his waist. 'Does Nur ad-Din ask you to dress in your finest clothes when you meet his wife?' she murmured in his ear. 'I cannot stop you from wanting her, Yusuf, but I will stop you from acting the fool. If I can see that you are infatuated with her, then others will, too.'

'There is nothing to see,' Yusuf lied.

'Then you will not go to her again?'

Asimat's words flashed through Yusuf's mind: 'I will help you, if you help me.' Did she want him to give her a son? And what would she give in return? Yusuf rubbed his forehead, trying to bring order to his thoughts. This was madness. Nur ad-Din was his lord. And yet . . . An image of Asimat's dark eyes flashed through his mind.

'I do not wish to speak of it,' he said at last. He pulled away and went to his trunk to retrieve a plain white caftan.

'If you do not speak to me, then I cannot help you. Tell me, my lord. What did she say to you?'

Yusuf sighed and turned to face her. 'She wants me to give her a son.'

Faridah's eyes widened. She came to him and took his hands. 'You cannot.'

'I know,' Yusuf snapped, then continued more softly. 'But she promised me—'

'What?'

Yusuf met her eyes. 'The kingdom.'

'This is madness. Remember what happened to

Nadhira. Nur ad-Din will have her stoned, and you executed.'

Yusuf nodded, but even as he did an image rose unbidden in his mind: the curve of Asimat's body beneath her caftan. Faridah frowned, then slapped him hard. 'How dare you!' Yusuf spluttered. 'Are you mad, woman?'

'It is you who have taken leave of your senses! I will not let you ruin yourself over this woman. We will leave for Tell Bashir.'

'No,' Yusuf said firmly. 'My lord has need of me.'

'You are not thinking of your lord, but of his wife. We will go. That is the only way to put her from your mind.'

Yusuf hesitated, and Faridah raised her hand again. Yusuf caught her wrist. 'Very well,' he said. 'You are right, Faridah. I will return to my lands until Nur ad-Din calls for me. I will think no more of Asimat.'

John crossed the sunny square at the heart of Aleppo and stepped into the souk where medicine was sold. Long ago Yusuf had told him that, for a price, anything could be bought in the souks of Aleppo, and it appeared he was right. The street that held the market was covered over with long strips of wood set half an inch apart, and diffuse light filtered through, illuminating a dizzying array of goods. John stepped around several herb-filled baskets that overflowed the small shops and spread into the street. Other stores sold more refined drugs – powders in clay pots and brightly coloured liquids in glass jars. John passed a thin Saracen who was boiling a deep-blue liquid over a small flame, sending the steam through a tube to collect in a glass jar, where it was now a pale green. John looked away just in time to avoid running into a doctor who was pulling a patient's tooth right there, in the middle of the street. Beyond the doctor, a dark-skinned man with a full head of bushy, black hair was holding up a jar containing a black, viscous substance and loudly proclaiming its ability to cure baldness.

John ignored them all, striding through the market until he came to a narrow alleyway that opened off to the right. He hesitated at the entrance, clenching and unclenching his fists. He knew that what he was doing was wrong, but what other choice did he have? He thought of Zimat, of what she had told him last night. He had to protect her, no matter what the cost. He took a deep breath and entered the alley.

The light was dimmer here, and John had not gone far when he tripped over the outstretched legs of a beggar. He began to offer his apologies, then grimaced in disgust and backed away. The beggar was a leper, his face and arms covered in sores that formed blotches of white against his darkly tanned skin. Amorphous bumps deformed his face, cruelly exaggerating his brow. He held out a mangled hand missing two fingers. 'Charity, good sir. Charity for a poor leper.'

'Stay back, devil,' John growled and drew his dagger.

'Leave him be, John.' John looked up to see Ibn Jumay standing in the alleyway. 'Leprosy is not a judgement from God, it is a disease,' the Jewish doctor said. 'So long as you do not touch him, it is not contagious.' He tilted his head, eyeing John quizzically. 'What brings you here, friend?'

'I came to see you. Yusuf told me that you have a practice in town.'

'Indeed. The man you were about to knife is one of my patients. Come, step inside.' He led John into a brightly lit room that opened off the alley. A broad table – large enough for a man to lie down upon – took up most of the floor space. The walls were covered with shelves lined with clay jars. John took one down and peeked inside to see black, withered leaves. 'Tea,' Ibn Jumay informed him. 'It helps with the digestion. But that is not what you are looking for, I'd wager.'

'No.' John put the jar back. 'I—I—' he began and faltered. He could feel himself flushing red. 'There is a woman.'

'Ah. You have got yourself into a bit of trouble, have you?' John nodded, and Ibn Jumay patted his shoulder. 'You are not the first, John. Nor will you be the last. Luckily, the laws of Islam are lenient in this regard. One moment.' The doctor went to the shelf on the far wall and began pulling down jars and looking into them. Finally, he found the one he was looking for and set it on the table. He scooped out a spoonful of dried leaves and dropped them into a pouch. 'Mix this with boiling water and have her drink it.' He met John's eye. 'It will cause her to expel the child.'

John felt suddenly nauseous. He lowered his eyes and fumbled in his coin purse for payment. He held out a dinar, but Ibn Jumay shook his head. 'That is not necessary.' He placed the pouch in John's outstretched hand.

As John stared at the pouch, he felt tears form and run down his cheeks. Finally, he dropped the medicine on the table. 'I cannot,' he mumbled and hurried out of the door. 'There must be another way.'

John strode through the gate and into the sunlit grounds of the citadel. A mamluk regiment was training on the field, and John skirted around them as he made his way towards the palace. He was almost there when Yusuf emerged.

'John!' he called. 'I was just coming to see you.' Yusuf frowned as he came closer. 'Are you well, friend? You look ill.'

'I am fine.'

'That is good, because we have a long journey ahead of us. I have decided to leave Aleppo.'

John felt his stomach tighten. He could not leave. Not now. His mouth was impossibly dry, but he managed to ask, 'When?'

'Tomorrow. I go now to take my leave of Khaldun and my sister. I will meet you in the barracks afterwards to arrange our departure with Qaraqush and Turan.'

John nodded. He watched Yusuf leave the citadel grounds, but when Yusuf had gone, John did not go to the barracks. Instead, he hurried to Yusuf's quarters in the palace. He found Yusuf's bedchamber empty. 'Hello?' John called. Faridah entered from the next room. She wore a thin cotton nightgown through which John could see the outline of her breasts and the curve of her hip. He looked away.

'Yusuf is not here,' she said.

'I know. I have come to speak with you.'

'We should not meet alone. You should go.'

John met her eyes. 'You said once that if I needed a friend, I could come to you. I am desperate, Faridah, and you are the only one who will understand.'

'What of Yusuf?'

'I cannot speak to him of this.'

Faridah studied him. 'You look terrible,' she said at last. 'Wait here.' She passed back into her room, and when she returned a moment later, she wore a green silk caftan. 'Have a seat,' she told him, and they sat across from one another on cushions. 'What is bothering you, John?'

John looked away. He felt suddenly awkward. 'I—I cannot leave Aleppo.'

'What do you mean?'

'There is someone—' John began, but could say no more.

'A woman?' Faridah prompted. John nodded, and Faridah smiled. 'This is a good thing! Yusuf is your friend, but he does not own you. You do not need to sacrifice your life to him. You should be with this woman. Yusuf will understand.'

'No. It is not any woman.'

Faridah arched an eyebrow. 'Who?' John lowered his eyes and did not speak. 'Who?' Faridah demanded.

'Zimat.'

'Yusuf's sister!' Faridah gasped. 'Are you mad?'

'She loves me. She desires a divorce from Khaldun.'

'Yusuf will never allow it. You are his friend, but you are still an ifranji. It would bring shame to his family.'

'Then what should I do?'

'You should leave Aleppo with Yusuf. It is for the best. Do not see Zimat again. Forget about her.'

'I cannot.' John paused and took a deep breath. 'She is pregnant.'

Faridah's eyes went wide. 'She carries your child? Are you sure?'

'Zimat says that the child is mine.'

'Then you must get rid of it. There are herbs—'

'No!' John said, more loudly than he had intended. 'I cannot kill the child.' He met her eyes. 'I will tell Yusuf. I cannot live with these secrets.'

'No. He will kill you!'

'Then we will run away, to the kingdom of Jerusalem.'

'And do you think Zimat will be happy amongst the Franks?' Faridah demanded. 'She is the wife of an emir, surrounded by luxury. What will her life be like as the wife of a simple soldier? What future will there be for your child?'

'Then what?' John demanded, his jaw clenched. 'I leave the woman I love? I leave my child to be raised by another man?'

Faridah nodded. 'If you truly love Zimat, then you must do what is necessary to protect her and the child.'

'And what about when the child is born? What if it has blue eyes or blond hair?'

'Pray to God that it does not.'

John stood atop the gatehouse of Tell Bashir, his wet clothes clinging to him and rain running off his nose as he stared out at the road from Aleppo. He held a long strip of leather, which he methodically wrapped and unwrapped around his right hand. The two mamluks on watch were hunkered down under their cloaks. 'What the devil do you suppose is hounding al-ifranji?' one of them whispered.

'Maybe he lost at dice.'

'Maybe he has lost his mind.'

John heard the words, but he paid no more attention to them than he did to the rain. It was seven months since they had left Aleppo and almost nine months since Zimat had told him that she had ceased to bleed, that she was with child. John expected news of her delivery any day, and so he stood here at the gate whenever he could, his eyes fixed on the winding road from Aleppo.

John thought he saw movement in the distance. He squinted, trying to penetrate the curtain of rain. He could just make out a group of riders at the edge of town. John turned to the men on watch. 'Someone is coming. Inform the emir and prepare to open the gate.'

The men scrambled away, and John turned back to watch the riders approach. As they drew closer, he could see that there were five of them. They splashed down the muddy street through the centre of town and up the short ramp to the gate, where the man in the lead pushed back his hood. It was Yusuf's younger brother, Selim. 'Open the gates!' he called. 'I come with news.'

John watched as Selim entered and was led into the citadel's keep. John bowed his head and took a deep breath. 'Please God,' he whispered. 'Let the child have dark eyes.' Then he descended from the wall and strode across the muddy courtyard to the keep. He went to Yusuf's chambers and found the door open. Stepping inside, he found Yusuf kissing Selim on each cheek. Turan stood to the side, smiling.

'John!' Yusuf exclaimed. 'Selim has brought good news.'

'Yes?' John asked, barely able to keep his voice from shaking.

'You remember my sister, Zimat? She has given birth to a son!'

'A son,' John whispered hoarsely. He turned to Selim. 'You have seen the boy?' Selim nodded. 'What is he like?'

'He is a healthy child.'

'And who does he favour?' John asked urgently. 'His mother?'

Selim frowned, confused by John's interest. 'The boy is only a babe, but he has his father's eyes.'

John sighed in relief. 'Il-Hamdillah,' he murmured. 'God be praised.'

Chapter 17

Yusuf could see his breath steaming in the air as he and John sat in the saddle atop a small rise just outside Tell Bashir. They had ridden out to inspect the harvest. It was autumn, and the fields were covered with golden wheat. Slaves moved between the rows of stalks, their scythes flashing in the sun. The wheat rippled in a sudden breeze, and Yusuf pulled his fur cloak more tightly about him. He thought of the panther he and John had tracked down in the mountains above Baalbek. How long ago was that? Yusuf counted on his fingers.

'What are you thinking of?' John asked.

'Time. It has been nine years since we left Baalbek.'

John nodded and gestured to the workers around them. 'I remember when I was a slave working in your father's fields. It seems like yesterday.'

'I was fascinated by you,' Yusuf chuckled. 'You were so foreign.'

'And I hated you. I hated all Saracens.' John sighed. 'We were so young then.'

'We are not so old now.'

'But we grow older.' John reached into his saddlebag and removed a book bound in finely worked black leather. He held it out to Yusuf.

'What is this?'

'A gift. You are twenty-three today.'

Yusuf frowned. 'It is just another day.' He tried to hand the book back, but John would not take it.

'Open it.'

Yusuf opened the book at random. The pages were covered with beautifully drawn Arabic script. He read: 'If a kingdom is divided against itself, that kingdom cannot stand. If a house is divided against itself, that house will not be able to stand.'

'It is the New Testament, part of our holy book.'

A smile tugged at the corner of Yusuf's mouth. 'You wish to convert me, John?'

'No. I want you to know your enemy.'

Yusuf looked at the book for a moment longer, then placed the palm of his right hand over his heart and bowed his head. 'Thank you.' He slipped the book into his saddlebag. 'I accept your gift.'

They left the fields behind and rode back to the citadel. In the courtyard a dozen young mamluks were training under the supervision of Qaraqush. Yusuf paused to watch them. The boys rode in a circle around the courtyard, firing arrows at a target that hung from one of the walls. Only one arrow had struck home so far, but the boys would improve with time. They were no older than ten, slaves newly taken from the distant Turkish steppes. By the time they reached eighteen and were freed, they would be skilled warriors.

Yusuf dismounted and handed his reins to John. 'I will see you at dinner after evening prayers,' he said, then entered the citadel's keep and went to his quarters. When Yusuf opened the door, his eyes widened. Faridah lay naked on his bed, her entire body covered with swirling patterns drawn with henna. She was well past thirty now and more voluptuous than when Yusuf had first met her, with wider hips and a softer body. But her hair was the same fiery red and her face unlined. She was, Yusuf thought, even more beautiful. 'Îd mîlâd sa'id,' she purred. Happy birthday.

'I am not a Frank, Faridah. To my people, the day of our birth is but another day.'

Faridah arched an eyebrow. 'Then you do not wish to receive your present?' She pulled a blanket over herself.

Yusuf went to the bed and pulled the blanket back. With his forefinger, he lightly traced the swirling patterns of henna, his finger moving down her stomach to between her legs. Faridah gasped, and Yusuf smiled. 'Allah has told us the greatest joy is in giving.' He began to kiss her when there was a knock on the door. Faridah rose and passed into her own quarters. Yusuf turned to the door. 'Enter!'

Turan came into the room, a letter in his hand. 'This has come from Aleppo.' Yusuf took the letter and went to the window, where he broke the seal. 'Is it from Nur ad-Din?' Turan asked.

Yusuf nodded. 'King Baldwin is dying. Nur ad-Din has called me back to Aleppo to help him prepare his campaign against the Franks.'

'Then you must go. I will tell Qaraqush and John to prepare our departure.' Turan headed for the door.

'Wait, Brother,' Yusuf called. 'I admit that I had doubts when I made you my second-in-command, but you have served me well these last few years. Now I have another, greater service to ask of you.'

'Name it, Brother.'

'The campaign against the Franks may last for many years. I want you to stay here, to rule Tell Bashir while I am gone.'

Turan frowned. 'I would rather fight by your side.'

'I know, but I need you here to make certain that my lands flourish.'

Turan hesitated for only a moment before nodding. He had changed greatly since Nadhira's death. 'Very well.'

'Thank you, Brother.' Turan left and Faridah re-entered the room. Her lips were pressed in a thin line of worry. 'Nur ad-Din has called for me,' Yusuf told her.

'I heard.' She met his eyes. 'And Asimat?'

Yusuf smiled to reassure her. 'You need not worry. She means nothing to me.'

NOVEMBER 1161: ALEPPO

Upon his arrival in Aleppo, Yusuf went straight to Nur ad-Din's apartments to present himself. He met Shirkuh in the antechamber, just leaving the king's quarters. 'Yusuf!' Shirkuh beamed and embraced him. As they exchanged kisses, Yusuf noticed for the first time that he was now taller than his uncle. 'How have you been, young eagle?'

'My lands flourish. And you, Uncle?'

Shirkuh frowned. 'Nur ad-Din has me riding across his kingdom and beyond to purchase more mamluks.' He shook his head. 'Our king is a man possessed. Gumushtagin has convinced him that Allah will not give him an heir until he rids our lands of the Franks. Nur ad-Din speaks of nothing but defeating them. He works without stopping. He has not left his study for days.'

'Surely Allah will favour such devotion.'

'Inshallah,' Shirkuh grumbled. 'Try to get him to rest, if you can.' He placed a hand on Yusuf's shoulder. 'You must come to Khaldun's to meet your nephew. I will see you there tonight.'

'Tonight,' Yusuf agreed. Shirkuh left, and Yusuf stepped forward so that the guards could search him. They took his sword and dagger, then led him into Nur ad-Din's quarters. Yusuf followed the mamluk through the first room, where he had dined before, and into Nur ad-Din's study. A massive desk dominated the room, covered with papers and maps. More papers had spilled on to the floor. Nur ad-Din leaned over the desk and marked an x on one of the maps. Yusuf noticed that the tips of his fingers were ink-stained.

'My lord,' Yusuf said quietly.

Nur ad-Din looked up and his face brightened. 'Yusuf! You have returned.' He waved Yusuf forward. 'Come, look at this.'

The map before Nur ad-Din showed the Frankish

425

lands. 'What are these?' Yusuf asked, pointing to one of the dozens of xs that had been marked on the map.

Nur ad-Din grinned. 'I have sent scouts into the Frankish lands. These are places where the terrain will give us an advantage. At that one, Hattin, our enemy will be exposed and without water. If we can lure them to one of these spots, then the battle will be half won.' Nur ad-Din stood straight and clapped his hands together with satisfaction. 'The time has almost come. Usama has been to the court in Jerusalem. He reports that Baldwin will die any day now.'

'Then we attack in the spring?' Yusuf asked eagerly.

'No. Baldwin's brother Amalric is said to be half mad, an idiot who stutters and laughs at nothing. The longer he reigns, the weaker the Franks will become. And I must be sure that the emperor in Constantinople will not intervene. We will wait a year, and in the meantime I will prepare an army the likes of which the world has never seen. That is why I have called you here. I want you to work with Gumushtagin to collect a special tax to help fund the coming war.'

Yusuf frowned. 'I will of course serve as it pleases you, my lord, but perhaps my talents could be better used elsewhere.'

Nur ad-Din shook his head. 'I prize your honesty, Yusuf. I need you to make sure that every fal collected makes it into my coffers. Gumushtagin is clever with money, but I do not trust him as I do you.'

Yusuf placed his hand over his heart and nodded. 'Thank you, Malik. I will not fail you.'

'Good,' Nur ad-Din murmured as he turned his

426

attention back to the map. He dismissed Yusuf with a wave of his hand. Yusuf was at the door when Nur ad-Din called out to him: 'Wait, Yusuf. There is one more thing. I want you to visit Asimat.'

Yusuf felt a sudden tightness in his chest. 'Asimat, my lord?'

'She suffered another miscarriage recently.' Nur ad-Din sighed and massaged his temples. 'She has been impossible these last months, and you always seem to cheer her.'

Yusuf swallowed hard. 'Very well, my lord. I shall do my best.'

John wiped nervous sweat from his forehead as he waited outside the gate to Khaldun's home. He and Yusuf had left the citadel after evening prayers, and the air had cooled with the setting of the sun. Still, John's caftan was soaked and his stomach was tying itself in knots. He had never been this nervous, not even on the eve of battle.

'How old do you think Khaldun's son is now?' Yusuf mused. 'He must be nearing his third year.'

'Three years and seven months,' John said quietly.

Yusuf glanced at him sharply, then smiled. 'Is that so? You never cease to impress me, John.'

The gate swung open, and they stepped into the court-yard, which was lit by torches burning in brackets on the walls. At the far end, Khaldun was striding out from his home to greet them. A young boy trailed behind him.

'Yusuf!' Khaldun called as he approached. The two men met near the fountain in the centre of the courtyard and exchanged kisses. Khaldun gestured to the boy, who was peeking out from behind his legs. 'This is my son. Ubadah, greet your uncle.'

The boy stepped out from behind Khaldun and bowed. 'Salaam 'Alaykum, Uncle,' he said shyly.

Yusuf lifted Ubadah from the ground and kissed him on both cheeks. 'Wa 'Alaykum as-Salaam, little man.' The boy giggled, and Yusuf set him down. 'I am glad to meet you at last, Ubadah.'

John had not moved from the gate. His body felt leaden, beyond his control. Ubadah had dark brown eyes, but other than that his resemblance to John was remarkable: the same straight, narrow nose; the same arch of the brow; the same square chin. The boy's hair was sandy brown – light for a Saracen. There was no doubt in John's mind; Ubadah was his child.

'Come, John,' Yusuf called. 'Introduce yourself to my nephew.'

John approached woodenly and knelt before the boy. His mouth was dry, and it was all he could do to speak. 'Salaam, little one. I am pleased to meet you.'

Ubadah stood wide-eyed, then his lower lip began to quiver. 'Ifranji! Ifranji!' he bawled and ran to Khaldun, who lifted him up and held him close.

'I am sorry, John,' Khaldun said, laughing. 'I fear I may have told my son one too many stories about the terrible Franks.'

John felt a tightness in his chest and suddenly it was difficult to breathe. He forced himself to smile. 'I understand,' he managed. Khaldun's laughter faded as he looked from John to his son. He looked back at John and frowned. John struggled to control his emotions as he met Khaldun's eyes.

'Where is my sister?' Yusuf asked, breaking the tension.

'She is not well,' Khaldun said, turning to Yusuf. 'She asked that you pardon her absence.'

'It is nothing serious, I hope.'

Khaldun shook his head. 'A passing indisposition.' Somewhere nearby, a muezzin took up his strident call. John looked up and saw that the light had faded from the sky, which was now an inky black, speckled with stars. 'It is time for the isha'a,' Khaldun said. 'We will pray here.' He pointed to a streak of white on the wall of the courtyard. 'I have marked the direction of Mecca.' As servants came out from the house with prayer rugs, Khaldun turned to John. 'You may wait in the gatehouse, if you wish.'

'I will stay and pray to my God,' John replied. He stepped back into the shadows near a side door of the house and knelt. He bowed his head but kept his eyes on the men before him.

Yusuf, Khaldun and Ubadah went to the fountain and began to wash their heads, arms and feet in preparation for prayer. They were joined in the ritual ablution by the Muslim servants and mamluks of the household. The men finished washing and stood before their prayer rugs, their backs to John. They began to pray, chanting the first lines of the rak'ah: *In the name of Allah, the Most Gracious, the Most Merciful.* John knew that the isha'a had four rak'at, taking maybe ten minutes. The men prostrated themselves near the end of the first rak'ah, and he quickly rose and silently slipped through the side door. At the door to Zimat's room he stopped. He pressed his ear against it, but at first he heard nothing over the chanting outside. Then he made out a faint sound – crying. John opened the door.

Zimat sat in bed, her knees drawn up to her chest. She looked up in surprise as John entered, and he saw that her face was streaked with tears. 'John,' she breathed.

'I feared you would have forgotten me,' he said as he closed the door.

Without a word, Zimat rose from the bed and ran to him, burying her head in his chest. 'How could I forget you? I see you every day in our son.' John held her and stroked her hair. He could feel the knots in his stomach begin to relax. Then Zimat pulled away from him. 'Why have you come back?' she demanded. She turned her back to him. 'Why did you leave me?'

John placed his hands on her shoulders. 'I had to. I could not take you with me to live amongst the Franks. Your son – our son – would have had nothing. You would have had nothing.'

'I would have had you.'

John gently turned her so that she was facing him. He lifted her chin so that he could look into her dark eyes. 'You can still have me, if you want me.'

'You know I do.' John leaned forward to kiss her, but she put her hand to his lips. 'But you must promise to never leave me again.'

John took her hand and kissed it. 'I promise.' He pulled her against him and kissed her. Her lips were even softer than he had remembered.

The door to the room started to open, and they jumped apart. Their son, Ubadah, stood in the doorway. His eyes widened, and then he screwed up his face and began to cry. 'Ifranji,' he bawled, pointing at John. 'Ifranji!'

Zimat went to him and swept him up into her arms. 'There, there my sweetness,' she cooed. 'He is not an ifranji. He is a friend.' The boy quieted, and Zimat looked to John. 'You must go.'

'But what if—'

'I will deal with my son and Khaldun. Go!'

John left the room and slipped back out into the courtyard. The men were prostrate, just finishing the final *rak'ah*. They sat up and murmured in unison:

Greetings to you, O Prophet, and the mercy and
blessings of Allah.
Peace be unto us, and unto the righteous servants of
Allah.
I bear witness that there is none worthy of worship
except Allah.
And I bear witness that Muhammad is His servant
and messenger.

Each man looked right and whispered, 'Peace be upon you.' Then they looked left and repeated the phrase. They rose. Prayers were over. The servants began to gather up the prayer mats while the mamluks headed back to the gatehouse.

The main door to the house opened and Zimat appeared in the doorway. She was still holding Ubadah.

'Brother!' she called to Yusuf. 'Welcome! Come inside and let us feast your arrival.'

John watched as Yusuf went to her and kissed her on both cheeks. 'It is good to see you, Sister.' He reached out and tousled Ubadah's hair. 'Your son is a handsome little man. He resembles his father.'

A smile tugged at the corner of Zimat's mouth. She looked past Yusuf and her eyes met John's. 'I know,' she replied.

'She is my lord's wife. She is my lord's wife,' Yusuf whispered under his breath as he approached the harem. At the entrance, the eunuch guards barred his way. 'I have come to see Asimat at Nur ad-Din's bidding,' Yusuf told them.

One of the guards nodded. 'Follow me.' The guard led him to Asimat's room and showed him inside. On the far side of the room, Asimat sat on a cushion across from one of her servants. They were bent over a games board, and stepping closer, Yusuf saw that they were playing shatranj. Asimat moved her horse – two spaces forward and one to the side – to threaten the servant's shah. She did not greet Yusuf.

'My lady,' Yusuf said and bowed.

Asimat looked up and frowned. 'It is you.' The servant rose silently, and Yusuf took her place. He could feel the servant's eyes on him as she went to stand by the door.

'Nur ad-Din says that you have not been well,' Yusuf said. Indeed, now that he was sitting across from Asimat he noticed dark circles under her eyes. Her hair, usually carefully combed, now fell unkempt about her shoulders. She was still beautiful, but damaged somehow.

'There is no mystery. I grow old and I have no son. That is all that ails me.'

'You are still young, Khatun.' He smiled. 'You will have a son.'

'By who? Nur ad-Din?' She laughed bitterly. 'He does not come to my bed any longer. He plants his seed in younger women. Who, then, will give me a child?' Yusuf looked away. 'Who?' Asimat demanded loudly.

'I only wished to cheer you,' Yusuf murmured.

'There is nothing *you* can do for me.' She met his eyes. 'You are a coward.' Yusuf blinked in surprise at the insult. 'I offered you everything, and you fled,' Asimat hissed, her voice low so her servant would not overhear. 'You will never be anything but the Emir of Tell Bashir, a god-forsaken fort in the middle of nowhere. You do not have the courage to be more.'

Yusuf felt his face flush red. 'I have courage, Khatun,' he said between clenched teeth. 'But I have honour, too.'

Asimat's eyes narrowed, and she searched his face for a long time. 'You have too much honour,' she said at last. 'That is why you will never be great.' She turned her attention back to her game and dismissed him with a wave of her hand. 'You may go now.'

Late that night, Yusuf stood with his back pressed against the stone wall of the palace, his bare feet clinging to a thin ledge of stone no more than six inches wide. He looked down to the ground far below, where white rocks at the base of the cliff that fell away from this side of the palace gleamed in the moonlight. He had crawled out of his window in the palace and was now making his way along the ledge towards Asimat's chambers. He inched his right foot further along the wall. As he did so, the piece of ledge beneath his left foot gave way. Yusuf teetered, his heart hammering in his chest, but managed to stay upright. Below him, the chunk of ledge clattered off the wall and disappeared into the darkness far below. 'By Allah,' Yusuf whispered to himself. 'What am I doing?'

He clung to the wall while his heart slowed. He knew he should turn back, but he could not. Asimat's words had stung and festered in his heart: 'You are a coward . . . That is why you will never be great.' He had to speak to her, if only to show her that she was wrong. He was no coward, and he would be more than the Emir of Tell Bashir. Much more.

Yusuf continued along the wall until he came to a window. He knew this was Shirkuh's chamber. It was dark. Yusuf slipped past and continued on his way. He traversed three more dark windows without incident and then came to a row of brightly lit, arched windows, which stretched along the wall for thirty feet. Yusuf peered inside and saw three guards on the far side of the room standing at attention beside a pair of double doors and facing out towards the window. Yusuf crouched down, trying to get below the windows, but it was impossible on the narrow ledge. '*Yaha*!' he cursed under his breath. There was no way to pass without being seen.

Or was there? Yusuf turned himself around so that his cheek was pressed firmly against the stone wall. Then he bent down until he could grip the rough stone of the ledge with his hands. 'Allah protect me,' he whispered and slid his feet off the ledge, lowering himself so that he hung from his hands, his body dangling over the rocks below.

Yusuf began to move slowly along the wall, shifting his hands over a few inches at a time. Looking up, he could see bright torchlight spilling out from the windows above. He was only a quarter of the way across, and already his fingers were beginning to burn with fatigue. Yusuf grit his teeth and kept moving. He glanced up – halfway there. He began to move faster. His hands were in agony now; his knuckles felt as if they were on fire. He reached his left hand a bit too far along the wall and it slipped off, leaving him hanging by one hand. He felt his grip slipping and looked down to the ground far below. Grunting with the effort, he swung his left hand back up to the ledge. He closed his eyes against the pain and forced himself to keep moving, one hand after the other. When he opened his eyes, the arched windows were behind him. He pulled himself upwards, his legs scrabbling against the wall, until he managed to get one foot up on the ledge. He stood slowly, pressing himself into the wall. He stayed there for a moment, panting and flexing his hands. When his pulse finally steadied, he moved on.

Asimat's window was the second one he came to. Yusuf peered inside, but could see nothing in the darkness. He hesitated for a moment, then squeezed through the narrow opening. He froze, his heart beating violently. To his left, he could make out a washbasin, and to his right, Asimat's bed. He crept towards it. Asimat

435

was asleep, lying on her back. It was a hot night, and she had kicked off her covers. She wore a nightgown of almost transparent silk, through which Yusuf could see the outline of her side, the gentle curves of her breasts and her nipples, dark against her pale skin. Her hair lay over half her face. She looked peaceful. Then she opened her eyes and screamed. 'Help! Guards!'

Yusuf knelt beside her and clapped his hand over her mouth. 'It is me, Yusuf,' he whispered.

Her eyes went wide. She pulled his hand away. 'What are you doing here?' she hissed. She looked away to the door; the sound of footsteps was coming along the hall. 'You must hide. Now!'

Yusuf ran back to the window and slipped through just as the door banged open. He pressed himself against the wall, out of sight. He could hear several eunuch guards troop into the room.

'What is it, Khatun?' one of the guards asked. 'What has happened?'

'It was nothing, a nightmare,' Asimat replied. Yusuf glanced through the window and saw that she had risen from her bed and was confronting half a dozen guards. He ducked back out of sight.

'Are you sure, my lady?' the guard insisted. 'I can leave a guard here if that will make you more comfortable.'

'That will not be necessary. You may go.'

Yusuf heard the guards march out and the door close behind them. A moment later, Asimat leaned out the window. 'Are you mad?' she demanded. 'Why have you come here?'

'I came to see you. I thought—'

'You thought what, you fool! Nur ad-Din will kill us both if the guards find you here.'

'I am sorry. I will go.' Yusuf began to edge away.

'No. The guards will be more alert now. You should wait. Come in.' Asimat disappeared back into her room.

Yusuf moved to the window and swung inside. Asimat was standing beside her bed, slipping a silk robe over her more revealing nightgown. 'Well?' she whispered as she tied the robe closed. 'Now that you are here, what did you come for?'

Yusuf moved closer. 'You said once that you would help me if I helped you.' He looked into her eyes – two black pools in the darkness. 'What did you mean?'

'You know what I meant.'

Yusuf shook his head. 'No. I must hear you say it.'

'Then you are not the man I hoped you were.' Asimat turned her back to him. 'There are some things that cannot be said. They are too dangerous.' She stood silently, her long black hair illuminated by the soft moonlight falling through the window. Yusuf's eyes moved from her shoulders to the curve of her hips beneath her silk robe, and down to her bare calves.

He swallowed, then moved to her and put his hand on her side. He gently turned her so that she was facing him. 'I am the man you hoped for,' he whispered and kissed her. Her mouth opened to his. He moved his hand to the small of her back and pulled her close against him so that he could feel her stomach and breasts against him. After a moment, he pulled away. 'I will give you a child,' he told her.

Her only answer was to reach out and run her hand through his hair. Then she pulled his head down towards her and kissed him, running her tongue lightly over his lips. While they kissed, she took his hand and placed it on her breast. Her nipple was hard. Yusuf's breathing quickened, and he felt himself stiffen. He kissed her harder while untying her robe and pulling it from her shoulders. He put his hands under her nightgown, encircling her thin waist, and then running them up her sides to grasp her breasts. She slipped her hand inside his caftan, and he gasped with pleasure as she grasped his zib. She moaned softly as he began to greedily kiss the long curve of her neck. He felt her breath hot in his ear. 'Give me a son,' she whispered, 'and I will give you a kingdom.'

Chapter 18

Yusuf sat in the council chamber, his eyes on the carpet before him. Nur ad-Din was talking, but Yusuf found it harder and harder to meet his lord's eye. Indeed, he hardly heard a word the king said. Yusuf's mind kept drifting back to thoughts of Asimat: the feel of her body as it moved under him, their whispered promises. He had visited her many times in the past months. Each time he swore to himself it would be the last. But always he returned. He shook his head, trying to clear his thoughts.

'Yusuf!' Nur ad-Din called. Yusuf looked up. He met Nur ad-Din's eyes, then quickly looked away. 'I was speaking to you.'

'I am sorry, my lord. I did not hear.'

'I see.' Nur ad-Din studied Yusuf for a moment. 'You look as if you had a long night, my young friend. Gumushtagin tells me that he visited you to discuss collection of the tax from Homs, but you were not in your chamber.'

Yusuf felt himself redden. Did Gumushtagin suspect something? Yusuf looked to the eunuch, seated beside

439

Nur ad-Din. Gumushtagin returned his gaze impassively, revealing nothing. 'I—I—' Yusuf began.

'With a woman, were you?' Nur ad-Din suggested. Yusuf nodded. '*Ah ha*! So you are human after all. I am glad to hear it. Your Faridah is beautiful, but one woman is not enough for a young man. You should enjoy yourself, just so long as you don't create any mischief. Stick to whores and virgins.'

'Yes, Malik.'

'Now, I was asking you about Baalbek. Gumushtagin tells me they have sent seven thousand dinars in payment. He says they could send more.'

Next to Yusuf, Khaldun, who was Emir of Baalbek, spoke up. 'That is all we have, my lord. I told Gumushtagin—'

Nur ad-Din raised his hand to stop him. He looked to Yusuf. 'You were raised in Baalbek, Yusuf. Can they pay more?'

Yusuf glanced at Khaldun, then nodded. 'Ten thousand.'

'Good,' Nur ad-Din said. 'I need every fal I can find to put our army in the field.' He paused and looked around the room at his emirs. 'War is coming. King Baldwin is dead.' There was a murmur of excitement. 'We will gather our men and watch the new king, Amalric. When he makes a mistake, we shall strike!' The men pounded the floor to show their approval. 'Now go,' Nur ad-Din told them, 'and bring me more men.'

Yusuf began to leave, but Nur ad-Din called for him to remain. 'I have a special task for you, Yusuf. It concerns our Frankish prisoner, Reynald.'

'He is still here?'

'His subjects do not seem eager to pay his ransom, and I begin to see why. I have had disturbing reports of his behaviour. It is said that he beats his servants, has raped one of them even. You speak Frankish. I want you to speak with him.'

'And what shall I tell him, my lord?'

'Tell him that I have treated him as a guest, but if he continues to spit upon my hospitality, then I will be happy to treat him as a prisoner.' Yusuf nodded. 'And Yusuf, take this opportunity to observe Reynald. He may be a savage, but he is a powerful man amongst the Franks. Find out what drives him, how he thinks. I wish to know as much about my enemy as possible.'

Yusuf reined to a halt outside the gate of a nondescript house, one of over a dozen sandwiched together on this narrow street not far from the citadel. A gap-toothed, blind beggar sat next to the gate, singing softly to himself. Yusuf looked to John.

'This is it,' John said as he slid from the saddle.

Yusuf dismounted and pounded on the gate. 'Open up!' he shouted. He knocked again, then stepped back to wait.

The blind man had stopped singing. He looked towards Yusuf with white, milky eyes. 'That is an evil place,' he lisped. 'I hear things at night, horrible things.'

The gate creaked open, and Yusuf turned away from the old man. A mamluk guard stood in the gateway, blocking the entrance to the home's courtyard. Yusuf nodded in greeting. 'We are here to see Reynald.'

The guard's nose wrinkled in disgust. 'He is in there.' He jerked his head towards the door on the far side of the courtyard.

'What is he doing?'

'Only the devil knows. We don't set foot in the house. It is an unclean place.'

Yusuf glanced at John, who shrugged. Yusuf turned back to the guard and handed him his reins. 'Look after our horses.' He strode towards the house, with John following. Yusuf reached the door and pushed it open. They stepped into a rectangular reception room, bare but for a large rush mat in the centre of the wooden floor. The house was silent. No one came to greet them.

'Is anyone here?' John called. 'Reynald?'

They heard the slap of sandals approaching, and a moment later a slave girl entered from a door to the right. She was a young Frankish woman, blonde and pale with a purplish bruise on her left cheek. She bowed when she saw them, then straightened and without speaking pointed down the hallway she had just come from.

As soon as Yusuf entered the hallway he heard something – a muffled whimpering. He turned to John, who raised an eyebrow. The noise grew louder as they continued on, the slave girl trailing them. Yusuf stopped at an open doorway at the end of the hall and saw the source of the muffled cries. A naked slave girl with a gag in her mouth was standing facing away from them, her hands against the far wall of the room. Reynald was behind her, grunting and panting, his breeches around his ankles and his hands on her hips.

'Excuse me, my lord,' John called out.

'I said I did not wish to be disturbed!' Reynald roared without turning around.

'Lord Reynald,' Yusuf called more loudly. 'I wish to speak with you.'

Reynald glanced behind him, and his face went red. He shoved the girl aside and pulled up his breeches. 'Mary!' he shouted at the girl behind Yusuf. 'Take them to the front and make them comfortable.' He turned to Yusuf. 'I will be with you in a moment.'

Yusuf followed Mary back to the reception hall, where she provided them with silk cushions and urged them to sit. She left and returned a few minutes later with tea. Shortly thereafter, Reynald entered, now dressed in a loose-fitting cotton tunic. He sat across from them. 'To what do I owe this honour?' he asked.

'Nur ad-Din has asked me to speak with you,' Yusuf said. 'The slaves who serve you are his property. They are not for you to use as you please.'

'What is the worry?' Reynald leered. 'They are spoiled now, anyway. Nur ad-Din can add them to the price of my ransom.'

Yusuf frowned. 'You have been our prisoner for nearly five years. Your countrymen do not seem eager to pay for your return.'

'The bastards! Patriarch Aimery has turned them against me.'

'Be that as it may, it does not appear that you will be leaving any time soon. Nur ad-Din wishes you to know that he will treat you as a guest so long as you behave as a guest should. If you continue to abuse his hospitality, then he will have you thrown in the dungeon.'

'I see,' Reynald grunted. 'So I cannot touch the girls?' Yusuf shook his head. Reynald glared at him. 'I cannot leave this place, and I cannot please myself. I might as well be in the dungeon. What am I supposed to do here?'

'I will bring you books, if you desire.'

'Books?' Reynald snorted. 'Books are for priests. I have no use for them.'

Yusuf's eyes widened. 'You cannot read?'

'I have spent my life in combat, not wasting daylight on books.' Reynald pointed a thick finger at Yusuf. 'That is why one Frankish knight is worth ten of you Saracens. You are too cultivated, too learned by half. You are practically women, with your silk robes, perfumes and bath-houses. No wonder you have to hide your women away in harems: so real men will not take them.'

Yusuf wanted to reach out and slap this uncouth barbarian, but he restrained himself. He took a long sip of tea, then set the small cup aside. 'Learning and cultivation do not make one weak. Throughout history, the civilized man has repeatedly triumphed over the savage: Alexander over the Persians; the Romans over the Gauls; the Prophet over his enemies.'

'Rome fell.'

'Only when it became corrupt,' John interjected.

'Perhaps that is why God has sent us,' Reynald said. 'He has called on a stronger race to wipe you corrupt heathens from this earth.'

'A stronger race?' Yusuf smiled in the face of the insult. 'Yet you are our prisoner.'

Reynald's cheek twitched. 'You defeated us through trickery at Jacob's Ford.'

444

'Strategy, not trickery,' John said. 'Perhaps if you had read more books, then you would know the difference.'

Reynald turned towards John. 'So you take his side against me? Do not forget that you were once my man, John, bound to me by oath. But you Saxons are all alike – faithless dogs. King William was right to crush your people.'

'At least my people have honour.'

'That is always the answer of the weak.'

'I am strong enough to beat you,' John growled.

'I'd like to see you try, you and your sodomite friend!'

John began to rise, but Yusuf put out a hand to restrain him. 'Perhaps we can settle this argument in a more civilized fashion,' he said to Reynald. 'I shall hold a tournament in the citadel. If you wish to prove your strength in combat, then you can do so there.'

'It would be my pleasure.'

'Good,' Yusuf said and rose. 'I will see you soon, Reynald. Come, John.'

Yusuf was at the door when Reynald called out to him. 'A tournament must have a prize. If I win, then I can do as I please with the women.'

Yusuf stopped and turned. He looked to the servant Mary, who stood in the corner, her eyes wide and her legs visibly shaking. He turned back to Reynald, and took a deep breath. 'So be it.'

Yusuf could hear the ring of steel on steel over the roar of the crowd as he paced in the dim shadows beneath the arena stands. In the ring, John and Qaraqush were facing off in the second to last round of the tournament.

Yusuf had sought the shade because he could not bear to watch his two friends fight. Above, the mamluks who packed the stands stood and stamped their feet, sending a shower of dust drifting down. There was a final roar, and then the crowd fell quiet. The contest was over. Yusuf stopped pacing and waited for John and Qaraqush to emerge.

Nur ad-Din had agreed enthusiastically to Yusuf's idea for a tournament. He had promised a twentieth of Reynald's ransom – a fortune – to the tournament's victor. Hundreds of mamluks had volunteered to fight. Yusuf had selected seven men to compete along with Reynald. That morning, John, Qaraqush, Reynald and al-Mashtub had all advanced. After a break for refreshments and prayer, the tournament had resumed with John fighting Qaraqush. As Yusuf watched, two mamluks removed a section of the wall around the ring, and John and Qaraqush stepped through, leaning on one another. Both men's chainmail was soaked with sweat. Qaraqush was holding his right wrist, which was swollen and red. John limped slightly and had a nasty bruise on his right cheek.

'Who won?' Yusuf asked.

'John,' Qaraqush grumbled. 'Damn near took my hand off.'

'It was a close match,' John said. 'I was lucky to win.'

'*Hmph*,' Qaraqush snorted. 'Luck my foot; you were better than me. I just hope you beat that Frankish bastard, if it comes to that.' He nodded towards Reynald, who was approaching the entrance to the ring. The tall, heavy-set Frank wore an open-faced helmet and an iron breastplate over chainmail. He ignored the three friends as he stepped past them into the ring. The huge mamluk al-Mashtub came next, wearing chainmail that left his bulging arms bare.

'Take care of that pig for us,' Qaraqush told him.

Al-Mashtub grinned. 'With pleasure.'

'Do not underestimate Reynald,' John warned. 'He made short work of his last opponent.' Indeed, Reynald had battered his first adversary into a bloody mess. The combatants' blades were blunted, but they could still do serious damage. It was not unusual for people to die in tournaments. 'Reynald is dangerous.'

'So am I.'

Yusuf stepped forward and kissed the huge mamluk on both cheeks. 'Allah protect you.' Al-Mashtub nodded and headed into the arena. The mamluks moved the section of wall back into place, closing off the ring behind him. Yusuf turned to John and Qaraqush. 'Come. Let's watch.'

They emerged from beneath the stands and went to a ramp that led up into the arena. The match had already started, but the crowd of mamluks parted readily as Yusuf made his way to the front row. John and Qaraqush squeezed in beside him. Directly across from them, Nur ad-Din was seated between Shirkuh and Gumushtagin. Yusuf nodded to the king, then turned his attention to the action in the ring, a circle of beaten earth some ten yards across, bordered on all sides by a low, wooden wall.

The two combatants stood a few feet apart, both already breathing heavily. Reynald's sword flashed in

447

the bright sunshine as he raised it high above his head before swinging down at al-Mashtub. The mamluk parried the blow, and the two men's swords locked together at the hilt. They strained against one another, but strong though he was, Reynald was no match for the size of al-Mashtub. With an audible grunt, the huge mamluk shoved Reynald away. The Frank stumbled backwards towards the wooden barrier that surrounded the ring. He slammed into it just in front of Yusuf, and his head snapped back, spraying Yusuf with sweat. The crowd roared. Reynald reached up to straighten his helmet, then gripped his sword with both hands and strode back towards al-Mashtub.

'Come on, al-Mashtub! Beat the son of a whore's face in!' Qaraqush shouted. He turned to Yusuf and added more quietly, 'I've got two dinars on him to win it all.'

'I'm not so sure,' Yusuf murmured. He turned to John. 'My money is on you to take the prize.'

'I'm not here for the prize,' John replied. 'I'm here for Reynald.'

The crowd roared and Yusuf looked back to the ring. Reynald had gone on the offensive, spittle flying from his mouth as he hacked down again and again, pushing al-Mashtub back across the ring. Finally, al-Mashtub sidestepped a blow and countered, catching Reynald in the side. The Frank stumbled back, bellowing in pain. The crowd stood, cheering. 'Finish him!' Qaraqush shouted. 'Finish him!'

Al-Mashtub advanced, sword held high. Reynald backed away, then, with a roar, he charged. Al-Mashtub hacked down, but Reynald parried the mamluk's blade before slamming into him, shoulder lowered. He caught al-Mashtub in the chest and drove him backwards, smashing him into the wall of the arena. Al-Mashtub raised his sword, but Reynald grabbed his arm, pinning it against the wall. With his other hand, Reynald smashed the pommel of his sword into al-Mashtub's face, crushing his nose and spraying the crowd with blood. He swung again, but this time al-Mashtub caught his wrist. The mamluk slammed his forehead into Reynald's face, snapping the Frank's head back. Blood ran from Reynald's broken nose, matting his blond beard.

But Reynald still had al-Mashtub pinned against the wall. The Frank grinned madly, then head-butted al-Mashtub, once, twice, three times. Al-Mashtub dropped his sword and his knees buckled. Reynald held him up, his left forearm under the mamluk's chin while he smashed him in the face twice more with the pommel of his sword. Finally, Reynald released al-Mashtub and stepped back. The mamluk slumped to the ground, unmoving.

The crowd fell silent. Reynald spit at al-Mashtub, then raised his arms and strode to the centre of the ring.

'The man is an animal,' Qaraqush whispered.

Yusuf turned to John. 'You are next, my friend. Allah protect you.'

John prayed silently as he knelt beneath the stands, his forehead against the pommel of his sword, which he held pointed towards the earth. He heard footsteps approach, boots crunching on the hard ground. 'Prayers won't do you any good, Saxon.' John did not need to open his eyes to know that it was Reynald who spoke. 'I'll see you in the ring.' John remained kneeling until he heard Reynald walk away. Then he crossed himself and rose.

John entered the ring to find Reynald waiting for him, his sword held casually over his shoulder. John ignored him. He walked to the centre of the ring and bowed towards Nur ad-Din, then he turned to face Reynald. 'I have a score to settle with you. It is because of you that I was made a slave. You sent Ernaut to murder me outside Damascus. You tried to kill me yourself outside Tell Bashir.'

'Maybe now I'll finish the job.' Reynald swung his sword from his shoulder and held it in front of him as he stepped towards the centre of the ring. John raised his sword, and the two men faced off only a few feet apart.

'Fight!' Nur ad-Din shouted, his voice drowned instantly by the roar of the crowd.

John circled to his right, and Reynald mirrored him, keeping his distance. 'Why do you serve that infidel?' Reynald asked, nodding towards where Yusuf sat. 'Can't get enough of your sodomite friend?'

John said nothing. He sprang forward and slashed at Reynald's side. Reynald parried the blow and countered with a vicious cut at John's head. John spun out of the way and resumed circling, but Reynald was no longer mirroring him. The Frank stood in the centre of the ring, turning in place to follow John's movements. 'Are you afraid of me, Saxon?' Reynald taunted. 'Come here and fight.' John kept circling. Suddenly Reynald charged forward, hacking down at John's head. John blocked the blow, and their swords locked. John strained against Reynald, their faces only a few inches apart. He could feel the Frank's breath hot on his face. Reynald's swollen, purple nose and blood-caked beard made him look like some crazed demon.

'Tell me, Saxon,' Reynald sneered. 'When you and the Saracen do it, do you prefer the bottom or the top? I bet you take it. You seem the type. Your father certainly was.'

John shoved Reynald backwards so that their swords disengaged. 'What do you know of my father?' he growled and resumed circling.

Reynald grinned, showing blood-stained teeth. 'I know he was a Saxon dog who got what was coming to him, strung up like the traitor he was.'

John's knuckles whitened as his grip on his sword tightened. 'Do not dare speak of my father!' he snarled. He could hear the blood pounding in his temples.

'Did you think you could escape your past by fleeing England, Saxon?' Reynald sneered. 'I know your story. A priest on pilgrimage from England told me. Your father was a traitor, plotting against the king with those other Saxon pigs. Your brother at least had the courage to turn him in. And you killed him for it. Stabbed him in the back, no doubt, like the cowardly dog you are.'

With a roar, John charged, hacking down at Reynald with all his strength. Reynald blocked the blow, and John swung again and again, driving his opponent backwards. Then John swung down, and there was nothing there. His sword bit into the earth, and a moment later Reynald's sword hit him in the side, snapping a rib. John staggered away, gritting his teeth against the stabbing pain that came with each breath. Reynald was on him immediately, swinging for his head. John blocked the blow but intense pain shot through his side, causing him to cry out. He tried to counter-attack, but Reynald easily knocked the blow aside, then stepped forward and punched John in the ribs. John gasped in pain and stumbled back until he hit the wall. He clung to it for support, the world spinning around him. He saw a flash of metal out of the corner of his eye and barely managed to raise his sword in time. John blocked the blow, but his sword went flying from his hand. A second later, the pommel of Reynald's sword smashed into John's face. He swayed and then slumped to his knees.

John hung his head. The pain that he felt was nothing compared to the shame that flooded through him. He had failed. Perhaps this was God's punishment for violating his oath, for killing his fellow Christians at Banyas. Or perhaps it meant that there was no God, only brute strength, and John was not strong enough. He felt cold steel pressed against his neck and looked up to see Reynald standing over him. 'Do it,' he whispered. 'Finish me.'

'That would be too good for you, dog,' Reynald smirked. 'Some day, you will burn for betraying your people and your faith, and I will be there to watch.' He spat in John's face, then kicked him in the chest, knocking him to the ground. John lay there unmoving, shuddering with each painful breath.

'I cannot believe it.' Yusuf stood in the stands, clenching the wooden barrier in front of him. Around him the crowd was silent as they watched Reynald walk to the middle of the ring and raise his arms in triumph. A mamluk hissed his disapproval, and soon the entire crowd was hissing. Across the ring, Nur ad-Din shook his head in disgust. Reynald just grinned.

'I will wipe that grin off his face,' Yusuf muttered. He stood on his bench, then vaulted over the barrier to land in the ring. 'I challenge you,' he called to Reynald.

The Frank turned to face him. 'Challenge me?' he snorted. 'I have already won your tournament. I have beaten the best you have to offer.'

'You have not beaten me.'

'And why should I? I already have what I want. The slaves are mine now, to use as I please.' He turned away and walked towards the exit of the ring.

'You said a Frankish knight is worth ten Saracens, yet you have defeated only three,' Yusuf called to him. 'Are you afraid to fight one more?'

Reynald turned back to face him. He took Yusuf's measure and then laughed. 'I will fight you, runt,' he said and raised his sword. 'And you are the one who should be afraid.'

Yusuf smiled and turned to Nur ad-Din. 'He will fight me!' he shouted in Arabic. The crowd roared.

'On one condition!' Reynald shouted over the crowd. 'If I win, then I go free.'

Yusuf translated the request for Nur ad-Din. There were shouts of protest and hisses from the crowd. Nur ad-Din raised his hand for silence. 'And if you lose?' he asked Reynald.

'If I lose, then I will abide by your rules so long as I am

453

your prisoner, and once I am ransomed, I swear that I will leave these lands. I will never fight the Saracens again.'

Nur ad-Din stroked his beard as he considered the proposal. Finally he nodded. 'I accept.' He turned to Yusuf. 'If you lose, then you will pay his ransom; one hundred and twenty thousand dinars.'

'I do not have half that sum,' Yusuf protested.

'Then you will return Tell Bashir to me.'

Yusuf looked to John, still slumped on the ground, then to Reynald, standing proud and defiant. He turned back to Nur ad-Din and bowed. 'Yes, Malik.' Again, the crowd cheered.

Yusuf went to John and knelt beside him. 'Come, let's get you out of here.' Yusuf took John's arm and helped his friend to rise.

'You crazy bastard,' John croaked. 'You don't have to do this for me.'

'I am not doing it for you. I do it for the slave girls in Reynald's household. This tournament was my idea. I thought Reynald would be beaten easily. Those girls do not deserve to suffer for my mistake.'

They left the ring and entered the dim area under the stands, where Ibn Jumay was waiting to take John. The doctor helped him away, and servants came forth bearing armour for Yusuf. He stripped off his caftan and slipped on a leather jerkin and breeches, then pulled the heavy coat of chainmail over his head. He strapped on his helmet and was sliding his left arm through the straps of a small, circular shield when Shirkuh appeared, a scowl on his face.

'Are you mad, nephew? If you lose, then you will have nothing.'

Yusuf met his eyes. 'I will not lose.'

Shirkuh stared at him for a moment, then nodded. 'Very well. But do not underestimate this man. He is a snake, and like a snake, he is dangerous.' Shirkuh kissed Yusuf on the cheeks. 'Allah protect you, young eagle. Do not fail.'

Yusuf re-entered the ring to the applause of the crowd. He crossed to where John's sword lay and picked up the blade of dark, curved steel. Then he turned to face his opponent.

'Come to avenge your Saxon lover, infidel?' Reynald asked.

'I have come to teach you a lesson, dog,' Yusuf replied as he adopted a fighting stance – knees bent, legs wide, sword held at an angle before him.

Reynald raised his blade. 'Come on then.'

'Fight!' Nur ad-Din called.

Yusuf sprang forward immediately, lunging at Reynald's gut. The Frank moved to parry, and Yusuf changed direction, spinning to his left and slashing down so that he caught Reynald on the side of his knee. He finished his spin and stood facing Reynald.

'Jesus!' the Frank cursed, limping slightly as he backed away. He flexed his knee, his face tight with pain as he straightened it. 'Infidel pig!'

'That is your first lesson,' Yusuf told him.

'I'll teach you something,' Reynald roared and charged. Yusuf retreated, moving back until the last second, when he jumped to the side. Reynald crashed into the wall of the arena, the wood splintering in the middle. Yusuf slashed across his back, and Reynald roared in pain. He spun around, his eyes wide and nostrils flared.

'That is your second lesson.'

Reynald growled and charged again, hacking down at Yusuf. Yusuf blocked with his shield, but the weight of the blow left his shield dented and his arm numb. He sidestepped the next blow and swung out, catching Reynald in the side of his helmet. The Frank stumbled back, his helmet dented and blood running down his face. Immediately, Yusuf went on the offensive, slashing at Reynald's waist. Reynald managed to parry, but Yusuf reversed the blow and hit the Frank just under his left arm. Reynald cried out in pain and lowered his sword. Yusuf swung for his head to finish him. At the last second, Reynald raised his bare left arm and knocked the blow aside. Yusuf heard a crack as the Frank's forearm broke. Grimacing in pain, Reynald swung up with his sword, catching Yusuf in the ribs and knocking him to the ground.

Yusuf looked up just in time to see Reynald's sword arcing down towards him. Yusuf blocked with his shield, but felt something snap in his arm. Reynald swung down again, but this time his sword bit into the earth as Yusuf rolled out of the way. Yusuf sprang to his feet and ducked under an attack. He parried another strike, but the strength of the blow sent his sword flying from his hand. He raised his shield and backed away until he came up against the wall of the arena. The crowd had fallen silent; Yusuf could hear the snap of pennants atop the arena.

Reynald grinned and raised his sword. 'Time to win my freedom.' His eyes widened in surprise as Yusuf pushed off from the wall and charged. He ducked Reynald's hurried blow and drove his shoulder into the Frank's gut, knocking him backwards. Then Yusuf brought his shield up, wincing in pain as he smashed it into Reynald's face. As the Frank stumbled back, Yusuf sprinted past and scooped up his sword. He turned to face his enemy.

Reynald stood unsteadily, his face a mask of blood. His left arm hung useless at his side. Yusuf's own arm ached with pain, and his ribs burned. Nevertheless, he stood straight and forced himself to smile. One of the first lessons he had learned from John was to never show pain.

'Have you had enough?' he asked. 'Or shall I teach you a final lesson?'

'You dirty son of a whore,' Reynald growled. He limped forward, swinging his sword backhanded at Yusuf's head. Yusuf dodged away, slashing at Reynald's back as he passed. Reynald spun around and came after him, but again Yusuf slipped away, scoring a stinging blow on Reynald's sword arm.

'Hold still, you cunt!' Reynald snarled. 'Fight me.' He swung at Yusuf, who ducked the blow and sidestepped another before backing away. 'Fight me!' Reynald roared and charged Yusuf. This time Yusuf stood his ground. At the last second he ducked and threw his body at Reynald's knees. The Frank flipped over Yusuf and landed hard on his back. Yusuf jumped to his feet and kicked his adversary's sword away. Then he placed a booted foot on Reynald's chest and held his sword to the Frank's face.

'Do you yield?' Yusuf yelled over the roar of the crowd. Reynald scowled and tried to rise. Yusuf stomped hard on his gut. 'Do you yield?'

'I yield,' Reynald wheezed.

'Louder!' Yusuf commanded. 'So they can all hear you.'

'I yield!'

Yusuf stepped away and looked about him. The crowd was cheering madly, men stomping and pounding on the wall around the arena as they chanted his name: '*Yusuf*! *Yusuf*! *Yusuf*!' He spotted Nur ad-Din and bowed low to his lord. Nur ad-Din rose and vaulted over the wall into the arena. He strode over to Yusuf and embraced him.

'Well done, Yusuf,' he whispered in his ear. 'I have not been blessed with a son of my own blood, but Allah has sent me you instead.'

Chapter 19

John crouched atop the gatehouse of Khaldun's home and looked down into the dark courtyard. He had only been to visit Zimat a dozen times since his return to Aleppo over a year ago; they both knew how dangerous each visit was. But tonight the sky was moonless and the streets dark. It was a night for thieves – or lovers.

John dropped down into the courtyard and pressed himself against the wall. After a moment he crept to the side door and slipped inside. As he walked down the hallway past Ubadah's room a board creaked beneath his foot. He froze. There was no sound of movement in the house, and he continued on to Zimat's room. He pushed the door open. The room was dark and he could just make out Zimat asleep in bed. John entered and closed the door softly behind him. He removed his boots and breeches, then sat beside Zimat, gently pushing a strand of dark hair away from her face. She smiled in her sleep. John kissed her lightly on the lips, and her eyes opened.

'You should not have come,' she murmured, but her smile said otherwise.

'I had to see you. It has been too long.' He pulled off his caftan and started to get into the bed beside her. Zimat pushed him back.

'Wait. Let me look at you a moment longer.' John stood naked, self-conscious as he began to harden. 'Your zib is happy to see me,' Zimat teased. 'Bring it here.' She pulled the sheets back, and he slid into bed beside her. 'I am glad you came,' she said as she laid her head on his shoulder. With her finger, she gently traced patterns on his bare chest.

John stroked her hair. 'I have news,' he whispered. 'Yusuf says the new Frankish king, Amalric, is gathering an army. I met him once, when I first came to the Holy Land. He was only a boy and now he is a king.'

'*Shhh*,' she said, putting her finger to his lips. 'I do not wish to discuss the Frankish king.'

'What do you wish, my lady?' Their eyes met, and her hand moved down his chest, past his stomach. 'That is what I was hoping for,' he murmured and rolled over so he was on top of her. He kissed her soft lips, her neck. She moaned softly. Then her body stiffened. Her eyes were wide with fright. John turned and saw Ubadah standing in the doorway. John had not seen him for months, and the boy was taller, his face thinner. He looked more like John than ever.

'Mother, what are you doing?' the boy demanded. 'Who is that man?'

'It is nothing, my son.'

Ubadah's eyes narrowed. 'It is him,' he spat. 'The ifranji! I will tell Father.' The boy disappeared from the doorway.

'No, wait,' John called. He grabbed his caftan from the floor and pulled it on as he chased after the boy. He caught Ubadah in the hallway and grabbed his arm. The boy began to scream: 'Father! Father!'

'Quiet,' John hissed, lifting the boy from the ground with one arm and clamping his free hand over Ubadah's mouth. He turned to move back down the hall when behind him a door opened. Khaldun stepped out.

'Ubadah?' he called sleepily.

The boy bit the hand John held over his mouth. ''Sblood!' John cursed and pulled his hand away.

'Father!' Ubadah cried. 'Help!'

John ran back to Zimat's room, kicking the door shut behind him. Zimat had pulled on a robe and was sitting on her bed, her face buried in her hands. John handed Ubadah to her, and she clutched the boy to her chest. 'We are lost,' she cried. 'Khaldun will kill us both.'

John found his belt and drew his dagger. 'I will not let him touch you,' he promised. He moved to join her on the bed and stumbled as the floor lurched beneath him. 'What is happening?'

The shaking grew worse, becoming a rolling as if he stood on the deck of a ship at sea. Dust drifted down from the ceiling, and the washbasin in the corner fell over with a loud crash. Ubadah began to cry. 'It's an earthquake!' Zimat shouted. 'We must get out.'

John took Ubadah from her, and they headed for the door. Suddenly it swung open, and Khaldun stepped into the room, sword in hand. When he saw John, his eyes went wide. 'You!'

Then the ceiling above Khaldun collapsed, and he

disappeared amidst the debris and dust. John put his arm around Zimat and pulled her back against the wall opposite the door. The shaking was so violent now that they could barely stand. They sank down against the wall, and John pulled Zimat and Ubadah close to him, holding them in his arms.

'God save us,' he whispered. 'Naudhubillah.' Then there was a loud crack above them. John threw himself over Zimat and the boy just before the rest of the ceiling collapsed.

'Oh, yes,' Yusuf breathed as he lay on his back in Asimat's bed with her on top of him, her hands on his chest and her hips moving rhythmically. She moaned in pleasure, then arched back as she began to move faster. The bed shook beneath them as they climaxed together. Asimat stopped and looked down at him, a smile on her face, but the shaking did not stop. Yusuf heard shouting and men running in the hall.

'An earthquake,' he whispered.

'You must go,' Asimat said as she rolled off of him. 'The guards will come for me.' Yusuf climbed from the bed and began to pull on his breeches. 'There is no time for that,' Asimat hissed. She took his other clothes and cast them out of the window. 'Go!'

Bare-chested and barefoot, Yusuf slipped out of the window just before the door to the room crashed open. 'Khatun!' a guard called. 'Come with us. We must leave the palace.'

Yusuf began to inch his way along the ledge. The trembling was growing worse, and after only a few feet he stopped to keep himself from falling, his fingers digging into the thin cracks between the stones. Still the shaking worsened. To his right, a section of the ledge, where he had stood only moments before, buckled and fell away, dropping down the sheer slope. Yusuf felt the earth roll under him, and to his left, a stretch of wall ten feet wide shook and then collapsed outwards, spilling stones and a screaming eunuch guard into the void. The man's cry was cut short as he hit the rocks below.

Yusuf managed to edge forwards and swing through the gap opened up in the wall. He found himself in a hallway and crossed to the far side, where he leaned against the wall, breathing heavily. Five eunuch guards rushed by, pulling two women in nightgowns after them. Not one of them even looked at Yusuf as they sprinted past and rounded a corner further down the hall. There was a deafening rumble and the corridor filled with dust as the ceiling in the hallway to the right collapsed. Yusuf pushed away from the wall and ran in the opposite direction, after the guards. He was rounding the corner when he collided with the eunuch, Gumushtagin. The two men staggered back, staring at one another in surprise.

'Yusuf!' Gumushtagin exclaimed. 'What are you doing in the harem?'

'I – I wanted to make sure that our lord was safe.'

Gumushtagin's eyes narrowed as he took in Yusuf's lack of clothing. 'You came straight from your room?' Yusuf nodded. 'You lie,' the eunuch hissed. 'The path across the palace is blocked. There is no way through.'

Yusuf opened his mouth to speak, but no words came.

Gumushtagin sneered. 'The Honourable Emir Yusuf – our lord will be most interested to hear what you were doing in his harem.'

Just then, the floor lurched beneath them, knocking both of them to the ground. The wall to their right collapsed outwards to reveal the night sky. The floor buckled and tilted sharply, sending them both sliding towards the gap. As his feet slid out into space, Yusuf managed to grab hold of a piece of the wall that still stood. With his other hand, he grabbed Gumushtagin's wrist as the eunuch slid past into the void. Yusuf strained to hold on to the eunuch as he dangled over the rocks far below.

'Don't drop me!' Gumushtagin squealed. 'Don't drop me!'

The jagged stone that Yusuf held to keep from falling was cutting into his fingers, and Gumushtagin's wrist was slowly slipping through his hand. 'Hold on to me!' Yusuf shouted, and the eunuch locked his free hand around Yusuf's wrist. Gritting his teeth, Yusuf managed to pull Gumushtagin up until he could grab hold of a section of the wall. Then, slipping his fingers into the cracks in the broken floor, Yusuf crawled up to a flat section. He reached back and pulled Gumushtagin up after him. The two lay there, gasping.

Again, the floor began to roll beneath them. Yusuf got to his feet. 'It's not safe here. We must get out of the palace.' He helped Gumushtagin up, and they made their way through corridors littered with fallen stones. The stairs leading to the ground floor were still intact. They hurried down, through the rubble-strewn entrance hall and out into the night. Yusuf looked back. Jagged holes had appeared in the walls of the palace, and to the left, an entire wing had collapsed.

He turned around. A crowd had gathered near a gap in the wall, where a section some twenty yards wide had fallen outwards. Yusuf started that way when Gumushtagin grabbed his arm. 'You saved my life. I will not tell Nur ad-Din what I saw tonight.' Yusuf nodded and turned to go, but Gumushtagin did not release him. He leaned close. 'I will say nothing, but I will not forget. You ruined my plans for Tell Bashir, Yusuf. If you cross me again, then I will tell Nur ad-Din what I know.' He released Yusuf. 'I will be watching you.'

'I understand.' Yusuf hurried on and found Asimat on the edge of the crowd, standing safe beside Nur ad-Din. 'My lord,' Yusuf said and bowed. 'Praise Allah, you are safe.'

The king had a far-off look in his eye. He did not appear to see or hear Yusuf. 'Allah has sent us a message,' he murmured. 'He is angry with me. We must attack. We must attack.'

'Go,' Asimat told Yusuf. 'Our lord is not well. I will tend to him.'

Yusuf waded into the crowd, looking for Faridah. Everywhere, servants and mamluks from the palace were on their knees wailing. Others hurried from person to person, looking for friends or loved ones. Yusuf found Faridah sitting with her head down and her knees drawn up to her chest. She was covered in grey dust. Qaraqush knelt beside her.

'Faridah!' Yusuf cried. 'Thank Allah you are well.'

She looked up. The right side of her face was covered in blood. Her eyes widened in disbelief. 'Yusuf,' she whispered as tears came to her eyes. 'You're alive!' He knelt down and embraced her. Yusuf could feel her shaking as she sobbed against his shoulder.

'I found her in the rubble,' Qaraqush told him. 'She was lucky to survive.'

'Have you seen John?' Yusuf asked.

Qaraqush hung his head. 'No. No one has.'

Yusuf nodded. He felt a pain in his chest as he clutched Faridah to him. Tears began to form in his eyes, and he released her. He would not let his men see him cry. He turned away and went to look out past the gap in the wall. The scene in the town below was hellish. Fires had spread, filling the air with black smoke and illuminating entire city blocks that had collapsed into rubble. Yusuf looked to the street where Khaldun's house had stood. He could not see the house amidst the rubble and clouds of smoke.

'Zimat,' he whispered.

Yusuf led Qaraqush and a dozen mamluks into the city, dodging past debris. The facade of the great mosque had collapsed outwards, spilling massive stones into the main square. A fire raged in the shattered remains of the mosque. Yusuf passed a soot-covered imam who was tearing at his grey beard and shouting repeatedly, 'Allah has forsaken us! Allah has forsaken us!'

Yusuf turned down a crowded side street. Some men and women were weeping openly. Others stood dumbstruck as they stared at the ruins of their homes. Here and there, men dug frantically through the rubble. Yusuf reached the end of the street and stepped past the broken gate to Khaldun's street. There were fewer people here, and the air was thick with choking black smoke. He passed a young girl covered in grey dust, stumbling down the centre of the street and calling loudly for her mother. Yusuf crawled over a pile of rubble that had spilled into the street from a collapsed building and came to the wall around Khaldun's home. The wall still stood, lit brightly by a fire blazing across the street. A eunuch guard sat in the open gateway, his head cradled in his hands. As Yusuf approached, he saw that the man's scalp was wet with blood.

'Where is my sister, Zimat?' Yusuf asked. The guard looked at him dumbly. 'Khaldun, your master. The boy Ubadah. Where are they?' The guard turned away, shaking his head. Beyond him, Yusuf could see that the home had collapsed into a pile of stones, wooden beams poking out here and there. Yusuf hurried through the gate, crawling on to the ruins. 'Zimat!' he called out. 'Khaldun!' He turned back to where Qaraqush and his men were waiting in the street. 'Search the rubble. Find them!'

Yusuf's men spread out across the remains of the house, and he crawled forward over the debris. He had scrambled far ahead of his men when he heard a sound, like the mewing of a cat. It came from a large mound of rubble just ahead of him. Yusuf put his ear against the mound. It was no cat that he had heard; it was a woman crying out, her voice muffled by the rubble. Hurriedly, Yusuf began to pull aside debris. The crying grew louder.

He pulled another stone aside and could see through a crack into a space beneath the pile of rubble. 'Zimat!' he called into the crack.

'I am here,' she called back weakly.

'Hold on! I'm coming.' Yusuf was frantically pulling stones away. He could see Ubadah, lying motionless, and Zimat's arms holding him. They were huddled in a narrow space in the rubble. He pulled another stone aside, and he could see Zimat's face. He grabbed a large, flat rock and straining, rolled it aside. Zimat lay before him, curled around Ubadah. Over them, shielding them both, crouched John. He was covered in dust, and blood ran from the back of his head. He looked up at Yusuf, and their eyes met.

Yusuf took a step back, his face pale. He blinked in disbelief. 'John?' he murmured. 'What are you—' He stopped as he realized what he was seeing. The blood began to pound in his temples. 'What is this?' he whispered.

Behind him, he could hear Qaraqush shouting: 'My lord, did you find something?' Yusuf turned to see the mamluk some twenty yards off, making his way towards them.

Yusuf turned back to John, who had extricated himself from the rubble. He had taken the boy from Zimat and was helping her up. 'You must go,' Yusuf hissed at John. He took Ubadah from him. 'Go!'

John nodded and scrambled away, around the pile of rubble. Yusuf put his head to Ubadah's chest and heard his heart beating. He turned towards Qaraqush. 'The child lives!' he shouted. 'Zimat too!'

The shouting awoke Ubadah, who looked about, confused. 'What happened?' He looked up and saw that Yusuf was holding him. 'Uncle?'

'Yusuf!' Qaraqush called. He had stopped only a few feet away. His eyes were fixed on something at his feet. 'You must come and see this. Leave the boy.' Yusuf handed Ubadah back to Zimat and stepped over the rubble to Qaraqush. The mamluk pointed at a gap in the debris. 'There.' Half of Khaldun's face was visible through a pile of masonry and fallen beams. His eye was open, staring sightless up at the heavens. Qaraqush put his hand on Yusuf's shoulder. 'I am sorry, Yusuf.'

Ubadah had broken free of his mother and now appeared at Yusuf's side. 'What is it?' His eyes fell on his father's face. Yusuf lifted up the boy and carried him away, but it was too late. 'Father!' Ubadah cried. 'What has happened to my father?'

Yusuf began to speak, then looked at Ubadah's face. The words died on Yusuf's lips. He did not know what to tell the child. His father lived, but Khaldun was dead.

The sky was beginning to lighten when Yusuf, covered in soot and dust, finally returned to the palace. His room was gone, so the guard at the door directed him to another, in a wing of the palace that had not been damaged. He entered to find Faridah waiting for him.

'Zimat and the boy?' she asked.

'They live.'

'Thank Allah.' Faridah crossed the room and embraced him. Yusuf stood stiffly and looked straight ahead while she held him. She let go and stepped back. 'What is it? What has happened?'

'John,' Yusuf whispered. 'He has betrayed me.'

'What do you mean?'

'Zimat's child – it is John's.'

'Does Khaldun know?'

'He is dead.'

'What will you do?' Faridah asked.

'My duty – I will avenge the honour of my family and of Ubadah.'

'By killing the child's father?'

'His father is already dead.' Yusuf strode past her to the window, where he looked out on the ruined city. Fires still burned here and there.

'You know better than that, Yusuf. The boy still has a father.'

'He must never know.' A tear ran down Yusuf's cheek, making a track in the soot. 'I will take John hunting. We will ride into the desert, and I will finish this.'

Faridah approached from behind and placed a hand on his shoulder. 'Do not,' she said gently.

Yusuf spun around and slapped her backhanded, snapping her head to the side. 'Quiet, woman!' he hissed. 'It is none of your business.' Faridah said nothing. Yusuf could see the red print of his hand on her cheek. After a moment he reached out and gently touched it. 'Forgive me.'

'I will. But if you kill John, will you be able to forgive yourself?'

Yusuf turned back to the window. 'I thought he was my friend,' he murmured. 'How could he?'

'Perhaps he loves her—like you love Asimat.'

'This is different.'

'Is it?'

'John is not just one of my men. He is my friend. Does that mean nothing?'

'It should – for both of you.' Faridah embraced him from behind, her chin on his shoulder. 'Do not do this thing, Yusuf. You will regret it.'

'I must.'

'No. You do not want his blood on your hands.'

'What I want does not matter,' Yusuf said, his voice trembling with emotion. 'The earthquake was a sign, a warning from Allah. I have been living without faith, without honour. It must stop. Friend or no, John must die.'

John rode along the ridge of a tall dune, lit gold by the sun setting behind him. Yusuf rode just ahead, the sand spilling away from his horse's hooves and sliding down the steep slope. They had been riding all day, leaving Aleppo far behind them to the west. They had come to hunt, Yusuf said, but he had ignored the few signs of game that John had pointed out. Yusuf had hardly said a word during the long journey. He rode with his eyes fixed on the distant horizon, and John followed, unwilling to disturb his friend's silence, afraid of what Yusuf might say.

The wind picked up, and John could hear the hiss of the sand as it blew towards them. He pulled a fold of his turban across his mouth and squinted against the stinging sand. After short time the storm passed, leaving him and his horse covered in a thin layer of grit. His horse shook its mane, sending sand flying. John blew his nose and picked grit from his eyes.

They rode down from the dune on to a flat waste of hard-baked sand, broken here and there with ridges of red, flaky rock. There was no vegetation, no life anywhere, and the only sound was the soft crunch of their horses' hooves on the ground and the gentle whisper of the wind. John spurred his horse up alongside Yusuf's. 'It reminds me of our trip to Tell Bashir, all those years ago,' he said.

'*Hmph*,' Yusuf grunted, his eyes still fixed on the horizon.

'We were so young, only boys. We have come a long way, haven't we, my friend?'

Yusuf glanced at him. 'A long way,' he murmured and spurred forward to ride ahead of John.

They rode out of the sandy waste and up a ridge of rock. Their horses' hooves clattered on the hard surface, sending pebbles skittering. At the top of the rise they looked down into a shallow ravine, a thin stream of water flowing at the bottom. 'This looks like a good place to camp,' John suggested.

'No, just a bit further.'

They rode north along the ridge while the sky faded from golden red to a dark violet speckled with innumerable stars. A new moon rose, bathing the landscape in silvery light. John could see his breath, drifting upwards in the night sky. He pulled his cloak more tightly about him. Still, Yusuf rode on, holding the reins with one hand while with the other he fingered the eagle hilt of his dagger. Finally, John rode closer and touched his friend's arm. 'Yusuf.'

Yusuf started. 'What is it?'

'We should make camp. Before the night's cold settles.'

Yusuf nodded. 'Yes, you are right. It is time.' He pointed to a wide, flat spot beside the stream below. 'Down there.'

They picked their way down a narrow track to the water's edge. 'I'll gather wood,' John said as he slid from the saddle. The wind had died, and the soft crunch of his boots in the sand was loud in the silence. Yusuf had also dismounted and was busy with his saddle. John wrapped his horse's reins around one of the bushes on the riverbank, and the horse lowered its head to drink. He removed its saddle and patted its side. Then he headed upstream to look for wood.

Some thirty yards from camp, he found a pile of dry driftwood. He knelt down and began to gather up branches when behind him he heard the unmistakable sound of a blade being drawn – the hiss of steel sliding against leather. He turned to see Yusuf, sword in hand. His friend's mouth was set in a hard line.

'What is this?' John asked as he stood.

'You know,' Yusuf said, his voice trembling. 'You lay with Zimat. Ubadah is your son. Admit it.' He took a step closer and raised his sword. His eyes had narrowed dangerously, and his lips were stretched back in a snarl. 'Admit it!'

John met Yusuf's eyes and knew that his friend meant to kill him. He had feared this day since the first time he

473

lay with Zimat. He would not fight it. He owed Yusuf his life and more. He sank to his knees in the sand. 'I lay with her. The child is mine.'

'How could you?' Yusuf shouted, taking another step towards John. 'I warned you not to touch her. I thought you were my friend!'

'I am.'

'You are a dog, like all Franks!' Yusuf kicked out, catching John on the chin.

John slumped forward, hands cradling his face, then pushed himself back upright. He spat blood from his mouth. 'I am a Saxon. And I am your friend.'

'I must kill you,' Yusuf said. His eyes shone with tears as he brought his sword to John's neck. The steel was cold. 'You have stained the honour of my family. You have betrayed my faith in you.'

John met Yusuf's eyes. 'Then we have both betrayed our masters,' he said softly.

'What do you mean?'

'You know what I mean.'

Yusuf lowered his eyes. The sword shook in his hands, the sharp blade drawing a thin trail of blood from John's neck. 'This is different,' he said at last. He drew the sword back, preparing to strike.

'I love her,' John whispered.

Yusuf began to swing down, and John closed his eyes. But the blow never came. John opened his eyes to see the blade hovering inches from his neck. Yusuf's face was contorted in a strange mixture of anger and pain, his forehead creased, jaw clenched and eyes wet with tears. He cast his sword aside and strode away.

John let him go. He finished gathering wood and then returned to their camp. Yusuf was sitting against his saddle with his back to John, staring at the dark waters of the stream. John dropped the kindling and set about building a fire. When the blaze was crackling, he pulled up his saddle and sat facing the flames. After a moment, Yusuf turned around. They sat across from one another, staring at the blaze in silence.

Finally, one of the logs burned through and collapsed, sending a spray of sparks into the night sky. John leaned forward to poke at the fire with a stick, then added another branch. He sat back and looked across the flames to Yusuf, who was still staring straight ahead, his features shadowy in the firelight. 'You asked me once why I came to these lands,' John said to him. Yusuf did not reply, and John continued. 'I was raised in Northumbria in the town of Tatewic, far from here, in England. It is a green land, so different from here. But my land too has been conquered, and by the same Franks who conquered the holy city of Jerusalem.'

'But you are a Frank.'

'No, I am a Saxon. My father was a thane, an emir amongst my people. Before the Normans came, we were a family of great lords. When William the Bastard claimed England for himself, my family joined the other thanes to fight him. We lost almost everything. Still, we were some of the lucky ones. The Normans killed hundreds. Worse, they burned crops and slaughtered livestock, leaving thousands more to die of hunger. We lived, but my father never forgot.

'He was a good man, my father. He taught us to fight

475

and to farm the land. He raised my older brother to follow him as thane; even after the wars, we still had a smallholding and a few serfs. He sent me to the nearby abbey every day to learn the French and Latin of our invaders. I was to become a priest.' John stopped, looking into the fire and battling old memories. It seemed he could see the face of his father in the flames.

'What happened?' Yusuf asked.

'My older brother was not satisfied with the little that was left to us. He made a deal with the Norman king. He accused the remaining Saxon lords in our county of treason, including my father. They were all hanged, and their lands seized by the Normans. In return, my brother was given the land of our neighbours. I could not forgive him. I killed him, my own brother.' John looked away.

'You did your duty,' Yusuf said quietly.

'Yes.' John swallowed. 'But killing him did not feel like justice. I could not forgive myself for what I had done, and I feared the Normans would hang me for a criminal. So I fled. The Pope has promised redemption to all who take up the Cross. I went to France and joined the crusade. I thought my capture at Damascus was God's punishment for my crime.' He looked away from the fire, to Yusuf. 'Now I know it was a gift. I will never forgive myself for what I did, but God has granted me a new life, a new brother.' Yusuf met his gaze. 'Can you forgive me, Brother?'

Yusuf's forehead creased, but he said nothing. They sat beneath the endless stars while the fire burned to nothing. When the last flames had vanished and the embers had turned to ash, Yusuf rose and stretched. He looked down at John. 'You know that you can never marry her.'

'I know.'

Yusuf nodded. He stepped over the ashes and held out his hand. John took it and Yusuf pulled him up. 'Come then, friend. Let us return to Aleppo.'

Chapter 20

Yusuf trotted up the long causeway leading to the citadel of Aleppo, with John riding beside him. They had ridden in silence during the long trip back from the desert. They passed through the gate and into the citadel grounds, where they stopped and dismounted before the stables. Yusuf met John's eyes as he handed him the reins to his horse. He took a deep breath. 'I—I wanted to say—'

John raised a hand, stopping him. 'There is no need. We said all that needed to be said in the desert. We are still friends; that is all that matters.'

Yusuf nodded. He reached out, and they clasped hands. 'I will see you this evening when we train the men.'

'This evening,' John agreed and led the horses to the stables.

Yusuf headed for the palace, skirting the field at the centre of the citadel, where a dozen mamluks were playing polo. One of them knocked the kura through the goalposts and whooped in triumph. Watching him,

Yusuf thought back to his childhood and the first time he had bested his brother Turan at polo. He shook his head. Then, beating Turan had seemed the most important thing in the world.

Yusuf entered the palace and went to his quarters. He was not surprised to find Faridah waiting for him. She took one look at his face and smiled. 'Thank Allah, you did not do it.'

'I could not.'

She crossed the room and kissed him. 'You did the right thing.'

'Yes,' Yusuf murmured.

Faridah released him and stepped back. 'Asimat has sent a message. You are to go to her quarters.' Yusuf frowned. 'You do not wish to see her?' Faridah asked. 'What has happened?'

'I do not wish to discuss it.' Yusuf went to the door. 'I will return soon.'

When Yusuf reached the harem, one of the guards informed him that Asimat was in the gardens. Yusuf left the palace and crossed the citadel grounds to the rose garden, where the trimmed hedges were in full leaf and full bloom. The guards waiting outside nodded to Yusuf, and he entered, winding his way towards the centre of the maze of pathways. Looking back, Yusuf could see the guards' heads rising above the hedges. Their eyes were fixed upon him.

Yusuf found Asimat at the centre of the maze, sitting beside a low, circular pool with water bubbling up in the centre. She smiled when she saw him. He bowed. 'Khatun.'

'I am glad you came,' she replied, standing and moving to him. 'I thought I had lost you in the earthquake, Yusuf. It made me realize something.' She lowered her voice. 'I—I love you.'

Yusuf stepped back. 'Do not say that.'

'Why not?' Asimat's brow furrowed. 'Do you not love me?'

Yusuf looked away. 'We must not see each other again.'

'What do you mean?' She grabbed his arm. 'Look at me!' Reluctantly, he met her eyes. 'You love me. I know you do.'

'It does not matter. I will not betray my lord.'

'It is too late for that. You have already betrayed him.'

'No.' Yusuf took her hands in his and spoke urgently. 'The earthquake was a sign, Asimat. What we are doing is wrong, but Allah has given us a second chance. We must return to the path of the righteous.'

Asimat pulled her hands from his. 'A sign from Allah? Do not be foolish!' Yusuf said nothing. He turned his back on Asimat, but she grabbed his arm, spinning him around to face her. 'You would give up the kingdom, then?'

'If I must.'

'I see.' Asimat stood straighter, and the warmth faded from her expression. 'You have greatness within you, Yusuf, but you fear it. To be great, you must be willing to seize your opportunity, no matter what the cost. You must be willing to betray anyone at any time. Anyone.'

'And you, Asimat? Would you betray anyone to see your son on the throne?' She nodded. 'Even me?' Asimat met his eyes, then looked away without speaking. Yusuf shook his head. 'It is no wonder Allah has cursed your womb. You are everything I despise.'

Asimat slapped him, hard enough to snap his head to the side. 'You do not love me, coward,' she spat. 'You never have.' She turned and strode away.

Yusuf did not move as she left the garden. He knew he had done the right thing, but he felt ill, sick to his stomach. He picked one of the blossoms – a damask rose – and smelled it. 'I do love you, Asimat,' he murmured. Then he dropped the flower and crushed it under his boot.

AUGUST 1163: ALEPPO

'Oh Allah forgive me; have mercy upon me,' Yusuf murmured as he knelt on the floor of his bedchamber. He prostrated himself, then straightened as there was a knock on the door. 'Enter!' he called.

John stepped into the room, then froze. 'I am sorry, Yusuf. I did not realize that it was time for prayers.'

'It is not,' Yusuf said as he rose. 'But praying brings me peace. Now, what do you want?'

'You are needed in the council room.'

'Do you know why?'

'Your brother, Selim, has come from Damascus with news. That is all I know.'

Yusuf hurried through the palace and up the narrow spiralling staircase to the council room in its high tower. Nur ad-Din was there, along with Shirkuh, Gumushtagin and Selim. Yusuf entered and exchanged kisses with his brother.

'Salaam, Selim. It has been too long.'

'He has brought good news,' Nur ad-Din said. 'King Amalric has made his final blunder. He is marching on Damascus at the head of an army.' He looked at the men around him. 'We will grind the Franks to dust against the walls of Damascus.'

'It is not all good news,' Shirkuh grumbled. 'The Christian army has a head start on us. Damascus might fall before we arrive.'

'We will reach the city in time,' Nur ad-Din insisted. 'And then we shall crush them – this time for good.'

SEPTEMBER 1163: DAMASCUS

Yusuf rode with Nur ad-Din and Shirkuh at the head of an army over ten thousand strong. They had been marching for nine days, heading west at first and then following the Orontes River south past the walled cities of Hama and Homs. After Homs, they had cut across the mountains, and today they would reach Damascus. Yusuf hoped that they would not be too late. The Frankish army had reached Damascus four days ago.

They were riding across a flat plain, following a gully that cut its way through the sun-baked earth, a thin trickle of water at the bottom. The plain seemed to stretch away endlessly, the distant horizon shimmering in the heat. Damascus was still hidden over the horizon when Yusuf saw a brown cloud rising high into the sky ahead.

'What do you suppose that is?' Nur ad-Din asked the emirs around him.

Yusuf squinted against the bright sun. 'It looks like smoke.'

'That it does.' Shirkuh frowned. 'I pray to Allah that we are not too late. If the Franks are in the city—'

'Then we must hurry,' Nur ad-Din finished his thought. 'Come!' He spurred his horse forward. Yusuf and the other emirs galloped after him, followed by thousands of mounted mamluks. The hooves of their horses drummed on the plain like thunder and sent up a tall plume of dust behind them. The city rose quickly above the oncoming horizon, the dark walls bordered by empty desert on the left and emerald orchards to the right. As they rode closer, Yusuf could see that the city was not on fire. The brown cloud came from the low hills to the west of the city, beyond the orchards.

Nur ad-Din raised his fist as he reined to a stop, and Yusuf pulled up beside him. 'I don't understand,' Yusuf said. 'There is nothing in those hills to burn.'

Shirkuh grinned. 'That is not smoke, Yusuf. It is dust, kicked up by an army on the move. The Franks are withdrawing.'

'Damascus has held again,' Nur ad-Din exulted. 'The Franks must have feared being caught between the walls and our army.'

'They are not far off,' Yusuf said. 'If we push hard, then we can catch them.'

'Patience, Yusuf,' Nur ad-Din replied. 'Our men have ridden far today, and we want them fresh for the fight.

We will camp in the orchards where there is plenty of food and water.'

'And the Franks?'

'You will take an advance guard and trail them, sending messengers back to keep me apprised of their movements. Keep your men out of sight. I want the Franks to think we have let them escape. Then, when the time is right, we will surprise them as we did at Jacob's Ford. And this time, we will not stop until we have driven every last Frank into the sea.'

SEPTEMBER 1163: PLAIN OF BUTAIHA

Low, rocky hills rose to either side of Yusuf as his horse picked its way along the floor of a ravine, walking in the footprints left by the Frankish army less than an hour before. He and his men had been following the Franks for two days, angling south-west across the plains and low hills that lay between Damascus and the Jordan River. Yusuf turned in his saddle to look at the forty hand-picked mamluks riding behind him. It was a small enough force that if they were seen, the Franks might take them for a band of raiders. Yusuf knew that further back, on the broad plain a quarter of a mile behind them, Nur ad-Din sat with his army, waiting for Yusuf to spring the trap. John was with them, riding in the baggage train where he would not be forced to fight his fellow Christians. Yusuf wished his friend were with him now.

Yusuf turned forward again. Ahead, the ravine turned to the north, but the trail beaten by the Franks headed straight on, out of the ravine and over the low rise before him. Yusuf reined to a stop.

Qaraqush rode up beside him. 'What do you think?'

'It is time,' Yusuf replied. 'We will follow their tracks.'

He spurred his horse up the gentle rise, then reined in sharply when he reached the top. A grass-covered plain lay before him, running towards the thin, silver ribbon of the Jordan River. The Frankish army was spread out over the plain, their steel helmets glinting in the sun, pennants snapping overhead. They had stopped to water their horses. As Yusuf watched, a knight near the edge of the army pointed to him. He heard shouting in Frankish, carried to him on the wind. Yusuf did not move.

'By Allah,' Qaraqush murmured as he rode up along-side Yusuf. The other mamluks joined them, spreading out atop the hill. On the plain, the Christians began to mount their horses. A single knight spurred across the plain, followed by three more, then a dozen. 'We should retreat,' Qaraqush said.

'Not yet,' Yusuf replied. Hundreds of knights with lances in hand were now charging towards them, fol-lowed by thousands of foot-soldiers. Yusuf waited until the closest knights were only a hundred yards off. 'Now!' he shouted as he wheeled his horse. 'Retreat! Back to the army!' Yusuf dug his spurs into his horse's sides and gal-loped down the hill, his men thundering after him. He crouched in the saddle, his head close beside his horse's neck as he raced along the wide ravine. He could hear the shouts of the Franks and the pounding of hooves. He looked over his shoulder to see the first Frankish knights cresting the hill behind him. '*Yalla*!' he cried and flicked the reins, urging his horse to go faster. '*Yalla*! *Yalla*!'

Yusuf rounded a last curve and rode out of the hills and on to the plain where the Muslim army waited. The line of men stretched for a quarter of a mile. Mamluks on foot stood in front, long spears in hand. Behind them were thousands of mounted mamluks and Bedouin warriors, bows at the ready. Yusuf spotted Nur ad-Din's banner at the centre of the line and headed for it. The line of foot-soldiers parted to let Yusuf through, and he pulled up before Nur ad-Din in a cloud of dust.

'They're coming! All of them!'

Nur ad-Din grinned. 'Our time has come.' He raised his voice to address the men around him. 'Prepare to fight! Allah is with us!'

Across the plain, the Franks began to pour out of the ravine, spreading out as they thundered towards the Muslim lines under a cloud of dust. Yusuf thought back to his discussions with John, long ago in Baalbek. Nothing could stand up to a Frankish charge, John had said. Yusuf looked to Nur ad-Din, who was still grinning fiercely. 'Perhaps we should retreat before the initial onslaught,' Yusuf suggested. 'To draw them in before surrounding them.'

'Retreat?' Nur ad-Din roared incredulously. 'No, we will stand firm, Yusuf. Allah will give us strength.' The closest Christians were nearing the line. Nur ad-Din drew his sword and waved it over his head. 'Let fly, men!'

Yusuf nocked an arrow to his bow and picked out one of the charging knights. He released the arrow and followed its path until it was lost amongst thousands of others. The arrows momentarily dimmed the afternoon sun as they arced through the blue sky. Then they fell hissing amongst the Franks. Yusuf saw a knight at the front of the charge take an arrow in the chest, but his armour was too thick for the missile to penetrate all the way to his flesh. Here and there knights fell, their horses shot out beneath them, but the Frankish charge did not falter. The knights rode on, arrow shafts protruding from their armour. The nearest knights were only thirty yards away now, and their deafening war cry rolled over Yusuf. '*For Christ! For the Kingdom!*'

'For Allah!' Nur ad-Din shouted back, and all along the line the men echoed his cry. '*Allah! Allah! Allah!*' Yusuf tucked his bow into his saddle and readied his sword and shield.

Then the first Franks hit them. Yusuf saw a knight speared off his horse by one of the foot-soldiers. The next knight suffered the same fate, and the next. Yusuf began to hope that the line would hold, but then a solid mass of knights hit the line at once. They smashed through the wall of foot-soldiers, trampling them underfoot. A knight charged towards Yusuf with lance lowered. At the last second, Yusuf jerked the reins and his horse stepped to the side. The knight's lance missed Yusuf by inches. Yusuf slashed out as the knight rode past, catching him in the throat and knocking him from the saddle. Yusuf turned to see another knight bearing down on him, and this time he could not avoid the long lance. He managed to block it with his shield, but the force of the blow sent him flying from his saddle to land hard on his back. Yusuf staggered to his feet, ready to defend himself, but there was no one to fight. The wave of Frankish knights had thundered past, driving the Muslim army before them and leaving carnage in their wake. Dead mamluks lay all about, many with the long shafts of lances protruding from their chests. Riderless horses wandered everywhere – some galloping madly in fear, others cropping at the grass. Yusuf edged towards a horse, but it shied away, eyes rolling, and galloped off. Yusuf heard a roar behind him and turned to see an endless stream of Frankish foot-soldiers pouring from the hills and surging across the plain towards him.

Yusuf ran in the opposite direction, after his retreating army. The dust thrown up by the fleeing mamluks and pursuing Christians was far off, but closer, only a hundred yards ahead, Yusuf spotted Nur ad-Din surrounded by twenty mamluks of his personal guard. Nur ad-Din had halted his retreat and was waving his sword over his head, trying to rally the remnants of his army. Dozens of Frankish knights swarmed around Nur ad-Din's guard, eager to strike down the Muslim king. As he ran, Yusuf glanced back to the Frankish foot-soldiers rushing across the plain. If Nur ad-Din did not retreat soon, he would be lost.

'Yusuf!' It was Qaraqush, riding up and leading a horse. Al-Mashtub and ten of Yusuf's men were with him.

Yusuf swung himself up into the saddle. 'To Nur ad-Din!' he shouted and spurred across the field. They hit the Frankish knights from behind. Yusuf cut down two men before they could turn to defend themselves. The other Franks scattered as the rest of Yusuf's men arrived. Yusuf rode up beside Nur ad-Din. The malik's face was pale and his shoulder was stained with blood.

'You are injured,' Yusuf said.

'It is nothing.' Nur ad-Din raised his voice: 'To me, to me! Stay and fight!'

'It is no use, my lord. Your army has fled. You must retreat.'

'I will not let these dogs defeat me,' Nur ad-Din growled.

Yusuf met his lord's eyes. 'They have already defeated you, Malik. Do not let them kill you as well.'

Nur ad-Din's shoulders slumped. 'Very well,' he whispered, but he did not move. All energy seemed to have suddenly left him.

Yusuf looked back to the onrushing mass of Frankish foot-soldiers, only fifty yards off now. One of the soldiers hurled his spear, and it landed only a few yards short of Yusuf's horse. Other Franks stopped and nocked arrows to their bows. Yusuf turned back to Nur ad-Din. 'We must ride, Malik!' He grabbed Nur ad-Din's reins and then spurred away, pulling the malik's horse after him. The guard fell in around them. They had not gone far when arrows began to fall all about them. One struck Yusuf's horse in the flank, and the beast stumbled, throwing him. Yusuf jumped clear and rolled to his feet. Nur ad-Din had reined to a stop, seemingly oblivious to the arrows striking the ground around him.

'Ride!' Yusuf shouted to him, but the king did not

move. 'Qaraqush, al-Mashtub! Get him out of here! We will hold them off long enough for you to escape.'

'Allah preserve you, Yusuf!' Qaraqush called as he grabbed Nur ad-Din's reins and led him away at a gallop.

Yusuf turned to face the Franks. 'Come on, men!' he shouted as he charged towards the enemy. 'For Islam! For Nur ad-Din!'

'Christ's blood! He's gone mad,' John whispered. The retreating Muslim army rushed past him as he sat astride his horse on a low hill, watching as Yusuf and a dozen men charged into a mass of thousands of Franks. The two sides collided, and for a moment Yusuf's charge held. From this distance, his men in their dark chainmail looked like a steel blade as they drove deep into the Frankish ranks, the foot-soldiers in their lighter armour dividing left and right. Then the charge faltered as one mamluk fell, then another and another. A moment later the cluster of Muslim warriors disintegrated, engulfed by the Franks.

John gritted his teeth as a blinding rage swept though him, obliterating all thought. He drew his sword and spurred down the hill, riding at a gallop past the long line of retreating Saracens. The mounted Frankish knights had given up the chase and had turned to looting the dead. John flew past them without a glance, heading for the mass of Frankish foot-soldiers. Their charge had stopped. As John drew closer, he saw through the dust shrouding the Franks that Yusuf was still alive and standing in a clearing with four other mamluks. The Christians had their backs to John; they were toying with Yusuf and his men, poking at them with long lances. Two soldiers turned at the sound of John's approach, but it was too late. His horse knocked one man aside and crushed the other under its hooves. He slashed to the left and right as he drove through the crowd.

'Yusuf!' he screamed as he pushed through the last few Franks and rode into the ring. Without stopping, he reached out and grabbed Yusuf's arm, swinging him into the saddle behind him before crashing into the Franks on the other side of the clearing. His horse pushed through the crowd, John hacking at the men on his right and Yusuf protecting their left. But the Franks pressed closer and closer. John felt a sword glance off the chain-mail on his side. Another slashed across his thigh, opening a painful wound. A flail slammed into his helmet, and he saw bright lights flash before his eyes. With a roar, he lashed out wildly. Then he was through, galloping out on to the plain.

'Are you crazy?' Yusuf shouted in his ear.

'You are my friend, I will not let you die alone.' John glanced over his shoulder to see that a dozen foot-soldiers had given chase on foot. They fell back, five yards, then ten, and gave up running. 'We've made it!' John cried. Then one of the Franks reared back and threw his spear. It missed, but a second spear buried itself in the flank of John's horse. The beast stumbled, then collapsed beneath John and Yusuf, who threw themselves to the side to avoid the crushing weight of the animal. They rose to see the soldiers rushing towards them.

'We'll never outrun all of them,' John said.

'Then we'll die fighting.'

'No. I owe you my life, Yusuf. It is time I paid my debt.'

Yusuf shook his head. 'I will stay with you.'

'Save yourself!' John roared and pushed Yusuf towards the distant Muslim army. 'Run, damn you!' Then John turned and sprinted towards the oncoming Franks. He sidestepped the spear of the first soldier to reach him and slashed at the man's throat, taking him down. A second Frank came at John with a mace, and John ducked the blow before cutting at the man's legs, sending him tumbling. The next two knights attacked John together. One thrust his sword at John's chest, while the other cut at his head. John parried the first blow and ducked the second, then threw his body into the two men, sending them all sprawling on the ground. John stabbed one with his sword, leaving it in the man's chest. The other was scrambling to his knees, sword raised, when John punched him in the jaw. The Frank's eyes went blank and he slumped to the ground. John took his sword and stood to see that the rest of the Frankish soldiers had formed a ring around him.

'Come on,' he growled, raising his sword. 'Come and get me, you bastards!' One of the soldiers rushed forward, but stopped short. John took a step towards the man. Then he felt something slam into the back of his head, and the world went black.

Yusuf jogged past the ragged remnants of Nur ad-Din's army. Some of the foot-soldiers were carrying companions or helping their friends to limp along. Others walked alone, heads down. Mounted mamluks rode amongst them, staring vacantly ahead, stunned by defeat. Bone-weary, Yusuf forced himself to keep running until he reached a small stream where the army had stopped to set up camp and count their losses. Yusuf knelt beside the water and began to scoop it into his mouth.

'Yusuf!'

He looked up to see Shirkuh approaching. Yusuf stood, and his uncle embraced him. 'Well met, Uncle.'

'Well met, indeed. I thought we had lost you, young eagle. Come, I will take you to Nur ad-Din.'

Shirkuh led him across the stream and to a tent. Inside, Nur ad-Din was sitting on a camp stool, his head in his hands. His shirt was off, and a doctor was busy sewing up the ragged wound in his shoulder. Nur ad-Din was mumbling to himself: 'I have built mosques and schools, given to the poor. Why has Allah punished me?'

'My lord,' Yusuf said, announcing his presence.

Nur ad-Din looked up and a smile spread across his face. 'Yusuf! You have survived. It is a miracle!'

'Yes,' Yusuf murmured, thinking of John. 'A miracle.'

'You saved my life, Yusuf. I am in your debt.'

'I only did my duty, Malik.'

'You were one of the few who did,' Shirkuh said.

'He is right,' Nur ad-Din agreed. 'You have proven your worth, Yusuf. When others fled, you stayed to fight for your lord and for Allah. You shall have new lands, and a new name to honour you. From this day on, you shall be known as Saladin.'

'Thank you, Malik,' Yusuf said. Saladin: righteous in faith. It was a good name.

'It is I who should thank you, Saladin.'

493

Two days later, the army of Nur ad-Din trudged into Damascus. There was no cheering as Yusuf followed the king through the gate and down the wide avenue towards the palace. The people lining the street watched in silence as the troops filed past.

Yusuf's father, Ayub, met them in the entrance hall of the palace. 'Welcome, Malik,' he said and bowed. 'Thank Allah, you have returned safely.'

'There is nothing to be thankful for,' Nur ad-Din grumbled. 'I have failed. My army is in tatters, and I shall be forced to make peace with the Franks. We shall never drive them from our lands.'

'I have news that will perhaps cheer you.' Ayub gestured towards a man standing behind him. The man was tall and thin, with prominent cheekbones and darkly tanned skin. His face and head were clean-shaven. Even his eyebrows had been shaved. 'Allow me to introduce Shawar, the Vizier of Egypt.'

'Greetings, Nur ad-Din,' Shawar said as he stepped forward. His voice was soft, and he spoke with a slight lisp. 'It is an honour to meet you.'

Nur ad-Din nodded. 'What brings the Vizier of Egypt to my court?'

'Treachery,' Shawar replied. 'I have been chased from Cairo, and the caliph is in the hands of traitors.'

'And what do you want from me?' Nur ad-Din asked, his voice weary.

'Your help to retake my kingdom.'

Nur ad-Din laughed bitterly. 'With what? My army is in ruins.'

'They are strong enough. The people of Cairo will welcome me. I am their rightful ruler.'

'I see,' Nur ad-Din murmured. 'And why should I help you?'

'Because I will send you a third of Egypt's revenues each year as tribute. And I will recognize you as my lord. You will be King of Egypt.'

'King of Egypt,' Nur ad-Din whispered. For a moment his eyes gleamed with the old fire. Then his shoulder slumped again. 'I am tired of war.'

'Send me, Malik,' Shirkuh urged. 'I will conquer Egypt for you.'

Nur ad-Din looked to Shirkuh, then back to Shawar. 'I shall think on it,' he said. 'You may go, Shawar.' The Egyptian nodded and was led away. Nur ad-Din turned to Ayub. 'I wish to bathe. And then I will eat.'

'Very well, my lord,' Ayub said. 'But first I have news from Aleppo. It is your wife, Asimat. She is pregnant.'

Nur ad-Din straightened, and a grin spread across his face. 'A child. A son perhaps!' he roared. He embraced Ayub and kissed him on both cheeks, then turned to Yusuf. 'Can you imagine that, Yusuf? A son, an heir at last!'

'A son,' Yusuf repeated. His son.

SEPTEMBER 1163: JERUSALEM

John awoke with a start as cold water splashed over him. He lay on his side on hard ground. His mouth was dry, his lips cracked, and his head ached as if someone had driven an iron spike deep into his brain. He winced as he gingerly touched his scalp and felt dried blood caking his hair. He cracked open an eye and saw that he was lying in a dim prison cell. Rough-hewn stone walls stood on three sides, and the fourth was closed off by iron bars. There were three other men in the cell – all Saracens. Two were unmoving, flies buzzing about them. The third sat against the wall, staring vacantly ahead. John looked to the entrance of the cell, where two men stood. One wore chainmail and leaned on the shaft of a tall spear. The other wore the dark robes of a priest.

'This is the one?' the priest asked. 'The Frank?'

'A Saxon, Father Heraclius,' the soldier corrected as he pulled open the cell door. 'He talks in his sleep, and he speaks their savage tongue.'

Heraclius stepped into the cell and kicked at John's leg. 'You awake, Saxon?' John rolled over on to his back, moaning at the pain in his stiff joints. The priest knelt beside him. The man was clean-shaven, with deep blue eyes and blond hair. He had an effeminate beauty about him. 'Do you understand me?'

John nodded. 'Water,' he croaked.

The priest snapped his fingers at the soldier. 'Bring water.' He turned back to John, reaching out and brushing John's long hair away from his eyes. 'Blue eyes,' he murmured. 'You are indeed one of us.'

The guard returned with a waterskin and handed it to the priest, who gently lifted John's head and held the waterskin to his lips. John drank greedily, the cool water a blessed relief. After a few swallows, Heraclius pulled the skin away. 'That is enough for now. Can you talk?'

'Yes.'

'I have come to care for your soul, my son,' Heraclius told John. 'You were captured with the Saracen army. I am told that you fought for them, that you killed many of our men. How did you come to be with the infidels?'

'I was captured at Damascus during the second crusade.'

Heraclius's eyebrows rose. 'That was fifteen years ago. You spent all that time amongst the infidels?'

'Yes.'

'And did you remain true to our faith?'

'I did.'

'That is good, my son. But you have betrayed your oath and imperilled your soul by fighting for the enemies of God. However, you may still be saved. Tell me, do you desire salvation?' John nodded. 'Then you shall have it.'

John looked away as he felt tears welling in his eyes. After all this time, he had finally found redemption. The stain of his brother's death, of the knights he had killed: it could all be wiped away. 'What must I do?' he whispered.

The priest smiled. 'You must burn as a traitor and a heretic. The fire will purify your soul.'

Historical Note

Eagle is based in fact. Yusuf ibn Ayub – or Saladin as he is known to history – was one of the greatest military and political leaders of his age, and his exploits have been celebrated by Muslims and Christians alike. We are lucky enough to have contemporary accounts of his life from people who knew him, including Imad ad-Din, who appears briefly in *Eagle*. However, we know relatively little about Yusuf's early life – the period covered in this book. We know that he grew up mainly in Baalbek and Damascus. He played polo, was interested in religious studies and knew many poems from the *Hamasah* by heart. There are stories of him drinking and consorting with prostitutes as a youth, and in *Eagle* I attempt to show why this deeply religious young man might have engaged in such behaviour. At the age of fourteen, he joined his uncle Shirkuh in the service of Nur ad-Din and was given a fief – Tell Bashir in this novel. Aside from a few brief stints in Damascus, he spent the next twelve years in Nur ad-Din's service. From these scraps of history I have woven together the story of Yusuf's early life.

The major events in the story happened much as I

described them. I drew heavily on William of Tyre's account for my description of the Second Crusade. Nur ad-Din did conquer Damascus without bloodshed, and he did surround and rout the Christians at the battle of Jacob's Ford in 1157. However, there were too many battles for me to include every one. The final battle in the book is actually a composite of two events. In 1158 Baldwin marched on Damascus and subsequently defeated Nur ad-Din's army on the plain of Buthaia. I combined this with Nur ad-Din's defeat at Krak des Chevaliers in September 1163, the point at which *Eagle* ends.

Most of the people who appear in the story are real. Turan and Selim were Yusuf's brothers and later his lieutenants. Ayub and Shirkuh were Kurds who entered the service of Nur ad-Din's father after being banished from Tikrit. Qaraqush and Al-Mashtub became generals under Saladin. Usama and the eunuch Gumushtagin were members of Nur ad-Din's court. Ibn Jumay, the Jewish doctor who John meets upon first arriving in Yusuf's home, really did serve as Saladin's physician. Less is known about the women in Yusuf's life, although it is recorded that he had a sister who was very important to him – Zimat in my story. Faridah is my invention, although women like her certainly existed. Asimat was Nur ad-Din's wife.

On the Frankish side, King Baldwin, the young prince Amalric, William of Tyre and Reynald de Chatillon were all – as far as we know – more or less how I have portrayed them. I have not exaggerated Reynald's cruelty. The story of him tying the patriarch to the roof of the citadel of Antioch is true. Reynald used the money that he extorted from the patriarch to invade Cyprus, where he and his men went on a rampage, looting churches, burning crops, raping women and cutting the throats of those who were too young or too old to be sold into slavery. Reynald is also known to have regularly raided in Muslim lands. In fact, although I moved his capture to the battle of Jacob's Ford in 1157, he was actually captured three years later while raiding cattle. He was confined in Aleppo for sixteen years before being ransomed by the Byzantine emperor Manuel for the mind-boggling sum of one hundred and twenty thousand dinars – this at a time when a mamluk's monthly wage was only three dinars.

The only major character who was not real is John. However, while John is fictional, much of his story is based on fact. Saxons like John did suffer greatly during and after the Norman invasion of England. As many as one hundred thousand men and women – nearly ten per cent of the population of England at the time – were killed in the Harrowing of the North, during which the Normans developed many of the scorched-earth techniques that they later used in conquering the Holy Land. Many Saxon warriors fled to seek their fortune elsewhere. Some made their way to Constantinople, where they eventually formed the Emperor's Varangian guard. Others headed for the Holy Land. And some, like John, no doubt ended up in slavery. After the failed siege of Damascus during the Second Crusade, there were so many captured crusaders in the city's markets that some were indeed sold for the price of a pair of sandals.

I have done my best to portray accurately the details of the world in which John finds himself – the food, the markets, the slaves, the mamluks, the desert. The poems that Yusuf recites from the *Hamasah* were quoted from C. J. Lyall's translations in John Cunliffe and Ashley Thorndike (eds), *The Warner Library, Vol. 2: The World's Best Literature*. I drew on contemporary accounts, ancient maps and modern archaeological research to describe the walls, gates, buildings and general layout of Baalbek, Acre, Damascus, Tripoli and Aleppo. These cities have of course changed since crusader days, but many of their greatest treasures remain. The Roman temple in Baalbek – the largest in the world – is still every bit as spectacular as I describe it. Aleppo's citadel, perched on a hill above the city, is a marvel. And the Umayyad mosque in Damascus is one of the great achievements of early Islam.

The Islamic world was in many ways more advanced than Europe at the time. While earlier practices like trial by fire persisted, this was also a society that had modern courts of law, psychiatric hospitals, brilliant philosophers and which, most spectacularly, invented modern medicine. Their doctors developed the germ theory of disease, techniques for removing cataracts and even medication for heart disease. Islamic medical books from the eleventh century were still being used in European medical schools into the early 1900s. Unsurprisingly, many Muslims, Jews and native Christians looked upon the Crusaders as dirty barbarians. One example of this attitude is the story that Ibn Jumay tells of the mad Frankish doctor whose only idea of medicine is cutting off body parts. I took the story from the autobiography of Emir Usama ibn Munqidh.

Of course not all Europeans were savages like this doctor or brutes like Reynald de Chatillon. Thousands were inspired by their faith to make the arduous journey to the Holy Land. And many of the Europeans who settled there adopted eastern ways, wearing caftans and turbans, bathing regularly, eating local foods and employing Jewish or Muslim doctors. They were part of a vibrant culture – Christian, Muslim and Jewish; eastern and western – which existed in the Middle East during the Crusades. While *Eagle* is a work of fiction, I hope that it does justice to the complexity of this culture and to the life of the man who represented the best it had to offer: Saladin.

Kingdom

JACK HIGHT

1164. The young warrior Saladin joins a Saracen army headed for Egypt. He finds there a land of wonders – from the ancient pyramids and the towering lighthouse of Alexandria, to the caliph's luxurious palace – but also a land of unparalleled danger. In Egypt, no one can be trusted, not even his family. Saladin is surrounded by enemies and haunted by a secret that threatens to destroy him.

Meanwhile, in Jerusalem, Saladin's closest friend, the former crusader John of Tatewic, has been branded traitor. Spared execution on condition that he serves King Amalric, he soon finds himself embroiled in court intrigue. Dark forces within Jerusalem conspire to seize the throne. As John confronts them, his loyalty to Amalric, and to his old friend Saladin, is put to the test.

Now read on . . .

www.jackhight.com

Chapter 1

John's head jerked to the side as he was slapped, and he blinked awake to the taste of blood in his mouth. He looked about, trying to orient himself, then groaned as the excruciating pain in his shoulders washed over him. He was still stretched out horizontally on the rack, his feet tied down with ropes at one end, his bound hands stretched too far above his head. He looked to his right. Just beside his head was the crank, every turn of which stretched his hands and feet a little further apart. He must have fainted from the pain after the last turn. Past the crank, John could see a small square window set high up on a stone wall. The light filtering through was dim. He was sure it had been day just a moment ago. How long had he been out? As he watched, a hand grabbed the crank and turned. John howled in pain as he felt his shoulders starting to dislocate. His vision dimmed and then someone slapped him again. His eyes blinked open to see Heraclius leaning over him.

The priest had high cheekbones, a thin nose and a delicate jaw. His deep-set eyes – as blue as the turquoise waters of Acre harbour on the day years ago when John had first arrived in the Holy Land – narrowed slightly as they studied his victim, betraying a grim satisfaction at the suffering he had wrought. Heraclius was handsome – beautiful even – but John had learned to hate the sight of him. The priest's thin lips stretched into a smirk. 'Stay with me, Saxon,' he purred in his heavily accented Latin. Heraclius was a half-educated country priest from the wild Auvergne in France, and he had a peasant's love of cruelty. He leaned forward to whisper in John's ear. 'Tell me, why did you fight for the Saracens? Why did you betray the cross?'

'I never betrayed the faith,' John growled through gritted teeth.

'Liar!' Heraclius hissed. 'You killed your fellow Christians. You betrayed your crusader's oath. You betrayed us, preferring to serve the infidel, the forces of Satan.' Heraclius placed his hand on the crank and John flinched. But Heraclius did not turn the crank; he made a show of studying it, running his finger lightly over its handle. 'The rack is a dreadful thing. A few more turns and your arms will be pulled from their sockets. You will be crippled, unable to lift a sword ever again.' He bent over so that his breath was hot on John's face. Their eyes met. 'You spent many years in Aleppo, Saxon. You know its fortifications, its weaknesses. Tell me: how can we take the city?'

'I have told you. The walls are strong. It will take a siege of many months. You will have to starve the people out.'

'No!' Heraclius snarled. 'There must be more: a secret

entrance, a weak point.' John shook his head. 'I see.' Heraclius sighed and then straightened. When he spoke again, it was in a louder voice, as if he were delivering a homily in church. 'All that happens is part of God's plan, Saxon, even your faithlessness. It was He who determined that the infidels would capture you, that you would betray Him by serving them. And it was God who delivered you into my hands. Do you know why? Because you have come to know our enemy, their cities, their people, their walls. You have been sent to us by God as the key to their destruction.'

'You are wasting your time,' John said. 'I know no secrets.'

'We shall see,' Heraclius murmured. 'Perhaps we simply need to find new ways to motivate you.' He looked up and called in a sharp voice: 'Pepin! Bring me the coals.'

John twisted his head to the side and saw a brawny, square-faced guard approaching, his hands wrapped in cloth. He carried a shallow bronze dish containing a layer of smouldering coals. He set the dish down on a low table beside the rack. Heraclius went to the table and took up a pair of pincers. He selected a coal and held it out, only inches from John's bare stomach. He moved the coal up past John's chest, towards his face. John tried to twist his head away but Pepin grabbed hold of his ears, holding him still. Heraclius held the coal just above the bridge of John's nose. The heat was intense – like the blast from an open oven – and within moments John felt as if his forehead were on fire. An acrid smell filled the room as his eyebrows began to singe. Heraclius bent close to John so that his smiling face was lit red by the glowing coal. 'Tell me about your master, this Yusuf,' he whispered.

John swallowed. 'He is the emir of Tell Bashir. His father is the governor of Damascus and his uncle, Shirkuh, commands the armies of the Saracen king.'

'And how did you come to be in his service?'

'I came to the Holy Land with the Second Crusade. I was captured at Damascus and purchased by Yusuf as a slave. He was only a boy then.'

'You saved his life at the battle of Butaiah. Why?'

John hesitated, his eyes fixed on the burning coal just inches away. 'Yusuf is my friend.'

'He is an infidel!'

John looked away from the coal and met Heraclius's eyes. 'He is the best man I have ever known.'

'I see.' Heraclius turned away and dropped the coal back into the dish. John exhaled. 'Oh, I am not done with you,' the priest said. 'Not yet.' He nodded to Pepin who placed the coals on a shelf at the end of the rack, just beneath John's feet. At first, the warmth was almost pleasant. Then John's feet grew uncomfortably hot, as if he had set them too long beside a fire. He twitched, trying to jerk his feet away but his arms were still stretched to breaking point, and the motion caused a spasm of pain in his left shoulder. He lay still and squeezed his eyes shut, his teeth grinding as he fought against the burning pain in his feet. He thought he could feel blisters starting to form on his heels. And then the heat was gone. Pepin had removed the dish of coals. A moment later Heraclius's face reappeared above John.

'What of Nur ad-Din, the Saracen king?' the priest asked. 'You met him, yes?' John nodded. 'How is he protected? Could an assassin reach him?'

'In camp, he is surrounded by the mamluks of his private guard. In Aleppo he rarely leaves the citadel. No assassin could reach him alive.'

'Do you swear it?'

John nodded. 'By Christ's blood.'

'We shall see.' Heraclius gestured to Pepin, who replaced the dish of coals.

The pain came more quickly this time. John's entire body tensed, and he began to squirm despite the pain in his shoulders. To keep from shouting, he bit his tongue so hard that it began to bleed. Heraclius watched impassively. John could smell burning flesh now, his own. 'I speak the truth!' he shouted. 'What do you want from me, you bastard? What do you want me to say?'

'There, there. I believe you,' Heraclius soothed. He frowned. 'I was wrong. You are not the key to defeating the Saracens. Pepin, take the coals away.'

The heat vanished. John relaxed, but his breath was still coming in ragged gasps. Heraclius walked away and came back with a wet cloth, with which he gently dabbed John's feet. The relief was so overwhelming that John almost passed out. 'Thank God,' he murmured.

'Do not thank him yet,' Heraclius said. 'Your suffering has just begun.'

'But you said you believe me!' John protested.

'And I do.' Heraclius set the wet cloth aside. He crossed the room and paused before a table covered with instruments of torture: thumbscrews, hooks for tearing flesh, metal claws known as Spanish ticklers and other devices whose use John hoped he would never learn. The priest picked up one of these last, a pear-shaped metal contraption with a wing nut at the top of the pear. 'Now that we have seen to what you know, I must see to your salvation. Your time amongst the infidels has stained your soul. We must wash it clean.' He began to turn the wing nut, and the pear expanded, four separate pieces of metal spreading out. Heraclius turned back towards John. 'You must suffer for betraying the faith. It is the only way to find salvation.' The priest nodded to Pepin. 'Hold his mouth open. He shall pay the price for breaking his crusader's oath.'

John clinched his mouth shut, but Pepin grabbed his jaw with one hand and pulled back on John's nose with the other. The second John's mouth opened, Heraclius shoved the metal pear in. It tasted of metal and blood. Heraclius gave the wing nut at the end of the pear a twist and it expanded slightly, forcing John's mouth to open wider. John gagged and coughed. He jerked his head side to side, trying to spit the pear out, but Pepin grabbed him by the ears and held him still.

Heraclius was smiling, clearly enjoying his work. 'The pear of anguish is an ingenious piece of work,' he said as he watched John squirm. 'It is especially useful for punishing blasphemers and oath-breakers. First, your jaw will dislocate.' Heraclius gave the wing nut another twist, forcing John's jaws further apart so that they began to ache. 'Then, the skin of your mouth will tear, disfiguring you.' He gave another twist. John's jaw felt as if it were going to snap. He clenched his fists, fighting

510

the pain. 'If I expand the pear all the way, then you will never lie again: you will be unable to speak.'

Heraclius was about to give the wing nut another turn when John heard the sound of booted feet approaching, echoing off the stone walls of the dungeon. Looking past Heraclius, he saw half a dozen men in mail enter the room. A tonsured priest in black robes was at their head. 'Stop!' the priest demanded. 'Leave that man be!'

Heraclius turned. 'The Patriarch turned the Saxon over to me. You have no authority here, William.'

'I have the king's backing and the king's men. That man is a Christian and a noble. Amalric was furious when he heard that you are torturing him.'

'I do not serve Amalric. I serve God,' Heraclius replied. 'The Saxon killed our men. He broke his oath as a crusader. He threw his lot in with the infidel Saracens. He must be made to suffer if he is to be redeemed!' Heraclius reached for the wing nut at the end of the pear.

'Stop him!' William shouted. Two burly guards grabbed Heraclius's arms and pulled him away. William went to the rack and pulled a lever, releasing the tension on the ropes that bound John's hands and feet. The guards removed the pear and began to untie John's bonds. He groaned in relief as he gingerly flexed his arms and legs, then gasped as a stab of pain shot through his left shoulder. William helped John sit up just in time for him to see Heraclius being dragged from the room by two soldiers. At the door, Heraclius managed to shrug them off. He straightened and turned to face John and William.

'This is not the end of this!' Heraclius spat. 'The

Saxon betrayed his oath. I will see that he goes before the High Court. And mark my words, William: he will burn!'

John awoke to the sound of a door creaking open. He opened his eyes and blinked against the bright light streaming in from the window above his bed. Yesterday, after his feet had been bandaged, John had been carried from the dungeon to this tiny room in the compound of the Knights Hospitaller. Overcome with exhaustion and pain, he had passed out as soon as they laid him in his bed.

Now he stretched out and rolled over, away from the wall. The door to the room was open and a lean young man in brown monk's robes stood in the corner. The monk was clean-shaven and tonsured, with sunken cheeks, a jutting jaw and protruding eyes. He was inspecting the contents of the bronze chamber pot. He sniffed at the pot and frowned. 'His black bile is weak,' the monk murmured to himself.

'Who are you?' John demanded as he sat up in bed, groaning at the pain in his left shoulder. The rack had done its work. John's arm hung limp at his side. He could not move it without suffering a horrible, stabbing pain.

The monk looked up from the chamber pot and smiled. 'Ah, you are awake. Good. My name is Deodatus and I am a doctor. Father William has sent me to tend to you. He says you have suffered grievously.' He stepped over to the bed and nodded towards John's feet, which were wrapped in strips of linen. 'May I?'

John swung himself around so his feet hung off the bed. Deodatus crouched down and began to unwrap the bandages. The soles of John's feet were covered in angry, red blisters that oozed a sticky, clear fluid. Deodatus gently touched one of the blisters, and John winced in pain. 'Your flesh is hot. Your humours are out of balance,' the doctor said gravely as he rose. 'I understand you were subjected to the rack?'

'Yes. I cannot move my left arm without pain.'

The doctor grasped John's left wrist with one hand and placed his other hand on John's shoulder. As Deodatus slowly lifted the arm, a sharp pain shot through John's shoulder, as if a white-hot iron had been plunged into the joint. ''Sblood!' John cursed through clenched teeth.

Deodatus shook his head, then went to a small, leather-bound trunk that he had brought with him. He opened it and took out a handful of dried roots, a mortar and a pestle. He murmured the Ave Maria as he ground the root to powder.

'What is that?' John asked.

'Daffodil root for the burns on your feet. It will draw the heat out.' The doctor finished grinding the root and went to the chamber pot, from which he scooped out some faeces. John's eyes widened as the doctor placed the faeces in the mortar and mixed it in with the daffodil root. The doctor approached the bed with the foul-smelling mixture and John drew his feet back.

'Keep that away from me,' he said as he wrapped the linen back around his feet.

'The faeces will help to restore your black bile,'

Deodatus assured him. 'It will bring your humours back into balance.'

John's nose wrinkled in disgust. 'Do you have any aloe?'

'What is that?'

'A plant. It helps to cure burns. The doctor Ibn Jumay says . . .'

'A Jewish doctor,' Deodatus huffed. 'His medicine will send you to the grave.'

'I'll take my chances with Jewish medicine. Keep that shit away from my feet.'

'Very well. But you are still too sanguine. I shall be forced to bleed you to reduce your heat.'

'No,' John replied firmly. 'You will not.'

Deodatus spread his hands. 'If you will not accept my aid, then I cannot be responsible for the consequences.'

'Fine. Forget about my feet. I am more concerned about my shoulder.'

'It is very bad. I fear the damage will fester, drawing foul humours to it.' Deodatus reached into the small trunk and pulled out a short saw. 'It must come off.'

John's jaw set. 'Over my dead body.'

'It will be,' Deodatus said, testing the saw blade with his thumb. 'If I don't take your arm, then you will die. I am afraid there will be no discussion. I am a doctor and it is my duty to save your life, despite you if need be.' Deodatus stepped over to the bed. He gripped John's shoulder and brought the saw blade down towards the joint. 'This will hurt.'

'Yes it will.' John grabbed the doctor's cowl, pulled

him forward and head-butted him. Deodatus stumbled backwards, his eyes wide and his nose dripping blood.

'You're mad!' he exclaimed. 'You'll dic if I don't take the arm.'

John met his eyes. 'Then I'll die. If you touch my arm again, you'll join me.'

'Damned fool,' Deodatus murmured as he hurriedly closed up his trunk and tucked it under his arm. 'God help you.' Deodatus fled the room, bumping into William on the way out.

Father William stood in the doorway, watching Deodatus go, then turned to John, eyebrows raised. 'What did you do to him?

John shrugged. 'The man is a quack. He doesn't know the first thing about medicine.'

'But that is the court physician!' William protested. 'Ah well, no matter. I have important news. Heraclius has managed to convene the High Court sooner than I expected. They will hear your case tomorrow.

John nodded. 'The sooner the better. I am ready to die.'

William frowned. 'God willing, it will not come to that. I have volunteered to defend you at the trial. I do not share Heraclius's belief that suffering is the only road to salvation. But if I am to defend you, then I must know the truth. How did you come to be in the service of the Saracens?'

John closed his eyes, his mind racing back to his first days in the Holy Land. 'I came as a soldier with the Second Crusade. I was captured at the siege of Damascus and purchased by Najm ad-Din Ayub, now the wali, the governor of Damascus. I served as a household slave and then as the personal slave of Ayub's son, Yusuf. I taught him to fight and he taught me their ways. After I saved his life, he freed me.'

'And why did you not return to your people?' William asked.

'Return to what? The lord I had served, Reynald, betrayed me at Damascus. It was because of him that I was captured. And the Frankish soldiers I had served with were brutes. Yusuf was different. He was cultured and kind. He was my friend. And there was a woman. She bore my son. I could not leave them.'

William nodded. 'I understand. So when you were captured at Butaiah, you were fighting for this Yusuf. He was your lord?'

'Yes.'

'Then you committed no crime. It was your duty to serve your lord.'

John looked away and his forehead creased. He thought of the men who had died at his hands. 'But all that Heraclius says is true. I killed Franks, more than one. I deserve to die.'

William studied John for a moment. 'No, you do not deserve to die,' the priest said at last. 'The men you killed were warriors. You met on equal terms and you fought to save a friend. I have seen Frankish knights kill young children, then claim it is God's work. Where is their trial? Heraclius and his kind are blind. They believe they are fighting a holy war, but they betray our faith with every defenceless man they torture, with every innocent they kill.'

516

'I am not innocent,' John murmured.

'You may be guilty, but death will not wash away your sins. You can only redeem your soul through action.'

'And what can I do?' John demanded bitterly. 'It is not only Franks that I have killed.' He paused, thinking back before the Crusade to his home in England, to the manor of his childhood. He looked up, tears now in his eyes. 'I killed my brother. Nothing I can do will bring him back. It won't bring any of them back.'

William crossed the room and placed a comforting hand on John's shoulder. 'You cannot save them, but you can save others. I believe that your captivity was no accident. God has a plan for you. He has sent you to us for a reason.'

'I am only one man.'

'Nevertheless, you might hold the key to our salvation. We cannot hold out against the Saracens forever. The only way the Kingdom can survive is if we reach an accord with them. You know the Saracens better than any of us. You have lived in both worlds, East and West. You have spent years at the court in Aleppo. You can speak to them as we cannot, understand them as we cannot. You can help to bridge the gap that divides us.' William squeezed John's shoulder. 'At least try. Do not throw away your one true chance at salvation.'

John's eyes remained fixed on the ground at his feet. 'And if I let them kill me? Will the fire not wash me clean as Heraclius says?'

'Look into your soul. Do you believe that suffering will save you?'

John thought back on his years in the Holy Land: the brutal march to Damascus; his capture and near death; the beatings he had suffered as a slave; his torture at the hands of Heraclius. None of it had washed away his guilt. 'No,' he said. 'Suffering will not save me.' He looked up. 'Show me what I must do, and I will do it.'

'Good!' William smiled and clapped John on the back. 'First, we must get you through this trial. Because you have been accused of breaking your oath, you will not be allowed to speak unless directly questioned. I shall speak for you. You have but to answer truthfully any questions that are asked of you.'

'And what are my chances?'

'God does not deal in chance. We must trust in Him. I will come for you tomorrow, when it is time.'

William turned to leave, but John grabbed his arm. 'You did not answer my question, Father. What are my chances?'

William sighed. 'Not good. Heraclius has stacked the court against you.'

'And if I am found guilty?'

William met his gaze. 'The punishment for treason is death.'

The bells of the Church of the Holy Sepulchre were ringing to call the canons to their morning prayers as John, his arm around William for support, hobbled into the audience chamber where the High Court was meeting. The thick rugs that carpeted the floor were a blessed relief to his blistered feet after the hard stone of the paved courtyard he had just crossed. The members of the court waited for him on the far side of the room. King Amalric sat on a simple wooden throne, the dome of the church visible through the window behind him. He was young, perhaps John's age, but whereas John was lean and fit, the king was heavy-set, pudgy even. He had a ruddy complexion, with straight hair the colour of straw and a slightly darker, thick beard. His piercing blue eyes met John's across the hall and the king laughed suddenly, an odd, clipped laugh that sounded loud in the silence of the hall. With a start, John realized that he had met him before. When he first arrived in the Holy Land, John had attended a meeting of the High Court and Amalric – only a child at the time – had been there. John had never forgotten that peculiar child with his clear blue eyes and his strange laugh. Now, Amalric was king.

Two men framed the throne and Heraclius and three others were seated on benches that ran along the side-walls. 'This is the High Court?' John whispered to William. 'The last time I attended, there were hundreds of men.'

'Only four are needed for a quorum,' William replied. He gestured to John's right, where a dour, bony man in gold-embroidered robes sat beside Heraclius. 'That is the Patriarch of Jerusalem. He is the one who turned you over to be tortured.' Next to the patriarch was a brawny, thick-browed man in chainmail, his black surcoat bearing the distinctive white cross of the order of the Knights Hospitaller: four arrowheads, all touching at the tips to form a cross. 'Gilbert d'Assailly is the Grand Master of the Hospitallers. He is an Englishman like you, but don't expect any mercy from that quarter.

He hates the Saracens with a passion. I have more hope for that man there.' William pointed to the opposite side of the hall where a man with steel grey hair sat straight-backed, wearing a white surcoat emblazoned with a red cross. 'Bertrand de Blanchefort is Grand Master of the Knights Templar and he is a man of reason. As for the king, his constable Humphrey, and the seneschal Guy' – he waved to the throne and the two stern middle-aged men flanking it – 'I do not know where they stand.'

They came to a stop a dozen feet from the throne, and John and William both knelt. 'Rise,' Guy commanded in a harsh voice. He was thin with darkly tanned skin. As seneschal, it was his duty to preside over the Court. 'Present yourselves.'

'I am Iain of Tatewic, called John,' John declared.

'Silence!' the seneschal snapped. 'You have been accused of oath-breaking. You are not to speak before this court.'

John opened his mouth to reply but William shot him a warning look. 'I am William of Tyre,' the priest said. 'I will speak for the accused.'

'Very well.' The seneschal nodded towards Heraclius. 'The accuser will present his case.'

Heraclius rose, bowed to King Amalric and then stepped to the centre of the hall, just in front of John. He cleared his throat and began. 'This Saxon, John of Tatewic, has betrayed his Crusader's oath, betrayed his faith and betrayed the Kingdom. For years, he served the Saracens of his own free will. By his own admission, he fought with them at Banyas and Butaiah. He killed dozens of his fellow Christians. He has committed treason against the Kingdom and sacrilege against the Holy Church.' He paused to look each judge in the eyes. 'For justice and for the salvation of his soul, he must die for his crimes.' Heraclius bowed again and returned to his seat.

The seneschal looked to William. 'What does the accused say to these charges?'

'He pleads innocent to treason and sacrilege.'

The seneschal looked to Heraclius. 'I understand you have a witness?' Heraclius nodded. Guy raised his voice to address the armed men who framed the entryway at the far end of the hall. 'Guards! Bring the witness.' A guard stepped out and returned a moment later with a short man in a loose-fitting burnoose. He had close-set eyes and a turned up nose that gave him a piggish appearance. A gruesome gash ran down the left side of his face, from his hairline to his jaw. The wound was recent, still angry and red, oozing blood near his temple. The man passed John and bowed before the throne. 'Present yourself,' the seneschal ordered him.

'I am Harold, a sergeant and vassal of the king.' Sergeants were Frankish landholders who in return for title to their lands in the Kingdom of Jerusalem, served as foot soldiers in armies of their lord.

'Do you swear by God that you speak the truth?' the seneschal asked.

'Aye, I do.'

The seneschal nodded. 'Heraclius, you may question the witness.'

Harold did not wait to be questioned. He pointed at

John. 'That whoreson killed my brother! And he did this to me.' Harold touched the wound on his face.

'Where was this?' Heraclius asked.

'The battle of Butaiah. We had routed the Saracens. My men were mopping up, taking captives for ransom, when he arrived on horseback like some demon out of hell. He rode into a company of over one hundred men to rescue a Saracen lord. They killed seven of our men and the two of them rode out again unscathed. I have never seen the like. He is no man; he is a demon in human flesh, a man possessed.'

'A man possessed,' Heraclius repeated. 'A demon who kills his own. Let us consign this demon to the fires from which he sprang!'

John noticed that the Patriarch and Gilbert the Hospitaller were both nodding their heads in approval. King Amalric was listening carefully, but his expression remained neutral. William addressed the King. 'John is no demon. He is a warrior and a good one. He only killed in defence of himself and of his Saracen lord, to whom he had sworn allegiance. His honour was at stake, not his loyalty.'

Heraclius shook his head. 'It was not honour that led him to kill his fellow Christians, but his depravity. What are the Saracens but the hand of Satan made manifest in this world? When the Saxon killed for his Saracen master, who was he killing for?'

'He fought for his lord, nothing more,' William insisted. 'How many of you here have killed your fellow Christians in France or England? Gilbert and Bertrand, you have faced one another in battle. You have killed one another's men. There was nothing heretical about that.'

'Yes, but I was not under a crusader's oath,' Gilbert replied. 'I had not sworn to fight only the Saracens and to aid my fellow Christians.'

'John's crusade was long over,' William said. 'It ended at Damascus, when our army was routed, and he was captured fighting for Christ. Now, at long last he has returned to the fold. Let us welcome him back. He has suffered enough.'

'He has not!' Heraclius shouted. 'His soul is at stake. Only fire can purify it!'

William's nose wrinkled in disgust. 'Torturing this man further will stain your black soul, Heraclius. It will not save John.'

There was a moment of silence and then the constable Humphrey stood. He was barrel-chested, with a handsome, broad face. 'This court is not fit to decide the fate of this man's soul,' he said, his voice low and rasping like the sound of steel on a whetstone. 'That is a matter for the Church. We are here because the safety of the Kingdom is at stake. I fear that if we let this Saxon live, more men will join the enemy. We all know of the Saracens' wealth. If there are no consequences for betraying the Kingdom, then what will stop them from buying the allegiance of our sergeants? We will find our own people turned against us.'

'Hear, hear!' Gilbert agreed.

'But John did not join the Saracens of his free will,' William pointed out. 'He was captured and enslaved.'

Humphrey shook his head. 'But he still chose to fight for them.'

'He chose to serve his lord, who was a Saracen. John is a man of honour: he could not do otherwise.'

'I too am a man of honour,' said the grey-haired Templar, Bertrand. 'If this man fought in service of the lord to which he was bound, then I am inclined to be lenient.' Bertrand's kind eyes met John's. 'Tell me truly, John: why did you fight our men?'

'I owed my life to Yusuf, the man I fought to save. I fought to repay that debt.'

'And if you had it to do again?'

'I would do the same.'

Bertrand nodded in satisfaction. 'I cannot fault you for that. Will you swear an oath never again to take up arms against the Kingdom, on pain of death?'

John nodded. 'I swear it.'

'I do not trust the word of this Saxon,' the Hospitaller Gilbert protested. 'All of his kind are deceitful.'

John spoke quietly. 'I am a man of my word.'

'*Hmph*,' Gilbert snorted. 'You have already betrayed us once. If we free you, how long before you betray us again?'

'I am no traitor,' John insisted. 'It was Reynald who betrayed me in Damascus and left me to die.'

'Prince Reynald?' the seneschal demanded. 'The former ruler of Antioch?' John nodded.

'You see!' Gilbert declared. 'He besmirches the honour of a brave man in order to save his own life. How can we trust this deceiver?'

John's hands balled into fists. He took a step towards Gilbert, but William put a hand on his shoulder. 'Not now,' the priest whispered urgently.

'Do you wish to strike me, Saxon?' Gilbert sneered. 'Release him, William. He needs to be taught a lesson.'

'Th-that is enough, Gilbert!' It was the king, Amalric. His voice was sharp and authoritative, despite his stutter. 'I have h-heard enough.' He looked to Heraclius. 'Do you have anything to add?' The priest shook his head. 'W-william?

'I ask only for lenience. If John has done wrong, then let him earn his forgiveness in service to the Kingdom.'

Amalric nodded to the seneschal Guy, who addressed them in a loud voice. 'The accused can only be found guilty by a clear majority – four or more votes. If guilty, John shall suffer the fate of a traitor. He will be crucified, then hung from the Jaffa gate for one week as an example. At the end of that time his body shall be burned.' The seneschal paused to allow his words to sink in. 'Patriarch, what is your verdict?'

The Patriarch stood stiffly. 'Guilty.'

Gilbert rose next. 'Guilty.'

'And you, Bertrand?' the seneschal asked.

'Not guilty!' the Grand Master of the Templars declared firmly.

The seneschal looked to Humphrey. 'Guilty,' the constable said gravely. John felt his mouth go dry. That was three guilty verdicts. He held his breath as the seneschal cleared his throat.

'I pronounce him not guilty,' the seneschal said. 'King Amalric will cast the deciding vote.'

John met Amalric's blue eyes. The king hesitated for a moment, then looked away. 'Guilty.'

John felt suddenly faint. William held his arm to steady him. 'I am sorry, John.'

John nodded dumbly. He stood with his head down, his eyes locked on the floor as the seneschal declared the verdict. 'John of Tatewic, you have been pronounced guilty of treason. Tomorrow, you will be crucified before the Jaffa gate.' Two guards came forth and took hold of John's arms. They began to escort him from the room but John stopped and pulled free. He turned back to face his judges who were already starting to file from the room. 'Wait!' John called. 'I challenge the judgement. I will fight to prove my innocence.' The judges turned to look at him wide-eyed. No one spoke.

William strode towards him. 'What are you doing? You can barely stand. How will you fight?'

'I will die either way. I would rather die fighting.' John raised his voice. 'I said I challenge the judgment. I will fight those who think me guilty.'

'But this is ridiculous!' Heraclius sputtered. 'The court has decided.'

'No,' the seneschal declared. 'He has the right to challenge those who voted against him. But to prove his innocence, he must defeat all four of them – or their chosen champions – in a single day.' He looked to John. 'Are you sure?'

'Yes.'

'Very well. Then we will meet in the courtyard tomorrow at noon and John of Tatewic will fight to prove his innocence.'

*

526

John stood in the courtyard of the palace, looking up at the dome of the Church of the Holy Sepulchre. The top of it had disappeared into the fine, misting rain that beaded on John's chainmail. He felt William's hand on his shoulder. 'It is almost time,' the priest whispered. John nodded and lowered his gaze to the courtyard, where a ring seven paces across had been chalked off in the centre. The stones that paved the courtyard were slick with moisture. That would work to John's disadvantage. His feet were a mess of torn skin and burst blisters; he had almost fainted from the pain when he pulled on his boots. The slick footing would further limit his mobility.

Across the courtyard, King Amalric, Gilbert and Humphrey stood in their mail. The seneschal was there too, along with Heraclius and the Patriarch, who had brought a champion to fight for him – Harold, the man with the long gash on his face. The seneschal held four straws, which the men were drawing to see who would fight first. When each had picked, the sergeant Harold held the shortest straw. He grinned and looked to John. 'Now you will pay for what you did to my brother.'

John did not reply. He turned and exaggerated his limp as he walked over to William. Anything he could do to make Harold overconfident would help. It was the only advantage that John had.

William handed John a three-foot sword with a wide blade of dark grey steel. John took it and slashed it side to side, testing its balance. The priest held out John's shield. John tried to lift it but a blinding pain tore through his shoulder. ''Sblood,' he growled and dropped the shield. 'It's no use. Find something to bind my arm to

527

my body. I don't want the damned thing getting in my way.' William untied the cord about his waist and looped it around John, cinching it tight so that it held his left arm pinned to his torso. 'My helmet,' John said.

William slid the iron, open-faced helmet over John's head. John turned and stepped into the ring where Harold was waiting. The sergeant was a squat bull of a man. He too had opted to fight without a shield. He held his sword with both hands.

The seneschal stepped between the combatants. 'The swords have been dulled to prevent serious injury. You will fight until one of you yields or cannot continue.' He stepped out of the ring. 'Touch swords and begin.'

To protect his vulnerable left side, John turned himself sideways, so that his sword was extended towards Harold.

'I'm going to enjoy this,' the sergeant said.

They touched swords, and Harold attacked immediately, charging forward and hacking down with a mighty, two-handed blow. John raised his sword and parried. As he turned Harold's blade aside, John stepped to the side and knelt, raking his sword left to right and catching Harold in the shins. With a cry of pain the sergeant fell forward, losing his sword and landing hard on the stone pavement. John rose and as Harold rolled on to his back, John knelt, slamming his knee into the man's chest. He pressed the edge of his sword against Harold's neck. 'Yield!' John shouted. Harold spat, catching John full in the face. John smashed his sword's hilt into the sergeant's face, splitting his lip. He hit Harold again, splattering the stones of the courtyard with blood.

'Enough! Enough!' Amalric roared. 'John is the victor.'

John used his sword to push himself up, wincing at the pain in his feet as he stood. He hobbled towards William who clapped him on the back. 'I can't believe it!' the priest exclaimed. 'God is surely with you, John.'

John shook his head. 'God has nothing to do with it. Harold was angry and overconfident. That won't happen twice.'

Across the courtyard, Harold had been dragged to the side, where he sat cradling his face in his hands. The other men were again choosing straws. The constable, Humphrey, held up the short one. Without a word he pulled on his helmet and drew his sword. Humphrey was about John's height and size, but a few years older. He carried himself with a warrior's assurance as he stepped forwards.

'Careful of this one,' William warned. 'The constable commands the king's armies. He is a formidable warrior.'

John faced off across from Humphrey. The two men touched swords and then Humphrey began to circle around the edge of the ring, forcing John to turn in order to keep his opponent in front of him. John gritted his teeth, each step as he turned bringing a stab of pain. Humphrey kept circling, refusing to close. 'Come on, you bastard,' John grumbled under his breath.

Suddenly Humphrey charged, moving so fast that John just managed to turn the constable's sword aside before Humphrey slammed into him, bowling him over. Humphrey landed on top of John and the two men skidded across the slick stone of the courtyard. John managed to throw Humphrey off but struggled to rise with his arm pinned to his side. Humphrey was already on his feet while John was still on his knees. The constable attacked with an overhead chop. John parried and Humphrey kicked out, catching him in the chest. John fell back into a somersault and landed again on his knees. Humphrey was right on top of him, charging with his sword held high. As Humphrey swung down, John threw himself forward under the blow, slamming into the constable's knees. Humphrey flipped forwards and landed hard, giving John time to push himself to his feet. Humphrey had also risen and the two warriors faced off.

Humphrey began to circle again. He was breathing hard and John did not wait for him to catch his breath. Gritting his teeth against the pain in his feet, he charged, thrusting for Humphrey's chest. The constable was caught off guard and just managed to sidestep the blow. John spun and slashed for his head. Humphrey jumped back out of the way of the blow but slipped on the slick pavement. His guard came down and John swung for his head to finish the fight. Somehow Humphrey managed to block the blow. Their blades grated against one another and locked at the hilt, bringing the two men face to face. John head-butted Humphrey who staggered back, his blond beard matted with blood from his nose. Again John attacked, putting all his strength behind a slashing backhanded blow. Humphrey managed to deflect the attack, but John's sword glanced off his blade and caught Humphrey on the side of the helmet with a loud ring, leaving a deep dent and dropping the constable to lay unconscious at John's feet.

The seneschal proclaimed the obvious: 'John is the victor.'

A moment later, Humphrey's eyes blinked open and focused on John. 'Well fought, John.'

John dropped his sword and extended his hand, helping Humphrey to his feet. 'I had more to fight for.'

'*Hmph*.' Humphrey pulled off his helmet and gingerly touched the knot forming on the side of his head. Then he bent down and picked up John's sword. He handed it to him hilt first. 'I like you, Saxon. I hope you live.'

Amalric and the Patriarch had already drawn straws. The king held the short one. He began to put on his helmet when the seneschal put a hand on his arm. 'Sire, do you not wish to choose a champion?'

Amalric shrugged off the seneschal's hand and pulled on his iron helmet, which was open-faced with a cross-shaped bar that extended down in front of his nose. 'N-no,' he stuttered. 'I will fight for myself.'

'But sire!' the Patriarch protested. 'You could be injured, or worse.'

'How can I condemn this man to death if I am not willing to risk my own life?' Amalric drew his sword and stepped into the ring. The king rolled his broad shoulders to loosen them. He was a large man, heavy-set and strong looking, and he was fresh, whereas John was already tired. At least, the pain in his feet was less now, although he dreaded what he would find when he removed his boots. He turned himself sideways to the king and raised his sword.

'God save you,' Amalric said and touched his sword to John's. The king attacked straight off, grunting as he hacked down at John's head. John parried but the force of the blow almost knocked his sword from his hand. He gave ground as Amalric hammered at him, chopping down again and again. John managed to spin away but Amalric was on him immediately, slashing for John's chest. This time John only deflected the blow enough to sidestep it. Amalric reversed the direction of his blade, sweeping it up towards John's head. John ducked and then jumped backwards to avoid a left cross from the king. Amalric was on him immediately, chopping down. John deflected the blow and slipped away to the centre of the ring. His right hand was numb from the shock of blocking the king's powerful blows. He was fighting a losing battle and he knew it.

John went on the attack, thrusting at Amalric's chest. The king knocked the blow aside and John spun, bringing his sword in a wide arc towards his opponent's head. His sword was met by the king's steel. John stepped back, then attacked again with a flurry of thrusts, but Amalric blocked each blow with ease. John was breathing hard and his arm was tiring. He had to end this fight soon and there was only one way to get close enough to strike.

John began to retreat, letting Amalric come to him. The king gripped his sword with both hands and levelled a wicked blow at John's side. John did not even attempt to block it. He raised his sword over his head and took the blow with a grunt, feeling a sharp stab of pain as a rib snapped. Before Amalric could recover, John stepped inside his guard and brought his sword down, slamming it into the crown of Amalric's helmet and leaving a deep dent. The king stumbled back, a trickle of blood running down his forehead. John attacked but Amalric recovered in time to parry his thrust. Their swords locked together and the king shoved John, who went reeling back across the ring.

John stood bent over and gasping, each breath an agony. Across from him, Amalric pulled off his ruined helmet and cast it aside. His blond hair was matted with blood. 'My lord!' the seneschal gasped as he stepped forward.

Amalric waved him off. 'Let me finish this,' he growled and raised his sword.

John did likewise. He straightened and forced himself to smile. He would show no weakness, nothing that might give Amalric an advantage. 'I am waiting, your Highness.'

Amalric grinned back, then charged with a roar. At the last second, John threw himself at the king's legs, but Amalric was ready: he leapt over John and landed on his feet. John rolled and began to push himself to his feet when the king's sword slammed into his back, knocking him flat on his stomach. Amalric stepped on John's sword hand, then kicked his sword away. John rolled on to his back and found himself looking up at the point of Amalric's blade. 'Well fought, John,' the king said. 'But the fight is over. Do you yield?'

John tried to rise, but Amalric stepped on his chest, forcing him back down. John looked past the king's blade to Amalric's blue eyes, and then to the grey sky beyond. So this was how it ended. John closed his eyes. 'I yield.'

*

John sat hunched over, his head between his knees, staring at the damp dirt floor of his cell in the dungeon beneath the palace. Today was the day that he would die. From somewhere close by came the sound of dripping water. 'Sixteen thousand, seven hundred and ten,' John whispered. 'Sixteen thousand, seven hundred and eleven.' He had started counting the drops last night, when he could not sleep. The counting distracted him from the horror of his coming crucifixion. 'Sixteen thousand, seven hundred and twelve.' How many more drops, he wondered, until they came for him? How many more until he died?

The sound of the dripping was swallowed up by the echo of footsteps approaching down the stone corridor. John shivered, despite himself. The time had come. The footsteps stopped outside his cell. He looked up and was surprised to see William on the other side of the steel bars. 'I have brought someone to see you,' the priest said.

John's forehead creased. 'Who would want to see me?'

William moved aside, and Amalric stepped into the pool of torchlight before the cell. John tried to stand but the pain from his blistered feet was too great. He sank back down. 'Forgive me if I do not rise, your Highness.' Amalric waved away the apology. 'Why have you come?' John asked wearily. 'Do you wish to see what a dead man looks like?'

'You are n-not dead y-yet, John of Tatewic.' Amalric produced a key and unlocked the cell. He pulled the door open. 'I have come to free you.'

John blinked stupidly. 'What?'

'I have pardoned you,' Amalric explained as he stepped into the cell. 'I can use you, John. You are a m-man of courage. You almost beat me y-yesterday fighting with one arm, after having defeated two great warriors.'

'You are wasting your time, your Highness. I will not fight the Saracens.'

'I do not want you to f-f- . . .' The king's face contorted as he struggled to get the words out. 'I do not need another warrior. I want you to serve at my court. I am surrounded by spies and intriguers. I could u-use someone from the outside, someone who is loyal to m-me alone. And y-you know the Saracens better than any of us. Who better to advise me? Will you serve me, John?'

John nodded. His mouth was too dry to speak. He had readied himself for death, and now he had been given a second chance, not only to live but to redeem himself.

'There is one condition,' Amalric warned. 'Y-you must swear n-never again to take up arms against the Kingdom or your fellow Christians.'

'I swear it.'

'Good!' Amalric began to laugh his strange, manic laugh. The outburst passed as quickly as it came. He stepped into the cell and extended his hand. John winced at the pain in his feet as Amalric pulled him upright. 'You are my man,' the king said and embraced John.

'Thank you, Sire.'

'William will show you to y-your quarters. For n-now,

535

you will stay at the Hospital of Saint John. I will see y-you tomorrow morning at the palace.' Amalric stepped out of the cell.

'So I am free to come and go as I please?' John called after him. 'What is to prevent me from leaving the city? From going back to the Saracens?'

Amalric turned and met his eye. 'Your word. That is enough for me.'

The king left and William entered the cell. 'Come,' he said. 'Let's get you to your quarters.' John put his arm over the priest's shoulder and leaned into him as they left the cell. They passed down the long corridor, then up two flights of narrow stairs and out into a courtyard. It was a brilliant autumn morning, the sky a deep blue.

William helped John across the courtyard and through the wide gate that led out into the city. John paused on the far side of the gate. Straight ahead stood the vaulted halls and churches of the Hospitaller complex. He looked down the road to his right to where a church loomed over a pig market. In the distance to his left a rocky outcropping rose up above the city: the Temple Mount. He could make out the mighty Dome of the Rock, its gilded roof glinting in the morning sun. William glanced at John's face and smiled. 'A pretty sight, isn't she? Welcome to Jerusalem, the Holy City.'